UNDER THE SIREN'S SPELL

"Shhhh," Jack urged, reaching up to put a finger on her lips. But she held his hand at bay, and then the melody captured him. It was light as air, yet thick as honey. Amber notes so pure they pulled him in. Jack Nelson had never felt so happy in his entire life. His flesh burned with pleasure while the faces in his mind shifted; he was guzzling from the finest, rarest booze ever refined. It burned so sweetly as it slid down his throat.

The song had stopped. That's probably why Nelson surfaced from the musical spell in time to understand. The fire wasn't in his mind. His throat burned. He opened his mouth but gagged on something rich and iron. Blood spilled out across the woman's chest, dripping like gory wax down her ribs.

"Wha-di-ya . . . ?" he gurgled as he slapped a hand to his neck and felt the hot flow and ragged flesh of his neck. He blinked and saw his blood on her mouth. She was grinning, and her fingernails dug into his back, dragging him back down for the fatal bite . . .

Other *Leisure* books by John Everson:

THE 13TH
SACRIFICE
COVENANT

Siren

JOHN EVERSON

LEISURE BOOKS NEW YORK CITY

A LEISURE BOOK®

August 2010

Published by

Dorchester Publishing Co., Inc.
200 Madison Avenue
New York, NY 10016

ISBN 10: 0-8439-6354-9
ISBN 13: 978-0-8439-6354-0
E-ISBN: 978-1-4285-0899-6

Visit us online at www.dorchesterpub.com.

ACKNOWLEDGMENTS

Memory, inspiration and imagination. Those are the three keys of a novel, and *Siren* was inspired by memories of mesmerizing music and my many visits to various beachfronts along the coast of California. The words formed far from the coast however, during my weekly writing nights in 2009 at Rizzo's in Naperville, IL. Thanks to Erika and the rest of the gang there for always keeping my glass at least half full! Thanks also to Cocteau Twins, whose otherwordly, ethereal music provided the perfect backdrop for many hours of this novel's writing when I worked at home.

There are far more people to acknowledge for their support than I possibly can here, but thanks to my family, Geri and Shaun, for allowing me to don my "fiction" hat and disappear for hours and days into my other world. Thanks to Don D'Auria and everyone at Leisure for indulging my dark dreams. Thanks also to Roy Robbins, Dave Barnett, Shane Ryan Staley and Mateusz Bandurski for putting together beautiful limited editions and translated versions of my work.

Thanks to my first readers, Rhonda Wilson, Paul Legerski, Martel Sardina and Bill Gagliani, for fixing so many of my fact and grammar gaffes; to Lon Czarnecki and John Borowski for porting my visions to the web and film; and P. S. Gifford, Bill Breedlove, Dave Benton, Erik Smith, Peter D. Schwotzer, Nate Kenyon, Edward Lee, Jonathan Maberry, Bryan Smith, Kresby, WIL Keiper, Brian Yount, Paul Mannering, Sheila Halterman, Deb Kuhn, Peg Phillips, the Mallecs and the Rentfros for encouragement and support and for always being there.

Siren

PROLOGUE

1979

Salt hung in the air like fog; the taste of the ocean filled Andy's mouth as she led him along the rocks. The stark light of the night sky picked up and followed the stitching on the denim of her jeans. It was all Andy could do not to grab at the shifting moon of her ass as she stepped up and down and across the labyrinth of seaside boulders, leading him to the secret spot she'd prepared. The place where she would release that denim. The place where they would share blood.

She was an older woman. A dark-haired, slim and sexy older woman named Cassie, whom Andy had met at the bohemian coffeehouse where he studied after school. She said she was twenty-three, but her eyes held a knowledge of things far older than her years. Andy had been both afraid and entranced by her attentions, but ultimately, the lure of her dark eyes had called him out. And tonight, he would perform a ritual with her. A spell, she said, to call to the earth a power from beyond. A power that she could use. A power that would benefit them both . . . *if* he did as she said. Bottom line: he didn't really care about getting a piece of the power . . . he just cared about getting a piece of her. She had haunted his dreams—waking and sleeping—for weeks.

"Here," Cassie announced. She turned to him and put her arms around his neck. Beyond her hair, he could see the waves breaking in faint white sparks against the rocky shoreline. "I can feel something strong here," she said. "There's power in this spot. I've known it for years."

Andy shrugged. It looked like any other stretch of this godforsaken beach to him. Even in the daylight nobody swam here; the beach was treacherous. And the bay had had more than its expected share of shark reports, even though few ever swam in it.

But when Cassie pressed two warm lips to his own, Andy forgot about the beach, and only considered the heat of the body pressing against his own. And the flash of passion in the eyes that stared back at him. She may have been older, but she was a little thing, all lithe and sumptuous against his chest, and as he stared down into her eyes, he knew that tonight, tonight . . . he would become a man.

For a seventeen-year-old boy, that's an amazing, wonderful, knees-shaking kind of thought.

Cassie, meanwhile, considered the spell she planned to cast. There was power in the ocean, the mother of all life. A heavy, deep, silent power. A power as treacherous and uncertain as it was vast. And there was something more in this place, though she wasn't sure exactly what it was. It sang in the air like a faint locust call.

She led Andy to an open space on the beach right at the tide line and emptied her bag onto the sand. With her hands she dug eight holes in a circle in the sand and set the stub candles inside them, a disembodied set of crow's feet in the center. She kissed Andy again and pushed him backward to relax on the ground. Then, with a smile, she got up again and walked along the waterline until she found what she needed. Returning to the circle, she threaded a twine of seaweed in and out, around the perimeter of candles.

Andy watched as she set more things inside the circle center—leaves and hair and bits of dark gnarled stuff that could have been flesh or vegetable. He wasn't sure, and didn't want to know.

Cassie lit the candles, which despite the protection of sitting deep in the sand wells she'd dug, flickered fast in the night breeze. She sat back on her haunches then, and surveyed her work. After a moment she nodded and reached into her leather handbag to withdraw a knife. Not your standard kitchen steak knife, or even a street fighter switchblade. No, this was something special; the blade tapered to its point in a curve that mimicked the swell of an ocean wave. Its dark wood handle was decorated in strange jagged characters surrounding a bloodred stone.

"Now we're ready," Cassie said. Her eyes danced with the reflection of flames.

"Tell me what to do," Andy said. He hated how his voice sounded small against the whisper of the surf. Somewhere, a night bird cried; in pain or victory, it was impossible to tell.

"We have the elements of air, fire, earth and water in our circle, as well as the seeds of life and death. Now we add the elements of blood—and passion—to complete the spell."

"Don't you need to say something, or wave a wand or . . ."

Cassie laughed. "I'll say a few things as we fuck, but really . . . the magic is in the combination. The trigger is my will, and *us*, being together . . ."

She leaned forward to kiss him and Andy's eyes rolled back. *God she tasted good in his mouth.* When she broke the embrace, she set the knife between them and stripped off her shirt, motioning for him to do the same. Then she stood, shucked her jeans, shimmied out of a pair of pink bikini panties, and they sat again, naked on the ground. Andy shivered as his butt touched the grit of the cold sand.

"Give me your hand," she whispered, and he did.

"Give me your life," she said, and drew the blade across his palm. Andy winced, but didn't say anything as the blood welled.

She sliced a cut in her own palm and then pressed their hands together, holding their arms out over the center of the circle of flame. "My life in yours," she whispered. When she relaxed her grip, drops of their mingled blood splattered the totems in the sand.

Then Cassie's breasts were warm against Andy's chest, and he was on his back, her hair curtaining his face, her mouth sucking in his tongue with a hunger he'd never known. He grew hard against her and in moments, she rolled him over so that now he was on top and whispered, "Now, Andy. Now."

Andy slid against the velvet skin of her thighs and felt the warmth of her against him. He pressed and shifted and felt a momentary pang of fear. What if he couldn't find the way inside her . . .

. . . And then warmth engulfed him and he was *there*. The feeling was amazing, as if a liquid hand had slipped around his cock, teasing and taunting him in a way real hands could never attempt. He pressed against her, trying to find his way deeper, closer to her. He kissed her, pushing into her mouth. She returned the probe of his tongue, but then her eyes flared and she pressed him back.

"Harder," she demanded. "Make me feel you."

He tried to comply but still she demanded more.

Andy stabbed into her faster, slamming against her with more force. Their skin smacked and echoed with the rhythm of the surf, and her cries crescendoed, tight, anxious gasps of pleasure. Still she insisted on more. She gripped him by the shoulders, lifting him and pulling him back. Her mouth lolled open as he followed her lead, and she moaned. "Grab my hair," she hissed.

He slid a hand into her hair and pulled her neck back in time with his hips. "My neck," she said then. "Slam me hard, Andy. I need to feel it all."

Andy slipped his hand from her hair and held both hands around her throat, gripping her like a rag doll. She held him just as tightly at the neck, guiding his passion, pushing him back to lift her head from the sand, and then letting go as he slammed her whole body beneath him. In seconds her cries grew uncontrollable as his passion released. As the first waves of orgasm engulfed him in a fever dream, he pounded into her faster, faster, faster, lifting her head and slamming her to the sand with him, a single body in desire. Her hands and thighs urged him on, her screams moved from "yes, yes" to guttural grunts and moans. He lost himself in the motion, crying out with her in sharp staccato bleats of pleasure.

He didn't notice immediately when her cries of ecstasy turned. But as his own wave crested, the echo of his partner died. As the euphoria slipped away like water through sand, Andy blinked and slowed, releasing his fingers from their grip on her throat as her own arms fell away from their grip on him.

Cassie was motionless beneath him, and he bent to kiss her. "Cassie?" he whispered. But the velvet of her lips didn't respond.

"Cassie, wake up," he urged.

The sand beside her black hair was dark, and when

Andy lifted her into his arms he felt the reason. The sticky, hot, horrible reason.

The point of the boulder that had been hidden beneath the sand glinted in the moonlight, its tip black with blood, and when he panicked and dropped her motionless body, Cassie didn't move. One arm lay pinned beneath her back while her legs remained twisted in an unnatural crouch. One thin drip of saliva slid down her cheek, and Andy saw that her breasts were still. Completely, unsexily still. No breath to raise them.

"Shit, shit, shit," he whispered, and bent to her chest. Her heart made no sound.

Andy pulled on his pants and paced the beach, jumping at every night sound. He thought of his hopes for college, his dreams of scholarships and football. His ticket away from this tourist-trap town. Every time he turned back to the light of the dying candles, those dreams changed to an image of rusted prison bars.

When he finally collapsed again beside Cassie's body, tears wetting all of his face and chest, she remained undeniably dead. He ran a hand over the white skin of her chest, and his hand came back slick and cold. He knew he couldn't leave her there. And he couldn't tell anyone what he'd done. Her life was over, no matter what. Why did his have to be over too? "This is not my fault," he cried out in anguish to the waves, though there was no one there to hear.

Under the midnight moon, Andy made his decision.

He was not going to die with her. Shoveling all of the candles and totems into her big leather shoulder bag, he lifted Cassie over his shoulder and, bag in hand, walked her body down the beach. There was a rock promontory—Gull's Point—that extended out into the black of the ocean, and he thought that would be as good a spot as any.

When he reached the edge of the rocky finger, he laid

her body down on the stone and took one last long look at her thin, still face.

His first older woman. Maybe his last.

"Shit," he whispered again.

Andy gathered some fist-size rocks and shoved them into her bag before dragging its long handles over her head and around her neck. At first, her head wouldn't slip through the hoops, but he screamed one long cry of anger and with a yank of pure fury, finally the leather stretched and gave way. The bag slipped around her throat, and strands of black hair specked with red were caught between his fingers. Crying silently all the while, he stuffed another rock into the bag. One thing you learned while living near the ocean is that things had a tendency to float.

He stuffed a couple rocks in the back of her jeans, and wrestled them partway up her legs before tying another heavy rock inside her shirt, and knotting that around her ankle. Satisfied that she would sink, Andy wrestled her off the ground again, and staggered to the edge of the rocky promontory. With a cry of anguish and pain, he lofted her away from the rock, to splash down and into the whitecaps just a few feet below.

She sank without a whisper. Andy ran. It was hours before his tears stopped.

Beneath the surf, Cassie sank and shifted with the fickle flow of current, finally coming to rest at the broken mouth of an old rotted ship's hull. Seaweed fanned her head as the rock-laden purse and jeans dragged her down. From the back of her head, dark blood seeped into the sea, the steady suction and push of the water releasing more of her lifeblood to the bosom of the first mother. The ocean accepted her body home.

Blood slid like smoky ribbons over the face of a snow-white rock next to her head. That rock protruded only slightly from the heavy brown sediment of a century. But as the blood coiled and diluted in the waves, some of it lingered like a stagnant cloud.

If anyone had been watching, they would have seen the white stone shift slightly. And a few minutes later, again. They would have seen something like a funnel appear in the muck, as the tip of the stone lifted, a cloud of ocean dust swirling away in its wake.

They would have seen the skeletal joint that held that rocky white finger to a hidden piece of bone beneath the mud, and they would have seen that mud shiver and slide away as the bone sought release and brought four more bony white appendages with it.

They would have seen that hand cradle the head of Cassie like a mother, only . . . instead of giving care, this hand was taking it. Feeding. Bony fingers stroked the softly swaying locks of her black hair.

Only, nobody was there to see.

Nobody saw that a century of sleep had at last come to the end, thanks to the call of Cassie's spell . . . and the power of her blood.

CHAPTER ONE

Today

The rock skipped across the waves like a bullet, skimming the surf and bouncing once, twice, three and four times before it finally hit its match, a whitecap with attitude. The stone disappeared without a fifth leap into the unrelenting ocean.

Evan shrugged and picked up another stone. An oblong one. Gray and smooth. This time, he only got two skips before the rock was stolen by the waves. Arm was tired, he told himself, and left the next stone where it lay.

The ocean stole everything. Leaning down, he picked up the hook of a crab claw and flung it into the foam.

Everything.

Evan wiped the tear from his cheek and walked on down the beach. The night hung on him with its own rushing silence, but Evan could still hear the sounds of his past. He could hear Josh out there, in the waves. His son. His baby boy.

Dad! Josh had called, voice filled with sudden panic. And then, *Dad?*

And then there'd been no sound at all.

"Stop it," Evan screamed, as he did nearly every night, angry at himself for more things than he could describe. But fear certainly topped the list. A long list of words came to mind actually: *fear, coward, chickenshit, weak, pathetic, loser, scumbag, fuckhead* . . . the words degenerated further with the acid heat of his tears.

Evan picked up another rock from the beach and flung it into the waves. But this time, he didn't stop to see how far it went before it fell. Instead he turned back toward the lights of home.

The rock skipped seven times.

The sound system overhead played a Georgia Satellites song and Sarah smiled to herself, because as she looked around the bar she thought that she might be the only one old enough to *remember* the Georgia Satellites. When the hick twang of her youth faded into the raspy growl and twining guitars of Foo Fighters, she saw the heads of several guys around the single pool table begin to nod with more gusto. The kids knew this one.

Somehow rock had left her behind thanks to an invisible anchor around her heart, holding her back. She could never escape her past. And wasn't that why she was here?

"Can I buy you a drink?" one of the pool boys asked her, and Sarah stared into the hopeful's eyes, not with honor, but with a simple question. *Why?*

Her days of one-night stands were two decades past, and she knew the lines along the sag of her jowls and the silvering web in her hair were just the most obvious indicator that time was *not* on her side. No guy with jet-black hair and pecs that dared his belt buckle to try to cinch tighter could possibly have an interest in her. Still, that guy did stand at her side, and put his hand on her shoulder, and offered her another beer.

What the hell? she thought, and asked for a Guinness. Maybe he saw the ring as her hand slipped easily around the glass.

"You married?" the man said, pulling up a stool. He didn't take his hand off her. Instead, he let it slip from her shoulder, across her back, to grip familiarly on her thigh.

She nodded. "For about as long as you've been alive," she said with a grin. She looked up at him with weary eyes, and maybe something there sent a chill of reality down his spine, because his easy hand slipped away. He threw down a couple bucks on the bar, nodded and slipped back to the pool table. From behind, Sarah heard low voices and laughter. She didn't turn around. There was only so much heartache you could absorb in your life, and she had had her fill. If someone were making fun of her now, for sitting here old and empty in a bar . . . she wasn't going to eat that. She wasn't going to do anything at all, except take one more pull on the edge of her glass. Okay, maybe two.

And then she'd go home. *Home is where the heart is*, she thought. "But where has my heart gone?" she answered herself aloud.

The sound system—*whatever happened to jukeboxes*—now pumped with the beat of Britney, and the voices in the bar around her began to pick up in volume. It was amateur hour, Sarah thought. Time for the adults to go home. She looked into the neon lights of the bar signs above her head, and smiled sadly at the sexy tattooed thing behind the bar who made no bones against sticking out her rack and flirting with the pool table boys for tips. Sarah looked back to her beer.

The foam on the latest pull of Guinness made her laugh. She couldn't have explained why, exactly. It just struck her as funny . . . all this dark, heavy liquid coloring the bulk of her glass and then this white wreath of bubbles trying to hold it all in. She knew about holding it in. That's why she was here. She held it *all* in.

"Something wrong with your beer?" a voice asked from behind her. Sarah turned slowly, afraid that the pool boy was back. But then the tenor of the voice sunk in, and she saw the hard line of his jaw, and the soft care in his deep-set blue eyes, and she shook her head.

"Nah," Sarah said. "The beer's just fine." She lifted her glass and drained half of it in one desperate pull.

"Let's go home, huh?" Evan said, and pulled her off the stool. She only stumbled a little, as the bells of the door rippled to announce their exit, just as they did nearly every night. Behind them, the bartendress with the rack rolled her eyes and cleared the bar. She gave little thought to why the old girl had to be escorted home every night. She just pulled her T-shirt tighter to smile falsely at the boys drinking Bud as they shot eight ball.

Damn drunks never left a good tip.

CHAPTER TWO

Loss is an all-consuming passion. Kylie could have told you that in a heartbeat, if she'd still had one.

"I never said I would take you with me," Abram yelled in the dark corner of the beachside club. Nobody around them seemed to hear the outburst, though the girl with the shock white hair and the short pink skirt heard him loud and clear. She heard him in the marrow of her bones.

On the stage, a short guitarist in glasses and a plaid shirt rambled his earnest way through CCR's "Have You Ever Seen The Rain," and Kylie suddenly wasn't sure if it was Abram's betrayal or the power of the song that made her cry.

But she knew what it was that made her tears split into a smile as Abram explained that he didn't have time for a relationship, he had an opportunity in the Bay Area, and he had to devote himself to that and make it happen. And maybe someday if . . .

Kylie ignored Abram's pathetic explanation for abandonment. Sucker 'em, suck 'em and dump 'em . . . she knew the drill. Now the plaid boy at the mic was singing, "Stop, children, what's that sound," and she was struck, not with the power of the old Buffalo Springfield lyric but with the memory of a group of Muppets singing a hippie song.

Just then, as Abram tried to make his best earnest, brow-crinkled face to explain his urgent need to leave her behind, Kylie began to laugh out loud.

Abram clearly was shocked and a little flustered. And as she kept laughing, the feeling building in her like an explosion—an explosion of emotion that only mildly included anything that should have resembled laughter—Abram faded away.

Kylie realized he was gone a long while later, after the laughter and the tears and a bad John Mayer song had ended. She should have known that Abram would leave her. They always did.

She slipped out the side door of The Sand Trap and walked down the empty sidewalk of Fifth Street toward the ocean. The moonlight was high in the sky and she didn't want to go home. There was nothing comforting about the idea of her empty bed right now.

She kicked off her sandals on the edge of the cement path and walked barefoot in the cold sand. In moments she felt the even-colder kiss of the waves rushing over her toes. From somewhere, far away, she heard the high, pure voice of a song.

Unconsciously she walked toward the sound. Music had always made her feel better in the worst of times, and this was definitely one of the worst of the worst. She had really loved him. She had loved all of them, to some degree, but this time, *this time* . . . she had thought it would be different. She kicked up a cloud of sand with her toes and laughed bitterly. It would never be different . . . because guys were all the same. They wanted one thing from a girl and once they got it a few times . . . they got bored. And then they wanted something else. *Someone* else.

The music seemed to be coming from down the beach, near the rocky finger that stuck out into the surf. Gull's

Point, they called it, since in the summer months the stretch of treacherous rock was almost completely carpeted in noisy flocks.

But now, the rocks were empty. Dark, jagged angles against a moody night sky.

Someone was there, Kylie knew. And she sang beautifully. Kylie couldn't make out the words, but the melody drew her, full of heartache and hope.

She reached the edge of the natural jetty, and carefully threaded her way down its length out into the water. The song came from just around the top, but to get there, Kylie had to walk all the way out to its edge, and then climb around.

The ocean was beautiful at night, she thought, as she stepped up on a boulder crusted with blackened algae. Between the quiet wash of the waves and the beauty of the song, she realized that she no longer felt angry at Abram. Or even sad. All the hurt and frustration of the day was stolen by the melody; the energy of the night seemed to slip away from her, and Kylie decided to rest for a moment on the rocks.

She sat down and stared out into the faint white crests, the tang of the ocean warm and alive in her throat. She breathed it in and let it all go. The music was everywhere, quiet but all encompassing, and she closed her eyes and let it take her to a better place.

Featherlight hands slipped up the back of her shoulders and Kylie relaxed and closed her eyes. She no longer cared. The music was inside her now, and its call was everything.

Kylie didn't feel the nails as they moved across her body, deftly stripping her of her clothes. She barely noticed them as they trailed across her chest and up her neck. Through a waking dream, she shivered, and struggled to break through the strange fog that enveloped her mind when the gold-flecked eyes suddenly stared into hers with the hunger of a predator, and she realized at last that she was exposed, and in danger.

But by then it was too late.

Kylie screamed once, as the song abruptly ended.

But only once.

Nobody heard as two cold hands dragged her body from the rocks and into the welcome embrace of the ocean.

CHAPTER THREE

Sunlight fingered the rumpled bedsheets. Evan woke with one beam across his face. He squinted at the claw of dawn. *So early.* In the morning, the nights felt too short . . . yet when he stared at the ceiling at two A.M., they seemed far too long.

Beside him, Sarah snored. She'd be out for a while yet. Since Josh's death, she'd been sleeping later and later . . . because she'd been at the bar more and more. Evan would have been worried she was cheating on him there and picking up guys . . . but more often than not it was he who showed up to take her home. They walked alone much of each night in their private grief . . . but they walked together still at the end.

He kissed her lightly on the forehead and slid out of bed to shuffle to the bathroom. A year ago, Sarah would have been downstairs already, rattling around in the kitchen and waking up both Evan and Josh with her happy noise. Eventually "her boys" would come straggling down the hall, yawning and stretching into a kitchen warm with the scents of eggs or grits and coffee, and they'd gather at the table to talk about the coming day.

Josh had been an eighth grader at Bayside, and talk of high school had already begun to filter into their break-fast conversations. Should he go ahead and take advanced-placement history? His grades allowed it, but if he went out for track and swimming, did he really want to subject himself to harder homework?

Evan pushed for him to do the AP classes; they'd get him into a better college, and Josh had generally rolled his eyes. "What makes you think I'm going to college, Dad?" he'd taunt.

Sarah would support him, sort of, piping up from the stove; "I don't see anything wrong with being a career lifeguard."

Evan stared at the dark circles under his eyes as he shaved and inwardly winced. What a difference a year made. The face that stared back at him looked thin and tired, and gray hairs now sprinkled his temples as well as curled amid the black fuzz of his chest. He had a slight paunch now—not bad for a guy in his forties, but he'd been tighter, healthier, a year ago.

Sarah still slept when he got out of the shower and dressed for work, her mouth slack and open against the pillow. Evan longed to wake her up, to kiss her with the kind of passion they'd once shared in the mornings; "Something to remember me by while you're at the office," she used to whisper as her anxious fingers released the belt he'd only just buckled. But he knew better. Those days were gone with his son.

He stopped in the hall for a moment, as he did every morning, to stare at the posters on the wall of Josh's room above the bed. They'd touched nothing in Josh's room since that day. The morning light trailed across an empty bed, and fingered a dresser covered in a jumble of books, magazines and rock band trading cards. Evan had been proud of Josh's interest in music; it had echoed his own. The two of them had often sat, side by side, at the piano or with the acoustic guitar, singing folk and rock and nonsense songs together. Evan grinned at the memory of Josh way back when he was five. Evan had made up a lyric about Josh catching a lizard tail in the bathroom and using it to brush his teeth. The boy's face had crinkled in disgust as he laughed and groaned, "No way, Dad, yuck! Gross!"

A tear threatened to escape the corner of Evan's eye, but he shook it away. And walked away. For the hundredth time he promised that soon, soon, he would go into that room with boxes. They had left it exactly the way Josh had left it that morning he and Evan had gone to the ocean. Sarah and he had thought somehow that still having Josh's room intact would give them a way to still have their son in their lives. A visual memory of the time when he was with them. But Josh's life and smell and sound had slowly leached away. All his magic was gone from that place now.

Neither Evan nor Sarah had moved on. They were as mired in their grief as the room was tied to the dusty artifacts of a life long gone.

"It's time to let go and put it away," Evan said to the empty hallway. But in his head he answered. *But not today.*

The shipping yard already hummed with activity when Evan pulled into the lot. He dreaded Thursdays, since the fishing boats always seemed to dock the heaviest that day . . . and that meant he'd be humping to keep up with the manifests and invoices and all the other paperpushing that working at a small seaport entailed. If you lived in a tiny port town like Delilah, you either worked in the fishing trade in some way or in the tourist-trap block of town. Once a secret duty-free port refuge for rumrunners, Delilah had grown to a minor legitimate port on the California coast where fishermen and small freight companies could dock with minimal fees and lots of personal attention. That lure rose and fell with the decades. Over the past twenty years, the town had sold itself more as a quaint tourist attraction than as a port authority.

The downtown still boasted some of the original Victorian houses built at the turn of the last century, and with a coordinated effort by the town fathers and some business owners, the main drag of Serenade Street had been retrofitted and polished up to look like a row of dollhouses. The long, sheltered arc of Hidden Bay boasted a good stretch of golden sand before deteriorating into miles of rock and boulders, and in the summer and fall months that lone stretch of beach filled with umbrellas and coolers, largely from tourists. The townspeople were all busy selling to the interlopers; they had no time to use their own beach.

Evan took the rock stairs up from the parking lot two at a time to climb to the "lookout" perch occupied by the Delilah Harbor Authority. He was late again; no matter how hard he tried lately, he couldn't seem to hit the decks on time. The weathered wooden screen slammed shut behind him and he cursed under his breath. The noise would alert Darren, who had been a pain in the ass about everything lately.

"Just coming off break?" his boss called from behind a pile of shipping records as Evan passed the port's "big office." *Big* was kind of a misnomer—Darren ran the yard from a ten-by-twelve room whose birch paneling and stacks of unfiled manifests made its space look even smaller than it already was. But . . . Darren did have the only office in the place.

"Yep," Evan answered, trying to keep his voice light. "*Break*fast."

He kept moving, not giving Darren the chance to lambaste him for not moving to the tick of the clock, and slipped behind his desk feeling like a scolded schoolkid.

Evan, Bill, Candice and Maggie all had desks in an open area they called "the bull pen" just beyond Darren's office. There was a small entry room beyond that where some of the ship captains came to go over their shipping manifests and complete other paper trail details. Not the least of which included paying port fees.

None of the workers at Delilah Harbor Authority spent the day at their desks, as they were always called upon to help out at the dock with something. Evan was a jack-of-all-trades when it came to serving as the chief accountant. He also could throw a mean rope anchor and heft a barrel of fish.

Maggie raised an eyebrow at him and grinned as she whispered, "You're going to get a detention!"

"I know, I know. I've gotta get a handle on it." Evan shook his head before confiding, "Sarah's just been out late a lot . . . reeling her in isn't always easy and then I can't sleep and . . ."

Maggie shook curls of wild chestnut hair across her eyes and then had to brush it away. "I'm not the principal; you don't have to tell me."

She smiled, a little sadly. "Andy said she's been up at O'Flaherty's a lot lately. You know, he can't come to bed without his beer either."

"I'm guessing he's not drowning in his though," Evan replied. Maggie opened her mouth to say something but then thought better of it. She didn't have an easy answer for that. Bill looked up from his terminal and pursed his lips, but though a wrinkle passed his brow, he didn't enter the conversation.

The room stayed silent for a while after that.

CHAPTER FOUR

Evan watched the water fill in the indentations left by his bare feet in the sand. The waves were constant, lulling, in their predictable low roar inward and whoosh of instant retreat, and yet at the same time unpredictable. During his stroll up the beach his feet hadn't gotten wet more than once, and yet now, his footprints suddenly glimmered with the wash of a strong surge of surf. Every few waves surged closer to his path.

After dinner, he'd walked the long stretch up Safe Harbor and now sat on a cold, blackened boulder that marked the beginning of Gull's Point. He looked back toward the twinkling lights of Delilah. The glimmer of his hometown barely registered against the brilliance of the night sky; the stars were out in full tonight, and the beach flickered with secret reflections.

Evan leaned back and stared at the sky, as he absently fingered the half charm chained around his neck. Josh had worn the other half, after presenting it to him one Father's Day, just a couple years before. A show of their solidarity, to wear two halves of a medal.

He looked down the empty stretch of beach and wondered, how many days and nights had he and Josh crisscrossed this sand? How many times had Josh tried to lure him into the water? How many times had he refused to go?

Josh had been a Pisces, and lived his sign; he'd always been in the water. As close as they'd been, that was one thing that father and son had never shared. Because while Evan loved the look and smell of the ocean, ironically, he was also an aquaphobe. Afraid of the water. More than afraid. Phobic. It was a crazy phobia for someone who lived near the ocean and worked at a port. But Evan had never been able to shake the paralyzing fear. He'd had it since he was a kid. It was more than that he couldn't swim; while he could walk along the beach and admire the view, if you asked him to take a swim, his heart began to pound, and sweat leaked from his pores like rain. His legs grew palpably weak at the slightest suggestion of walking into the ocean to let the waves carry him. Even at home, his bathing consisted solely of a shower . . . he would never relinquish his body to a bathtub. Friends never understood why he refused invitations to their hot tub parties, and he could never have admitted that it was because he was afraid of immersing himself fully in water. At least, he couldn't have explained before last year.

Evan had lived with the phobia all of his life without needing to explain it to virtually anyone . . . until the day that Josh had died.

He shook the water from his eyes and tried to think of something else. Something that had been good with him and Josh, something that had nothing to do with water. Some last thought he could console himself with, before he put his plan in action. Because he'd decided before kissing Sarah good night that he was actually kissing Sarah good-bye.

Evan looked out at the place in the bay where Josh had gone under for his last time and considered the distance between there and where he stood. At the same time, the happy memory of him, Josh and an acoustic guitar took shape, and he blinked back saltwater as he remembered the day that he and his son had sat alone on the deck behind their house, singing "Daydream Believer" and whatever other simple songs Evan could figure out on the acoustic guitar.

He began to sing "Forever Now," remembering one of his favorite songs from Psychedelic Furs. Josh was into more modern stuff, but he had always liked how Richard Butler's voice had rasped and twisted in time to the fuzz guitars and wild saxophones of that '80s band. Oddly enough, Evan had been able to both play and sing some of the band's signature songs without too much embarrassment on guitar.

Evan stared up now at the night sky and sang. The song's bitterly hopeful lyric—a wish to hold one moment in time forever—rang true in his heart, and he felt himself choking up. At the same time, in a bit of a mental "bait and switch" maneuver, he steeled his legs and courage and prepared to run—for as long and as far as he could—straight into the ocean. Evan had considered drowning himself in the place where Josh had died so many times; it had become as normal of a thought to him as breathing. And he didn't want to wait any longer.

He wiped a tear from his cheek, and let the song and the moment go, and let the rhythm of the surf take over the night again as he started to run down the sand, a kamikaze to the ocean. If he could only get far enough into the water before his legs refused to work, the gentle surf would make short work of him. It would be an appropriate way for Evan to die.

Only, there was something more now.

As his struggling melody ended, another voice colored the night air. A beautiful, sensually fluid voice. Evan peered

down the empty beach and then back to the jumble of
rocks that made up Gull's Point. She was close, he could
tell that much, but he couldn't see her. The sound she
made though . . . it melted his heart. And his body. Evan
paused his run to the water almost the instant it began
and walked back to the boulder he'd been singing on. As
if in some distant dream, he felt himself relax again into
the questionable comfort of the boulder's seat, even as he
yearned to move closer and find the source. It embarrassed him to know that she had probably heard his
feeble attempts at song—maybe even felt the need to
sing to blot out the amateur attack of his singing. Still,
embarrassment aside, he had to meet the owner of that
voice! After enjoying the music pulsing in the air all
around, Evan pushed himself out of his reverie and
threaded his way around the rocks, hugging to the sharp
side of the point so that he didn't end up in the waves.
There wasn't much of a path to the point's tip, but it was
walkable if you were careful. Once there, something of a
lookout space existed; a flat oval spot on the rock that
protruded into the ocean where you could stand dozens
of yards out into the water, and watch the far horizon.
Lovers came there to watch the sun rise and set. And to
do *other* things, he supposed.

As he rounded the last obstacle in his path, his heart
stopped.

And started.

And stopped again.

Evan forced himself to breathe, slowly. Quietly. The
moonlight illuminated the woman's back and Evan
found himself yearning desperately to caress the creamy
skin that lay there, naked to the night, just steps away.
The woman rested her head on an elbow. The slope of
her ribs leading to her waist to the sumptuous rise of her

hip was as perfect as any artist's rendering of a nude in the moonlight that Evan had ever seen. He struggled not to be gauche and stare at her ass, but . . . Jesus . . . there was a naked woman lying on the ground here, singing! And the globes of her ass were absolutely kissable. How could he not stare at her? Especially when most men's magazines would have paid top price for the opportunity to photograph her. If the front side of this girl was anything like the back, she could demand any fee for voyeuristic entrée.

She had more than a perfect ass though. She had a pitch-perfect voice. And *that* may have been more attractive to Evan than her body. With the gentle rush of the surf around them, she sang a plaintive and unidentifiable melody that chilled and warmed Evan to the bone at the same time. He felt feverish with the sound, aching to run to her, to hold her in his arms and not because of the attraction of her body. Her music drew emotions in torrents from his heart. Her song, quite simply, played him.

The sound reached high into the night and then dipped, and Evan gasped at the impact of that melody.

And with the interruption of his gasp, the music abruptly ceased. The woman rose to her feet in a heartbeat, glanced around behind her. Her eyes narrowed as they focused on the spot where Evan stood on the beach. Without a second look, she suddenly stepped up on a jagged rock and dove off into the water a few feet below.

Evan was left with an impression of darkly luminous eyes and pouty lips framed by a long tangle of dark curls; her hair fell halfway down her back when she stood. He'd also caught a hint of softly curved breasts, and his belt easily felt tighter in the five seconds it took for her to turn, look and leap.

The moment was broken then and Evan darted across the open lookout area himself. It wasn't safe to swim in the bay alone; certainly not at night. He looked out across the gently chopping whitecaps and didn't see her anywhere.

"Miss?" he called after a moment. "I didn't mean to startle you," he continued. When she didn't surface, he called, "Come back to shore, it's dangerous out here at night."

His voice was answered only by the rush of water that surrounded Gull's Point, washing in and away from the beach. He stayed there, calling out to the mysterious woman, but she never answered. As the minutes ticked by, he realized that she might never be coming back. Why had she jumped like that? He asked himself over and over. What if her head had struck a rock below the surface? Or what if she couldn't swim, like him? Maybe that's why she wasn't resurfacing. Evan began to think that he might have inadvertently helped send a woman to her death.

The surface of the water betrayed no woman, only whitecaps.

Eventually, Evan threaded his way back to the beach from the edge of the point, his own attempt at suicide forgotten. Or, at least, put temporarily on hold. Planning your own death was one thing, but seeing someone else take their life—because she had never come back to the shore—that made Evan's stomach turn over. He walked back across his own footprints in the sand, the image of the woman disappearing into the waves playing over and over again in his head.

He prayed that she were all right, but he didn't believe she could be.

CHAPTER FIVE

The sign on the old wooden door read VICKY BLANCHARD, MD, but to Evan, it said something else entirely. He read it as "Dr. Blanchard, Head Case Doc."

He thumbed down the latch on the front door handle and entered the small waiting room in the converted Victorian. Once, the room had probably served as the formal "sitting" room, where lovers sat and conversed in stilted dialogue as matriarchs and chaperones looked on. Evan could only imagine the conflict between the flirtatious words that the couples had *wanted* to say and the formal dialogue they'd been *forced* to masquerade behind. Talk about a torture chamber . . . Now, it acted as a waiting room for Delilah's only psychiatrist. It hadn't been built for that purpose, and was definitely "cozier" than your average waiting room. But, Evan generally found himself waiting alone, thumbing through an issue of *Cosmo*. Dr. Blanchard was pretty good about not double-booking. So he never waited long. Or, perhaps, he was just one of the only ones in the small town crazy enough to subject himself to a head doctor.

Not like he'd done it by choice. In the aftermath of Josh's death, the company mandated that he keep his bi-weekly appointment if he wanted to keep his job. After skipping work a dozen times last year because he couldn't get out of bed, it was head doc or the highway.

Evan wished that he could have forced Sarah to take the same treatment. He hadn't turned into a raving fanboy of psychiatry, but he had to admit, his conversations with Vicky had helped him cope when things turned really black.

The inner office door opened, and the head doc in question stuck her head out. "Wanna come on back?" she asked sweetly. Dr. Blanchard couldn't afford to keep a receptionist on staff full-time just to send her occasional patients back to the "chat" room.

He followed her down a short hallway to a spacious office. The doctor's desk dominated the room in front of the floor-to-ceiling windows, but two couches bordered the walls on either side, and two leather-cushioned chairs perched in front of the dark wood desk. Once, this space had probably been the old house's family room.

"You know the drill," she said, slipping behind her desk. Evan felt kind of ridiculous talking to her at times; she could have been his younger sister. Dr. Blanchard stood a not very imposing five foot two, and weighed about as much as a coatrack, he theorized. She talked with the lilt of a high school sophomore; full of happiness and overexuberance.

Still, if you had to pour out your troubles, who better to drown in them than a former cheerleader, Evan had speculated on more than one occasion.

He plopped down in one of the chairs (she offered the couches, but he'd never felt right about lying down while talking to her) and raised an eyebrow as she pulled out her pad of yellow notepaper.

"Do you ever look at any of that stuff you write down after I leave?" he asked.

She raised two deep-blue eyes and stared back at him as if in shock. Then she laughed. "No, not usually." She winked, and then shook her head. "But that's really not the point here."

"I know." He smiled. "This is about me, not about you."

She pointed a long hot pink fingernail at him and smiled. "Right. Now tell me why I shouldn't have you committed this week."

"Well, actually, maybe you should," Evan began.

"Would you like to explain?"

"I think I saw a woman kill herself," he said.

"Tell me what happened."

Evan ran through the story of walking on the beach the night before, hearing the strange naked woman singing, and then watching her dive into the water to vanish without a trace.

"How are things with you and Sarah?" Dr. Blanchard asked.

"Apropos of nothing?" Evan laughed.

"I'm just curious . . . how are things with you two? The last few times you've been here you've said that her drinking has really increased. I'm just wondering . . ."

"You're just wondering if I'm hallucinating because I've been sharing the bottle with her, or because I'm desperately wishing she'd come home . . . or not leave home at all?"

She let a wry wrinkle crease her smile before answering. "Transparent, huh? I don't get to ask by-the-book questions like that very often. Sorry."

"You think I'm by the book?"

Dr. Blanchard shook her head quickly. "The book says nothing about men who see naked women diving into the ocean."

"So am I crazy?"

"I'll reserve judgment on that for now. Tell me about Sarah."

"Whose psychiatrist are you anyway?"

"Who is the most important woman in your life?" Dr. Blanchard asked. And then with a wicked smile, she held up one finger. "And don't say me."

"Sarah." He grinned. "And she's not good." His smile fell instantly. "I'm pulling her off a stool every other night. And she won't talk about it."

"I'd like to talk to her," Dr. Blanchard said gently.

"I'd like to bring her," he answered. "But we can't afford it—my insurance won't cover it. And she wouldn't come if we could."

Dr. Blanchard nodded. "I think you're under a lot of stress right now . . ." she began.

". . . So I'm imagining naked women on the beach?" he finished.

"That's not what I meant."

"No? Did you mean that you totally believe me when I tell you I saw a nude woman last night lying on the rocks who sang in the most beautiful voice I've ever heard—even though I couldn't tell you a single word that she sang—and that I watched her jump into the surf to drown in the waves? Is that what you meant?"

"You didn't see her drown," Dr. Blanchard said after a moment.

Evan laughed. "No, that's what makes it all bearable, isn't it? There's no evidence that I killed the woman, is there?"

"You didn't *kill* anyone," Dr. Blanchard spit back at him. "You couldn't *save* Josh. That's all. And if *anything* happened last night . . . then the fact is, you couldn't save her either. But you didn't kill anyone. And you have to admit that it's entirely possible that if you did see a skinny-dipper last night, that she was embarrassed and swam as far and as fast as she could before she let anyone see her face again. She's probably safe at home right now with her husband and kids, and her cheeks are flushing red every time she thinks about that guy last night who spotted her."

"Nice try," Evan laughed.

"I'm serious."

"Okay," Evan said. "So I saw a desperate housewife."

"Maybe."

Evan watched her face twitch. For a psychiatrist, she seemed to have no ability to keep her thoughts to herself; her facial muscles telegraphed every emotion she experienced. Inwardly he laughed; maybe that's why she was practicing a hundred miles from any major city.

"Evan," she said finally. "I've told you this before. But . . . what happened last night really just underlines it."

She leaned her elbows on the desk and sought to meet his eyes with her own in a gaze that was both serious and uninterruptible.

"You need to face your fear," she said. "How long have you been aquaphobic?"

Evan almost laughed as soon as she said it. He still hated that word. It reminded him of Aquaman, and thus seemingly meant something about how he was scared to death of watery superheroes. That's not what she meant, but the unbidden image made him laugh.

"I've never been able to swim," he said. "You know that."

She nodded, one faint wisp of blonde hair trailing over her nose. She didn't move to correct it. "Yes," she said, "but when did it become a problem? When did you realize that you simply couldn't ever swim? That you were afraid of water?"

Evan didn't even pause to think about it. "I've always been afraid of the water," he said.

"But you live by the ocean," Dr. Blanchard said, for

the umpteenth time poking at the root of his phobia. Only he could decide, ultimately, to uproot and face it.

Evan shrugged. "I just always have been afraid of it. And then I moved here, and it got worse."

"The woman, unveiled. The water, unprotected . . . The vanishing . . . Don't you think that maybe, just maybe, this is all a sign?" Dr. Blanchard hazarded. It sounded like bad Freud, but it made a certain amount of basic sense too. She continued, "Don't you think it's time to face your fears? Don't you think it's time to touch the water? You've been hiding from this since Josh died. The longer you hide, the longer you can blame yourself for that day. You need to release, forgive, and move past that horrible day. And the only way to do that is to forgive yourself."

Evan felt the bile rise in his throat. They'd been here before, he and Dr. Blanchard, and he thought he'd gotten past this piece of her paint-by-numbers psych test. Apparently not.

"I didn't see the woman last night out of guilt," he said. "But at the end of the day, I *did* kill my son."

Dr. Blanchard nodded her head. "So. We've basically gotten nowhere over the past year."

Evan didn't answer at first, and then looked up at her. "A year ago I didn't see women jumping to their deaths," he said.

"Nor did I," she said. "Nor did I. And I'd completely love to keep it that way."

She looked at him hopefully. "Here's what I think," she said. "I think you need to take swimming lessons."

She shifted behind the desk, and at the end of her fidgeting, she pulled one lone blue-jeaned leg up from beneath and slapped it on the top of the desk.

"Look," she said. "You've been coming here for a year.

There are good reasons that you've been upset, but it really is time to move on. Your son is not going to come back to you, and you are *not* responsible for his death. You were afraid of the ocean before you ever blamed it. Now you have to face both of those issues, and there's not a lot here that I can do for you." She paused for a minute, and then smiled. "In all honesty, I think you just need to go out and walk in the ocean. I'd recommend that Sarah be there with you. The two of you insist on suffering alone, when you should be together. Seriously, Evan, at this point there is nothing much that I can do for you. I can listen. I can give you some advice on what you need to do to help Sarah. But what do you need to do for you?"

She lowered her head and gave him the widest, most intelligent look of her eyes that she had. He could almost ignore her freckles.

"You need to face your fear. And your fear is the water. You need to go back there."

"I'm there every night," he said. "You know that."

"You're not *there*," she said. "You're *next* to there. You're just torturing yourself by looking at the scene of the supposed crime." She looked at him and shook her head. "If you want to put Josh to rest, there's only one way for you to do so. You have to get *off* the beach. And I don't mean avoid the beach. You have to follow your naked woman. You have to go into the water. That's where your answers lie. Not on the sand. And not here."

She motioned to the sterile confines of the office with its plastic potted plants and white-painted window frames. "I can listen to you for as long as you like, Evan," she said. "But I don't think I can help you anymore, if I ever could."

CHAPTER SIX

The house was empty when Evan came home, and to-night, he didn't feel bad about that. He stood in the door-way of Josh's room and stared at the Katy Perry poster on the wall. Dr. Blanchard was right about one thing—his life had become that of a bystander. Every day he looked at the shrine to Josh's life, his room. And every night he walked the beach and relived all the accusations that the place brought him. But it was like a film loop, playing over and over. He was frozen, not moving on.

He went to the kitchen and warmed up a plate of beef stew from the weekend. Sarah cooked most of the time, but Evan crocked up a mean stew on occasion and after sitting for a few days, the meat and spices marinated to get even better. He sat there at the kitchen table and stared out into the last glow of sunset as the beef melted on his tongue. Something had to change, he knew that.

But not tonight, he backpedaled a few minutes later. He pulled on his beach sandals and slipped out the back door.

The night air raised goose bumps on his arms as Evan walked down Butler Drive and arrived at the dry mounds of sand and spiky brush that marked the start of the beach. He trudged through the loose sand until he reached the waterline and then slipped off his sandals to walk along the water's edge. His night walks had been a ritual ever since he and Sarah moved here, over a decade ago. On the surface, it didn't make any sense that a man petrified of water would taunt himself by skirting its edge every single day, but Evan was fine with the ocean, as long as you didn't tell him he had to enter it. He loved the smell of the seaweed and salt that clung to the air, and the gentle, repetitive rush of the waves was the best sedative known to man. He slept soundly after his walks; or, at least he used to, when he wasn't retrieving Sarah afterward.

Tonight he walked a little faster than normal, a pace more determined than strolling. He wouldn't have admitted to himself where he was going, but his destination was clear.

Gull's Point.

The dark finger of rock jutted out in front him like a shadow in the night and, deep in his heart, he hoped that he'd see the woman again. Evan held his sandals tight. He'd need them for crawling around on the rocks.

He covered the half-mile walk in record time, and wiped the cold perspiration from his forehead when he set his first foot on the path down the point. He kept listening for a hint of music in the air, but the only sound was that of the surf. Carefully, he threaded his way down the rocks until he reached the end, the flat lookout where, last night, he'd seen the woman leap into the waves. Had she drowned?

She wasn't there tonight.

Evan laughed at himself. *Of course she wasn't there.* If Evan's fears were true, then she was at the bottom of the bay, and sooner or later, her body would probably be discovered floating to shore. And if Dr. Blanchard's theory were correct, then she was just a local skinny-dipper who was probably too embarrassed at being discovered to return immediately to the scene of the crime. Either way, she wasn't coming back here anytime soon.

He sat back and stared at the moon for a moment, and caught his breath. He'd walked faster than he realized to get here and his breath was labored.

Evan hadn't told Sarah about the woman last night. He told himself it was because she was out of it when she got home, but maybe it wasn't so clear-cut. Sarah wasn't the jealous type, normally, but, there was something about seeing the woman—and not just her nakedness—that had made him feel . . .

He began to hum to himself, the same melody he'd sung last night just before the woman had appeared. "Forever Now." Even just humming the song brought out emotion in him, and he let the melody die halfway through the first verse and chorus.

There was going to be no woman tonight. No song. No perfect pearl skin. Evan rose and threaded his way back off the point, carefully stepping between the jagged edges of black rock laced with gull dung. He began to walk toward home, though with something of the opposite in urgency to his journey here.

He'd only gone a few foot-dragging steps when something made him pause. Wishful thinking?

No.

There was the song again. His blood chilled and warmed from its very first notes. He looked out at the waves and saw only darkness. The rocks betrayed no movement. But the song. *The song was everywhere.* Evan didn't know which way to turn, but he knew he had to get closer to its source. He had to see her again. Talk to her. *Such an amazing voice* . . .

He started back toward the point, but then stopped;

the music didn't seem to be any closer as he walked toward the point, maybe it was even farther away. Again he scanned the dark beach and darker rocks and waves, but the moonlight didn't betray any sign of the singer.

Evan closed his eyes. The sound washed through his brain like the ocean over sand. He realized it was even stronger when he just relaxed and listened . . . and so he did. A smile grew unbidden on his face, as he followed the pure, perfect soprano notes. They trilled, crystalline like birdsong, before plummeting to the sonorous call of a whale before swirling back to dreamy octaves of more traditional verse. Beauty in dichotomy. Beauty in symmetry. Her voice swam effortlessly through curls and twists in melody, a sweet, dangerously alluring exercise in music. He couldn't make out any words per se, but she was singing *something*. And whatever the syllables meant, they made his heart tremble with joy and then cringe with sorrow. The song was bittersweet madness, and Evan let himself be lost in its beauty.

After a while, he knew which way to go, and he moved toward the sound. He felt drunk, groggy in the way you only feel after amazing late-night sex, the warmth and lust cooling but transposing into something more than simple physical ecstasy and release in the soul. Evan walked. He didn't open his eyes, but it was almost as if he could see anyway; the music brought him visions of lightning cracks in deep, somnolent purple and mountains of lush emerald and ocean waves that shimmered with the coolest, gemlike blue ocean waves that . . .

. . . lapped at his chest and sprayed his face with foamy salt.

Evan opened his eyes at the splash of a wave and saw her. The woman floated just a few feet away, dark eyes glinting in the moonlight reflecting off the ocean. Her tongue moved against white teeth as she trilled an exotic melodic riff, but suddenly Evan wasn't under its spell any longer. He was feeling the cold of the water on his skin and panic rose from his heart to his head like an electric current.

Evan screamed. The woman's eyes opened wide, and then she dove beneath the waves.

His own eyes popped as she disappeared and left him to realize how far into the ocean he had walked, completely unconscious of his path. How could he have done this? He'd never even felt wet until he'd opened his eyes to stare into hers. Evan's arms flailed for balance against the steady rush of the low waves, and he realized that he hadn't stopped screaming since the moment he'd felt the splash of saltwater on his face. Struggling for control, he forced his feet to step back, and back again toward land.

The woman hadn't resurfaced, but Evan didn't care about her anymore. All he could feel was the electric prod of panic. His heart beat in triple time. His chest burned and he couldn't catch his breath.

Evan turned away from the ocean to face the shore. When he saw that stretch of sand, safe haven, he stepped through the water faster. His heart pounded so loud in his ears, he imagined his valves giving way in an explosion of blood. In his mind he saw himself collapse here, just yards from shore, clutching at his heart as the water dragged him back to its murky, hungry depths. He forced himself to keep going, one step at a time. When the waves crested only as high as his thighs he began to run toward the beach, even though the fear warned him that he could fall and be dragged by the current back out to sea.

He *had* to get back on land. Now.

And then, he was there.

Evan collapsed on the wet-packed sand and struggled to control his breathing. It was difficult because as soon as he realized he had made it to safety, he began to cry. His chest heaved in ragged gasps and he closed his eyes and counted, using the power of slow, steady numbers in his struggle to regain control. He lay there on the sand for several minutes, willing his heart to slow down. He felt a fire beneath his ribs that threatened to consume him. He counted, and focused on the numbers. One, two, three . . . with each number, he slowed his breathing a little more. Finally, after pulling in a long, deep breath, he stood up, and stared back out into the ocean.

Waves crested and capped for as far as he could see, until the moonlight did no good and the water's surface was simply black.

No woman's head bobbed amid the breakers. Shaking his head in disbelief at what had just happened, Evan decided to join Sarah at the bar, as soon as he changed clothes. Only, tonight, *he* was having a drink.

CHAPTER SEVEN

June 3, 1887

Sometimes Captain James Buckley III felt like a pirate. During the long stretches between ports he had to keep driving the men, or they got sloppy. If they had their way, the deck of the *Lady Luck* would be littered with fish bones half the time, and the masts would hang loose with untethered sails. Not that he had a crew full of lazy louts, but . . . men will be men. And men without reason to keep things shipshape . . . didn't bother. When you're out on the waves, day after day . . . housecleaning doesn't seem very important. After all, who's watching?

Captain Buckley provided them the reason. Private "Three Hands" Nelson was getting a taste of the reason— one that he'd remember for many voyages to come—right now. The crewman was tied to the main sail, and periodically, when he felt like it, Captain Buckley would wander over and take a couple cracks at the boy with the whip that hung from a hook on the wheelhouse cabin. Right now, the lad's back was a series of red lines and welts and a fair amount of dried blood. 'Twas getting about time to release him back to his quarters for a day to recover.

It was brutal, yes, but the boy would learn a lesson he'd not soon forget. And the rest of the crew got a good brush-up reminder of who was captain each time they passed by the mast.

Served two purposes to give your crew a floggin' once in a while. They learned a bit of respect, and it kept the ship in shape.

One of the crew came running around the wheel-house. Jensen was his name. Cauldry's younger brother. Buckley had hired him on Cauldry's recommendation, even though the kid was greener than grass when it came to working a fishing rig. But Jensen actually *looked* green now. "Captain, we've just pulled in a net that I think you should see." The boy seemed to be biting his lip as he said it. His Adam's apple bobbed.

"All right," Buckley said, doing his best to sound put out by the interruption, though, in truth, he was curious about what could have riled up the boy up so badly. Seamen, no matter how young, didn't tend to be easily rattled. "Show me."

They walked to the stern, where a large net lay open on the deck. Silver minnows bounced and flipped in the air like popcorn. But at the far end of the pile of dying fish were Buckley's men: Jensen, Travers, Reg and Taffy.

Travers bent over something in the net, and Taffy kept stealing glances over the first mate's shoulder, but then looking away.

"Over here, Captain," Travers called. Buckley stepped around the puddles and lumps of broken seaweed near the net and bent over to look at what his first mate had found. His first thought was that they had netted a rib roast from depths of the deep blue. Chunks of bloody red meat hung off yellowing strips of curved bone. But his eyes followed Travers's hands, and he saw that the ribs sprouted an arm, and at the end of that arm dangled a gnarled, raw lump of something that may have once

had fingers. Travers was twisting at one of those appendages and the juice of bloated death dripped red from his
arm as he did.

"We got us some kind of half-eaten shark or baby
whale here?" the captain mused, but Taffy shook his head.
Then the white-faced crewman pushed away from Reg
and went to hang his head over the side of the boat.
Taffy never said a word, but from the sounds bleeding
over the side of the hull, he didn't need to.

"Naw," Travers said, strangely quiet. "Not unless
sharks have taken to wearing rings." The first mate held
up a shiny gold band with a black stone in the center.
"Looks like we found Rogers, sir. And something's eaten
him up pretty bad."

"Damn," the captain said, shaking his head. His voice
sounded flat as he pronounced, "He was a good man. I
wish we'd gotten to know him better."

Rogers had just joined the crew at their last dock. Few
of the ship's men would be able to remember much about
him for the funeral service, when they gave him the last
rites and pushed the chewed-up body back over the side.
Rogers had kept to himself and stayed belowdecks much
of the time, serving as cook and cleaner for the ship. And
then one morning, he just hadn't been around.

Buckley slapped a hand on Jensen's shoulder. "Go get a
sheet to put the man in," he said. The boy nearly tripped
as he twisted around to comply. He was back in moments. "I pulled this from my bed, sir."

"You'll be sleeping cold tonight then," the captain
responded, but motioned for him to lay it out on the
deck. Buckley bent to help Travers and slipped his hand
beneath one of the corpse's ribs. The lower half of the
man was missing, as was the head.

Travers grimaced, but grabbed the carcass by the

ragged bone that stuck out of the carnage where the neck should have been. He and the captain hefted the sodden weight onto the old sheet, which quickly stained a pinkish red. Two thin chunks of flesh fell to the deck as they moved their former crewmate and the captain nodded at Taffy. "Throw 'em in here."

The crewman bent to retrieve the pasty hunks of skin and muscle. Taffy touched the flesh as if he were picking up a steaming pile of manure. His face remained white as chalk after his trip to the edge of the hull. He dropped the pieces of Rogers onto the gruesome cage of ribs and quickly wiped his fingers on the edge of the sheet. Then he made a beeline for the ocean again.

Buckley and Travers folded the sheet end over end, and then again, tying the edges together, until Rogers was little more than a lump of laundry tied up in a bloodstained bow.

"Shall we throw the fish back, Captain?" Reg asked quietly, and Buckley laughed. "Hell no, lout, what would we do that for?"

"Because it's not right, sir. There are still little pieces of Rogers . . . and his blood . . . all over the catch. If we sell this batch, we're selling our cook for people to eat too, sir."

"Fish is fish and a catch is a catch," Buckley said, pointing to the silver fish in the net that had also held their former cook. "Rogers is gone and that's a good haul he brought us. We're taking it to shore. Now get it cleaned up. We'll have a service and say our last words for Rogers after dinner tonight." He turned to Cauldry and raised one eyebrow high. "How's that stew comin', cookie?"

Cauldry had taken over Rogers's duties the past two days, and so far had not successfully made anything qualifying as edible.

"I'll go check, sir." He dashed belowdecks again.

"Right," Buckley said. He nodded at the men who were pulling the net away from the sheeted body, and followed the boy down belowdecks to his cabin. As he opened the door and stepped inside, he grimaced at the odor of fish and something musky and rank. Working on the sea—living on the sea—made you immune to a lot. But Buckley had never grown to love the smell of fish. Thank God that "fishing trawler" was not the *Lady Luck*'s full-time occupation. He opened a small door in the wall above his bunk and pulled out a brown jug. Pulling off the stopper, he inhaled one bittersweet draught of alcohol and smiled as his nose cleared.

Then he took a long swig and sighed as his throat burned from the liquor. There were crates of the stuff on board right now, headed for port just north of 'Frisco. But the best . . . the best bottles never left the captain's quarters. He breathed out a mist of aged tequila, corked the bottle and checked the lock on his door. The captain then stripped off his jacket and shirt, and then carefully folded his pants to set in the corner.

At last, he turned to his bunk, and the reason he had come down here in the middle of the day. It hadn't been to drink. Two eyes sparked like lightning as he bent to touch the woman lying prone on his bed.

She jerked against the ropes that bound her wrists and ankles, and her head flew angrily from side to side, silken raven hair drifting and kinking across her face in black seaweed tangles. But she didn't make a sound.

She couldn't.

A leather strap gagged it all inside her.

"How is my little songbird today, hmmm?" the captain said, as he bent to kiss the exposed skin of her neck. With rank, came privilege, he thought, and without the pretense of love or foreplay, crawled on top.

CHAPTER EIGHT

"On my clock, eight thirty comes before nine o'clock,"
Darren called, as Evan slipped into the Delilah Harbor
Authority office. He closed his eyes and stifled an equally
smart-ass reply. He hated it when Darren tried to be
funny.

"Sorry," he said instead. "I promise I'll get back on
schedule next week."

Bill looked up at him with a twisted grin as Evan threw
his bag under his desk and powered up the ancient computer. One of these days, the shipping yard was going to
lose all of its records—Darren wouldn't spring for regular
data backup service, or computers that had been manu-
factured in this decade. Windows 95 was just fine for what
they needed to do, their boss had said on many occasions.

"He's not going to cut you any more slack, you know
that, right?" his friend asked.

Evan nodded. "This weekend I'm turning the corner.
I'm going to clean up Josh's room, Sarah and I are going
to have a long talk . . . next week things'll be different."

"Uh huh. I've heard that before."

"I mean it," Evan insisted. "I can't do this anymore,
I've gotta . . ."

Bill pulled a finger across his neck and Evan suddenly
knew that Darren had walked right up behind him.

"I've got a special project for you today," the shipping

master declared, and handed Evan a ream of paper. "These have to be cross-referenced with the files on Trans-Global for the past five years. They're calling for an audit next week, so I need to you get these in place before you leave today." He dropped the stack of paper in Evan's palms with a slap, and walked away.

Bill winked at him. "Told ya he was done. Meet you for a beer tonight at O'Flaherty's?"

Evan nodded. "Sure."

"Let's say eight o'clock? Looks to me like you're going to be busy until then."

Evan elbowed his friend in the shoulder. "Thanks a lot. Wanna give me a hand?"

Bill shook his head and laughed. "I didn't pull detention. This one's all yours."

There was already a roiling cloud of smoke drifting ghostlike along the ceiling when Evan slipped into O'Flaherty's. While California state law prohibited smoking in bars or any other public place, Delilah thought of itself as something of a sovereign state. Nobody was going to complain about smoke at O'Flaherty's and the cops weren't going to come down on it. Hell, half the force smoked cigars in the back room on Saturdays.

Evan stepped past a clog of giggling college girls and moved deeper into the recesses of the bar, which wound through two connected rooms, each with cloisters of jabbering people gesturing and indiscriminately sloshing alcohol on its long, dark plank floors. Some stood around tables, some just loitered in the middle of the walkway. The sound of the crowd was louder than the music on the speakers; Evan couldn't quite tell what song was even playing, he just felt the remote pounding of drums and thudding movement of a bass line.

A hand reached out and grabbed him by the shirt collar. Bill yanked him into a cubby, cut off from the walkway by a stained-glass window. Evan slid onto the stool and sighed.

"Long day in the morgue?"

He nodded. "I thought I'd never get through that stack."

"Teach ya to be late."

Evan grinned. "I promise I will be in at eight thirty A.M. on the dot on Monday."

"Well then, drink up, 'cuz we got two days to kill first," Bill said, and motioned for the waitress. After she took Evan's order, Bill cut to the chase.

"It's worse, isn't it? With Sarah, I mean."

Evan nodded. "Yeah. I'm dragging her home almost every night. And then I can't sleep."

"Need to get her some help, man."

"You think I haven't tried?"

The waitress slipped a foaming glass of Anchor Steam in front of Evan, and he took a deep swallow of the amber brew before saying anything else. Then he put down the glass and looked at his friend. "Right now, I need an ear myself."

Bill looked surprised, but simply said, "Lay it on me."

"I've been seeing this woman, down by the beach . . ." Evan began.

Bill raised an eyebrow, and Evan laughed.

"Not like that." He described the first night he'd stumbled across the nude woman singing on the rocks, and his fear that she'd drowned when she'd suddenly jumped naked into the water and disappeared, not to reappear.

"Naked chicks never drown," Bill commented. "They're water nymphs. They always float."

Evan shot him a look, but went on to tell him the story of the previous night, and of "waking up" while standing in the middle of the ocean.

Now his friend looked interested. "*You* walked into the water?" he said incredulously. "Up to your chest?"

Evan nodded.

"You're afraid to put your fuckin' *toe* in the water," Bill said.

"Thank you for overstating the obvious. That's why I wanted to talk to you. I don't understand it, or how it could have happened. Her voice was just so incredible, so powerful, that I had to get closer, I guess. I got lost in her song and had my eyes closed, and was just . . . I don't know, I was in a different place. It was kinda like I went sleepwalking."

Bill's forehead wrinkled, and he took a sip of his beer before answering. "You ever sleepwalk before?"

Evan shook his head, negative.

Bill leaned in and spoke softly, but firmly. "You know what I think?" he asked. "I think you saw the Siren."

"What are you talking about?" Evan laughed, and Bill grinned.

"The Siren of Delilah," Bill said. "She's been luring men to their deaths out there by the point for decades."

"A Siren, like in mythology?"

"Yep. You mean to tell me you've lived in this town all these years and you've never heard the stories?"

"I don't pay a lot of attention to urban legends," Evan said, and took another swig. "I don't believe in ghosts."

"The Siren's not a ghost," Bill insisted. "She's some kind of sea goddess . . . she lures men to the water, and most of the time, they never return."

"Then how do you know they went into the water in the first place?"

"What do you mean?"

"If they don't return, how do you know they ever went into the water?"

"Now you're just being difficult." Bill shook his head. "I can't believe you work at the port and haven't heard of the Siren. Some of the fishing trawlers won't even dock here after dark 'cuz they're so superstitious."

"I've never heard of a shipwreck since I've been here," Evan said. "Isn't that what Sirens do? Lure ships to crash on the rocks and shit?"

Bill nodded. "Sometimes. But they also lure men into the ocean. We haven't had a shipwreck here in ages, that's true. Though there were some a long, long time ago. Plenty of wrecks down there off the point."

"I hesitate to ask, but . . . what makes you or anyone else think there's a Siren haunting the bay now? Seems like a pretty 1800s kind of superstition."

"You'd think so, wouldn't you? But hell, man, you've lived here long enough to know this town. We may be just up the coast from San Francisco, but . . . there's a reason the rumrunners used to dock *here* instead of there. We're off the beaten path. A little backwoods. And you know what? People do disappear around here periodically. You've read about them in the papers and probably just didn't pay any attention 'cuz you didn't know them. But whenever it happens, I can tell you what the old guard are saying. They're shaking their heads when the police statements theorize about runaways who moved on and accidental deaths in the ocean. They're saying one thing: the Siren is swimming again."

Evan took a long draught of his beer, and then slammed it, empty, to the wooden shelf before them. "You *know* how ridiculous that sounds, don't you?"

Bill shrugged. "Is that any more ridiculous than an aquaphobe who goes sleepwalking into the ocean to chase after a naked chick? I mean, *really*, Evan."

"The music lulled me . . ."

"Exactly. What do Sirens do?"

"Never mind." Evan shook his head. "You're not going to convince me that this woman is some weird monster. The whole situation was a little odd, it's true, and she has a beautiful voice. But that's where it ends."

Bill shrugged. "Suit yourself."

The two men were silent for a moment, and then Bill laughed. "Okay, you win."

"What are you talking about?" Evan said.

"The whole Siren thing. It was a good try, and you had me going—but c'mon now. Tell me what really happened at the beach. Is this all a long way around you telling me that you are seeing another woman?"

"No—"

Bill shrugged. His face looked completely open, understanding, empathetic. " 'Cuz I understand, if you are. I know things have been tough with Sarah since . . . the accident, but really, Evan, I don't think that— "

"No, I'm *not* cheating," Evan insisted. "I wasn't making up a story."

"Okay." His friend didn't sound convinced. Instead, he abruptly changed the subject. "So you think the 49ers are going to do it this season?"

"Sure," Evan said. "Why not?" He ordered another beer, and didn't bring up the woman again.

CHAPTER NINE

There was a comfort in the familiarity of the wrongdoing . . . that's how Evan looked at it. Every night he walked the beach. Every night the sand stuck between his toes and every night he knew it was just an exercise in avoidance. He was expert at that. He knew that the right path was to move on . . . to step aside from the life that he'd built with Sarah all these years and start a new one. A life that didn't involve Josh. But . . . he couldn't seem to *go* there, as much as his mind said that it was the right place to be. He walked instead through sand that didn't care about Evan or Josh or Sarah . . . sand that had withstood the rush of a hundred thousand tides. Sand that didn't care if Evan's son had died here, fucked here or slept here . . . it didn't matter.

To Evan, it mattered. He wanted to connect with those places that his son had been . . . those places that his son held dear. And so he walked the beach again and again. Sometimes it seemed as if a whole world were against them. And sometimes it was just the way of life. Tonight he walked along the tide and imagined his son out in the surf, riding the waves. Josh had taken to the surfboard like a fish; he could twist on a wave like nobody.

Evan used to watch and envy his son's natural acclimation. He wished that he could be so free in the water; for him it was like watching a bird in the air. The motion seemed natural, but magical at the same time.

The thought of Josh on the waves made him want to cry, but Evan just walked farther down the beach. Down away from memory. Down away from Sarah. Down away from the fear that maybe, just maybe, he could have done something to change what was. What *is* . . .

He saw the black shadow of Gull's Point and shook his head. He would not sing tonight. He would not tempt the woman who had made the past couple nights so disturbing.

Evan picked up a rock and threw it sideways to skip across the waves. It bounced once, twice, thrice . . . and disappeared.

The emptiness of the waves washed over him and he felt his loss more than ever . . . the vastness of the world was upon him in the night, and Evan cried. He looked out into the mist of the night, to the horizon, black with empty promises of something that might be tomorrow. Black with . . . nothing. Evan cried and he wished for more.

There *was* more.

There was music. He heard the sweet, gentle notes crest the waves like dust. Quietly yet still strong . . . the sound somehow rose above the rush of water and he listened. He felt the music move his heart and, more importantly, his soul. He tried to ignore it. The music of the naked woman could not impact his life . . . could not come between him and Sarah. Yet, he could not deny its beauty, its purity. The sound was everything Evan had ever wanted. He closed his eyes to shut it out, but the motion only allowed the sound to cling deeper to his soul . . . she was inside him, and he could not say no to force her out.

Evan felt his breathing increase, and he knew that he could not deny her call. And then . . . there she was. Walking out of the waves just in front of him. She strode across the sand, naked and beautiful . . . perfect. Her eyes were deep and dark . . . yet bright somehow. Her breasts looked full and firm . . . desperately longing for him. Her legs posed long and strong, gently curved calves sculpted to muscular thighs, leading across the delta of her sex to the pit of her belly. Her thighs shimmered with wetness, and begged for him to look between, to the place that wanted him . . . the place that dripped with the ocean, and would, in seconds, drip with him . . . if he let her.

She was in front of him, and she put cold hands on his shoulders. He could not deny her . . . he drew her close, and his clothes were instantly damp with the embrace. She felt small in his arms, and yet strong. Her arms fit within his as if she were just a girl, but her breasts pushed against him with an urgency and a fullness that said she was no *girl*. She said nothing, but her lips spoke enough. They nibbled at his ear, and then slipped to his neck.

"No," Evan said at first, but he was unconvincing . . . and then her lips were on his, and his tongue met hers, and "no" was not at all what it said.

Evan kissed the naked woman who pressed against him as if she were the first woman he had ever kissed. His entire body seemed to melt with her touch, and thoughts of Sarah fled like dreams of a past life. His moment was here, now . . .

He couldn't deny her, and her hands helped lift his shirt, and fumble the zipper down on his pants. And then he was naked on the beach as well, pressing against her . . . flesh meeting like heat and cold do—first drawing apart and then melting together. They were like opposites, sea creature and land, but he wanted her more than anything. Her tongue moved against his teeth and lips and he accepted her, drew her in. She was everything he desired; cool and hot in equal measures. She was a fever dream.

He drew her down to the sand and never broke their

embrace, his hands exploring her back and ribs and yes, her butt—which was softer than any pillow he'd ever laid his head against. Her own hands explored him too, and he felt himself grow to steel against her . . . so hard that he couldn't think of much more than quenching himself within her . . . using her secret place to soothe the heat she'd inspired.

Her lips didn't allow him time to think about it for long, as her fingers slipped up from his ass to his head, and pulled him tight to her, urging him inside. And he complied, slipping into that place he'd only gone to with Sarah for years . . . he moved within her as if it were his second home. Her body offered an exotic attraction, yet also instant familiarity and pleasure, his cock driving deeper and deeper into her, desperately trying to find her core. Evan took the woman as his own, and her moans of pleasure echoed above the surf like carnal music. When at last he was spent, and slipped out of her to gasp exhausted on his back in the sand, she leaned over and kissed his belly, and then his chest, licking around his nipples to arrive finally at his neck, and then his lips. He tasted the salt of his own sweat on her mouth, and then she began to sing.

Evan felt himself drifting off to sleep in the comfort of her melody, and despite his eyelids' desire to close, he smiled and whispered, "Who are you?"

She paused and with a voice that seemed to come from inside his soul, she answered, "Ligeia."

CHAPTER TEN

Evan woke to the moon overhead, its light sharp and piercingly white in his eyes. A cool night breeze swept the beach, and he shivered. Goose bumps peppered his arms, and he realized that he'd been sprawled out there, nude on the sand, visible to anyone who might be out for a late-night stroll. For how long?

"Shit!" He rolled to a crouch and looked around, but spotted nobody. What time was it? He hurriedly brushed the sand off his skin and pulled on his pants. Once half dressed, he located his cell phone and checked the time. 11:34. Not too late, but late enough. Thank God it wasn't three in the morning.

Evan shook out his shirt and then slipped it over his head. He scanned the beach again, and nobody looked to be around, including the woman. Ligeia?

A sick feeling grew in the pit of his stomach as the memory of their coupling played out in his mind like a pornographic movie. He had cheated on Sarah. God . . . why? Things had been difficult with them this year, but even when they'd grown distant he'd never really *wanted* another woman. He swallowed, as if the act would wash away the memory, but instead he tasted the musky, salty flavor of Ligeia. He began walking quickly toward home and felt grains of sand chafing between the cheeks of his ass. He needed a shower, but he needed to get to the bar to pick up Sarah, if she hadn't come home yet. All of the euphoria of sex was gone; Evan felt like a jerk. A jerk in a hurry. He began to jog along the beach and then up the street to his house.

The lights were out as he followed the walk to the front door. He unlocked it and slipped inside. "Sarah?" he called. But there was no answer.

Damn. He ran to the bathroom and turned on the shower. Then he stripped out of his clothes for the second time that evening. Leaning over the sink, he stared hard at himself in the mirror. "Cheater," he said to his reflection. Brown eyes looked away from his accusation. His face looked thin to him, and Evan pursed his lips. Her taste still clung to him, and he quickly covered his toothbrush with paste and tried to scrub Ligeia away. Then he stepped into the steaming shower and did the same with his body. He was tempted to use Sarah's loofah, but it just seemed too much like one more betrayal to scrub the sweat of another woman from his body with his wife's bathing aids. Instead he doused himself with soap and scrubbed fast and furious, leaving his skin raw.

He toweled off and redressed, throwing his beach clothes to the bottom of the hamper. Then he ran back out into the night to find his wife.

Sarah's eyes were bloodshot when Evan found her at O'Flaherty's. She was talking to a beefy balding guy whom Evan vaguely recognized as one of the port's dock workers when he walked up.

"Hey, baby." She grinned feebly as he pulled up a stool. "Thought you weren't gonna come tonight." The dock man faded back quickly when he realized the situation. Evan laughed to himself. *Sorry, pal, not gonna take advantage of my drunk wife tonight.* Though, he mused, if he let it happen, it would sort of even the score between them.

No, he didn't think Sarah would go home with another man, even if blitzed. She was loyal and true; with way more character than apparently he had.

"Sorry, babe," he said. "I dozed off. Ready to go?"

She nodded and he took her elbow to help her down. Sarah leaned heavily against him, and he supported her with an arm around the waist as they walked unevenly toward the door. "I think my butt's asleep," she mumbled. "Maybe you can rub it for me when we get home."

He saw the look of sodden lust in her eyes, and rubbed her ass for a second through her jeans. "Sure," he said. For a moment he panicked . . . how could he make love to Sarah tonight? After . . . But then he shrugged off the fear. He knew that she was not going to be in any condition once he got her home and undressed. And he was right.

Less than fifteen minutes later, Sarah was lying facedown in their bed as Evan pulled off her pants and socks.

The room was filled with the gentle noise of her snoring. Evan lay down next to her, but every time he closed his eyes he saw the face of Ligeia.

It was a long night.

CHAPTER ELEVEN

June 4, 1887

Private "Three Hands" Nelson was not a happy seaman. His back was scabbed and sore. It hurt to move and he had to stifle a moan every time he bent over. The captain had made an example of him yesterday. Yes, sir, he certainly had. Well, Nelson didn't cotton to such things sitting down. He was going to get even. The private wasn't called "Three Hands" for nothing. On land, they said Jack Nelson could be shaking your hand while patting your shoulder . . . while at the same time slipping the green out of your wallet. A life on the streets of the Tenderloin District in San Francisco made a lad industrious. Or dead.

The captain had found a bottle of 'shine in Nelson's possession, and an open crate in the storeroom. Buckley had offered the private the chance to come clean, but Nelson had refused to explain and so the captain had taken him to the whipping post. The truth was, he had nicked the bottle from Taffy—Nelson would never have been so stupid as to pry open a crate of cargo and leave it visibly tampered with that way. And he wouldn't have taken the bottle if he'd realized how stupid Taff'd been. But he had his pride. Nelson didn't admit to stealing the bottle in the first place, but wouldn't say where he'd gotten it. And so,

Captain Buckley had tied him to the deck for a daylong whippin'. Regular sadist, their captain was.

Thing was, now "Three Hands" had a score to settle. If he was gonna be punished for something he didn't do, then he was going to do something like what he was punished for. And that's what he was about now. Nelson slipped through the lower decks without a sound. That was extra difficult with his back hurting the way it was, but Nelson was strong. The crew was all topside. He knelt before the door and tried the knob. Locked, as he knew it would be. He slipped out the pin from his back pocket and slipped it in the keyhole.

A locked door had nothing on Jack "Three Hands" Nelson. He smiled as he felt the latch click over. The door eased open and Jack took one fast look behind him. Satisfied that he remained unseen, Nelson slipped inside the captain's quarters and pulled the door shut. If the captain wanted to take something out of him, he'd take something out of the captain. He knew the ol' bugger kept the best 'shine locked away for himself. Could smell it on his breath at dinner every night. Well, ol' "Three Hands" would just help himself to a bit, and keep it hidden away beneath a loose board he'd found near Taffy's billet. Rough justice, indeed, if 'twere found!

The captain's cabin stank of fish and something else, something sweetly rotten. *Jesus*, Nelson thought. *For a militant asshole, the captain lived like a slob.*

Captain Buckley's quarters weren't huge, but the space was a damn sight better than the cluster of bunks that the men shared just down the walkway. On an old boat designed to move cargo, there was no place for fancy crew quarters. The captain and first mate got doors in front of the closets their bunks were housed in, and that was it.

Nelson waited for his eyes to adjust to the dark. There

was a porthole on the other side of the room, but it was curtained over. Odd, to leave the room in darkness for the day. He stayed in a crouch and moved across the room. It hurt to be on all fours, but he was less likely to knock something over this way.

The smell was stronger as he approached the captain's bunk—did the old sadist *sleep* with the damn fish, as well as net them? Nelson's hand brushed up against something on the floor. He squinted in the dark but couldn't make out what it was, though it felt cool and damp. He yanked his hand back. Maybe it was fish guts.

Something moved in the dark, and Nelson's heart stopped. Someone was here! He leaned toward the bunk, trying to see . . . anything.

The shadow moved again, and the whites of two glimmering eyes reflected back at him in the dark. Nelson could just make out the body now. The wrists were tied with a rope knotted to the fore of the bed, and as he followed the outline of the shadowy form down, he could see that the feet were tied apart—one to each corner of the bunk. Satisfied that there was no danger from this quarter, the private leaned in to stare into the woman's eyes. She made a whimper deep in her throat as he drew closer, but she didn't speak.

"What's your name, girl?" Jack whispered. Again she only grunted softly.

"You bastard," Jack quietly cursed the captain as he saw the reason for her silence. "Stay quiet," he warned, and reached his hand behind her head to release the gag.

He could see her a little better now as he pulled the restraint from her mouth. She stretched her jaw and ran a tongue over her lips to moisten them, and probably to take the taste of the gag away. Her eyes were wide and slanted just enough to look exotic. Mediterranean? Eastern? He wasn't sure. Her nose was thin and delicate, and her lips—now wetted—pouted thick and wide above a narrow chin. Jack ran a finger from her neck across the pit of her arm to cup one soft breast in his palm. Absently, he thumbed her nipple and it grew hard beneath his rough touch.

"So our captain has his own private plaything, does he now?" Jack murmured. He reached to the head of the bed and worked her wrists free of the rope. "And he likes to tie up more than just his crew. Hmmm. I wouldn't have given the old man credit."

The woman sighed as her arms were released and drew them to her chest in a pointless attempt to cover herself. One of her hands covered Jack's, and she stared at him with wide, questioning eyes.

"I'm not gonna hurt ya," Jack promised. His mind was racing now, trying to think of how he could work this situation to its best advantage. "I can help," he finally said. "Not much I can do while we're at sea, but once we're ashore . . ."

Her hand moved up his arm. He nodded. "Mmmm hmm. You understand." He ran a calloused hand over the velvet-soft flesh of her left breast, and then traced the faint down of her flesh to the place where the hair should have mounded, a tantalizing hidden gate to her sex. But when his hand met her crotch, he found it smooth. With one finger he traced the soft folds of her cleft and whistled softly. "Our captain keeps you bare in every way, eh? Does he shave you himself?" Nelson laughed softly and continued his private explorations, slipping a hand beneath her ass and cupping the cheeks before pulling back to hold her womanly "virtue" like a guard.

The woman sat up and cupped his face with her hands. Jack moved to embrace her, but she gently pushed him back, and began to work the buttons of his shirt. He grinned, and let her undress him, groaning a little when the shirt pulled at the scabs on his back.

He stood and undid his belt, relieving himself of the pants in a moment. Then he was sitting naked on the bed with her, and she ran her hands across his shoulders. He winced, and she looked confused. Her fingers moved lightly over his wounds and she raised a dark eyebrow, but still, said nothing.

That was all right with Jack; he had a momentary touch of panic as he realized what would happen if the captain walked into his private quarters right now.

But the woman drew him down in a kiss, and he quickly forgot his fear. He'd never been with a woman like this; so small, but so voluptuous at the same time. He sucked on her lips and then trailed his tongue down her neck and shoulders before boldly moving still lower, to chew gently on her nipples like soft fruit. Her hands were all over him, drawing him up and on top and at last in. He gasped at the warmth of her. As he bucked and moaned, the woman moved to meet him, but her eyes never left his. Wide and limpid, she stared unblinking at Jack as he moved quickly atop her to orgasm, and then collapsed against her, head on her breast.

Her hands stroked his hair and in a whispery voice, she began to sing.

"Shhhh," Jack urged, reaching up to put a finger on her lips. But she held his hand at bay, and then the melody captured him. It was light as air, yet thick as honey. Amber notes so pure they pulled him in. Lured him to a place that swam with light and lust, liquor and love. Jack Nelson had never felt so happy in his entire life. His flesh burned with pleasure while the faces in his mind shifted; he was suckling at his mother's breast, drinking from the delta of a snow-white whore; guzzling from the finest, rarest booze ever refined. It burned so sweetly as it slid down his throat, opening up his chest with heaven fire.

The song had stopped. That's probably why Nelson surfaced from the musical spell in time to understand. The fire wasn't in his mind. His throat burned. He opened his mouth but gagged on something rich and iron. Blood spilled out across the woman's chest, dripping like gory wax down her ribs.

"Wha-di-ya . . . ?" he gurgled as he slapped a hand to his neck and felt the hot flow and ragged flesh of his neck. He blinked and saw his blood on her mouth. She was grinning, and her fingernails dug into his back, dragging him back down for the fatal bite. She'd torn out his throat with her teeth!

Jack Nelson had lived twenty-three long years surviving the subterfuge of thugs in the back alleys of San Francisco, and he'd be damned if a woman—a woman still half shackled to a bed, damn it—was going to take him down with her teeth!

His body felt drugged and the pain in his neck unbearable. But Jack slammed one of his arms against hers, breaking her embrace, and then pushed away from her, catching her with a blow to the chest that propelled him away and out of her reach for a split second. He pushed off the bed with his knees, and fell to the floor. From behind him, the song began again, and Jack struggled to ignore it, to not hear. He rose to a crouch, but only moved a couple feet when the languor took him, and his muscles turned to jelly.

Jack slumped back to the wood, and felt the blood pumping away; the floor at his arm felt warm and wet. Just there, in front of his face, something else lay on the floor. Whatever he'd bumped on the way in, he realized. The end looked like a ragged butcher's nightmare, bloody and raw and gouged up. He saw the meat had hair on the flesh, and he struggled to rise again to see more. Some last part of him wanted to understand what he'd stumbled upon before he died. He knew now that he would die here. Jack Nelson had been downed by a woman's mouth. He laughed, almost, but blood gushed out of his throat when he did, and it turned to a long, horrible choke. The coughing woke him slightly from the woman's spell, and he lifted his head through the song to follow the flesh of the gory lump on the deck to make out a naked knee and a hairy shin. The foot was missing its toes; there were bloody stumps left behind, just as the top of the leg's thigh had been chopped away from whomever's body it had once walked with.

The song continued all around him, light and sweet, and dreams of golden fields cascaded in Jack's mind, as hands grabbed him by the ankles and began to drag him back to the bed.

With some fleeting remnant of his consciousness, Jack saw one more abandoned part lying near the bed, as the woman pulled him up from the floor.

A man's head.

It lay on its side on the wood planks, but Jack's last conscious thought recalled the ragged torso they'd raised with the nets yesterday. He knew that face.

"So that's what happened to Rogers," he mumbled.

And then the song ended, and her teeth were on him, and Nelson knew no more.

CHAPTER TWELVE

"Here it is in black and white," Bill said.

Evan looked at the newspaper on his desk and raised an eyebrow. The first article to catch his eye at the top of the page read DELILAH TURNS ON THE RED LIGHT.

"Here *what* is, Bill? The city council wants to change the zoning on West Avenue to allow a massage parlor? I didn't realize you'd been waiting for this. Tired of driving to San Francisco for your five-fingered oil treatments?"

Bill rolled his eyes. "Puh-leese. All you've gotta do is go up to O'Flaherty's after midnight if you want a good feel. Guys'd be stupid to go pay for it when all they gotta do is pop for a drink." He pointed to a smaller piece on the right corner of the page. This one read KYLIE REYNOLDS, 22, MISSING. The article was short, with a mug shot of the local girl, who hadn't come home from a night out at The Sand Trap with her boyfriend several days ago. The boyfriend was quoted as saying he'd broken up with her that night and he hoped she hadn't done anything stupid. Police said they'd welcome any information that would lead to finding the girl.

"Yeah, so?" Evan shrugged. "What about it?"

"Chalk another one up to the Siren," Bill said.

"You can't be serious. Every time someone goes missing in this town, it's the fault of some mythological harpy?"

"A Siren is not a harpy. Get your Homer straight."

Evan laughed. "I didn't realize you were so literary."

Bill didn't laugh. "Look, Evan, I know it sounds ridiculous. But if you ask people around Delilah—people who've lived here their whole lives—they're going to tell you they believe that something is out there near the point. Some call it a Siren; some probably say it's a sea monster. But Siren rings true to me. There have been disappearances out there for as long as I can remember. The papers just say the currents out there are dangerous and pull people in. But there are stories from the early 1900s of rumrunners crashing into the rocks out there, and every now and then, one of the sailors would survive and get to shore. You can go look this shit up—every survivor who ever swam in from one of those wrecks talked about hearing a beautiful woman singing. And the next thing they knew, they were swimming for their lives in the waves."

"Sounds like they were drinking too much on the job."

Bill shook his head in disgust. "You believe in God, Evan? Heaven and hell, all that shit?"

Evan nodded.

"So. You believe in a great invisible tooth fairy in the sky, and horned demons running around a land of brimstone and lava where the dead burn in agony 'til the end of time? And you probably believe in a purgatory, where the souls go who weren't quite bad enough to warrant demons repetitively sticking pitchforks in their eyes to sweat out their sins until they can get to the secret land of harps and honey. Is that right?"

Evan grimaced. "I wouldn't exactly describe heaven and hell like that."

"Read your Milton. And Revelations is a hoot too."

"Did you take one of those online courses in English literature this week, or what?"

"Just think about it," Bill said, ignoring the dig. "You

believe in all this invisible shit that nobody has ever seen, but you can't believe in a real flesh-and-blood creature that has been written about for hundreds of years here on earth that people have reported seeing over and over again?"

Bill turned back to his desk and shook his head. "We don't know it all yet, man. And we never will. There are secret things still on this earth. Be careful."

"Be careful."

Bill's words echoed in Evan's head as he walked the beach after dark that night. He hadn't told Bill about his tryst with Ligeia. He had intended to; he needed to talk to *somebody* about it. But after their conversation about the missing girl, it just hadn't seemed like the right time.

So tonight his heart remained a mess of guilt and lust. He had toyed with the idea of not going out, but... walking the beach was what he did. And he did want to see her again. He pledged to himself that he would not let his guard down again though. He needed to talk to her. To find out more about who she was, and to apologize for last night. Because he had made love to her under false pretense. He was married; he couldn't say "happily," because the past year had been the worst one of his life. But not because of his wife. He loved her and did not want anyone else. Even if Ligeia had given him the best sex of his life, bar none.

But he was married. Not available.

Tonight the waves were quiet, the whitecaps few. A chill wind blew in from the northwest, and he shivered. A gull called out once somewhere nearby, lonely in the dark. Evan shoved his hands in his pockets and stared at the white glints of moon reflecting off the wet pools disappearing into the dark sand ahead. Night crabs scuttled out of his path and along the waterline like furtive spiders, darting to snatch pieces of seaweed or fish and then disappearing down holes in the sand. The beach was quiet at night, but never empty.

Evan bent to pick up a miniature conch shell, speckled pink and brown and horned with some impressive spikes on its thicker end. Even after all these years, he never tired of bringing home interesting shells; Sarah had glass jars throughout the house filled with his finds. He slipped it in his pants pocket.

He walked near the point now, and slowed his pace, stopping before he reached the finger of dark rock. He bent to retrieve a small, flat stone and skipped it across the quiet ocean. One, two, three, four . . . five . . . . six times! A smile creased his lips—Josh would have been proud. They used to compete on how many skips they could get out of a stone.

The memory cascaded into myriad snapshots of their times at the beach. Playing Frisbee, skipping rocks, falling together in the sand laughing, sitting out by a campfire, late, Evan strumming on the guitar . . .

Unconsciously, he began to sing another of their favorite songs, from the band Industrial Disease. "Let me touch you now, forever, just this one last time . . ." But he couldn't complete the lyric. His throat closed. He teared up every time he sang that song anymore.

Somewhere else, as if in answer to his aborted song, a melody picked up. But the melancholy of Evan's tune transformed to light in its mirror. The voice moved high in the sky, almost like a wordless birdsong. And then it swam deep, a contralto cresting just above the waves with a sweetness that made Evan's knees tremble. He wanted to slip to the sand and lose himself in the perfect sound. Whoever this woman was, Ligeia had the most amazing voice he had ever heard. Why she wasted it out here on nobody, he couldn't fathom. Unless she simply came out here to practice? With a range so wide and a depth so beautiful, Evan couldn't imagine that she didn't sing professionally. Though he didn't know of any famous opera stars or the like living in Delilah. And he'd never heard of a singing star named Ligeia.

Evan looked for her on the rocks of the point and was about to start climbing the treacherous path to walk out into the bay, when he realized that she wasn't on the rocks tonight. A faint smear of ivory bobbed and moved in the water beyond the point, and as he stared, Evan saw that she appeared to be lying on her back, floating in the water, and singing to the stars. Every now and then he could see her arms break above the water, or a pale knee lift out of the waves and then disappear again to allow her to maintain her dreamy swim atop the waves.

Evan moved closer to the water; his whole body yearned to be nearer to the source of the music. Ligeia's song was hypnotic; he closed his eyes and felt her fingers play across his body like he were an instrument. The night seemed to warm around him as he surrendered to the sound, and opened his heart to the beauty of her song. The melody swam in his veins like liquor, expanding the reach of his consciousness, while at the same time rendering him numb to all distraction.

He was glad he had not followed his initial promise to himself to avoid the beach. He needed to stand next to her again. Even if he never touched her body again, Evan needed to listen to her song. His breath seemed to slow and speed up with the slipstream movement of the music, and he took another step nearer to where she sang. Evan was lost in the sound, and didn't even open his eyes to see where he was walking. He only drank in the sound and sighed, as it filled him up and then slipped away to leave him desperately aching. Ligeia's music played the emotions like a harp, and yet, Evan couldn't even have defined a single word of what she sang about. There *were* words and familiar syllables. But she sang in some other tongue, he thought. A language that was more beautiful than any he had ever heard. Somehow, the foreign sounds still gave him meaning; he felt as if he were on a ride through a powerful story—as she sang his heart quailed in fear and then rejoiced to the point of ecstatic pain at some lost piece regained. Evan moved closer to the sound and smiled as he realized the truth of her voice, the ultimate truth of the sound—music was a communication that went beyond words, and whatever she was saying, he understood the feeling, if not the words.

And then the music stopped, and Evan felt hands slipping around his shoulders. He gasped at a sudden chill, and opened his eyes . . .

. . . to see waves all around him!

Suddenly he fell out of the dream world and realized that he was neck-deep in the ocean, the water lapping like deadly acid around his face. Ligeia swam just before him, her fingers outstretched to play around his shoulders and slip up into his hair. But in five seconds Evan went from lolling in heaven to standing in hell. His gorge rose and his heart tripled its beat as his eyes went wide. He didn't see Ligeia as she rose and fell with the water. He only saw beyond her—the black waves and the panic overwhelmed him as completely as her music.

Evan opened his mouth and screamed.

A wave sloshed past at that moment, and the tip of a whitecap dashed him in the face, leaving him with a mouthful of brine. His scream turned to a choking cough and he lost his balance. Evan's head slipped beneath the waves, his eyes bulging wide and his arms flailing. Everything was dark, and his nose and throat filled with the cold seawater. He gasped for breath and only took in more water, choking silently beneath the night waves.

This was Evan's worst nightmare. Ever since he was a child, he'd woken up some nights in cold sweat, the memory of being trapped beneath the water still frozen in his eyes. And now, after all this time, it had come to pass. He tried to reach the surface, but his feet couldn't seem to find the bottom, and his head only poked out from the water for seconds before the current sucked him back down.

A hand found his arm, and then another slid around his waist. Ligeia. She smiled at him beneath the water, and leaned in to give him a kiss. Evan shook his head no, no, no—he was drowning!

And then her lips were on his, and Evan felt . . . relief.

His lungs no longer felt the fire of seawater and his throat didn't burn with salt. Ligeia's eyes bored into his own like brown pools of mystery, and holding him tight to her body, she swam him to the surface.

"Oh my God," Evan gasped as their heads broke the water. He clung to her like a baby and she carried him to firm ground until he could stand comfortably, the water lapping only as high as his chest. She faced him, the water moving her hair between her breasts to cover and then unveil with a rhythmic tease. "Thank you," he said. "I thought I was going to drown. I'm so afraid of the water and I've always been afraid of drowning and I don't even know what happened. I heard you singing and somehow I just kind of sleepwalked into the water, but I can't swim, and . . ."

"Shhhhhh," she said, and pressed a finger to his lips. Her other hand moved beneath the ocean, and slid along

Evan's right thigh. She kissed him again, and Evan felt a surge of heat as her tongue entwined with his. Then he realized that her hands were working at the belt on his jeans, and he shook his head, breaking the kiss.

"No," he said. "I came out here partly because I wanted to tell you . . . what happened last night was wrong, and I'm sorry. I'm married. And she's a wonderful woman. I love her . . . We can't . . ."

He gripped her arms and tried to push them back, but she was already pulling down his zipper, and then dragging the pants down his legs under the water. Fingers reached between his legs to cup and caress him, and Evan found it difficult to refuse the touch. But he steeled himself again, and pressed her back. "No," he said again.

Ligeia shook her head. Her eyes questioned him, her brows raised. And then she opened her mouth and began to sing again. She sang of sex and raw animal need.

She sang in a whisper against his ear, and then as she threw her head back in a scream, she urged him harder with her hand. In moments, she'd pressed him inside her, with the ocean as her lubricant.

Evan felt out of control, as if someone had put his mind in a box and shoved it on a shelf with a hole cut in the side for him to watch himself. Because this amazing, sexual creature was making love to him in the ocean and he couldn't stop his body from meeting her. The night seemed to shimmer and shift with a danger that only made the action more erotic. Ligeia's song stilled every doubt in Evan's head, and all he could see were her eyes, dreamy and dark. He sucked deep on her lips and then moved to taste the salt of her nipples as she clung to him and slid her body up, down and around him as if he were the pole, and she his mermaid dancer. Her orgasm came while Evan was lost in his own internal fireworks, and her voice cried out with a sound that was both pure in its expression of pleasure and thick with its animal celebration of lust.

Evan closed his eyes as she held him, and whispered to him softly of dreams. "When I was a little girl," she said at one point, "I prayed that I would meet a man like you. And now that I have, I don't want to ever let you go."

He tried to respond, to tell her that he was taken, that she would have to let him go. But he couldn't get up the energy. Instead he only rocked with her some more in the water, relishing the velvet touch of her skin against his and the sweet stories of desire that she told.

Evan woke on the beach again, still wearing a sodden shirt, but naked from the waist down, one pant leg still hung up on his ankle. Ligeia was gone, and the moon had slipped across the sky.

"Holy shit," he breathed, a wild rainbow of conflicting emotions raging inside him. "What am I gonna do?"

Pulling his cold, wet pants over goose-bumped thighs, Evan felt the fingers of panic rising up again in his heart. Tears welled in his eyes as he began to walk home, praying that Sarah were safe.

When he slipped inside his house ten minutes later, still wondering how he would explain the wet clothes, it was three A.M. He turned off the light in the kitchen and walked down the hall to their bedroom, praying that Sarah would be there.

Her light snores filled the room as he entered. Evan let out a sigh of relief. At least she had gotten home okay without him. He stripped off his clothes and decided to let them dry in the garage . . . He hoped she'd never know.

Evan walked naked to the garage and draped the jeans across the back of his car. He laid the shirt on the hood.

In the morning, when they were a little drier, he could figure out what to do with them.

Evan went back inside and got in the shower. He stood under the spray for a minute, thinking about the night. His cock felt thick and sated, as it always did after good, strenuous sex. As he thought of Ligeia's fingers in his hair, he felt his groin tingle and his manhood begin to ready itself for action once more.

"No," he whispered, getting out of the shower and drying off. He walked back down the hall to the bedroom, where he slid between the sheets next to the woman who had made his life worth living for as long as he could remember. But right now, his body wasn't thinking of her. He hated himself for what he felt in his heart.

What he felt was a betrayal of everything he had spent his life building, and the worst part was, he didn't really care. It took everything in him not to get back out of bed and walk back to the point. To call her name. Even though he loved and cared for Sarah, Evan wanted only one thing now, and knew that he would go back to her tomorrow night, no matter what the cost.

As he slid into a dream of her song, he knew that at that moment, he would give up everything for this woman. With every fiber of his body, Evan wanted Ligeia.

CHAPTER THIRTEEN

"I think I'm in love with her," Evan said.

Bill raised a hamburger to his lips and raised an eyebrow at the same time. He chewed, letting the silence stretch before answering.

"She feels the same?" he asked finally.

"I don't know. We haven't really talked much."

"Right. She talks with her body. Didn't your momma ever tell you to watch out for girls like that?"

Evan grinned, just barely. He had asked Bill to lunch at Cheeseburger Central because he needed to talk to somebody about last night. And his weekly appointment with Dr. Blanchard wasn't until Monday. "I've never felt like this before," he said, before biting into a South of the Border Burger. Guacamole oozed out of the bun to splat on his wrist.

Bill only stared at Evan's burger. "That's probably because you're eating avocado on barbecued beef. It's not right, you know? Burgers should be slathered in ketchup, mustard, onions, a bit of lettuce, maybe some cheese. But jalapeños and green shit? Looks like a seagull just shit on your meat."

"I'm serious," Evan protested. "I can't get her out of my head. It was the most amazing thing last night. She made me feel . . ."

"Like a real man, I know. We've all been there."

"Not like that. I mean . . . when she sings, everything in your head just slips away. I can't begin to describe it. She's got the best voice I've ever heard. Hell, twice now I've just gone sleepwalking into the ocean to get closer to her when she was singing. And you know how insane that is for me, of all people."

"She lured you into the water again last night?" Bill put down his burger. "Tell me you didn't go in again."

Evan laughed. "Fully dressed. The clothes are in the backseat of my car right now; I didn't want Sarah to find them."

"This is bad, Evan."

"Tell me about it. I don't want to hurt Sarah, but I have to be with her again . . ."

"That's the worst thing you could possibly do." Bill blotted the grease from his hands with a heavy brown paper napkin, and then grabbed Evan's arm. "Look. I know you don't believe this shit, but think about it, huh? You're scared to death of the water, and this woman can sing and make you go zombie and just wade right in? You think that doesn't play along with every Siren legend ever? She's got her claws in you now, and the next time, you may not walk out of the ocean alive. The Siren doesn't just mate with men, Evan, she eats them, soul to skin."

"What the fuck are you talking about?"

"Why do you think Sirens have lured sailors to crash their ships on the rocks? It's not an accident, Evan. Read your history. Hell, read your literature. The Siren needs men. But she doesn't want a husband. She needs us to breed. And she needs us to feed." He punctuated his pronouncement by picking up his greasy burger and tearing off a large chunk of meat. As he chewed, Bill urged, "Tell me more about what she said to you last night."

"It's hard to remember, honestly," Evan said. "It was

all like such a dream. I know she told me that now that she'd found me, she didn't want to let me go."

Bill choked back a laugh. "Yeah. I bet. She is going to suck you dry, man. Whether you believe she's a Siren or just a girl on the make, they all share that part in common. She's a woman. Tell me this—does she always show up at the same spot on the beach?"

Evan nodded. "Yeah, always right around the point. She swims in the bay just north of it. Why?"

"I'm curious," Bill said. "I'd like to see it."

"You've seen the point a million times."

"No," Bill said. "I want to bring my gear and take a dive out there."

"And accomplish what?"

"Maybe I'll find me a Siren of my own." Bill grinned. "Maybe Ligeia's got a sister."

Evan rolled his eyes and finished his burger. "I'll take you there tomorrow afternoon if you want."

"Perfect," Bill said. "And do me a favor? Try to keep it in your pants tonight—unless you're at home? Take Sarah out for a date or something."

CHAPTER FOURTEEN

Evan carried the black rubber flippers for Bill, who trudged down the beach with a black wet suit and an air tank flung over his shoulder. The sun blazed in the sky and there were a scattering of bathers dotted up and down the golden sand. It was a Saturday afternoon and the weather was perfect; if Delilah had been built a little closer to any other cluster of habitation, the beach would have been jam-packed. As it was, there were plenty of open spots for towels, though there was a gang of kids building sand castles right at the section of the beach Evan pointed out to Bill.

"That's the place," he said, looking back and forth between an invisible spot on the sand, and the black rock wall a hundred yards away. "We ended up, um . . . in the sand right about here both times, because she swam in from right out there."

Bill walked past the beach towels and set down his equipment. Then he set himself down with a dull thud. "Damn," he said, "that shit's heavy when it's not in the water." He stripped off his shirt and checked a meter on the air tank. Bill pulled out some goggles and tubing from a knapsack. Then he stood back up and stepped into the wet suit.

"I don't know what you think you're going to find out there," Evan said.

"Nothing, I guess. I just wonder if she's got some kind

of visible 'lair' out there. Nobody's ever really tried to hunt her down—everyone just talks about how she's out there, somewhere . . ." Bill shrugged. "And anyway it's a good excuse to use the equipment. I haven't gone diving in weeks."

"You're not going to find anything down there, you know?" Evan said. "But if the hungry Siren decides to come after you when you find her white picket fence on the bottom of the ocean . . . what are you going to do?"

"Swim like hell," Bill said. With that, he pulled the mask on over his face and trudged off, flippers flopping, into the water.

There was nothing quite like slipping below the ceiling of the ocean on a bright summer's day. Why didn't he do this more often? Bill smiled to himself as he kicked his long rubber pseudofeet and pushed against invisible walls with his arms to move out into the bay. Soon the rippled shadows of the surface waves evened out as the distance from air to sand grew deeper, and he moved through a blue-green window.

Fish scattered as he approached them, though some of the slower, larger ones only seemed to hang in place and watch sagely as he went by. The sand of the beach quickly gave way to a darker bottom littered with rock and fronds of seaweed. Bill kept the black shadow of the point's base in his sights to the left. According to Evan, the woman had consistently appeared just off its edge, right about in line with where he swam now. He swam along the bottom slowly, looking for . . . who knew what. Bones? A deep hole?

He chuckled inwardly at this swim. At his core, Bill was a pragmatic, realistic guy. He was not the one you'd point to in a crowd and say, "Yeah, now there's a guy who believes in spooks." But Bill had grown up with the deaths and they had happened too regularly to be written off as mere happenstance. This coastline had a long and desperate history, and the wild stories of a century ago were echoed in the events of the now, even if people didn't put quite the same wild-eyed spin on it.

At least not publicly.

It wasn't a huge surprise that Evan had never heard of Delilah's Siren, because he hadn't grown up here like Bill had. And . . . well . . . people didn't talk openly about it. Nobody was going to admit that they believed in something so patently ridiculous. But those who lived through the '80s in Delilah . . . they knew. They knew about the bodies. They knew about all of the missing-persons reports that had stacked up month after month, year after year, until one day after Delilah weathered a hurricane-like storm, those missing corpses had surfaced to dot the beach like the debris of broken homes that lined the streets in town.

Rotted arm bones, empty skulls, bodies only days or weeks in the watery grave—they had all washed ashore in the heart of the black scream of wind and torrential rain. They called it the worst storm California had seen in a hundred years. And certainly, where Delilah was concerned, the most gruesome.

The press blamed sharks for the deaths and a tornado-like churn of the bay for unearthing the ragged bodies of "drowned swimmers," but Bill knew what shark teeth did to a body. The day after the storm had torn half the roof off his parents' home, he'd been walking the beach to escape the nightmare the winds had left behind. And next to an old rotten piece of timber, he had stumbled across a dead man half buried in the sand of the shoreline. Bite marks covered his body, some of them showing on skin bruised in a rainbow of past pain, some of them showing by omission—by the missing flesh—wet, pale pink meat gaping where the muscles had been ripped away completely from the bone. After he had gotten over the initial urge to puke, Bill had crept closer, scattering the sand crabs feasting on the stinking carcass to look closer at the grotesque thing that had once been a man. And he knew that it was no shark that had done this.

The purpling bruises on the man's naked torso and thighs didn't resemble the wide snout of a shark's maw in any way. They looked to be just about the perfect size to have been created by a human mouth. Bill didn't know of any other animal that left tooth marks like that. He still woke some nights with the sight of that mangled man in his mind. For a while, after the "Death Storm," the Siren's tale had been openly discussed in Delilah. The stories that went back to crazed sailors describing her with their dying breath were all rehashed. But, in the end, the stories died down as the townsfolk focused on the more immediate tasks of burying the dead and rebuilding their homes. Sometimes she was whispered about on the grammar school playgrounds, or in the backyards of Cub Scout leaders during den meetings. But those who believed didn't risk the ridicule of those who came to Delilah after 1984, and the storm of the bodies. They kept that horrible superstition to themselves, stayed away from the beach at night and nodded to themselves when they read stories in the newspaper of another "missing person."

When Bill had been a kid, the missing persons had all come home. And they hadn't been pretty.

The ocean floor dropped off, and Bill suddenly hung in watery space midway between the blurry surface and the dark ground. The shadows lengthened as he followed the slope and he realized that the drop-off also marked the edge of the far end of the point. He was out in truly open water.

Bill swam easily through the depths, enjoying the feeling of effortless motion. Scuba diving was a lot like free fall, he thought. You entered another world entirely, and gravity seemed to slip away.

After a few minutes, he turned back. The ocean floor seemed a never-ending field of rock and occasional sea frond. He decided to use the drop-off shelf as a reference; he'd swim out a couple hundred yards, swim back, move to his left a few yards and repeat the process. Not knowing what he was looking for, he wanted to crisscross the area well.

The second time he swam out, he saw nothing of interest besides occasional nosy, colorful fish. One fist-size puffer fish followed him for a long time, its almost-human blue eyes staring at him unblinking.

The third time he swam out, he began to tire of the exercise. Evan was right; this really was a fool's errand. Even if there was a Siren, what made him think he could find her lair? What made him think he really wanted to? The image of the purpling skin of the dead naked man he'd found on the beach as a child came to mind and a shiver convulsed his spine.

He did not want to wash back ashore looking like that.

Bill was about ready to call it a day when he saw the shadow beneath him. The ocean floor had been slipping by as a murky blur of rock and plant life, with the occasional dart of fish . . . but all of a sudden the landscape turned dark. A black maw in the earth.

Bill kicked and turned around, circling the dark. Then he began to swim down, into the shadow. As he drew closer, he could make out the outline of irregular, jutting shapes. There were rocks and plants masking his view, but as he touched the bottom and ran a hand along one twisted piece of timber, the object of his examination suddenly took clear shape.

He had found one of the wrecks of Delilah's Hidden Bay. His hand touched the splintered, overgrown remains of the bow, while the open blackness that had drawn his attention was actually a gaping hole in the ship's midsection. It had sunk and settled sideways, with its breach to the sky. The wreck looked older than the ocean itself; Bill would never have been able to tell it was a ship if he hadn't put his hand on a piece of its timber. The ocean floor had closed in around it, digesting it a foot at a time, until every broken plank had been steadily overgrown and changed shape in a coating of plants and rock, silt and shells.

If Bill had been on land, he'd have whistled. Instead, he kicked his feet back off the silt and swam along the hidden lines of the wreck, nodding to himself as he saw where it emerged from the mud of the seafloor and where the seafloor grew around it.

He ducked under an overhanging rock—the last finger of the point that extended deep below the surface—and began to swim toward the hole in the ancient ship's hull. He couldn't tell what kind of boat it had once been, but it surely wasn't a pleasure ship. Its hull was too broad, the curve of its mostly hidden deck too long. Maybe the finger of rock he'd just passed had been the death of this boat; a treacherous underwater knife to the heart. A ship in a storm that buffeted up against that?

Bill aimed straight for the center of the wide black hole in the boat, and was halfway through when something slipped through his legs. He felt the tickle before he saw the cause; just a brief, seductive brush against the inside of his wet suit. He flipped around in the water and saw the cause.

The water around him filled with the shimmer of pink and purple translucent shapes. They hung and shifted around his body like a cloud.

A cloud of jellyfish. Big-ass jellyfish. One brushed across his head and then another trailed tentacles across his throat.

"Shit," Bill mouthed. He gently moved his arms back and then swooshed them forward, trying to push his body slowly through the water without angering the cloud. They looked beautiful—ghostly explosions with arms that hung like alien wraiths in the water.

All you needed was a bunch of jellyfish stings and you could kiss that next cheeseburger at Cheeseburger Central good-bye. Good-bye for good. A school of large, poisonous jellyfish was death to a diver. Deceptive, slow-moving death.

Bill moved his flippers slowly, carefully, trying not to kick the school up and along with him. A globe of pinkish flesh slid around the side of his breathing mask, and Bill stopped breathing for that moment, eyes gone wide and scared.

He wasn't afraid of *a* jellyfish. He was afraid of an *army* of jellyfish.

Carefully he kicked out his feet, and the black hole of the wreck drew away to become nothing but a shadow near the ocean's floor again.

A handful of the poisonous school followed the swirl of his feet, but once he'd drawn a few yards away Bill kicked out in earnest, and in seconds had left all of the creatures far behind. *That'd be rich*, he thought. *Man found dead of jellyfish stings; priceless wreck discovered nearby.*

Bill kicked his legs harder, aiming at the shore where he knew Evan waited. There were very few things he'd found that were worth risking your safety for.

Irrefutable proof of the legend of a deadly sea creature who chewed men up for fun was not one of them.

CHAPTER FIFTEEN

∞ ∞

June 4, 1887

It was hard to be a man and not love women. But it was harder to be a man and *live* with a woman. Captain James Buckley III had found the solution.

Love a woman. Live with a woman. But keep her bound and gagged until her services were needed. No harm. No haranguing.

Some would have called him cruel. A horrible pig of a man.

Buckley just called himself expedient.

He grinned at the thought and patted his intellect on the back—expediency is the heart of brevity and brevity is the soul of wit—and fumbled his key into the lock of his quarters. *A captain's prerogative should always include a nooner,* he thought. Or, in this case, a midafternooner.

Burying Rogers, the cook, last night had given him an appetite for the cause, he thought. He would have been too ashamed to have admitted to the wooden erection he had grown as they lifted the bag of body parts and swung it over the side of the ship to sink in the depths. But admit it or not, there it was. The remains of Rogers's body had excited him in a brutally sexual way. Buckley knew who had dined on the cook's softest flesh. He knew because some of that flesh was still here, in his cabin. And he was responsible for having thrown the other pieces overboard, unfortunately just hours before they ended up back on the ship in its nets. He wasn't excited by the bag of body parts, but any thought related to her excited him.

And while she chewed other men to the core, she took him TO her core. In a way no other woman ever had. She was amazing—an animal. The key to being a man was acting like one, Buckley thought. You had to show the woman who was boss. Even if that meant a gag and chains. And from those tiny, frantic mewling sounds she made every time he climbed into his fish-stinkin' bunk with her, she enjoyed it, he figured.

Buckley entered the cabin and carefully shut the door behind him. Sometimes she got angry when he woke her from a dream. But as he stepped into his cabin, some sixth sense told him that she wasn't dreaming. Something was *wrong*. Used to the small space in the dark, he stepped in four strides to the bulkhead window and drew the curtain there. The room filled with weak gray light, and Buckley swore.

The bed he shared with her was empty. The gag lay abandoned on the stained and stinking sheets. The ropes that had bound her hand and foot this morning were unraveled.

Where she had gone was a mystery, though there were only so many places you could hide on a ship drifting at sea. The reason for her freedom was clear enough though.

On the floor, next to the well-gnawed thigh of Rogers, lay the openmouthed face of "Three Hands" Nelson. The thief looked as if he'd been surprised at the end, and Buckley's first thought was *good riddance*.

But now Nelson's surprise could be the captain's undoing. *Damnitall*, Buckley complained. Another deckhand gone—that was surely going to cause some talk among the men. More importantly, how the hell was he going to recapture the damned creature and get her back in his bed where she belonged? Some men would have suggested a tall glass of bourbon and some sweet talk to catch a woman, but Buckley was of a different stripe. And this woman wasn't going to come back quietly. He knew that for damn certain.

He dug into a drawer in the bureau near his bunk and tossed a series of ropes and flogs and clips and such over his shoulder, until he found the tool he'd been looking for. He uncoiled the long, wound rope of leather and ran it across his palm with a satisfied grin. Then, bullwhip in his hand, Captain Buckley stepped back onto the deck outside of the captain's quarters and headed toward the storeroom.

If you wanted to catch a clown, look in the spotlight. If you wanted to catch a Siren, look in the dark recesses near the sea. The captain lit a candle and walked into the ship's hold, stacked with crates and crates of rum. The room had an almost claustrophobic feel—from floor to ceiling, wooden boxes filled the womb of the *Lady Luck*, and Buckley was always surprised at just how much liquor they managed to squeeze into his hold before he left Mexico and pulled out the fishing nets to mask his true trade from the port authorities.

He stepped into the deep shadows of the crates and whistled. He tried to hum a tune his mother had once sung to him as a child. He'd found it soothing, though it hadn't ever quite been up to par for those on the outside of the relationship. They said she couldn't carry a tune. But he'd wanted his momma to know that what she did mattered. In the end, it didn't really matter what his momma had sung to him. It all sounded pretty much the same to Buckley.

Some said he was tone-deaf, but he just figured that he

really didn't appreciate music. That's why he'd found it such a beautiful irony when just a few weeks before, the Greek man had led him to the hidden room that he'd stashed the singing woman in. Supposedly the woman had been taken in the middle of the night from where she wandered along Delilah's beach and would never be missed.

"Don't take that gag off, whatever you do," the wizened dark-skinned man had insisted. "The sound . . . it is death to a mortal man. Mark my words."

Buckley had marked them, but not surprisingly, hadn't listened. On the other hand, it hadn't seemed to matter. He had released the bonds on the beautiful woman's mouth and instead of hearing the litany of verbal abuse he was used to from a female, he'd instead heard a long, tremulous ululation that, he supposed, seemed like the thing that others called music.

For him, it was only noise. A hair-raising exercise in interruption that prevented him from reaching the reason he'd bought the woman from the Greek in the first place. When she sang, he found he couldn't complete the deed with her. His exertions simply stretched out in a frustrating infinity until he grew tired of the effort. Certainly her song had an impact on his manhood, but really, enough was enough. He quickly found out about the impact her song had on others though. On the first night of her new captivity he'd slept with her in a hotel in Delilah before they'd broken port, and a man had smashed down the door in the midst of Buckley's rutting. The captain had leaped for his gun, but he quickly saw that the man meant no harm—his eyes looked vacant and he only stood there, rapt at the hotel bed while she sang.

In moments, her mouth had been on the poor fool's neck, and blood drenched both the bed and voluptuous body Captain Buckley had so recently been enjoying. He watched with shock and awe as she chewed out the man's throat. There was nothing he appreciated more than the danger of savagery—Buckley had always longed to be a big-game hunter. Instead, he used his lust for blood as a means to keep a group of ruffians to work.

He tied a leather strap around her head and made sure it fully covered her mouth as soon as he got her back to the ship and stripped off the robes they had draped her in.

She needn't sing to him, or play coquette behind the pretense of civilized clothes. She was brought to his ship with only one purpose in mind. Robes would only slow that purpose.

But her insistence at singing caused the captain to ultimately keep her mouth in check. Aside from its impact on slowing the arrival of his orgasms, he couldn't have the men wondering who was in the captain's cabin besides the captain. The answer of "a woman" would have torn the ship apart. Nor could he afford for them to be smitten with the strangely euphoric effect her song seemed to have on other men.

And so she remained gagged and tied to his bed for hours on end until he returned to release her.

But, apparently, someone else had gotten wind that she was there and decided to release her without the captain's orders.

Buckley thought of the remains of Nelson and laughed.

Some men could handle their women. And some couldn't.

"Here, kitty, kitty, kitty," Buckley growled, threading his way among the crates of liquor. In his hand, the whip itched to be swung.

"Here, kitty, kitty," he said again.

Buckley laughed and licked his lips. He loved nothing more than the chase. And when you lived on a ship in the ocean, there were only so many places the prey could hide.

CHAPTER SIXTEEN

It was more than sex, Evan told himself as he walked down the beach. He stifled a yawn; tonight he'd tucked Sarah in bed before he took his walk, so it was already past 10:30. She had an early morning meeting and had wanted to turn in by ten. He had toyed with the idea of not walking the beach tonight but . . . he couldn't stay in his family room. On the couch trying to watch the ten o'clock news, he'd just kept fidgeting.

Evan couldn't say he *loved* her; he'd hardly spoken to her, despite the intense animal sex they'd had on the beach twice. Yet, when he thought of Ligeia, Evan's whole body warmed. He *needed* to be with her, with every cell in his body. After arguing with himself for fifteen minutes, he finally shut off the TV, slipped on his sandals and slipped out the sliding glass doors off the kitchen.

The surf was gentle and quiet tonight, and Evan didn't dally on his way to the point; he walked fast and with purpose; no stone skipping.

When he reached the place where he'd awoken naked at three A.M. just a couple nights before, he stopped and looked out at the dark horizon. Water stretched as far as the eye could see, merging into the black of the night-time sky. The point blotted out the stars to his left like a hole in the world.

"Ligeia?" Evan said softly. His voice barely seemed to

carry past his lips. He hoped that she would come tonight. Last night, after Bill's dive, he had not walked down here. While he told himself that Bill's was a fool's errand, and Ligeia was just some exotic singer living down off the beach somewhere nearby, he had to admit that he was starting to be sucked into Bill's irrational explanation for the power of her music. And her affinity for water. Did he really believe that the woman he came here to meet lived at the bottom of the ocean?

Evan laughed at his own internal question. Uh, *no.* But then why had he been worried that Bill's dive near the point would somehow make her angry at him?

"Ligeia?" he called again, a little louder.

Of course, he thought to himself, if he didn't believe there was something more than human about her, why did he just assume she would show up whenever he decided to walk the beach? As if she were some kind of genie he could invoke by his mere presence?

He frowned, suddenly fearful that maybe she wouldn't be here tonight. After all, it was later than the past couple times he'd found her, and he hadn't come at all last night. Bill had come to their house for dinner, and then the three of them had gone down to O'Flaherty's for a couple hours. They had taken over the lone ratty pool table in the back of the bar and played the night away, laughing and enjoying the company in a way they rarely did anymore. Sarah hadn't gotten drunk either—her eyes still sparkled with humor, not liquor, on the walk home. For once, she had been the one to have to wake Evan in the morning; he'd been groggy half the day.

"I missed you," a voice whispered in his ear.

Evan jumped. Ligeia was there, right next to him. Her voice had nearly sent him out of his skin, but when he looked at her, he felt instantly calm again. And aroused.

She stood naked in the night, arms at her side without shame. Her long dark hair fell in wet ringlets across her shoulders, but didn't cover the swell of her breasts. Her belly glistened with moisture; the curves of her waist and hips were preternatural. She was a muse incarnate, a modern Venus.

"We're going to have to take you shopping for a new outfit." He grinned.

Ligeia smiled and leaned in to kiss him. "Do you really want to cover me?" she said, biting his ear. "I think you're the one who needs a change in clothing."

Her fingers began to pull at his shirt, and Evan put his arms in the air for her to lift it over his head. In seconds his pants joined the shirt on the sand, and Evan held Ligeia tight to him, her soft flesh pressing his in all the right places. He felt desperate to have her then, immediately. He wanted to take her standing up, and he grew against her, edging up to do just that.

She pushed him back slightly and laughed. Her voice was crystalline and beautiful, just like her song.

"I want you in the water," she said.

Evan's heart stopped. His erection instantly lost its steel. "Um . . ." he began. She pressed a finger to his lips and knelt in front of him to press her lips to his belly, and below. "It was so good last time, you know?"

"I told you," Evan said, feeling stupid as he did so. "I don't like the water. I never have been able to—"

His words were interrupted by his own moan at the feeling generated by her oral attention.

"Shhhh," she said. "You will come with me."

"I'm aquaphobic," he insisted. "I can't help it."

"It didn't stop you before," came her reply. And then her mouth was full again, taking him deeper.

"I can't . . . explain it," he gasped, having trouble keep-

ing the conversation up while other things were *up*.
"When you sang . . . the world just . . . disappeared."

The warmth that engulfed him suddenly slipped away,
and her hands moved from his thighs to his shoulders as
Ligeia stood. The tip of her tongue brushed his lips,
sending a tremor down Evan's back, and then she opened
her mouth. A tremulous note emerged, vibrating low,
just at the point of hearing. Her head dipped, and her
eyes met his with a look that demanded his lust. Gold
freckled the brown of her eyes like a cat's. Her gaze was
electric. The melody rose from a whispering basso to a
tremulous soprano. She sang without real words; yet there
was meaning there. Evan's mind filled with first a deep
sadness, and then a great, overpowering need.

Evan's transport this time was instant. He barely noticed that she led him into the water. When she pulled
him under the waves, their bodies locked as one, all he
could see were her eyes. All he could feel was her mouth
on his, her body moving against him, holding him tight
and then releasing. The song had disappeared, replaced
by her kiss, but Evan drifted in the ocean, letting Ligeia
do the work, swimming and screwing at the same time.
Her fingernails pressed against his back painfully as she
reached her climax, and he felt his own release cresting
too. They spasmed together beneath the surface, but as
he opened his mouth unconsciously to scream out his
pleasure, Ligeia kicked once, and brought him to the air.

"Oh my God," he gasped, spitting out a mouthful of
seawater. He could only think of one word to describe the
feelings pulsing through every vein in his flesh. *Rapture*.

Ligeia held him easily, keeping them both afloat. Her
lips were wide, happy. Evan let himself drift in her care,
oblivious to all fear of the water. His phobia seemed to
melt away completely at her touch. "That was the most

amazing . . . ever," he said, heaving and gasping to catch his breath.

She pulled him tight to her breast. Her hair stuck to his cheek. "Come with me tonight," her voice whispered in the dark. "And you will have me like that always. Every day. Yours forever."

Evan's stomach clenched. "Ligeia, I . . ."

"Forever," she promised.

"I'm married," he said. "To a wonderful woman. I love her. I shouldn't be here at all."

"You're mine now," she said simply, with a shrug that preempted all argument. Then she flicked her tongue across his eyelids, nose and lips. Ligeia began to hum, and Evan's panic subsided instantly.

The wind blew against them, raising the fishy smell of the ocean depths, and he shivered. Ligeia gripped him tight to her, legs scissoring his and working him back between her thighs. When he entered her a second time, the force of her moan hit Evan like his own orgasm. Her voice broke all around him in short staccato squeaks. Mellifluous, high and almost birdlike. "Mine," she moaned more than once.

Evan couldn't help himself. His need for her grew so heavy, he joined her in promises.

"Yes," he said. "Yours."

CHAPTER SEVENTEEN

The door slammed behind Evan with a hollow snap, and he knew right away that something was wrong. Darren's office was empty, though the lights were on. He stepped into the bull pen, and all of the desks were empty, though the computer screens all glared with light. Bill's chair was pushed away from his desk, as if he'd left in a hurry; its back hung up on the front rim of Maggie's desk.

"Huh," Evan murmured. All of their cars were in the lot, and he hadn't seen anyone up on the dock. No ships were in this morning, though a couple were due, he knew.

He looked out the back window to the dock and confirmed that nobody was in sight. The pier extended out into the water without a single tie-up so far today. It was a beckoning finger into the ocean that remained unanswered.

"Huh," Evan said again, and went to his desk to turn on his computer, which was obvious in its off-ness. He was late again. And this time, he had apparently missed something big. *I'm going to hear about this, I bet.*

As the Windows 95 logo lit up the screen, he noticed a handwritten note on a Post-it dangling from his monitor.

Evan—

There's been an accident. We're going up the beach near the point.
—Bill

"What the hell," Evan said to the empty office. What kind of accident would have sent the entire office out to the beach? Images of blood on the sand, the crumpled body of a water-skier lying a dozen feet from its severed leg filled his mind. Steeling himself for the worst, he exited the back door and took the stairs down to the beach two at a time.

As soon as he passed the fence that walled in the cargo area of the port, Evan saw his workmates. They were huddled down near the point, but Evan didn't pay attention to what they were looking at. His eyes were trained on the ship out in the water, not far off the beach. He couldn't tell how large the craft was, but it was a cargo carrier, without a doubt. Probably the one he'd known was due in overnight, its berth filled with Mexican produce. A green machine, they called it in the bull pen.

This one wasn't going to be delivering much green though. Not with its bow head down in the bay. The port side of the craft faced the beach at an awkward angle—ass up, as it were. The water wasn't deep enough to swallow the craft here, and it had apparently run aground during the night.

There were flashing lights cutting the air beyond the sand, and as Evan drew closer he saw that there were blue-shirted cops kneeling down in the sand as well as Bill, Darren, Candice and some others.

Bill saw his approach and motioned him over. "You've got to hear this," he whispered as Evan met him just outside the circle of gawkers.

"What's going on?" Evan asked.

"Ship sank early this morning, just before dawn. They never even used the radio; Maggie saw them out here this morning after she got in. She happened to take a look out the bathroom window and saw a damn ship face-down in the drink, you know? She freaked out!"

"What happened?"

"Ha." Bill grinned dourly. "That's what I wanted you to hear."

His friend grabbed him and dragged him into the circle surrounding a body on the beach. Paramedics hunched over the bloody mess that Evan quickly realized was a man. It was just like his dream—the sand sated with blood. The emergency team had run an IV into the man's arm, and were doing something at the victim's neck.

"So . . . what?" Evan asked after a minute. Nobody was saying anything, but the body on the beach jittered and spasmed periodically, so he knew it wasn't a corpse . . . yet.

"The guy was talking a minute ago," Bill said. "They couldn't shut him up. I wanted you to hear."

"Well, it doesn't look like he's going to say much now," Evan observed. "So what's the deal?"

Bill opened his mouth to speak, but then stopped as a low moan erupted from the sand. "She was there!" a rough voice insisted. The voice sounded about like what you'd expect after gargling a cup of bleach. "I saw her. She was beautiful and . . . I swear to you . . . she was nekkid as a jaybird. I seen nekkid chicks before but she . . ."

The voice trailed off into a fit of wet coughing, and the paramedics leaned over, trying to shush him.

"She sang the most beautiful song . . ." the man cried out. Evan saw his legs stiffen, and then one hand reached up and grabbed the pale shirt of one of the paramedics. "She sang . . ." The voice stopped, and then the hand slipped away from the paramedic's back. In its place was a long red smear.

There was a flurry of motion, and one of the ambulance drivers tried CPR. But the man was gone. Bill pulled Evan back from the crowd. "He was one of the crew on a small freighter coming in from Porto Huevas. They were almost to dock early this morning, rounding the point when they heard music. The captain slowed the ship and edged closer to shore, and the guy on the beach was with him. He said that she sang like an angel . . . and they tried to get closer. Then the ship hit something . . . but neither one of them did anything, because all they could do was listen to the woman on the rocks. Singing."

Bill looked at Evan and opened his eyes as wide as he could. "Did you hear me, Evan? These guys crashed their boat and stood there on the deck as it went down because they were totally in a trance because of some woman on the rocks singing. Does that sound *at all* familiar to you, Evan?"

Evan shrugged. "Sounds like they got drunk and sleepy and wrecked their boat on some rocks," he said. "Not sure that a naked singer has a lot to do with it."

Bill took him by the shoulders and shook him. "Wake up, Evan. I know it sounds crazy, but hell . . . you've been with her. BEEN with her. No normal woman has the kind of effect on men that this chick does. C'mon, man. When have you ever been able to set foot in water deeper than a sidewalk puddle?"

Evan looked out to the ass end of the boat that stuck out from the bay and refused to answer.

"She's dangerous," Bill said. "Do you know why that man just finished bleeding to death?"

Evan shook his head.

"Because she bit him," Bill announced.

"So she's a vampire?"

"No! Sirens eat the flesh of their victims. That's how it works. That's why they lure ships to shore. For sex and . . . food."

Evan pulled his shirt away from his neck and showed Bill his bare skin. He ran a finger around his throat and shook his head. "I've had sex with her," he said in a low whisper that the others couldn't overhear. "And she's never bit me."

"Maybe you're sour."

"Then I've got nothing to worry about, huh?"

Evan started to walk away, and then stopped. "Hey," he called. "What happened to the captain?"

"She ate him," Bill answered without a trace of a smile. "I'm serious. That's what he said. She ripped out his throat and chewed off his lips. Was in the middle of ripping into his guts with her teeth when our guy back there tried to stop her. If he'd been smart, he would have just taken a dive and headed for shore while she was busy."

"Every man for himself?"

"Sometimes that's the only way to survive."

Evan, Maggie, Bill and the rest of the dock staff returned to the harbor office one by one, and the day crept by. Nobody seemed much inclined to talk about it, yet, obviously the man's death impacted them all greatly. Darren didn't even mention that Evan had been late. He simply disappeared into his office and hunched behind a stack of files and papers.

Outside, a coast guard cutter flanked the half-sunken ship, most likely to keep away the curious while the wreck was investigated. Maggie made a lot more trips to the bathroom than usual and every now and then just announced, "They're still there."

Evan was glad when the day was done, though he dreaded his first stop of the evening. It wasn't home, unfortunately. Tonight was his weekly appointment with Dr. Blanchard. He felt stupid for going. People could brag about how their weekly trips to the chiropractor kept them upright, but nobody really wanted to admit that they needed a shrink to keep moving through the days. Somehow, mental health remained taboo in a country where there was a head doc on every corner. Somebody was keeping them in business and most of those somebodies probably didn't have nearly as much reason as Evan to need help. Most hadn't lost a child.

Evan cringed as he walked up the sidewalk to Blanchard's door. He was still embarrassed about coming here, and knew if it hadn't been a demand of his employer, he never would have continued coming. Still, Blanchard had helped him, he had to admit that.

And today, he really needed her. He wasn't quite sure how he was going to tell her that, but he did. There was too much going on for him to pretend to be fine tonight though. Tonight, he needed someone to talk to. And after the scene at the beach today, he just couldn't bring himself to tell Bill.

Evan followed Dr. Blanchard into the office and eased into the maroon cushioned chair near her cherrywood desk. Everything about her office seemed to have a trace of red in it, he'd noticed, even down to the faint but unmistakably fake additional color added to her lips.

"I had sex in the ocean with a Siren," he blurted out.

Dr. Blanchard tried to hold it back, but couldn't. Her professional composure disappeared and she laughed outright.

"A what?" she gasped.

"A Siren," he repeated. "I'm not joking. Last night, I

went down to the beach, and a woman sang to me and it was so beautiful, so moving, that I walked right into the ocean with her, and we made love out in the surf. She even pulled me underwater while she came. And I went with it. I came with her, while my face was under the waves."

"This is a new tactic," Dr. Blanchard said, after forcing down her smile. "From a man petrified of the water, not to mention living life, to a man who is, pardon my French, fucking a force of nature in the ocean?"

She waited for Evan to respond, and when he only stared at his shoes, she continued. "Why did you say that?" she asked more gently. "What's going on?"

"I know it sounds ridiculous," he said. "But I've never been more serious in my life. The woman I told you about last week? The one who I thought drowned? Well, I went back to the point and she was there again. And she sang to me. So beautifully that I forgot everything. She led me right into the ocean. She could have led me into hell for all I cared. But last night, I think she killed a man. Two men, I guess."

Dr. Blanchard quietly pulled her notepad down to her lap and slipped the cap off her pen. Today, she thought, she might need some records.

"Okay, slow down," she said. "Let's start at the beginning . . ."

CHAPTER EIGHTEEN

June 7, 1887

Things didn't feel right. Sometimes, you could just tell. Taffy hauled the rope down hard and shifted the sail.

Sometimes, things didn't feel right 'cuz the sea was scary calm, and you just knew a deadly storm was brewing out in the west, and it was just a matter of time until that quiet turned to squall. You hightailed it to shore then, if you could, because nobody wanted to end up as so much meat in Davy Jones's locker. There was an electricity in the air during those times that raised the hair on the back of your neck. You just *knew* that lightning was poised to strike.

But Taffy had a different feeling right now. This wasn't a seaman's itch about the coming temper of Mother Nature. This was the kind of itch that kept you up at night searching the shadows for the beast you knew was out there. Somewhere close enough to slither out and kiss you. He'd had this bad feeling in his gut, truth be told, since the day Rogers had turned up missing. It had gotten worse when they'd pulled some of that boy's carcass up in the nets. Taffy didn't believe in coincidences; everything happened for a reason. Everything was connected. Now Nelson seemed to have disappeared into the drink. The thief had gotten hisself a captain's whuppin' and the next day, he was gone.

Coincidence?

He grinned, but it wasn't a happy grin. He'd been with Buckley on the sea for a couple years now, hoisting and hefting. The captain ran a tight ship; some called him mean as a widow's tit, but Taffy had always called him brutally fair. He'd had respect for the man, though Buckley kept to himself and didn't share his rum with anyone. They all knew he had it; you could smell it on his breath at dinner. But it was his ship, and if the captain wanted his nip, the men couldn't complain. Captain's prerogative.

Still. Something had changed this time out. The captain disappeared at odd times during the day, just . . . left the deck. Not a word to anyone. His usual surly stand-offishness now seemed simply rude and mean. And the atmosphere about the ship was different. There were the strange noises at night he'd never noticed before. Rogers had said it was just the ship settling, a light creak that seemed musical in its rhythm.

But Taffy had sailed this ship too many times. The noise didn't sound at all like boards creaking with the waves.

It sounded like muffled music.

Kind of like what he'd been hearing just now, from down here in the hold. Taffy slipped between the wooden crates, his ear at the ready. The ship swayed and dipped, slowly, easily, and Taffy's feet adjusted without thinking. But as they hit the low end of the trough, he heard a noise. A scraping. From his left.

He wove between another stack of crates in a crouch. A smile creased his cheeks as he moved. He felt like a mouser. And who knows, maybe he was on the trail of a large rat. They grew big as cats on these boats when they found easy food and no predators. But they didn't hum, Taffy thought. And damn it if that sound just now had sounded like a light, airy, feminine bit of absentminded musing.

But there were no women on this ship, so *that* was impossible. Or was it?

Maybe they had a stowaway?

The creaking came again, just on the other side of the square box that Taffy stalked behind. He nodded and decided to make his move. Springing into action, he twisted around the angle of the box, arms at the ready to grab and take on anyone or anything.

He saw the shadow before he knew what it was and his hands darted out to nab. But at the same time as he reached, a heavy rope flipped over his head and caught at his lower back, and with a snap, drew him right into the figure he'd grasped at.

"You!" that figure bellowed. The pressure on the rope suddenly released, and Taffy staggered backward, his hands tingling from their brush with the captain's shirt.

"Stand up," Buckley hissed, and Taffy did, like a soldier, full attention. "What are you doing here?"

Taffy felt caught and yet . . . he'd done nothing wrong. Stifling the urge to apologize, he countered, "I could ask the same thing, Captain. Exactly who did you think you were going to catch?"

Buckley scowled, thick gray eyebrows meeting above his nose like a bitter squall. "I asked you first," he said. "But I'll tell you anyway. I'm trying to find the scoundrel on this ship who's hitting our cargo. I thought it was Nelson, and maybe it was . . . but he's gone now, isn't he? Or is he? Maybe he's just hiding out down here, drinking us dry, while the rest of us work our arses off to bring what's left of our cargo to ground."

Taffy couldn't help it. He laughed. "That's the most foolish thing I've ever heard," he said. "Nelson was—is, I hope—a good man. He wouldn't dip into the hold. None of us are going to keep our places on this ship for very long if we don't deliver the cargo we're paid to sail."

"Ah, but I caught him with a bottle already," Buckley growled. "And where there's a sip there's a drink, if you catch my meanin'. Now tell me why I shouldn't include you in my list of drunken suspects. What're ya doin' down here in the hold when you should be pitching the mainsails for dusk?"

"I heard something," Taffy said. "Like there was someone down here."

The captain suddenly looked interested. "Heard something, didja? What'd ya hear, boy?"

"I've been hearing things ever since we last docked at Delilah. The other men, they tell me it's the old boards, but I don't buy it. We've sailed together too long, Captain. And this ship don't sing like that in the middle of the drink. Something's changed since we docked at Delilah."

"All that's changed is my crew's interest in the cargo," Buckley growled, pointing a thumb at the stairs. "Get above deck."

Taffy woke in the wee hours. The crew quarters sighed with the snores of hard-worked seamen and the unmistakably nasal wheeze of Jensen. The man never drew a breath that didn't sound vaguely tortured. Taffy didn't know how the man worked on a sailing ship with the rasp that plagued his every exertion, but the thick seamen seemed to muddle through. Taffy didn't know what had awakened him, but he slipped his feet over the edge of the bunk and decided to take a walk. He could use to lose a little water over the side.

He stepped down the dark corridor that led from the crew quarters to the ship's head. He took a lantern hung in the hallway to light the way as he closed the door to the small room and released his bladder into the hole that led straight to the sea.

After, as he stepped back into the corridor, he heard a noise and paused. Something quiet, urgent and soft broke the stillness of belowdecks at night. The sound grew slow and heated and desperate. It made him smile as his crotch grew tight. It drove him, made him move toward the bow of the ship. He passed the captain's quarters and then let himself into the storeroom just beyond. The ship's storeroom was a tight space just at the curve of the bow, not big enough to carry cargo, but big enough to store some small supplies for their voyage. This was the odd-shaped space where odds and ends and the crew's supplies were stowed. The front area was piled high in ripped nets and fishing supplies. The crew didn't do much fishing—despite their official charter—but they had to have the implements available to make their case, if they were ever questioned. Every now and then they had to pull in a catch and stow some evidence to support their claim that they were a fishing rig. If the authorities ever wanted to check the hold, they were dead. So they needed to keep some fish on hand for when they docked. Reg led them in a day of trawling the depths at the end of every trip before they'd head to port. He'd grown up a fishing brat, helping his pa drive a rig in 'Frisco for years. Now he helped them fill out a token catch each time they delivered rum to the ports of California. The catch was definitely more trouble than it was worth on the face of it, but it kept their record clean as a legitimate fishing rig.

Taffy held the lamp up over the shambling stacks of

supplies and stinking nets and stepped awkwardly between the mess. The light flickered in long shadows off
the curved boards of the hull, and Taffy shook his head
at the empty air between him and the dark crevice where
the two walls of the ship met and joined. There was nobody here.

"*mmmm-hmmmmmmmmm*"

Something moaned. Or creaked. Or . . . *sang.*

"*mmmm hmmmm mmmm hmmmmm,*" it came again.
The sound sent shivers down his body, and Taffy closed
his eyes for a moment, imagining the porch of his
momma's home back in Georgia at the turn of the war.
She'd brought mint juleps to the tables there, and served
the men from the troops when they came home for relief
in between skirmishes. She'd been a saint, he thought.

Taffy rounded the corner of a stack of old food crates,
and caught his breath. There, spread-eagle on the wooden
planks, lay the most beautiful woman he had ever seen.
Her hair cascaded across her shoulder in raven curls that
just about kissed the pink pucker at the top of the swell of
her chest. Her breasts lolled wantonly, creamy full in the
orange lamplight. Taffy thirsted for a taste of them with
the first glimpse of her untethered nipples. Above the soft
flow of her neck, her lips swelled thick and warm, heavy
as a woman just rolled over from a bout of passion. Her
hands said why. They reached between her legs with obvious intent, covering her sex, or perhaps exploiting it.
She moaned and whimpered like a bitch in heat, and with
every low and high exclamation of pleasure, Taffy felt his
spine melt. He almost collapsed to the ground at her
sound. Instead he moved closer and grinned, reaching to
undo the front of his pants. If there was an opportunity
to be had here in the middle of the night, in the middle of
the ocean . . . he was *not* going to pass it up.

Taffy stepped closer, the wheeze in his chest loud, but the woman seemed oblivious to his approach, despite the sound and the fact that his lamplight flickered brightly over her naked torso. She kept her eyes closed and reached deeper with her arm, calling out with louder and louder gasps as she did so. Taffy knew she had to know he was there, yet she brazenly continued to enjoy herself despite that. Clearly she wanted him to enjoy her exploration of herself, and he grinned—because he did enjoy it. He did very much, indeed. His pants were loosened and slipping down the thick muscles of his thighs as he shifted step by careful step closer, and he recognized the sound he'd heard earlier that day from the far reaches of the ship's hold. That musical, wavering, beautiful bit of noise that said "female" and "heaven" and "take me."

He set the lamp down on the deck and crawled between her legs, unconscious of how brazen the act may have been. She had not said a word to him, or even acknowledged his presence, and he was going to mount her? Her song drew him to her, low and quiet and needful, she hummed and whimpered and moaned—a music that seemed to fill the hold with a passion so thick you could mire yourself in it. Her voice was amber, and he dove in without regret knowing that he'd be trapped.

As Taffy let his body touch hers, the woman's eyes opened, and the golden-flecked brown pools drew him in like magnets. He leaned to kiss those pouty lips, and her hands slid from between her thighs to grip his back. She pulled him closer and drew his need to her own with an ease that he respected.

This woman, whoever she was, knew what she wanted, and he was happy to oblige. He slid into her, gasping at the warmth and comfort he found there, and took one thick nipple between his teeth as he drove his hips against hers.

That song, that amazing sound that was her, began to vibrate around him and he could almost see the colors change against the wood of the ship, from scintillating purples to deep, wanting crimson flares to yellow exclamations of passion. His eyes no longer saw the real world, but only registered its shades of passion.

When her fingernails dug into his back, he arched into her, and when her teeth bared and bit at his neck, he only moaned, stupidly assuming she thirsted for a taste of him.

What she thirsted for, unfortunately for Taffy, was his blood.

He only cried out once when she ripped out his throat and drank from the fountain of his heart. With her hands she grabbed him by the head and gave a fast, furious twist. The snap of Taffy's neck echoed through the hold like a gunshot; he was not nearly as flexible as his name implied. Ligeia relaxed as the seaman's life flowed into her like wine. She twisted and ground beneath him, leveraging his weight against her crotch as she drank and enjoyed the weight of him against her. He had died hard, and she used him. Soon she grew slick with his blood and for a time oblivious to the musty confines of the ship, smelling only the flower of his iron and the heat of her excitement.

After her song had spent, Ligeia rolled the heavy seaman over, his eyes white and dead in the flickering oil lamp he'd left behind, and she bent at his throat to slake another need. Hunger trumped all pleasure. With teeth that hid edges sharp as razors she fed on his flesh, closing her eyes to revel in the warm, salty taste of his muscle and blood.

"Hmmm," she moaned, as she separated the head from his spine. Strangely, this one's body didn't seem to hold on to his head with quite the possessiveness that she was used to, and she enjoyed the jellylike warmth that she buried her mouth on as his face fell away.

The ropes slipped around her wrists with ease. She may have been otherworldly, but she too could get lost in her passions. And not for the first time, it was her undoing.

"So . . ." Captain Buckley grinned, a long, wicked smile in the orange shadows cast by Taffy's lamp.

"You thought you would stay on my ship and take my crew did you?" The captain shook his head, and the woman's eyes widened, her blood-spattered cheeks drawing up in full comprehension of her miscalculation.

"You could have taken to the sea," he said, hog-tying her without regard for the long, sticky pink bits of flesh from Taffy's corpse that still clung to her. "You could have escaped. But I knew—I knew . . . with this many men in one place, locked at sea . . . you wouldn't leave. Not right away. Like rum to a drunk they were for you. You shoulda hedged your bets, my Siren," Buckley said. His teeth gritted against one another like chalk against a rough board. "But I have to say, milady, I am getting tired of cleaning up after your messes. And I am beginning to run short on crew."

Buckley left her tied tight and helpless in the corner while he slung Taffy's body over his shoulder. For once in his existence, the crewman mimicked his namesake and hung like a warm, boneless blob over the captain's shoulder. Buckley took the steps up to the deck as fast as he could, and after a quick look back and forth, virtually ran across the boards to the edge of the ship. He let Taffy's body fall to the dark waves below without a second thought, and then grimaced as he ran a hand across the warm stain that covered his chest.

Another shirt ruined.

Since Ligeia had entered his life, Captain Buckley had

disposed of a lot of shirts thanks to her feeding habits. Cursing silently, he slipped back down the stairs to retrieve his prize. He and she had some catching up to do after spending the past couple days apart. And he intended to catch up in the worst possible way. Captain Buckley considered the leather strap that had lain abandoned near the fishy stink of his bunk for the past two nights and smiled. His girl would be home again with him. She had a nasty side, that was for sure. But they suited each other in that. And after all, he'd paid for her, hadn't he? He intended to get his money's worth.

Oblivious to the music in her moans, the captain carried her naked form down the black shadow of his ship to the squalid confines of his cabin.

When he closed the door, he shut out the last of her hope. Tears streamed like the spray of the ocean down the captain's bloodied back, but he didn't care. He only positioned her lush body on his bed and began to strip off his own ruined clothes.

"Now," he said. "Now you will earn your place on this ship."

CHAPTER NINETEEN

"I think maybe we should go away somewhere," Sarah said.

Evan looked up from shoveling a mouthful of curried rice into his mouth and gave his wife a quizzical look. They'd been having a quiet dinner at Ocean Thaid, their favorite restaurant, and Sarah had been quiet up to now. She'd been picking at her pad prik instead of attacking it.

"I know you can't take a lot of time off right now, but maybe if we took a short vacation, even just a long weekend . . ."

His first thought was not for Sarah, or about the difficulty of asking Darren for time off right now, when he was on the boss's shit list and it was their busiest port time of the year. No, Evan's first thought was that if they went away, he wouldn't be able to spend his nights with Ligeia. *Ass*, he mentally kicked himself.

"We might be able to figure something out," he said aloud. "Did you have someplace in mind?"

Sarah shrugged. "Not really. I'm just feeling so . . . I don't know the word . . . trapped? Like, we're running the same maze over and over every day, and there is no exit."

"Very Sartre of you."

"You've been hanging out with Bill too much."

He grinned and took another bite as he thought a moment. "We could take a long weekend in San Francisco if you just want to get away," he finally suggested. "Or maybe spend a couple days in Napa?"

Her face brightened. "Napa would be good. I want to get away from water."

Evan felt his own smile diminish.

"We don't have to," Sarah said, recognizing that something about the idea didn't set well with him. "But I thought you'd like to get away from the ocean a bit too. It's like we're on a bad cycle and can't stop."

Evan nodded. "You're right. I'll talk to Darren about it tomorrow. Maybe we can even go this weekend."

Sarah suddenly started eating her noodles with visible relish. "Thanks," she said. Her eyes sparkled in the warm low light. "I really need this."

Their conversation turned to other things, but for the first time in weeks, it seemed they were actually having conversation, and Evan realized how much he'd been neglecting her. He really did need to get her out of Delilah, away from the constant reminders of Josh. Guilt at the reason he was reticent to go caught in his throat like a golf ball, but he fought it away.

Across the table, Sarah was still talking, and he forced himself away from thoughts of Ligeia stretched out naked in front of him on the beach to pay attention. It was a difficult thing to stop thinking of her, and last night she had not appeared when he'd gone to the beach. He'd stayed there for over an hour, the panic slowly growing that he might never see her again before he returned home, disconsolate, to spend a restless night next to his snoring wife.

". . . they said it was the first wreck on those rocks in more than eight years," Sarah said. She stopped, looking at him expectantly.

Evan shook his head in agreement, wondering what the question was he'd missed. "Yeah, it's been a long time since they had a point accident. Ships these days have plenty of technology to make sure they don't rip up their hulls on reefs."

"So what did these guys do wrong?"

"Asleep at the wheel," he said. In his mind he saw Ligeia standing naked on the top of the point, breasts jutting out in the dark like beacons of lust. A human lighthouse of doom.

"I'd guess they were just distracted," he concluded. "They just weren't paying attention to where they were going."

After dinner, Sarah took Evan's hand and led him away from the car. The night was warm, a humid night breeze ruffled the short sleeve of her shirt as she walked. Evan felt a return of his love for her, and longed to hold her, just hold her there under the stars. As it turned out, that was her intent too. She led him off Center Street to the small park in the middle of town. A bronze statue of a fishing boat and Delilah's first founding captain dominated the small square, and Sarah pulled Evan under the canopy of a tree and put her arms around his neck.

"I've missed you," she whispered.

He frowned. "I've been here."

"Not really," she said. "This last week or two . . . it's like you've been somewhere else half the time. And honestly . . . we both have been gone for a long time."

He couldn't disagree with that, and didn't have to, as Sarah kissed him. She pressed against him suggestively, and then with a wink offered, "Take me home?"

The answering machine light was blinking red when they walked back into the kitchen. Evan started across the dark floor to answer it, but Sarah grabbed his hand.

"It'll wait," she whispered, turning him to face her. Then she pulled her shirt over her head and smiled. "I won't."

Evan laughed and doffed his own shirt before pulling her tight to him. Then with a deft, long-practiced hand he released her bra. "Pushy sex kitten tonight, huh?"

"Are you complaining?"

"Not on your life." He bent to kiss her gently and her tongue slipped into his mouth with a more urgent demand. She burned hot tonight in his hands and worked clumsily at his belt buckle as she moaned softly into his mouth.

Evan walked backward to their bedroom as Sarah ran her hands over him. She hadn't been this visibly turned on in months . . . maybe years, he thought.

In minutes they were both naked on cool sheets, and the familiar scent of her arousal filled Evan's head with lust and warmth. It was so good to be close like this with her; Sarah had been the center of his existence for longer than he could remember, and they had grown distant over these past months. As he slipped inside her, it was like coming home after an extended, tiring trip. After his recent nights on the beach, her flesh felt different, as if he had to rediscover the feeling of his wife. For all her energy, Sarah ground against him with a slower, less-fevered need than Ligeia.

"Oh God, Evan," Sarah cried out beneath him, and he ached to release with her. He tried to focus on the O of her mouth and his own impending release, but as it hit and the waves of pleasure sent him away for that split second of euphoria, he saw himself riding not his wife, but the dark, hungry body of Ligeia. As Sarah's mouth opened in a final scream of passion, Evan saw Ligeia, her eyes full of black mystery, her lips lush and demanding and her teeth . . . white and wide and . . . sharp. His orgasm ended with a cool chill as he struggled to refocus on Sarah, who was here, instead of Ligeia, who was not.

He rolled off his real wife, blinking away the image of his feral "water wife" and forced a smile as he leaned to kiss Sarah. "Good?" he murmured.

She nodded, a dreamy smile already covering her face.

He started to slip out of bed, but she put a hand on his shoulder and whispered, "Stay with me?"

Evan took her in his arms and kissed her again, letting her snuggle into him, and rest her head on his shoulder. In moments, Sarah was fast asleep, but Evan couldn't let go. He lay wide-awake in the dark, his mind filled with images of Ligeia. Images of lust . . . and hunger.

CHAPTER TWENTY

The mornings came hard after a night of good sex. Evan still felt completely drained as he finally turned off the alarm after three hits to the snooze button. Sarah was already in the shower, and so he padded into the kitchen to make a pot of coffee. As he poured in the grounds, he noticed the red light on the answering machine still blinking. The message Sarah had stopped him from listening to last night (not that he'd minded the interruption)—he'd never come back in to play it.

He poured the water into the back of the coffeemaker, hit start and then clicked the message button on the answering machine. Bill's voice drawled from the tiny speaker.

"Hey, people, where are ya at? Screening calls, huh?"

Evan smiled. Bill's paranoid assumption if someone didn't take his call was never that they weren't actually busy doing something else, but that they *must* be avoiding him.

"Listen, Evan—I just thought you'd get a kick out of this. After the wreck by the point the other day, the city council decided at its meeting tonight that they're going to have a beacon erected out there on the rocks. Talk about knee-jerk reactions! We don't have an accident out there for years and then there is one and . . . pow, there goes the view! Anyway . . . just thought you'd be interested. Pretty soon when you take your night walks you're going to get hit in the face with a nice red radio tower beacon instead of starlight. They call that progress. Anyway . . . see you tomorrow, I guess."

The line went dead and Evan stood still, thinking about the implications of the beacon. If there was construction going on out at the point over the next few weeks, would Ligeia still come around? A chill ran up his spine at the idea of losing her now. If he were a girl who liked to walk the beach naked, singing . . . well . . . he wondered if there were a bunch of guys lounging around by the point all day, would that keep her away at night?

Evan heard the shower shut off in the other room and shrugged away the thought. Nothing had started yet, and he hoped to be able to see her tonight after missing her the past two. For now . . . he had to get through another day.

The port was humming with activity as he pulled up to the lot. Bill was running up and down the dock shouting at various dockhands, while scribbling stuff down on a pad of notepaper. A large ship—the *Ting-Ho*—had come in at dawn, and there was plenty to do; this wasn't a local freighter, but an international. And when a ship like that came into Delilah—someone outside their normal runs of local commerce—things kicked into high gear. Service with a smile—they wanted this trade back. Delilah had a small trade route happening with fishermen and rumrunners. Had since Prohibition. But they still hoped for bigger fish to fry as a port town. The fishing trade was diminishing, and the liquor boats could dock anywhere. All that drew anybody to Delilah was habit and a love of old-town architecture. The place did look good at sunset with all those turn-of-the-century Victorians dotting the long hill of Main.

But looking good didn't contribute to the tax base.

Evan hurried up the steps to the office and kicked on his computer. He was on time for once, but with the boat in dock he still felt late.

"Darren said to grab a #2790 form and have a talk with the ship's portage officer," Maggie said. She breezed through the empty staff office on her way to the kitchen, and was already retracing her steps with two mugs of coffee in hand before Evan had found the requisite paperwork. Someone was getting the A+ treatment!

"Chop chop," she laughed. "Cargo's a-wasting!"

Cargo, in this case, turned out to be nothing worth writing home about. While the freighter hailed from Taiwan, it carried a wealth of widgets that were of no interest to anyone but manufacturers. No cool electronics filled this hold, no. Instead it was crammed with stacks and stacks of tiny plastic fittings and wires and computer chips, all boxed and crated and jammed as tightly as would fit from wall to wall and floor to ceiling in the hold.

You always liked it when a foreign ship came to port, because more often than not, you could score some kind of cool gadget or gimmicky bit of merch. But while this one carried lots of tech, it didn't haul anything worth carrying away. This boat didn't carry any DVD players or knockoff iPods. It had digital fun, yes, but only if you had a manufacturing division that needed the absolute basic raw materials to build something worthwhile out of.

Evan spent the morning walking the cargo hold and spot-checking inventory as the crew unloaded the hold, row by row. The short Oriental crew chief, whose name was Ying How or something similar, two syllables that hit the ear like a one-two punch—Evan couldn't have repeated it exactly—told him all about their reasons for coming to Delilah.

"Everything is on way to businesses in northern California," the man said, gesturing at the crates. "Home boss say it cheaper to come here to the little town and send on trucks than to go to San Francisco and use trains."

Just the kind of story that Darren liked to hear; Evan grinned to himself. "We hope you'll stay here a day or two and enjoy yourself," he heard himself saying.

Ying How shook his head. "We are back to water fast. Must pick up return parts. In-out, In-out, you know?"

The man raised one thick black eyebrow, and Evan nodded. He did understand, but despite that, when the man said, "in-out, in-out," there was only one thing he could think of. And it had nothing to do with freight.

By three P.M., the *Ting-Ho* had docked, unloaded, undocked and sailed.

By six P.M., Evan had returned home, kissed his wife, checked the mail and changed clothes.

By seven P.M., he was itching to return to the beach. Sarah beamed at him all through dinner—some lemon chicken concoction she'd gotten the recipe for from her friend Yovana. He complimented it and absently polished off his plate.

But throughout the whole conversation (he couldn't have told you what they talked about) his only thought was on whether Ligeia would be at the beach tonight.

When he slipped on his sandals at 8:30 and announced he was taking a walk, Sarah pouted. "You won't be too long, will you?" she asked. Her eyes told him that she didn't want him to leave at all. Last night had really impacted her, he guessed.

"Not too long," he promised, feeling like a heel. In his heart, he hoped that he would be seeing Ligeia . . . and if he did, he knew that he wouldn't be home until long after Sarah had gone to bed.

He kissed her, and her arms held him tight, tighter than normal. She really wanted him to be with her tonight, he could tell.

"I love you," he said, giving her a quick peck on the lips. "I'll be back."

The beach was loud tonight, Evan thought as he walked quickly down the line of tide debris. Storm coming, he supposed. The breakers were capping white as far out as he could see, and the rush of the sea felt like a tangible roar in the air.

Evan skipped a stone absently, but it sank before it completed three skips. The water was too hungry tonight.

When he reached the point, Evan took a breath and held it absently. He was convinced that she wouldn't appear. The water was wild; he'd been gone for a couple nights (not that she came to see him, but still) . . . he was sure that he would go away crushed.

Evan reached the curve of the beach that dipped inward and then led back out to the finger of the point and stopped. He could walk down the long rock face, but he hadn't the past couple times. And now . . . he just wanted to wait a while. Absently, he began to hum, knowing in his head that the past times he'd started singing, she'd answered.

It didn't take very long.

The air suddenly vibrated with warmth, and Evan felt his lower back quiver. His chest ached, instantly, at the sound of her voice. He knew it was her before five notes had sounded. The gentle trill shimmered in the air like an aural fog, and Evan felt instantly euphoric. She was here! He couldn't tell where; her voice seemed to slip out of the sky from everywhere at once. Beautiful, wanting and slow.

And then her hands were on him, massaging his shoulders and slipping down his ribs to hug him from behind. He sighed, and turned to meet her.

"You've been gone," she said. "I missed you."

"I was here a couple nights ago, but you didn't come," he said.

"I was here last night," she whispered in his ear. Her tongue strayed quickly from words to exploration.

"I'm here now," he said, and her tongue found his, and they stopped talking. Like before, she was already nude, her body dripping with the moisture of the ocean. Evan pulled her to him and felt her dampness through his shirt. He cupped her ass and ground himself against her pelvis, without any feeling of propriety. They both knew why they were here and he wasn't going to waste their time with games.

But this night, instead of stripping him instantly, Ligeia pushed his chest away from hers. "Come with me tonight," she said.

"Where?"

"Come with me to my home. Stay with me. Swim with me."

Evan shook his head. "I know you got me in the water before but . . . I really don't like it. Honestly!"

She ran a finger from his left nipple to the center of his crotch. "I could make you love it," she promised.

A fleeting thought of Sarah crossed his mind, and Evan shook his head. "I can't go tonight. I don't have much time," he said. "Where do you live anyway?"

A thin smile creased her face. With one hand she gestured out to the water just beyond Gull's Point. "There," she said. "And everywhere."

Evan felt a pang of unease in his gut as she pointed to the water. Did she really mean to say that she lived in the ocean? Bill would have told him to run, run fast! Or was she just being coy, teasing him with vagaries and hints?

She pressed up against him and with a darting tongue wet his lips, and then his earlobe. "I've been waiting for you for a long time," she whispered.

Then she was undoing his shorts and pulling off his shirt, and Evan didn't think about where she slept when he wasn't there. He only wanted to "sleep" with her now. They lay down and the sand was cool on Evan's skin, but Ligeia burned against him, her hands slipping up and down and around his body, exploring him with fluttering touches and urgent grabs. He nuzzled her breasts and teased with his tongue before swallowing one; her nipple was thick and hard in his mouth and she cried out as he bit down, gently, slipping a hand between her thigh from behind and then riding it up into her warm cleft. Then she wouldn't wait anymore and she straddled him, the moonlight reflecting off the sweat on her skin as if she were covered in diamond dust. She was glorious in the night, and Evan came with barely any provocation. But she didn't let him go, only continued to ride him, slowly, easily, as if they had all night. Evan could feel himself losing it, his moment long past. She began to sing. As always, her melody hinted at the lost and exotic, perhaps in part because the words were indistinct. Did she sing of love, or a foreign childhood? He couldn't be sure. The beauty washed over him easily, and he surrendered to it fully, closing his eyes and disappearing in the colors and sensation it brought to him. Evan had always been in love with music. It had been his truest, dearest love since he was a child. When he tried pot as a teen, he had to do it while wearing headphones and listening to Rush or Kansas or Styx . . . some kind of ambitious progressive rock that worked inside him with the drug to produce . . . a grand euphoria that only the smoke and the music combined could create. If he drew in a hit without the music, he felt instantly nauseated.

Ligeia's song reminded him of those long-gone days of smoking with headphones on, black lights raising strange and wonderful colors from the rock posters pasted across his bedroom walls. He had not felt this good in twenty years. Yet, this was better than then. This was stronger, natural . . .

Two hands helped him up from the sand, and Evan smiled dumbly as Ligeia continued to sing, her lips moving across his chest, barely touching, and then coming up to hum strong in his ear. He could feel his erection somehow returning, and she pulled him to follow her as she stepped backward toward the water. "My turn," she said, her eyes glinting with want.

"Oh no," he said, fear suddenly rising in his gut like a sudden fire. "Not again, I—"

"You shouldn't refuse a woman who wants you," Ligeia said, tilting her head down to look at him with eyes that brooked no argument. "You should thank her, and listen to her song; her music tells you what you need."

With that she opened her mouth and let out a brazen moan of passion that sent shivers down Evan's spine. So raw, so feral, so . . .

Ligeia's cry turned into a brooding, throbbing snippet of melody. Her eyes never broke contact with his as she stepped close, rubbing her breasts against his chest, moving her lips within centimeters of his, all the while working a magic of melody that turned his bones to jelly. When she pulled again he didn't protest, but followed her into the dark water once again. Ligeia wrapped herself around him in the water, pulling him close and impaling herself on him, taking him inside her with a single thrust. Her song rose and fell with their rhythm, until at last she gasped with her impending orgasm and stopped singing to lock her lips on his. As Evan's eyes opened wide, her face filled his vision, and then they were beneath the water, moving as one in a free fall of sexual frenzy that kept thoughts of water far from Evan's mind. All he could think about were the amazing bursts of pleasure shooting from his groin through his spine. Sex had never been like this for him, ever. And now he was giving himself to a woman whom he barely knew. A woman who insisted on taking him in the ocean. A woman who his best friend claimed was some kind of water witch, a Siren.

He broke her kiss to laugh at that stray thought and instantly regretted it. Evan's mouth filled with cold brine and he tried to spit it out but only succeeded in drawing more ocean in through his nose. His eyes widened with the panic that had kept him from stepping more than a foot into the waves for most of his life, and his hands broke from their hold on Ligeia's firm ass to flail like a maniac in the water. He only succeeded in pushing himself away from her, his only life preserver, and in seconds he had plummeted from the peak of euphoria to the depths of panic. Evan opened his mouth to scream, where nobody would ever hear. Evan was going to drown, just as he'd always known he would.

Ligeia slipped up from beneath his writhing form, darting between his thighs to crawl up his chest in the water. She locked her arms around his waist, and pressed her lips to his. Evan pushed her away, struggling without reason to be free so that he could . . . what? Suck in more water? Panic didn't leave room for logic. He tried to shake free of her embrace, but Ligeia didn't let go. Her eyes bore into his beneath the black water, and somehow in the black of night beneath the ocean he could see the sparkle there, the life spark just centimeters away. Her tongue darted into his mouth and the closer that she clove to him, the more the fear dissipated. It slipped away like ice propped near a flame. In seconds, Evan stopped fighting her, and held her tighter. He clung to her like a life preserver, and in return, she moved her legs around his waist again. Her tongue wrestled playfully with his own and he couldn't—wouldn't—believe it, but somehow from the depths of panic, after being inside her twice already in a half hour, he slipped in again. Ligeia's face grinned with victory, and this time she held him tighter and moved against him slower and made the moment stretch into what seemed like an hour.

When at last she pushed back from his mouth to gasp a soundless "O" in the waves, Evan had already moved beyond the boundaries of the place he called sanity. He started to take in water through his nose again and coughed, pulling horrible seawater into his lungs, but then she was back, pressing her lips to his hungrily, thankfully, and in seconds with strong thrusts of her feet they surfaced and bobbed above the waves. The lights of Delilah were distant fuzzy orbs on a faraway horizon and Evan wondered idly how far into the depths they had gone. Exhausted, he didn't wonder how they would get back. He trusted Ligeia implicitly in the water. She had made him do things there he never thought possible. She had given him the best moments of his entire life in the place he hated with all of his being.

"Come home with me now," she whispered.

Evan's eyes widened, and suddenly that blissful euphoria slipped away. His spine broke the water, which trickled down his vertebrae and suddenly felt like ice.

"Ligeia, don't . . ." he began.

"Don't you want this for always?" her voice murmured in his brain like a foggy echo. Her hands had grasped his own and worked them against the soft, tight skin of her butt with a wanton disregard for propriety. She moved his hands up from the gentle slope of her ass, and then brought them between their bodies until she guided his fingers to cup her breasts. "Don't you want this?" she echoed again.

Evan felt as if he were on a bad drug high; her voice reverberated over and over in his brain like a bad trip. "Don't you want to take me every night like this?"

"Yes," he answered without thinking. "Yes. But . . ."

"Then just say yes, not but," she said.

Evan touched Josh's medal on the thin chain around his neck as his mind flashed to an image of his son's room, yellowing pictures on the wall, Psychedelic Furs poster tucked in one corner like a guilty pleasure hidden beneath the garish poses of more "today" popsters like Lady Gaga and Black Eyed Peas and Snow Patrol. He saw a vision of Sarah, passed out in their bed like a corpse, the only suggestion that she still breathed being the moisture at the side of her mouth, shimmering slightly, ever so slightly that you'd have to stand for moments watching it to see in the gentle cascade of midnight breath.

Leave his memories of Josh? Leave his home—his sad, desperate crypt of a home with Sarah?

"No," he answered at last. "I can't, I—"

Ligeia's eyes flashed in the night and she shoved him away from her with his denial, set him adrift in the ocean.

"No, don't—" Evan cried out, but then she returned to him in a heartbeat, and drew him close.

"You can't stay adrift forever," Ligeia whispered in his ear. His neck tremored at the briefest rush of her lips. "You have to choose a direction and swim," she said. "But tonight . . ." She kicked against the loud roar of the surf, and started to drag him in the direction of the shore. "Tonight I will choose for you."

Evan relaxed, slightly, and felt his heart yearn suddenly for the shore.

"Tonight, but not forever," she warned.

CHAPTER TWENTY-ONE

"What am I gonna do?" Evan complained.

"I don't see the problem," Bill answered, raising a pint and miming a toast. "You've got a wonderful wife who loves you, and you're fucking a sea devil in the ocean to boot. I'd say you've got the horns by the bull."

"You're a jackass," Evan spit. "You know I don't want to hurt Sarah."

"And yet you drop your clothes on the beach virtually every night to get down with a chick who basically you know only by name and the feel of her tits," Bill retorted. "Where does she live? How old is she? What does she like to do on a Saturday night? What's her favorite food? Who are her favorite authors? Favorite movies? I'm not going to ask favorite positions, because I bet *that*, you could answer."

Bill tilted back the beer and slammed it back on the table as he burped. "Answer me a single one of those questions and I'll let you off the hook. But you can't, can you?"

Evan didn't answer. He looked away and watched the bartender serve two blonde women at the long wooden bar that cut O'Flaherty's in half. They giggled and shimmied onto their chairs with a unified motion that suggested they were performing a ritual. Evan knew where that ritual would lead in three or four more hours when the hour grew late. They were here to score, and tomorrow, they'd be comparing notes and laughing about the inadequacies they'd uncovered in their latest conquests. And next week, they'd be here again, same place, same time, same modus operandi. No commitments, no change.

"No, I can't," he admitted. "I know almost nothing about her."

"I know a lot about her," Bill said. "But you don't want to hear it."

"Fuck that," Evan laughed. "You think I'm boning a freaking piece . . . a piece of mythology," he laughed.

Bill looked at him and the crags above his nose looked deeper than normal. Bill wasn't old, but the mark of thousands of days in the seaside air and subsequent nights in the bar had begun to leave their toll. "Yeah," he said. "Yeah, I do. And it scares the hell out of me."

"Look," Evan said. "I found a woman who loves the water." He grimaced. "Granted, for reasons which we won't go into here, that, in and of itself, makes me queasy, and it's all kind of amusingly ironic, but that's not the part of her that I have fallen for."

"You don't have to talk about that part," Bill suggested, raising his glass. "Although, if you have pictures . . ."

"Fuck you, you recalcitrant. No pictures. But I could describe the way her ass curves right into the small of her back like . . ."

Bill put up his hand. "Enough!"

His friend shook his head and had another sip of beer before he continued. "I know you guys have had a rough year, but . . . I just don't know what to say about you cheating on Sarah. I mean . . . what has she ever done to you?"

Bill held up a hand before Evan could answer. "I know the lure of a hot chick by the ocean, don't you think I do? But . . . I think you're going to get hurt. I think Sarah's going to get hurt. I think your dick is going to get hurt.

And I don't want to be around to see any of that, ya know? Especially your dick."

Evan opened his mouth to answer and found he had nothing to retort.

Bill shrugged his shoulders and drained the second half of his pint. "Sometimes it sucks to be your friend. You get the chicks and I have to tell you *not* to score. It's just not right. I'm the single guy."

"Yeah, well, that's because you talk to the likes of them." Evan motioned at the blondes at the bar, but he realized as he turned that they weren't on their stools any longer. And a moment later, he understood why.

"Hey there," one of them said to Bill, running a hand over his broad shoulders. "My friend and I were just wondering, how would you like to join us at the bar for a quick drink? Her name's Christine, and she is just in for the week visiting. I wanted to show her some local color, you know?"

Evan figured that color was probably pink, and it didn't really matter whether it was local or not, but he didn't blame Bill too much when his friend held up an index finger and suggested, "I'll be back in a minute . . ." before leaving with the girl who seemed at least ten years his junior. *Whatever.* Evan couldn't throw stones, after all . . . he was getting fish on the beach.

"What the fuck am I doing?" he asked himself, pulling a long swig on his beer as he watched Bill stumble across the room to ease his ass onto a bar stool in between the two unnaturally bright-haired bottle blondes.

Evan hoped Bill didn't have a lot in his wallet, because he figured, at the end of the night, whatever was there, was going to be gone.

That said . . . it was hardly the time for Evan to be parochial. He put down his glass, dropped a twenty on the table and started out of the bar, clapping Bill on the shoulder as he went. "Good luck," he murmured, but didn't stay to hear the answer.

He was headed toward the beach and he knew what kind of luck he needed to be successful there. He just needed to show up. Evan took Fifth Street toward the ocean and prayed in his heart and his groin that Ligeia would be there, once again, to greet him.

CHAPTER TWENTY-TWO

June 9, 1887

The *Lady Luck* cut through the water like a knife through red meat—quiet and clean and lethal. Captain Buckley held the wheel and his fingers sweated as he pressed it to the right, praying that Ligeia would feel his intention. He was headed toward shore. It was time to dock, and she was always more amorous when they were near the land. Not docked . . . then she grew distant. But just before docking . . . she was amazing. Desirable, delectable . . . decadent. It was almost as if she had the urge to "spawn" when she approached land. Given her pedigree, maybe that was exactly it, Buckley thought.

He had left her in the cabin, retied and gagged after she finished gnawing on the thighbone of Rogers. It was probably the last day until he had to dispose of the thing. The cabin had begun to smell too strongly; the men would get suspicious. And she had a new recruit for her hunger regardless. The body of Nelson now lay in his cabin unblemished, except for the blood that had pooled and congealed beneath the wounds. The cabin reeked with the stench of iron now, both old and newly bled. Buckley knew that it was time for Ligeia to move on to her new meat, though he didn't relish the disposal duty of the old.

Buckley wanted to talk to her about her killing habits,

and come to some agreement on when and how and who. He wished she could communicate with him, logically, in the same way, but he understood the limitations she faced. For one, he kept her gagged. For another, she wanted to kill him and didn't speak even when the gag was removed. Plus, she was nocturnal it seemed; when he was awake, she was ready to sleep. They were at an impasse, he thought. They were opposites and opposites attract. Buckley loved his twisted, torturous girl, and he aimed to make every moment of her captive journey desirable. Perhaps, eventually, she would grow to love it.

"All you have to do is ask," he murmured, quiet beneath the gravity of a growing insanity. "I would give you anything." The fact that she'd killed two of his men briefly troubled his mind, but he answered himself. "There are some things that don't lend themselves to examination. You just have to follow your gut. My gut says . . . you will always be mine, 'til death do us part."

Buckley smiled as he envisioned the nude girl lying on his bed right now, waiting for him in the shadows. He turned the wheel and guided the boat toward the distant light of shore. If he'd been paying any attention, he might have noticed that he was alone on deck; his crew had quietly disappeared. They had turned their sights to a different mission. Of late, they had become concerned with the hidden cargo of their captain, though they weren't sure on what it was. But it was not hard to realize that their leader had become preoccupied with something else. And it was time that someone found out exactly what the captain was up to. Because . . . it seemed as if the ship had become a dangerous home for its crew. Rogers had disappeared. And then Nelson. And now Taffy.

In the cargo hold beneath their oblivious captain, the remaining men appealed to the first mate. They gathered in a circle around Travers. The faint light from a handheld lantern cast orange shadows on his face. Travers looked like he were burning.

"He is keeping something from us," Jensen insisted. "He doesn't speak except in mumbles and cryptic phrases all day, and then he disappears below. Meanwhile, our mates are disappearing. Don't you think it's just a wee bit strange? We're a fishing boat with a secret hold. And men are starting to 'fall off the deck' every other day. I don't buy it. Something about our cargo is dangerous."

"What would you have me do?" Travers asked. He'd been with Buckley for the better part of six years, and the *Lady Luck* felt more like his home than the tiny flat his wife kept up in the half a year he was away from it. He'd always felt safe here, but he had to agree with the men. Things weren't feeling so secure anymore.

"I say we go up top right now and demand that he tell us what's what," Reg said. The beefy crewman beat a fist into a broad ham of a hand. "If we all go together . . ."

Travers shook his head. "That's called mutiny," he said. "Or, at least that's how Buckley would see it. If you go at him with a gun, he's not going to roll over, he's going to fight." The first mate pursed his lips a bit, considering.

"Let me try to approach him first," Travers suggested. "I'll feel him out quietlike tonight. Not combative. I've been with Buckley a long time. He's tough, but deep down he's a good man, I think. If there's something worse than bad luck in all this, well, I think he'll give me some warning."

The captain remained quiet at dinner, though Cauldry had actually managed to season a stew that didn't taste like well-worn shoes. Jensen suggested that the fill-in cook looked good in an apron, and Reg made the sign of the devil at the both of them. "Don't start with any of that stuff," he complained. "We have enough unnatural going on around here."

Cauldry cuffed his younger brother and motioned for Reg to shift over on the long plank they used as a dinner seat. He pulled out a pair of dice from beneath the dark stains of his once-white apron (he may have learned how to cook, but he surely hadn't learned how to be neat at it) and tossed them on the table.

"Any takers?" he asked, and at that, the captain, who'd stayed silent through all the tomfoolery, stood, nodded at the men and left the galley. The chatter stilled as the men all watched Buckley walk out. Then they turned, again as one, to look at Travers. He rewarded them with a tortured smile, nodded himself and rose.

"I'll see what I see," he promised, and followed the captain.

Behind him, the voices of a nervous crew letting off steam rose again. But there was a forced element to it, as if they were trying just a little too hard to act naturally free and fun.

Buckley's cabin door was just closing as Travers reached it.

"Captain, a minute?" Travers called, and put his hand on the door to stop it from closing. "I'd like to talk to you."

Buckley's face poked around the narrow gap. The captain raised a brush of a salt-and-pepper eyebrow and simply said, "What do you want?" He didn't let the door budge inward an inch.

"Could I come in for a moment, sir?" Travers asked. "I'd like to talk to you in private."

"Not now," Buckley answered, gruff as ever.

Travers heard a thump from behind the captain, and

pressed again. "It will just take a minute, sir, but I'd like to talk out of earshot of the men."

Again the thump, and the captain shook his head, violently. "Good night, Travers," he said, and began to push the door shut. Travers didn't let it close immediately. He wondered about the thumping behind the captain. Could somebody else be in the cabin? Just as he framed that thought, he heard something else from the dark behind Buckley's head.

"*Ehhhhhiiieeeahhhhh*," came a thin, wavering sound, just barely audible. It could have been a ghost or a girl—it was high-pitched and forced . . . yet, strangely soothing for all its intensity.

"Good night!" the captain shouted savagely, and pushed his shoulder into the door.

Travers staggered back from the door, shocked at the captain's response. He'd never acted like this before. He leaned against the wall across from the dark wooden frame of the captain's cabin and mused.

Buckley had absolutely not wanted him to enter the cabin—a place where Travers had gone many a time for private chats. The first mate stared down at the floor, and noted a couple dark spots just in front of the captain's door. As he looked closer, he noticed more of them, a faint trail that led across the planks and toward the stairs to the deck. He crouched down, and touched the larger of the spots, moving his finger back and forth across the wood. It didn't feel wet, not anymore. Still, when he pulled back his finger, it looked to be stained a dull, gritty red.

From beyond the captain's door, again he heard the high-pitched sound, followed by the low but unmistakable bark of Buckley.

The old bastard had someone in his cabin! Travers

performed a quick mental survey and confirmed that the entire crew—what was left of it—was currently behind him in the galley. "Hmmmpfh," he said to himself, and slowly followed the trail of spots up the ladder and across the deck. They disappeared before he'd gone but a couple steps; the sea was constantly spraying the boards above deck.

But he'd seen what he needed to. They had led from the stairs in a straight line toward the edge of the ship.

The captain had carried something from his cabin to toss overboard. Something that leaked. Something dripping a liquid that looked an awful lot like . . . blood.

"Hmmmpfh," Travers said for the second time, and looked toward the dark hole leading back belowdecks. Somehow those stairs didn't look as friendly and welcoming as they normally did.

Home wasn't seeming quite so sweet tonight.

CHAPTER TWENTY-THREE

San Francisco rose like a wraith city out of the bank of fog. The drive across the Golden Gate Bridge was dreamlike—the world below faded to invisibility, while white streamers of fog slipped through the steel cage of the bridge's arch work with lazy speed.

"They call it the City by the Bay, but it should be the city in a cloud," Sarah laughed.

"It'll burn off by lunchtime," Evan promised. "It's supposed to hit eighty today."

"I hope so," she said. "I want to go to the park."

One of Sarah's favorite places in the world was Golden Gate Park—when they were first married, they had spent many hours there walking the long, winding paths, sipping tea in the small café overlooking the water in the Japanese Tea Garden and exploring the scents and vibrant colors of the rose garden. The park was an amazing expanse of winding walking trails that led to the de Young Museum, a music concourse, Stow Lake and botanical gardens. Eucalyptus trees stretched to the sky throughout, refreshing the air of the place with a fresh, vibrant tang. After a day of walking, you could end up on one end of the mile-and-a-half-long rectangle at the tie-dye capital of the world, Haight–Ashbury, or at the other, down near the beach. Sometimes they'd have dinner at the Beach Chalet, right there on the edge of the sand to close a perfect day, watching the sun set over the ocean, as the chill of night swept in. Some places had three or four seasons during the year; San Francisco could have three or four seasons in one day.

"Well, fog or no fog, first stop is the wharf," Evan declared. "I'm dying for some crab!"

Evan always called "first stop" as Fisherman's Wharf— where they would grab a claw or two of crabmeat from one of the vendors along the sidewalk. Then, fortified with the tender, rich meat, they'd browse past the line of wax museum/T-shirt shops/boat-ride tourist traps, and walk up past the cable car drop-off to Ghirardelli Square for Sarah's weakness. Chocolate.

San Francisco was all about the food for them in the first few hours, as they snacked and shopped and slowly made their way to Chinatown, where they'd lunch on dim sum.

Today, the wharf was quieter than usual . . . the fog still lay heavy on the street, giving everything a gray, indistinct, dreamlike feel. Sarah held his hand as they walked down the sidewalk, taking in all of the tourist shops selling cheap fleece jackets to combat the unpredictable cold spells. You never knew if two hours from now the weather was going to warm up or drop twenty degrees when you were down near the bay.

They walked down to one of the piers and Evan got a cup of crabmeat, but Sarah strayed from her usual and asked for a crab cake.

"Cake?" he ribbed her. "What is this, a birthday party?"

She leaned up and kissed him on the lips with a knowing look in her eyes. "No," she said. "Anniversary."

"Huh?"

"I figured you forgot but . . . our first date was twenty-four years ago today."

"It was?" Evan frowned, trying to remember.

"Lout." She punched him. "Glad it made such an impression on you. I used to get cards and fancy dinners on this date to commemorate it, but now"—she sighed dramatically—"he doesn't even remember."

"No wait, I do, I do," he said, starting to nod.

"I've heard that before. What did it get me? Laundry to do and dishes to wash. Woo-hoo."

Evan leaned in and bit off a piece of her crab cake just before she put it in her mouth. "There," he said. "We shared our anniversary cake, just like at the wedding. And I've given you a lot more than dirty dishes."

"Oh yeah," she said. "I forgot. You give me a dirty bathroom too."

He shook his head and dodged. "I remember that trip. We went to the wax museum and took the ferry out to Alcatraz. God, we were tourists."

Evan moaned in pleasure at a bite of crabmeat. "Damn," he said. "I can never get enough of this place though."

They ate and walked, enjoying the smells and quiet conversations and rows of fresh crabs on display, aproned kiosk keepers hawking their particular stylings of the ubiquitous sea creature. Evan at last tossed his napkin and shell into a garbage can. "Do you want to go to the wax museum today, for old time's sake?"

"Are you serious?" Sarah laughed, looking at him sideways to see if he was pulling her leg. They'd both avoided the waterfront display of kitsch for years.

"Yeah, why not?" he asked. "They might have a statue of Johnny Depp by now for you to drool over."

"You just want to see if they have Paris Hilton," she answered, rolling her eyes. "Trust me, she'll be dressed in this display."

"Actually, I was hoping for a Jenna Jameson career retrospective." He grinned.

She punched him in the shoulder and yanked his hand, pulling him toward the crosswalk. "Let's go before you make me mad."

The museum felt old. Even though it had been completely renovated at the end of the '90s, walking inside its doors was like stepping into another world; one that had been mothballed for decades. Whether it was the velvet drapes or the fixtures or the shadows that rested dully on everything but the spotlighted displays, Evan just felt like they had stepped off the street and directly into the past.

"Wow, some things never change, huh?" They stood in front of a display recreating the pitchforked farm couple from the painting *American Gothic*. The dour look of the two figures gave him the creeps.

Sarah squeezed his hand. "It looks just like us!"

"What, old and crotchety?"

She laughed. "No, old and still in love, silly!" She leaned up to kiss him.

"Hmmm," he answered, after her lips broke away. "I'm not sure anybody has ever intimated that *American Gothic* exudes romance."

"It's all how you look at it," Sarah explained. "See, you're seeing them as a grumpy old couple, and I'm seeing them as two people who've faced the world together and won . . . and now, weapon in hand, it's like they're giving the world a dare. Just try to stop us."

"Um, right," Evan said. "I'm sure that's exactly what Grant Wood meant when he painted it. C'mon."

They walked through the Hall of Religions, which included the long table with wax figures of Christ and all of his apostles. "That was here the first time we came," Sarah said.

"That was probably here fifty years ago when they

opened this place," Evan laughed. "I'm telling you, except for the *Titanic* display, I think all this stuff was here before."

"No way," she said. "Beyoncé, Mike Myers, Angelina Jolie—and yes, I saw how you studied her lips—there's a ton of new stuff."

"Well, it all seems old!"

They circled around the red velvet drapes and stepped into the wide circle of the Chamber of Horrors, where stacks of skulls lined the walls and a guillotine hung at the ready. "This has gotten a lot bigger," Sarah said.

Evan nodded, looking at the grim, manic skull of the Crypt Keeper, a persona replicated from the classic HBO *Tales From the Crypt* series. It seemed a little ironic that a figure replicated in a wax museum was that of a fake creation in the first place. "Yes, I guess it has. And bloodier, I think!"

In the corner, an ax-murdered victim grasped for purchase at a rope with hands that no longer were connected to a full body. The man was missing below the waist, where the "flesh" was red and ragged. Sometimes wax could be too realistic.

"Ew," Sarah said, and moved closer to Evan. He stepped her through the horror show display and into another small, dark room. Here, the tableau was of a rocky seaside. The back wall was painted a deep midnight blue, and tiny pin lights reflected back from a faraway horizon that was supposed to represent a town.

In the foreground, a woman lay on her side, head on her hand. She was nude, and Evan's eyes were drawn to her instantly. The sculptor had gone into great detail on the figure, capturing a mole on the woman's left breast and even the tiny ripples of pink that made her nipples look truly human. Her hair hung in long black ringlets over her shoulder, nearly covering her right breast, and her abdomen was pocked by a thin shadow of a belly button. But beyond there, her figure grew strange, as her skin changed to silver scales at her hips. In place of a woman's legs and most private part, she was transfigured into fish, with a long silver tail.

"There's your boobage," Sarah laughed, as she read from the display sign about the figure. "You can look all you want but you'll never get any from her! She's a woman with no entry."

"Just my kind of luck," he laughed. "I finally find the perfect woman, and she's built like a Barbie." He dodged a backhand, and observed, "Kind of racy for the wax museum to do a naked mermaid."

"Not a mermaid," Sarah said. "She's a Siren."

Evan's heart tripped. Sarah didn't notice his face lose color as she was looking at the sign.

"'The Siren has been represented in many ways through the years,'" Sarah read. "'While initially depicted as a bird or fish with the head of a woman, over the centuries in art and mythology the Siren became more humanized. Some accounts described her as either completely female, or most similar to the mermaid, with alluring upper-body female features, but with a fish tail in lieu of legs. In one famous painting, she and her two sisters are shown lying sated on a beach filled with the corpses of the men they have lured with their song to serve as their dinner. This depiction is shown here, in a famous creation on loan from the Française Museum de la Wax.'"

Around the wax woman, the beach was littered with the torsos of men, some of them showing the yellowed struts of ribs peeking through mangled, half-chewed flesh.

"Kind of puts a whole new spin on fishing, doesn't it?" Sarah asked. "Here you men are always out there reeling in the fish, and here's a half-fish woman who's reeling in the men. And not because she likes 'em or wants to date 'em . . . she's just hungry."

Sarah laughed, pleased with herself, but Evan didn't join her. He was staring at the dark eyes of the Siren, and picturing Ligeia on the beach. He heard Bill's voice insisting that Delilah had a Siren. "If you know what's good for you, you'll stay away from that beach at night or you're going to be fish bait," Bill had said at one point. "She may be putting out right now, but in the end, it's you that's going to be giving it up. You can't trust her."

Evan's reverie was snapped by a punch in the shoulder.

". . . Evan!" Sarah stood next to him expectantly. "Hello, earth to Evan? Could you take your eyes off the wax boobs for a minute?"

"Sorry," he recovered. "I was just thinking of something."

"What you could do with a wax woman in your bed after the lights go out?"

"Hmmm? No, I've got one of those already, who needs two?" He dodged away from her, and kept moving right into the next display, which thankfully included nothing horrific at all. Unless you considered the clown grin of Lucille Ball horrible.

They moved through the rest of the museum quickly; Sarah was anxious to get down to Chinatown, and Evan was anxious to just . . . get away from the place. For some reason, seeing the depiction of the Siren had really bothered him. In the back of his head a nagging voice kept asking, "So what, Evan, do you really believe that the girl you're banging is a mythological harpy?" He shook his head absently, trying to remember the feel of her hands on his back. No, she was no Siren, but he had to admit . . . she was a little strange.

"How many women do you s'pose sit out on the point singing every night in the nude," Bill had asked him at one point, and Evan had shrugged. "It only takes one," he'd said. "Yeah, one to lure you into the water just before she eats you," Bill had said. "That's the only one you'll ever need."

When they stepped out of the shadowed confines of the museum back onto Beach Street, it was as if they had exited into a different city from the one they had entered. Instead of the dreary gray morning, the sky shone a rich, bright blue, as the last wisps of white cloud fled like lost sheep across the sky.

"And here's why I love this place." Sarah smiled, turning around and around on the sidewalk, with her palms to the sky. "It's a mystery and an enigma."

"Four seasons in one day?" Evan smiled.

"Yes. And . . . chocolate. So much good chocolate. If only I could find my way . . ."

He laughed, took her by the shoulders and pointed her the opposite direction down Beach. "You'll find your Ghirardelli that way, ma'am," he said, and in minutes they were trudging up the hill toward Ghirardelli Square. Not much later, they were trudging again uphill toward Columbus, and then after passing the tempting street-side cafés of North Beach they started down the other side of the hill toward Chinatown. No matter how much amazing food you ate in San Francisco, you were always hungry for more, because you just . . . kept . . . walking . . .

Sarah and Evan walked all afternoon, picking up a full bag of junk along the way, from chocolates to small wooden Buddhas to a couple books from City Lights Bookstore, the classic beatnik book haunt in North Beach that Ginsberg once had called home. They lunched in Chinatown and then walked back toward the wharf to have a beer at the San Francisco Brewing Company's dark wood bar. Evan had threatened to play the piano, but Sarah's impending embarrassment was saved by a man from the Netherlands who struck up a conversation with them about the difference between American microbrew beer and Scandinavian outlets. Hops was mentioned frequently, and Sarah looked increasingly bored as the men's discussion grew ever more animated.

Finally, after they'd left the bar to walk back toward the center of the city, as the sun set and the breeze blew in the crisp, cool hint of night, Evan threw in the towel.

"I'm not going to be a hero," he gasped. "I'll admit it. I can't walk anymore. I vote for a taxi to dinner."

Sarah laughed, but she didn't protest. "I'm with you. I don't think I have any heels left."

Evan hailed a cab, and they both groaned a sigh of relief as they sank into the vinyl of the car's backseat. Evan gave the cabbie the address, but needn't have. They were headed to one of the prime tourist traps of the city, and the driver would have known it simply by name. Dinner, of course, had to be at the Beach Chalet. After a short ride through the mess of the trolley tracks and tourists and heavy traffic of Market Street, they had left the core of the city behind and were soon sitting at a table overlooking the dark, ominous shimmer of the ocean. Just down the beach, someone had built a small bonfire, and the smoke from that flickering orange flame, mixed with the twilight fog, gave everything around them a surreal vibe. The beach had an eerie stillness here at dusk, with a couple of joggers passing by as if moving through the vague backdrop of a dream, but otherwise, there was nothing between them and the night but the tiny lights of a boat, seemingly sitting still out in the water. Sarah pulled Evan away from the cool wind and the sand and up the steps to dinner.

Inside the restaurant, they sat in warm lighting, with a revolving team of waitresses willing to cater to their every whim.

"I love this place," Sarah said for the fifth time that day.

"I'm with you," Evan said, reaching his hand out to take hers. "And I love you."

She put her hand on his, resting against the table. "I love you too, Evan. I know I haven't been any good these past few months. Thanks for sticking with me through all of this."

A chill froze Evan's heart as he thought about just *how* he'd been sticking with his wife lately. He wasn't proud of what he'd done with Ligeia. And yet, as he sat there looking at the faint crow's-feet playing into the skin beside his wife's eyes, and took in the love that stared back at him, colored by a constant sadness, he knew that he wouldn't take it back if he could. He loved Sarah. He owed her almost every happiness in life that he could remember. But right now, he was itching to get back in the car and drive an hour north to Delilah, so that he could get out on the beach at nightfall. Because there was another woman who was giving him some happiness that Sarah, for all her well-meaning heart, could never give.

But that wasn't going to happen. Instead, the dark slowly swallowed everything around the Beach Chalet as they sat at a table by the window and looked out on the ocean.

After dinner, Sarah pulled him down the wooden steps and onto the sand. "Let's take a walk," she suggested.

"Haven't we done enough of that today?"

"Not on a beach," she reminded.

They slipped off their shoes and walked barefoot in the sand down to the tide line. There the sand turned hard and walkable thanks to being saturated by the occasional wave that pushed up high onto the beach.

"You can see my footprints in the sand," Sarah enthused.

"And you can see mine," Evan said, grinding his heels in to make the imprints extra large. "We won't be famous," he said, "but at least someone will know we've been here."

"I don't care if *I* was here," Sarah said, her voice colored by sadness. "I just wish that Josh still *was* here. He deserves to be here. He should be with us."

Evan felt his throat fill with emotion, and his voice cracked when he first opened his mouth to answer. "I know," he said. "I want that more than anything too. But I made sure that couldn't happen."

A silence took over the moment. They had managed to avoid talking about Josh for most of the past six months, and whenever one of them brought it up, the conversation stalled. They had cried together in the beginning, before the guilt had overtaken Evan, and he couldn't stand to talk about it anymore. It was all his fault, after all, he thought every time his son's name came up between them. And she must hate him for that.

"Evan, don't think that way," she said. "It was an accident. I know that."

He couldn't answer her. After a few awkward moments, they turned and returned in silence to the deck of the chalet.

After leaving the beach, they took a cab to the hotel, and Sarah undressed Evan at the foot of the bed, her brown eyes sparkling in the faint light that streamed in the windows from the city outside. "I love you," she whispered, and leaned in to kiss him.

In his heart, Evan felt a dagger stab and twist.

"I love you too," he said.

In moments, he didn't feel quite so much like a hypocrite, as his wife moaned her appreciation, and his own excitement peaked.

Afterward, they lay together in bed, arms entwined, and Sarah cried, just a little while. "Sometimes it's hard," she said.

"I know," he said. "It's like he's with me every day, but every time I go to say something to him . . . I know he's gone."

Her arms gripped him tighter, and her eyes closed. "It's not right that we're still here, and he's not," she whispered.

Unbidden in his mind, Evan pictured himself naked on the sand, with Ligeia's breasts rolling and moving provocatively in the air just tantalizing inches above his mouth. He struggled to blink away the obscenity.

"No," he said. "No, it's not right. Not right at all."

CHAPTER TWENTY-FOUR

"You think you're someone?" Ralph asked, the auto shop owner's belly jiggling like a damn tidal wave beneath his stained red shirt. "You haven't been someone since the day you set foot in here and said you needed a job. That was the day you gave up *being* someone. Now? You're mine, and as my own personal grease monkey, I'd like to see you get some *work* done."

Ralph pointed across the garage at the car raised up on a hydraulic lift so that a mechanic could get beneath it easily. "Like . . . maybe . . . have that Corvette ready to roll by tomorrow at seven A.M.? And don't mouth no bullshit about overtime to me . . . you've been taking long enough to fix shit as it is. You don't go home tonight until that car is purring like a damn cougar, and I mean the female kind. I want that car to sound like she's in heat when she pulls out of this garage."

Terry didn't know what to say. Actually, he did know what to say, but he also knew he couldn't say it. Because saying "take your donkey dong and stick it up some other horse's ass" would no doubt get him fired. Fast, and final. And let's face it, Terry needed the job. He didn't change spark plugs for kicks; he was trying to support his momma and younger brother Jimmy here. He kept his mouth shut through Ralph's little hissy fit, and when he felt like spitting . . . well, he just coughed into his hand and wiped it on the back of his pants.

Damn he hated this job.

He hated oil and he hated spark plugs and he hated filters and fluid sticks and everything else that went with being a mechanic. Terry had wanted to be anything but a grease monkey. Before everything had turned to shit, he'd been taking business courses at the junior college. He had read the Jim Collins books on creating and sustaining a successful business. He thought *Good to Great* would help him be at least more than average as a low-level business drone. But in the end, he realized that all the highly touted "be successful in business" concepts were a lot of hot air. The long and the short of it was, if you licked ass and did something people liked, they bought your shit. And if you didn't? You starved.

That didn't really help Terry to make the million bucks he wanted to drag back home like a bear to his cave with a carcass.

Ralph spit on the floor and motioned toward the Corvette once more. "Make sure it's done in the morning, or you'll be looking for a new shop to tinker in."

Terry knew that looking for a new shop would be difficult since this was the only one within twenty miles that had any automotive bent at all. Still, it wasn't the most motivating message. Ralph grumbled something else and moved out of the shop toward the front door for the night.

As soon as the owner left, Terry walked over to the front door and cranked up the volume on the radio. If he were going to be stuck here for the night, the least he could have was the blaring, soaring guitar leads of Boston echoing through his head like the glory of six-string heaven.

Damn, they were good.

Terry pulled out a tool drawer as the room echoed

with the twining guitars of the best music to get high to . . . ever. He even tried to get beneath the body of the 'Vette. It was a sweet car, but you know . . . when someone tells you *"ya gotta"* at eight o'clock at night, you pretty much don't *wanna*, no matter how sweet it is. Terry saw a lot of cars in his business, but not many as hot as this one. Damn—this was one expensive ride. He climbed into the driver's seat and enjoyed the slight cushion of the black leather-wrapped steering wheel beneath his hand. Then he popped the glove box and riffled through the owner's manual and oil change coupons there. At the back of the compartment was a stack of gold coins. Terry picked one up and saw an imprimatur of a nude woman with the words "Lusty Lady." Peep show money. He smiled. He'd pocket it if he knew where it would be good.

Then he climbed out and popped the trunk. 'Vettes had almost no storage space, but he was curious. The tiny space looked empty on a first glance, but then Terry saw a scrap of glossy red paper was trapped in the crack of the fake floor. He popped up the flooring to see if anything was stored beneath.

Bingo.

A lurid pile of magazines were stacked in one corner. On the cover of one, an icy blonde with breasts the size of cantaloupes held her chest with her own two hands, red lacquered nails glistening wetly against her skin like wounds. Around her belly, two black male hands reached, kneading her groin. The title was *Chocolate & Cream*.

Terry riffled through the handful of titles, uncovering *Cuckold Dreams*, *MILF 17* and *Deirdre's Dirty Secret*. The latter featured a busty redhead with a dildo as long as her arm on the cover. He pulled the pile of porn from the trunk and shut the lid.

Instead of working *on* the car, Terry did some work *in*

the car. He took the stack, climbed into the 'Vette's slick black leather seat, shucked his pants down and tilted the seat back. And then he got to *work*.

By eleven o'clock, the 'Vette was still up on the lift, and Terry woke up from a long nap populated by kinky girls wearing leather corsets and blindfolds. The magazines were spread throughout the interior of the car on the dashboard and passenger seat, opened to his newly found favorite photos. He gave a long yawn and shook his head, and decided he'd best clean up and get underneath the car before midnight.

Stashing the magazines back in the trunk, he decided to take a walk and a smoke break to wake up. Ralph's shop—Under Your Hood—was just off the beach, and Terry often took short jaunts to the water and back just to get away from his asshole boss. A quick cigarette and a few breaths of the sea air always brought his urge to scream "take this job and shove it" under control. The beach had saved him from losing a steady paycheck many times.

Terry lit up and walked the sandy path from the back parking lot of the car shop over the weedy no-man's-land beyond. The path rose and the sound of the surf grew louder, and then Terry was over the dune, and trudging down to the hard-packed sand of the beach. The ember of his smoke burned exceptionally bright tonight; the clouds had rolled in and promised a midnight storm; the normally brilliant sky loomed ominous and closed. One cloud bank glowed slightly, the light of the moon behind it, but aside from that and a few lights off the shore from seaside homes, the night was black as tar.

Somewhere nearby, Terry heard music, and wondered if kids were camped out on the beach, sneaking booze or toking up. He grinned, remembering the many times he'd come down here with friends back in high school. He began to walk toward the faraway sound, thinking that he'd give the delinquent kids a scare before heading back to work. Nothing more frightening than an adult stumbling across a teen party when you're a teen. He grinned and blew a cloud of smoke across the beach. This could be fun.

The music seemed to be coming from near the point, though he didn't recognize the tune. It seemed strangely quiet and stark for party music, though Terry had to admit, very pretty. All of his frustrations with Ralph faded the closer he got to the sound. Hell, maybe instead of scaring off the kids, he'd sit with them and have a drink. Fuck it if he ended up fired tomorrow . . . he was tired of this place and this job anyway. Maybe it was time to drift on.

He slowed as he reached the curve of the beach that ultimately led out onto the rocky wall that was the finger of the point and looked around harder. He didn't seem to be any closer to the source of the music, and he still hadn't seen the lights of a campfire or flash or anything. Where the hell were these kids? Out on the rocks? Usually when teens partied on the beach, they lit a small fire to stay warm, and on a night like this, to *see* one another. Unless it was a couple—in which case, perhaps they didn't want to be seen. Terry grinned at that. Maybe this was even better than he thought—maybe he'd catch some seventeen-year-old skin doing the nasty! He almost laughed out loud when he imagined the squeals his appearance would bring when he caught that little glimpse of heaven.

He slowly did a 360-degree turn in place, peering hard at the sand, trying to find some faintly moving shadows that he somehow hadn't picked up on yet. He started to turn quicker once his vision reached the ocean, assuming that the music wasn't coming from out in the water . . . but then he stopped.

What was that flash out in the dark water? It looked white, but not like a whitecap. Terry squinted and stepped closer. Damn if it wasn't a chick out in the water! Skinny-dipping by the look of it. He could see her legs kicking out above the water, and when her body moved up and out of the waves, he could see nothing but creamy skin. No suit.

Nice.

He couldn't see anyone swimming near her, and the beach appeared empty. Still, the faint but seductive music seemed to come from nearby. It was all around him, and he closed his eyes, trying to identify which direction it came from. Instead, in the dark space behind his eyelids, it seemed to amplify and grow, sparking pinpoints of light and swirls of ambient fog that lit his brain like a psyche-delic drug.

"Damn, that shit's intense," he murmured, and opened his eyes.

There was a naked woman standing five feet away from him. Her pale skin dripped with the ocean, and dark hair hung in wet, knotted curls across her neck and down her chest. Despite the gloom of the sky, her eyes reflected a shimmering light. They sparked tiny motes of fire while staring hard at him, unblinking.

Terry's gaze slid from her face to her breasts though, because it was hard to ignore a pair like that. They looked firm as fruit, and his throat salivated at the thought. God he wanted to bite into her. Look at those tits! He could suck those . . . and look at that tummy—flat, tight . . . mmm. Terry imagined his tongue licking the salty water from her belly button and then dipping its way lower to lave between her thighs . . .

She was singing.

In the midst of Terry's unapologetic sexual perusal of

the woman, it occurred to him belatedly that the music he'd been hearing for the past few minutes was not coming from a boom box secreted somewhere in the sand. It was coming from this woman, here, five steps away.

Okay, three.

One.

Her hands slipped up his arms from elbow to shoulder, and all the time her lips kept gently moving, her voice a trilling, gentle massage. Her song slipped into the clouds and then slid back down, a warm and potent melody of loss and love, pain and need. He could feel himself respond to the song, as much as to her skin, and he put his arms around her, drawing her wet body to him without thought.

In seconds his lips were locked to hers, and without knowing her name, Terry ran his hands down the cool, slippery skin of her waist and across the enticing swell of her ass. He slid a finger between her cheeks, and was poking the swollen folds of her sex from behind before he'd even ended their first kiss.

This was moving fast, he thought, too excited and surprised by his luck to question why a naked woman would walk out of the ocean and throw herself into his arms and then, without a word, unbutton his shirt and start to work on his belt.

He helped her with the latter, eager to get to the business at hand, because this was likely to be the best business he ever *got* in hand. This chick was fuckin' magazine-spread material. He flashed back to the skin mags he'd been looking at a couple hours ago and thought, *Nah, they got nothing on this bitch!* He had a moment of panic when he wondered, after all of his exertion in the car, if he'd be able to perform now that the real deal was right here.

But then she sprung him from beneath his jeans into

the night air, and shifted her legs to let him press against her, impaling herself on him as she sucked his tongue into her mouth, and his worries dissolved like desert clouds.

She moved over him with an aggression he wasn't used to; most of the girls he'd been with were happy to let him do all the pushing and shoving, so it was strangely exciting for a woman to be pushing and grappling him to the sand. And she did. She forced him with her hands on his shoulders first to his knees, weaving her fingers into his hair and pressing his head to her groin, and after he'd satisfied her immediate musky need there with wet laps of his tongue, she'd straddled him atop the cold sand, and her teeth sparkled white against the night as she threw back her head and opened her mouth to moan her appreciation at his movements beneath her.

"Damn, baby, you are amazing," Terry said, as his moment came.

The woman said nothing, only shifted her hips against his and increased her rhythm, again tilting back her head to stare up at the cloud-covered sky. This time, instead of moaning, she began to sing again, and as Terry felt his nerves electrify and pulse with an amazingly intense orgasm, his ears suddenly turned to jelly as well; her song made his body want to melt. The blur of clouds and dark and sand turned into a landscape so faint and indistinct with her song that Terry couldn't even move his hand to hold her as she began to fall toward him.

Her mouth brushed across his with a wet kiss, but then continued on to nuzzle his ear, and finally his neck. All the while she sang a whispery song of sated seduction and he felt paralyzed by its melody. Her hands slipped up his arms and gripped him as she pushed her breasts to his chest, pressing into him so hard that he really, for a moment, felt they were one.

And then the pain began.

The kiss at his neck, so warm and blissful after the big O suddenly turned hot, in a slap-at-your-neck-to-stop-the-mosquito kind of way, except that Terry didn't feel like he could move his hand to do the swatting, both because she was holding it and because her song was almost holding him in a weird trance. But then the heat grew to excruciating pain, and he opened his mouth to cry out. He had only just begun to scream when her lips fastened down on his, and he tasted the iron of his own blood in his mouth. His eyes opened, and he saw her suddenly in a new light.

Her eyes weren't brown with a strange sparkle to them. They were yellow, somehow reptilian. Like fish eyes. Her nose no longer looked patrician, but hawklike pointy, and her arms weren't flawlessly creamy, but blotched; a mélange of intricate streaks of dark pink scars and brown discolorations amid the white. And as he struggled to break her violent kiss and peered lower, suddenly drinking her in for seemingly the first time, he saw that her hips didn't curve seductively quite as he remembered at his first glance. They slimmed down from her waist and tapered into something silvery blue and geometrically shadowed. Something that was not two legs, but a solid tail of shimmering alienness, a heavy tail pinned between his legs. The beautiful woman who had pushed him to the sand was not beautiful at all; in fact, she wasn't really a woman. Her ass ended in fish scales.

Terry started to gasp "what the fuck" but the woman had already broken their kiss and bent to his throat again.

This time, when she lifted her face back up, there was a string of skin—or severed vein—hanging from her mouth, and her cheeks were spattered with tiny red pinpricks from the spray of Terry's blood. His cry had ended in a gurgle, and now, as the pain overwhelmed him, he stared at her through a fog, watching his blood drip from her wide, thin lips to run down the slope of her breasts to stain her nipples. He struggled to speak, to ask why, to beg mercy, something . . . but all that came out was a thin whisper; a faint rasp of sound. Terry tried to lift an arm, but it wouldn't move. He tried a leg—maybe he could unseat her. But again, nothing happened.

She opened her eyes wider and stared down into his, her mouth opening and revealing a row of sharp lower teeth painted in blood. "Mmmmm-ooo-oooooh," she sang, leaning down to whisper her melody straight into his right ear.

Terry couldn't fathom how, or why, but with that song, all the shrieking pain that pulsed through him seemed to slip away, and all he wanted was for this amazing woman to lie down on top of him and be part of him.

But she wasn't thinking quite the same way. Instead she leaned down and kissed the side of his neck that she hadn't already torn out. And . . . she tore out THAT side. When she rose above Terry again, her cheeks expanded, chewing on the rich flesh of his neck, Terry only saw her with a flicker of consciousness. He saw the piece of bloody skin hanging from her mouth like crimson tissue paper. He flashed back to the image from the skin mags earlier, of a woman tied in a chair with a ball gag in her mouth and raw red welts covering her chest. SHE LOVES THE PAIN, the caption had read.

Terry didn't love the pain. But it didn't matter. Ligeia bent down to chew on the flesh of his neck and shoulder again. And Terry didn't stay conscious long enough to complain.

CHAPTER TWENTY-FIVE

"So how was the honeymoon reunion weekend?" Bill asked as soon as Evan walked into the office on Monday morning.

"Gee, didja miss me that much?" Evan laughed, setting down his things on the desk. "Maybe I could turn on my computer and put my lunch in the fridge before we play twenty questions?"

"Okay, but hurry up," Bill said. "Nosy-bodies around here want to know."

"You mean, *you* want to know."

"Not me. Maggie wanted me to get the dirt."

Across the room, Maggie's head peered out from behind her computer monitor. "Try another one, Lug Nuts," she laughed. "You're the only nosy-body around here."

Evan walked down the short hall to stow his lunch in the fridge, then returned to finally punch his computer on with one finger and sat back in his chair with a sigh. "It was great," he said to Bill. "You know how much we love San Francisco, and the weather was perfect. We spent the first day down by the wharf—even did the wax museum, which we haven't done in like fifteen years. And then on Saturday, we hung out in Golden Gate Park all afternoon. Yesterday, we drove up to Muir Woods and messed around on the redwood walking trails for a few hours. We got back around nine last night. It was hard to get up this morning, but . . . I'm really glad we went."

"Sounds like a nice weekend," Candice offered, looking up from her computer to put in her two cents. "You two deserve it."

"See—there *was* another nosy-body." Bill grinned. Candice bounced a crumpled piece of paper off the back of his head.

Bill stood up and picked up the paper ball, launching it back from whence it came. He caught her in the temple, and the ball bounced off her computer screen and into her lap. "Delinquent," she grumbled.

"You started it," he pointed out, before coming over to kneel privately at the edge of Evan's desk.

"So . . . how was it?" he asked more quietly. "Is Sarah . . . ?"

"She's good," Evan acknowledged. "She had a really great time, and we talked a lot. Way more than we have in the past six months combined probably. I think we made some real progress."

Bill raised an eyebrow. "Do tell."

"This weekend we're going to start packing Josh's room."

"You've been saying that for months."

"I know," Evan said. "But this time, we both mean it. We've been living in a circle—doing the same thing every day, not letting it go, not moving forward. It's killing both of us in different ways."

"So . . . packing Josh's room is going to change all that?"

"Well, that, and other stuff. She's going to stop going to O'Flaherty's, and I'm going to stop spending hours on the beach."

Bill looked unconvinced. "Oh really?" he said.

"I'm serious," Evan said. "We have to change how we're living, or we're going to both self-destruct."

"And you're going to give up your time on the beach . . ."

Evan nodded. "I'm going to take a last walk tonight."

"That could be the most dangerous walk you ever take," Bill said, and then pushed himself up from a crouch to stand. He pursed his lips, shook his head slowly, and then walked back to his desk and bent over to fish something out from underneath. He stood back up with a copy of the *Daily Delilah* in his hand. He opened the front page, and then turned another. Finally, he smiled, and nodded again before bringing the paper over to Evan's desk. He threw it down on the desk and pointed to the article at the top of page five.

"Another one," he said. "You might want to read this before you take your walk tonight."

The headline read: BEACH MURDER INTERRUPTED TOO LATE

Evan skimmed the article beneath.

Terry Brill, thirty-four, was found early Saturday morning on the beach near the point. Brill, an auto mechanic who worked for the Under Your Hood shop on Bay Street, was reportedly working a late shift Friday night when he was last seen alive.

Police report that at approximately 12:15 A.M., Brill's body was discovered by a local man walking the beach.

"I had just gotten out of band practice, so I took a walk along the beach," David Benton told the Daily Delilah. *"I saw this woman lying down on the sand ahead of me. I thought she was making out with a guy and I was going to steer clear of them. But she looked up at me all of a sudden, and I realized two things. Number one, she was*

completely naked, and number two, her mouth was drip-
ping with what looked like blood. She looked like a ghoul.
That's when I got kind of nervous."

Benton, who plays bass in a local hard rock band, says
that when the woman saw him approaching, she stood
up and fled, diving into the ocean. He said she disap-
peared under the water and he did not see her return
to the beach. When he reached the woman's partner, he
found the man dead, apparently of blood loss from mul-
tiple wounds in the shoulder and throat area.

"The sand was covered in blood," Benton said. "The
guy looked like someone had chewed his throat to gristle.
There wasn't much left between his head and his chest."

Police reports state that Brill's corpse appeared to
have been mauled by wild dogs or wolves.

"We are looking for any evidence that would lead us
to find the woman reportedly seen with the body by Mr.
Benton," Police Chief William Gagli said. "Her connec-
tion to the deceased is unknown. At this time, Mr. Benton
is not a suspect in the case."

According to Ralph Maggiano, Terry Brill was work-
ing the late shift alone on Friday, finishing an engine job.

"He always took his smoke breaks on the beach," Mag-
giano said. "I always told him those things were going to
kill him one day. This is a tragedy for Terry's family, as
well as for our shop," Maggiano said.

Evan looked up with a smile. "I know that Maggiano
guy," he said. "Had my car fixed there last year. I can just
hear the rest of this quote: 'This is a tragedy, yep. We're
really sad. By the way, does anybody know where I can
find me a new mechanic? We got *work* to do here!'"

Bill grinned, but only slightly. "I showed you that for a
reason, Evan."

"Because you're obsessed with deaths on the beach?"

"No." Bill rolled his eyes. Then he whispered, "Because I'm obsessed with the concern that you are going to be another one of these deaths on the beach if you don't stop walking it at night. *Capisce*?"

"Look," Evan said. "You had me going before and actually had me believing for a little while that she caused a shipwreck! But I've been with her since then. She may be a little strange, but she's not a killer. You worry too much. And you believe in mythological creatures. These are not two qualities that serve you well together."

Bill presented him with the middle finger and stepped back to his desk. "Just trying to help, man. But . . . do what you're gonna do. Just don't come crying to me when you wash up all bloody on the sand tomorrow. Oh . . . wait a minute, that's right. Most of the victims just disappear without a trace. Good luck with that."

"If I'm washed back up on the beach, I don't imagine I'll be crying anymore. And anyway, I have no intention of disappearing," Evan said.

"I'm sure that's what Terry Brill said when he went out for a smoke break."

CHAPTER TWENTY-SIX

Evan's stomach flip-flopped as he walked along the cold night sand. He was nervous about this conversation. Maybe more so than of any conversation he'd ever dreaded having. He'd never been good at breaking up with girls before he'd met Sarah, and this was not going to be easy. How do you tell a sex goddess that you're not interested in indulging in her charms any longer?

Especially when you really *were* still interested.

Evan couldn't lie to himself. He wanted Ligeia as much as ever. And he certainly didn't *want* to give up his nightly walks by the surf—they'd been his tonic to wash away the stress of the day for years now. But . . . if he had any hope of saving his marriage—of saving Sarah, really—he had to stop this. He had to be true again to his wife, and he had to be there for her at night, when she was at her most vulnerable. His absence every evening had helped her climb into the bottle. Evan knew, in that sense, he'd failed her on the most critical level. He hadn't been there when she really needed him.

When they had run around in San Francisco, he'd seen his old Sarah come back. The Sarah he'd fallen in love with. And while making love to her would never compare to the strangely powerful eroticism of Ligeia, it was what he wanted. He couldn't deny the power of Ligeia, but he wanted to be with his wife every night, comfortable (some would say boring) in their bed. He wanted to hear that familiar slap of his body against hers, in a rhythm only they could devise together. He wanted to smell the sweetness of her breath as she drifted off to sleep each night, and cuddle in to the warmth of her at two A.M. when he woke from a dream.

Ligeia brought him more ecstasy than he had ever imagined possible, but Evan couldn't imagine living with her night after night. Hell, he didn't even know *where* she lived. He didn't know anything about her, except that she sang like an angel and screwed like a demon. Just thinking about her body touching his gave him an instant erection. *Damn*, he murmured to himself. *How am I going to do this!*

But Evan knew he had to end this, and work on breaking the negative cycle of depression he and Sarah had fallen into over the past year. Because if he didn't, he wouldn't have Sarah to wake up to anymore at two A.M.

They couldn't go on forever the way they'd been. Something bad was going to happen. Hell, less than a month ago he'd been planning to throw himself into the waves to ensure that something bad *did* happen to him. Something permanent.

But Ligeia had shown him that there was still hope to be had, pleasure to be derived from his life. Of course, her assumption was that he'd continue to derive that pleasure with her, but for Evan . . . as good as Ligeia was, he still felt allegiance to Sarah. She needed him more than she ever had, right now. And so tonight, Evan was determined to change their downward spiral. Step one was to say good-bye to the hottest girl he'd ever kissed. Step two was to walk away, never to return.

His stomach lurched again as he thought that sentence. His body wanted to feel her touch again. Breaking up was not on the program there. And how he would hold himself back when she turned up naked and beautiful, dripping with saltwater and reeking of pure lust . . . he had no idea. Nevertheless . . .

Evan reached the first boulders near the point and scooped a handful of stones from the high tide line. Then he sat down and flung them one by one into the water, granting the waves a smile of pleasure each time a stone managed to survive more than three skips before sinking many yards off the shore.

"Let me touch you now, forever," he murmured, sidearming rock after rock with a fatalistic precision. "Just this one last time . . ." he rasped, dragging out the last words in a melancholy prayer.

He scooped up another pile of pebbles, and rooted through them to find the stones with the flattest edges. In his mind, he heard Josh challenge him to a "skip-off." His son had carefully selected five flat, rounded stones and encouraged Evan to do the same. "Whoever gets the most skips buys the ice cream," Josh would challenge. And then they'd each throw, alternating attempts and calling out the number of skips at the end of each toss: "Three, six, four . . . seven!"

Age was no benefit or handicap on the stone-skipping game, and Evan won as much as Josh. Though Evan still seemed to pay for the ice cream afterward most of the time.

"You don't give me enough of an allowance," Josh would complain once they were inside the red- and white-striped Sweet Shoppe in downtown.

"Mmmm hmmm," Evan would reply. "That should teach you not to make bets you can't cover."

"Just skip the stone." Josh's voice seemed to whisper now in his head, a ghost who refused to lose. Evan did, and watched as the thin rock bounced across the waves four, five, six, seven and finally eight times before disappearing into the black.

"Ha!" Evan shouted, oblivious that there was nobody else in sight. "I did it, I did it," he laughed. "I win," he whispered in a voice that bordered on maniacal.

Then he looked around and the sun of his daydream faded. The sound of his son was gone, and all that he could see were the endless black waves of the ocean and the dark, cold sand beneath the unforgiving night sky.

He opened his hand and the remaining rocks and sand trickled out. "Damn," Evan whispered. As he stared out at the water, he could see his son's hand opening and closing in the air, just before it disappeared from sight for the last time. His eyes misted over, and he choked as again he said aloud, "Damn."

He clenched his fists and tried not to remember, tried to push that day off. He had relived it too many times and he refused to succumb again tonight. He had a difficult enough thing to do tonight without seeing his boy die, again and again, before his eyes. The chest heaves began again anyway, as they always did. Evan doubled over and choked, trying unsuccessfully to stem the tears. And finally, he just gave in, and let them all out like a slow sprinkler on the sand. "Josh, baby, I miss you," he cried, and clenched his arms to his own chest in a mock hug. "I love you, buddy," he whispered, though nobody was there to hear. "I love you so much."

Once Evan had regained control, he looked at his watch and saw that it was past ten o'clock. He'd been waiting for Ligeia almost an hour. A first.

Standing up, he walked up to the narrow path that led onto the gray shale of the point. He stepped over white and green piles of gull shit and made his way to the finger's far edge, where the black depth of the ocean merged with the sky in a claustrophobic trick of emptiness that felt ultimately close.

"Ligeia?" he called out to the ocean.

His voice was only greeted in a whooshing quiet. But Evan wasn't content. He tried again and again, struggling to make his voice heard over the rush of the surf. Evan called until his voice cracked, and he realized the futility of what he was doing.

She wasn't coming.

He had assumed that she would just be here, as she had every other time he'd come to the beach over the past few weeks . . . but . . . not tonight.

Evan threaded his way back to the beach and stood again on the sand, looking out at the hungry, dark water ahead. He prayed she was just busy tonight, but he worried that Ligeia was angry with him for taking Sarah on the trip. When he had told her the last time they had been together that he was going to be gone for a few days, Ligeia had not looked pleased. If anything, she looked cheated on. How ironic was that?

Dismayed, he began slowly walking back down the beach toward the road that led home. He could just stop taking this walk and the end result would be the same. He would have broken things off with his "mistress." He laughed bitterly to himself. *Mistress*. The word sounded ridiculous when used by him to talk about someone related to him. He was not the kind of guy who would ever cheat on his wife, he thought. But yet he *had*. Many times now. He remembered again their first night together on the sand and shrugged. For the amount of sex that had been doled out over the past year of their marriage, nobody would blame him. Still . . . it wasn't who he wanted to be. It wasn't what Sarah deserved.

He couldn't break it off with someone by simply not showing up. He needed to close this chapter of his life. He needed to say good-bye to Ligeia. He owed it to her, and needed it for himself.

When Evan got home, Sarah was waiting, sitting in the easy chair, sipping a cup of Earl Grey. She looked up at him as he closed the sliding glass door and said simply, "Hey."

"Hey," he answered, and knelt by her chair. On TV, the weatherman was calling for rain tomorrow afternoon.

"Gonna be a slow day for you tomorrow, I think," she said. Her voice was warm with the threat of sleep.

"Doubt it," he said. "Big shipment from Oregon due in tomorrow. Rain or shine, we're on the dock."

"Ugh," she murmured. Then she put a cool finger to his face. "You've been crying," she said softly.

"Yeah," Evan said. "Sometimes you just have to let it out."

"I know," she said, and set down her tea. Then she held her arms out. "But you're supposed to let it out with me," she said.

He shifted into her embrace and laid his head on her chest. She smelled warm and sweet, of lavender and honey. He felt his eyes well up for the third time tonight, and let go again.

"I love you," he whispered, and felt his heart choke beneath the words.

Her hand stroked his hair. "I know, baby. And I love you too."

Ligeia didn't come the next night. Or the next.

Evan started to wonder if he was really whacked— maybe she had simply been a fever dream, a warped hallucination to force him to refocus his priorities and fix things with his wife before it was too late.

He had promised Sarah in San Francisco that he would stop hanging out half the night on the beach, and so far he'd not kept it. He had to stop going there, but he couldn't without saying good-bye. Unless she had already gone. Moved on to some other guy while he'd been in San Francisco, assuming if he was taking an anniversary trip, that he'd be rekindling with his wife and would have no need of a mistress anymore.

That had turned out to be true, in the end, and perhaps she had seen the writing on the wall.

On Wednesday night, he tossed a hundred stones into the ocean and vowed that he would stop coming after one more night.

On Thursday night, Ligeia was waiting for him.

"I was beginning to think you were nothing but a dream," Evan said, as he walked up to her. She stood like a sentinel on the sand. A gorgeous, nude statue. A perfect sculpture of sex incarnate. When he spoke, she smiled, and his heart melted along with his groin.

"I'll always be here for you," she said. Her voice echoed in his brain, ripples of meaning spreading down his spine like a drug. The warmth of joy at seeing her spread through every pore.

"Ligeia," he began, holding out his arms to hug her.

She pressed herself against him, and he felt the wetness of her body soak into his clothes. Her lips brushed at his ear, and he shook his head, taking her arm with his hand to pull her back.

But she stepped back on her own and smiled at him. She looked almost like a child with the grace and innocence of that smile, and she took his right hand in both of hers. She pressed her hand against the cool velvet of her belly, brushing his fingers up and down on her skin. Not childish at all.

Evan felt his resolve weakening with the tantalizing feel of her flesh against him. But no, he knew this had to stop. He tried to get himself under control, but before he could say a word, Ligeia spoke again.

"You're going to be a daddy," she said, putting her hands on his shoulders and moving her face in close to his.

"Huh?" Evan gulped.

She ran his hand back and forth across her abdomen and said it again. "You're going to be a daddy. I'm pregnant with your child."

"Oh shit," Evan said. The words fell out before he could stop them, and he saw the pain crease her forehead as he said them.

"It's not that I—" he started.

She put a finger to his lips. "You don't want a baby?" she asked quietly.

"I want *my* baby back," he gasped, and pulled away from her. He turned his back and looked toward his house, so far down the beach.

"I don't want to start over," he said. "I did it once, and I don't want to do it again. I just want my boy back."

Ligeia's hands wrapped around his chest, moving from under his armpits to rub his belly and reach all the way up to cup his chin. At his back, he felt the cushion of her breasts, and hated himself for how much he wanted her right now.

"Ligeia," he began.

"Shhhh," she said, and unbuckled his pants. "You are confused. I am here now, and you are mine now. That's all you need to think about."

Evan struggled to say no, but then his pants were on the sand. His shirt slipped over his head, and her breasts were against his chest. He felt the warmth of her tongue and the world began to tilt sideways yet again.

"We will raise a family together," Ligeia said, as he entered her there on the sand. She was wet and open to him, and he found her talk of children and future somehow even more erotic than the simple promise of enjoying the salty taste of her breasts in his mouth forever. He rode her quick and desperate on the cold sand and kissed her longer afterward than before, as the sweat cooled on his back and raised a chill.

Ligeia's eyes locked on his and with a knowing grin, she raised an eyebrow. "You will come with me now, yes?"

"No," Evan said, brushing his lips to her cheek. Then he pulled back and met the intensity of her gaze with the look of a wounded puppy. "I can't. I love Sarah. And she needs me now, more than ever."

"*I* need you," Ligeia hissed, and pushed him off her. Then she rounded on him and pressed him to the beach beneath her.

"*You* need me," she insisted. "You know that. Your time with her is through. She had you for that time, but that time is done. My child is yours. Will you just walk away from that?"

He lay back on the cold sand and stared into the dark between the pinpoints of stars above.

"I have to," he whispered. "I don't want to . . . but I need to."

Evan rolled to his side and looked at the woman who lay on the beach, offering herself to him, not only tonight, but forever. Offering him . . . everything.

"Ligeia . . . I barely know you," he began, and instantly regretted it.

"You know me more than any man has known me in a century," she hissed.

"A century?" Evan laughed. "You don't even look . . ." His retort was stopped by the press of her lips to his own. When she drew back, she sounded angry.

"Come with me," she said. "Come with me and raise our child. Don't make me do this alone."

"I'll help you how I can," Evan began. "But first I'll need to know your address. Hell, I don't even know where you live and you say you're having my baby . . ."

"I live in your heart," Ligeia said, and tried to press him again to the sand. "And I always will."

"I have to go," Evan said, and pushed away from her to grab at his shirt. He shook the sand free and stood up. "I can't be with you for this," he said. "I have to take care of my wife now."

He stepped clumsily into his pants and felt the dampness of their sex saturate his underwear and then rub back accusingly against his skin as he buttoned his jeans.

Ligeia didn't move from her prone position on the sand. Her eyes flashed with anger.

"You are mine now," she said tersely.

Evan shook his head. "No," he said. "No, I'm not. I'm sorry. I can't do this anymore. That's what I came to say tonight. We have to end this. Good night, Ligeia. Good-bye."

He closed his eyes and couldn't believe how cold he was being in walking away, but was there any way to walk away that wasn't cold? When you were done, you were done and that was that. There was really no nice way to couch it.

Evan walked down the beach toward home, while a cold, horrible lump grew in his belly. He forced himself not to look behind him because if he did . . . he was afraid he would stop and return to her. Was it true? Did she carry his baby? Could she know already? That seemed unlikely. Was she just hoping?

How stupid he had been to have sex with her over and over, assuming that she was using protection. "Damn it," he cursed under his breath. If there'd been a wall nearby, he would have punched it. The anger—at himself, as much as at her for tricking him this way—grew inside him until the cold sickness melted, replaced by fire. If Ligeia were pregnant, and decided to make an issue about it . . .

He turned around and looked back at the beach, to where he had left her.

The beach was empty for as far as he could see. The waves rushed the shore in dirty white explosions of foam, and rolled back again, up and down on the sand, the empty sand from here to the shadow of the point.

Evan wiped a spot of water from his eye and shook his head. What was done was done. He prayed his weakness wouldn't come back at him to ruin what he needed to try to fix. And he needed to start that fixing now.

He turned back toward Delilah and began walking. In a minute, that determined walk turned to a slow and then more urgent jog. He had to get back to Sarah. A kaleidoscope of feelings fought for voice in his heart: guilt, lust, love and hope all mixed into a warring cloud of pain. "I'll never do this to you again," he promised aloud, as he ran. As soon as he said it, a piece of him railed, wanting desperately to do it again. He shook his head violently, trying to argue away the desire.

Behind him, a shadow slipped out of the waves to move swiftly across the beach. Far behind, but not so far as to lose sight, a figure fell in step to keep pace with Evan, padding softly, wetly across the sand and up the walking path that led to Fifth Street.

If Evan had not been so lost in his internal war of emotions, he might have noticed that the shadow followed him all the way home.

CHAPTER TWENTY-SEVEN

June 10, 1887

The storm hit with hardly any warning. If the fury of the wind hadn't howled through the ship like a banshee, the crew might have been more attuned to what happened in the captain's cabin. But by the time the screaming began, their hands and ears were locked to other tasks. Tasks like keeping the ship above water. Nobody had any interest in visiting Davy Jones's locker in the dead of night. And running shorthanded in a storm was a recipe for a voyage to the bottom of the sea.

It had been a sullen, quiet evening on the *Lady Luck* as she slipped through low breakers, easily on course to dock by morning. The crew, what was left of it, had watched Travers follow the captain out of the galley. They'd also seen him return a couple minutes later, and silently climb the ladder up top. Reg pushed back from the table and followed the first mate. "I'll see what's what," he told the rest.

Travers stood at the bow of the *Lady Luck*, staring out across the waves. He didn't say anything when Reg stumped across the deck to join him.

Reg stood next to the first mate for a few seconds, watching the waves, and Travers didn't volunteer a word. He looked lost in some private war.

"Clouds gatherin' fast," Reg observed.

Travers nodded, and a gust of wind blew a long twine of hair across his mouth. "Storm brewing," he said.

"What'd he say?" Reg asked.

Travers shook his head. "Nothing at all."

"We need to all corner him," Reg answered. There was steel in his voice.

"He's always been a good captain."

"That was then. This is today. We don't live in then."

Travers didn't say anything more, and Reg didn't press him. After another silent minute, he pushed away from the bow and slipped back belowdecks.

"Well?" Jensen said upon his return. Reg rolled his eyes and choked a bit for effect as he relayed, "'e says the captain's always been a good egg."

Cauldry smirked and hissed. "Tell that to Rogers."

"So much for talking to the captain," Jensen grumbled.

"Looks like I'm elected," Reg announced. "And I ain't taking no for an answer." A peal of thunder shook the boat, and the flash of lightning flickered through the dark galley.

Just as Reg stood, Travers yelled down to the men. "All hands on deck," he bellowed. "We got a storm on us. She's brewin' up fast!"

Cauldry and Jensen leaped up and started toward the ladder.

"I'll get the captain . . . after we have a word or two," Reg promised, and left in the other direction.

The ship yawed and shifted beneath his feet as Reg walked the narrow corridor to the captain's cabin. Another dull thunderclap sounded in the distance, and he felt the planks shiver. Maybe there would be no time to talk tonight after all, he thought. This felt like one wicked squall comin' on. He raised his hand to knock on the captain's cabin, but then paused.

He heard a noise from inside. The kind of noise that made a man feel . . . like a man. It was high-pitched, and rhythmic. And it absolutely was not the moan of their gravel-voiced captain. Reg pressed his ear to the door, and a slow smile drew across his face as he eavesdropped on the unmistakable sounds of a woman quickly approaching orgasm not far from the other side of the door. Mixed in with her cries were the heavier, deeper but equally satisfied groans of a male.

Reg felt his manhood shift at the sounds, and pulled back from the door. So. The mystery deepened. The captain had brought a woman on this trip. How he had kept her secret from them these past couple weeks he had no idea. Though as he thought back, he realized that Buckley had been absent from the deck more than usual these past few days. The wheels in his head clicked over, and his grin widened. No wonder the ol' man had been so hard on Rogers about snooping and thieving around belowdecks. He didn't care about the liquor, he was protecting another kind of vice. He stepped back and leaned against the wall until the faint noises coming from inside the captain's quarters diminished. The ship dove in a sudden roll again, and Reg took that as his cue.

"Captain," he called out, at the same time issuing a quick rap on the cabin door. "We got a storm on us. All hands on deck."

Reg didn't wait for Buckley's reply, but turned and walked down the hallway. But instead of heading toward the galley, he quickly stepped in the opposite direction. Reg slipped behind a stack of wooden moonshine crates in the hold, and turned to keep an eye on the path he'd just made. It didn't take long for the captain's door to open. Buckley hurried out, straightening his shirtsleeves, and went up top.

Still smiling, Reg waited a beat, and then came out of hiding. The next time he talked to the captain, he was going to have something to talk about. Something the captain couldn't brush off.

He tried the knob of the captain's door, and found it, not surprisingly, locked. Reg wasn't perturbed. He reached into a back pocket and pulled out a fishhook. He pressed it against the door frame and pressed until the curve of the hook was nearly straight and then pressed it into the slit of the lock. It didn't take much jimmying to trip the tumbler.

Reg cracked a grin and turned the knob, quiet as could be. Then he pushed it open and slipped inside, pressing the door instantly shut behind him.

The first thing that hit Reg was the smell. The captain's quarters were rank, that was for sure. At first he thought that it was simply the odor of raw fish, but then another stink revealed itself, and he squinted his eyes and shook his head in disgust.

"My God," Reg whispered. "Is he raising maggots in here?" The putrid scent hung thick enough in the air to make him gag.

As if in answer, he heard a whining squeal from the dark just ahead. Holding his nose with two fingers, he stepped carefully through the dark toward where he knew the captain's bunk was. The room was nearly pitch-black; but Reg saw in the dark like a cat. And in a moment, he'd forgotten the stench, as he dropped to his knees to look at the shadowy form on the captain's cot.

"Sooo," he said, staring down at the woman. She was naked and tied to the walls. Apparently the captain was worried about his little morsel swimming away. Reg ran his fingers across her cheek, and found a strip of leather running from the back of her head, down her jaw, to her mouth.

"He's really making sure you don't announce yer presence here, eh?"

Reg leaned forward until he was sure the woman could see his eyes. He could certainly see hers; they glittered almost catlike in the dark. "Just you stay quiet and I'll let you out of this," he promised. "But one loud word from you and it's back on, you hear?"

She didn't move, and he took that as his cue. Reg pulled the gag from her mouth and smiled as she took a couple of heaving breaths. "Thank you," she whispered.

"So the captain's keeping you here, eh?" Reg said.

"Do you suppose I enjoy being tied up and left in the dark?" she challenged.

"What would ya give me if I set ya free?"

"Your heart's desire," she laughed, softly. "What is it you want?"

"Right now? I want you."

"Then you can have me," she said. "But release my hands at least, first. I like to feel the man that I'm with."

Reg followed her arms with his fingers to the knot of the rope and undid the bindings by feel. After fumbling a bit, at last he freed her wrists, and she drew her hands down to her waist. As she kneaded her skin, the woman began to sing softly, and Reg found himself lost in the whisper of her voice. She sang sweetly, light as air. He couldn't make out the words, yet they made his heart bleed with desire. He wanted to protect this beautiful creature. To hold her and save her and nurture her. He leaned in to kiss her, and she flicked a tongue across his mouth, and continued to sing.

Reg leaned back and smiled, indulging her. But then

the ship shivered, and he remembered what was going on outside.

"We don't have much time now," he said.

"No," she said. "I know." She drew him close, and breathed upon his eyes and nose before slipping her mouth over his. She started to kiss him softly, lips warm and full, barely touching, but then grew more urgent, sucking him inside her with an urgency that Reg had never before experienced. She left him breathless, and when she broke away from his mouth and ran her hands down his chest, Reg gasped with an abandon he had only imagined.

"What is your name?" he whispered, as fingers slipped below his belly button to trace the workings of a man with the sensuality that only a woman could provide.

"Ligeia," she said. "I am and always have been, Ligeia."

Reg positioned himself back over her and found his entry without help. "I'll do whatever I can for you, Ligeia," he promised, pressing himself within her. She gasped at his entry, and then ran sharp fingernails down his back until her hands cupped his ass in a stranglehold, nails pinching so hard that they could draw blood.

"I know . . . you . . . will," she moaned beneath him, and then her mouth was on his, and then she was kissing his neck, and shoulder, and . . . neck.

And then Reg screamed. Because her kiss was not a kiss, but a bite, hard and mean. He pulled back and slapped at her, but in a heartbeat the sensual creature beneath him was no longer a girl, but a monster, all teeth and claws.

"Stop!" he screamed, but her fingernails ripped his face and bit into his chest like daggers. He punched at her, repeatedly, but he never seemed to hit her in a way that counted; he caught her in the chest and the shoulder, and even once in the jaw, but Ligeia only smiled each time, showing long teeth that opened in a shark's smile and dove for his flesh.

She did not miss her mark. Reg pulled away in stinging pain, slapping a hand against the warm stream at his neck with complete shock.

"Why?" he gasped, blood already streaming into and out of his mouth.

"Why did you come in here?" Ligeia said, grinning a crimson smile at him while holding his head in a vise between her hands. "Because I can." With that she dove back to his neck and sucked at his life like a leech. Reg would have protested, but already the feeling had left his hands, and as he feebly tried to push her away, the pain only exacerbated in his head. And so he leaned back and let her have her way. Just as he would have had her do, for him.

In seconds he was dead.

Ligeia undid the ropes that held her feet for the second time in a week. But this time, she vowed that she would not be a man's prisoner again.

Never.

She rolled herself over Reg's body and stepped past the half-rotted corpses of Rogers and Nelson on the floor, free for the first time in more than twenty-four hours. She stretched, and then retrieved a robe that Buckley had given her when they'd first boarded the *Lady Luck*. She strapped it around her waist and decided to go see what men were left.

She would never leave the ship, not while there were men to be played. To be hunted.

She could make things mighty difficult for her previous captor if he had no crew left to run the boat.

Ligeia smiled at that thought, and let herself out of the captain's chambers. She had spilled first blood, and now she was primed for a chase. As she stepped into the passageway, she saw her next victim, but as it turned out, he didn't give her much of a run for her money. He looked puzzled at her sudden appearance, though unafraid. He should have been.

Ligeia grinned, teeth still warm with the iron of Reg. She began to trill a quiet song as she advanced on the man.

"Who are *you*?" First Mate Travers said to the bloody half-nude woman exiting the captain's quarters.

He never did find out.

CHAPTER TWENTY-EIGHT

The waves crashed and broke in the restless sea; an abyss of frighteningly empty proportion. A mile or a thousand away, the horizon slipped down to close the gray of the day in a perfect kiss. In between—in between—was the horror. Two pale young hands reached out from churning turmoil, two hands without a face grasping at the gray sky for air. Evan stood rooted to the beach, desperate to run into the angry waves to grab those hands, to pull them out of the maelstrom, but somehow, his feet wouldn't listen. They remained rooted to the sand, trembling like jelly. With every attempt he made to dash into the water, his legs locked and shivered and threatened to spill him to the beach. But they would not move forward. From the turquoise blue of the waves a dark head suddenly shot up and a thin, frightened voice yelled in pure terror, just once, "Dad, please!" And then the head was gone.

Evan surfaced from the dream with tears on his face. He wondered if he would ever stop reliving the nightmare in his sleep. It came almost every other night, and had since the night after Josh's death. For a while, he'd worried it would drive him mad, and he'd started seeing Dr. Blanchard. In the distance, he heard someone call his name. He wiped his cheeks dry, and then heard his name again.

"Evan!"

It was Sarah. And she sounded upset.

God, from one nightmare to the next.

He rolled out of bed and staggered to the bedroom door, wearing only his boxers. He passed Josh's room, dark and quiet as always, and reached the family room. Sarah was there, wearing her heavy pink robe and holding a cup of coffee. He could see the steam in the shadows of the dawn light.

"Evan, what the hell?" Sarah asked. With her free hand, she pointed out the front door. He stepped past her and looked. His heart leaped as he registered the sight.

The white cement of their porch was marred with an offering. Or a warning. Evan wasn't sure which.

The cement was covered by a pile of hand-size silver fish. They were fresh; a couple still twitched and spasmed, sending dead ones to slide across the concrete. Dead fish eyes stared at Evan like an accusation. He grimaced and looked away.

"What the hell?" he echoed.

"That's what I said," Sarah answered. "Why the heck would someone pile fish onto our stoop?"

Evan shrugged. "High school prank? I dunno."

"Well, that's just creepy," she said, wrinkling her face in disgust. "Could you get rid of them before the flies come? I don't want to smell these things come dinnertime."

"Could I get dressed first?" he asked, and she shrugged, before walking back to the kitchen.

Evan stood at the door a minute longer, staring at the dull, vacant eyes of the fish. The eyes looked angry, accusatory. In their reflection he could see the events of last night, on the beach, as he turned his back on Ligeia and left her to the water. Abandoned her.

In his heart, he had no question about where the fish

had come from. They were here for him. A gift from Ligeia. But . . . what did they mean? Was it a spiteful good-bye? Or simply a way for her to let him know that she knew where he lived? What was she trying to tell him?

He closed the door and went to pull on a pair of sweat-pants, so that he could scoop up the dead fish with a shovel and bury them in the compost at the back of the yard, though the neighborhood cats would likely tear them to shreds before they decomposed. Still, no point in wasting a chance at good fertilizer. But he had to wonder if this particular fertilizer were tainted in a way that would poison the soil instead of enrich it.

Evan shook away the thought and pulled on his clothes. Sarah remained in the kitchen, nursing her cof-fee like an addict. She was not a morning girl, and it took her a shower and a solid pot of the black stuff before she was ready to talk about anything. As he passed her on his way outside, he looked at her profile in the gray morning light and a chill cascaded down his spine. She looked so fragile and soft as she sat there at the kitchen table, just staring out the sliding door to their backyard. She looked so alone, and Evan longed suddenly to hold her, to crush her to him in an embrace to prove to her that he was hers and hers alone.

Sarah had no idea what he had done to her. No clue why anybody would send them fish. The thought drove a sick pit in the center of his stomach. Again, his fault. His weakness that threatened the equilibrium of their life. He didn't want to hurt Sarah any more than he already had. He wanted to move beyond these last few weeks of his strange, but undeniable betrayal and bury it with the fish—bury it with the past, really, all of it. Once and for all. They could never erase the memory of Josh, nor would they want to. And he would never outlive his guilt at his son's death. But they had to somehow get past the daily anchor of the pain; they had lived in a purgatory for too long. Evan figured he and Sarah had thirty or forty good years left to muddle about on this earth, and he didn't want to spend them anchored in this horrible, recriminating cycle they'd slipped into since Josh's funeral.

Evan dug a hole in the musty compost pile mix of coffee grounds, old grass clippings and rotting bits of food that somehow had escaped the scavengers. After he'd cleared a hole two or three feet down, he dumped in the pile of fish from the plastic bag he'd carried them in and covered the hole back up. The gray of the morning fog was just starting to lift, and he felt better as he tamped down the last bit of earth.

After he put the shovel away, he stepped back into the house. He walked into the kitchen behind Sarah and put his hands on her shoulders, giving her a squeeze.

"It's time," he announced. She looked up at him with a crinkle of confusion.

"Tomorrow morning, we are going to start converting Josh's old room."

Sarah only nodded and took another sip of coffee.

"I know I've said it before, but we need to do this, for both of us."

"I don't know if I can help," she answered. "I'm not sure I can put his things in a box."

This time it was Evan's turn to nod. "Go shopping in the morning," he suggested. "Let me take care of the worst of it. Then you can work with me to redecorate it, to make it new again."

He brushed a tear from her cheek, and she leaned into his hand. Wordless, he held her, and caressed her shoulder with his free hand. "I love you," he said.

The day passed slowly. Evan was on a paper-trail mission and that meant lots of time at the desk, sorting through forms. Plenty of time to think. And his mind always seemed to come back to the ocean. And a woman.

"How's it going?" Bill asked him in the afternoon. "You've been pretty quiet today."

Evan shrugged. "Woke up with a pile of fish on the stoop this morning."

"Hmmm," his friend said. He leaned in to talk softer. "Well, that seems normal. Especially when you're dating a sea creature. Maybe it's the Siren equivalent of roses."

"I don't think so," Evan said. "I broke up with her last night."

"Uh oh. In that case, I suppose you could consider it the marine equivalent of dog shit on your stoop. Be glad she didn't set the fish on fire. That woulda stunk. 'Course in your neighborhood, nobody woulda known the difference."

"Very funny," Evan said. "Do you think I should try to go talk to her tonight?"

"Do you want to make up with her?"

Evan shook his head. "I've gotta end this. I told Sarah that tomorrow we're cleaning out Josh's room. It's really time to move on. You know? On every level."

"Then let it be," Bill said. "You're not going to make her any happier by going out there, raising her hopes when she sees you, and then telling her a second time that no, you're breaking up. Trust me, dragging it out never makes it easier. You've told her once, so now move on.

You dropped your bomb, she gave you her little love token, and hopefully that's the end of it."

Evan nodded. "I hope so."

Bill went back to his desk, but in his heart, Evan knew that a pile of fish wasn't going to be the end of it. Ligeia was more tenacious than that. But what she would do next . . . he had no idea. A shiver raised the hair on the back of his neck. He had no idea.

CHAPTER TWENTY-NINE

"I brought home some boxes from work," Sarah said, as Evan stood in the center of Josh's old room, coffee cup in hand. "I stacked them up in the garage."

Evan nodded absently at his wife as he looked around the room, eyes roaming from posters to light fixtures to the jumbled desktop. He wasn't sure where to begin.

"That's fine," he said. "Thanks."

Sarah rested a hand on his shoulder, and planted a peck on his cheek. "You're not mad at me for leaving you here to do this for a while, are you?"

"No, I understand," Evan insisted, though in his heart, he was a little miffed that Sarah was bailing on this part of the journey. They both needed to put away the pieces of their son's life—him doing it for her wasn't really going to help her with that. And he could have used her hands in putting it all away. Symbolically if not in practice. He wasn't looking forward to this. Hell, he'd spent a year avoiding it.

"I'll be back by lunch," Sarah promised. "By then I probably can be more help to you."

"Okay," he agreed, as she gave him a quick kiss and disappeared out the doorway. He didn't miss how her eyes lingered on the walls of the room that one last time, or how she blinked quicker as she did so.

Once he heard the garage door close, Evan took his

own deep breath and circled the room a last time. And then he began.

First step was simply to start removing things from the walls and piling it on the bed. And so the Snow Patrol poster turned into the first victim, as Evan slipped his hand beneath the paper and forced the tape away from the wall. He didn't know why, but he carefully removed the tape from the poster and rolled it up to set on the bed, as if he were going to rehang it at some point. But Evan had no intention of doing that. Still . . . he handled Josh's things as if they were his own. Carefully. With love.

And piece by piece, the posters and plaques and other knickknacks all came down until the room began to look a little bare, though there was a good pile forming in its middle.

Evan went to the garage and found the pile of boxes Sarah had contributed; a handful of midsize copy-paper boxes and slightly smaller boxes that held the coffee pouches Sarah's company used in their lunchroom. He left most of them in the hallway outside Josh's room, as he filled one of the coffee boxes with the trinkets he'd pulled down from Josh's tackboard. Pictures of Josh with Tiendra, the girl he'd taken to junior prom. And of him with the guys, probably freshman year, all lined up waiting for the starting gun at a track meet. Then there were the key chains that he collected, with logos ranging from popular movies to rock bands. And the snakebite kit, still wrapped in its plastic sleeve that he'd found at a garage sale for its kitsch value. The old 1960s vintage kit had a red label at the top that read RIP, SLASH, SUCK! SURVIVE!

Evan and Josh had both laughed over the block letters and assorted exclamation points when they'd found it sitting in a box in someone's dank garage. For fifty cents, Josh had had to have it.

Just below that, Evan plucked a handful of buttons, most of them things that Evan himself had picked up over the years. He smiled as he pulled off the Japanese-animation vixen who posed as a sultry coquette advertising Matthew Sweet's classic *Girlfriend* album. Geez. Evan had picked this one up himself back in college. Of course, that's where the rest of these came from, he realized, as he pulled off a tiny Psychedelic Furs "Pretty in Pink" button and a spooky gray-tone "Lonely Is An Eyesore" button, advertising an ethereal collection by the '80s English label 4AD.

Evan misted up for the first time then, thinking about the music he and Josh had shared. They'd always been close, but music was where they really connected. And Josh had been as fascinated with the "antique" mystery of Evan's old LP collection as Evan had been with the new stuff that Josh brought home on his iPod. Music wasn't a generation-gap indicator for them, it was glue. Evan pocketed the buttons, instead of putting them in the box to pack away.

They had been his originally, and now they were his touchstones to countless nights spent in front of the stereo, playing music with his son, both of them closing their eyes and nodding, living in the beats.

In the corner, the acoustic Washburn guitar still sat, covered in dust. Evan remembered all the times he'd kicked back on the floor, trying to pick up the basic rhythm and chords on that guitar while a song played on the stereo. Later, Josh had taken lessons, and had gotten better than his old man, though neither one of them were ever performance-ready musicians.

Evan picked up the guitar now from its stand, and with a sharp burst, blew the dust in a cloud from the instrument's neck. Then he sat on the bed and strummed it, wincing slightly at the out-of-tune disharmony that jangled through the room. Holding down the seventh fret of the second largest string, he began to carefully tune the guitar by ear. Once he was satisfied that the instrument was at least mostly in tune with itself, he began to strum an easy song he'd played a lot when Josh had been a baby.

"Don't you know / I love you so / never never never gonna let you go," Evan sang quietly.

"And when you're big / it won't be long / I will still be singin' this song . . ."

He stopped abruptly, to wipe a tear from his left eye. Evan could still remember the time that he'd written the simple ditty, when Josh had still been an infant, lying in a baby seat. The boy had waved his chubby arms in the air as Evan played, almost as if he were keeping the beat.

"Don't you know / I love you so / never never never gonna let you go," Evan whispered, setting down the guitar and picking up one of Josh's swimming trophies. He set it in the box, and then set another trophy next to it, and a third, before he couldn't keep up the bravery anymore. He sat down on the floor of his son's room and let the tears flow freely, finally, and held his face in his hands.

"I'm sorry," he choked to the empty room. "I'm so, so sorry."

Evan let out the grief; he'd grown accustomed to letting the tears have their way. For a while after Josh's death he'd tried to be brave and hold them in, but once he'd begun letting the tears out as they came, he'd found that the periods of *awful* lasted less and less. He had discovered the cathartic impact of tears.

And so now he sat there in the middle of his son's floor, and cradled his face in his hands and bawled like a baby. The sooner it came, the sooner it would be gone.

Thump.

Something crashed against the window. Evan sniffed and rubbed a hand across his eyes and nose, trying to clear his face. What the hell had that been? It was loud; sounded like it nearly busted the glass.

He got to his feet and started toward the bedroom window, still covered partially in the charcoal gray drapes that Josh had picked out for himself.

Evan had his hand on the drape to pull it back when another smack hit the window.

Thud.

He jumped back. "What the hell?"

Now his heart was pounding. Who was throwing things at his window?

Evan gingerly pulled back the draperies and looked outside. The morning was shaping up to be a lovely shade of slit-your-wrists gray, and he had no doubt that a storm would roll in before dinner.

The edges of his view were obscured by small evergreen shrubs, but Evan could see the open grass of the yard directly in front of him, and the empty asphalt of the street beyond. The Aramonds' brick ranch across the street looked as quiet and deserted as everything else he could see from this vantage point.

"Hmphff," Evan said, and released the curtains. He decided to go outside to have a look.

The neighborhood seemed still as midnight when he stepped outside; strange for a Saturday, but it was pretty cool and blustery. Not exactly a day that called out for an outing to the beach!

Evan stepped off the stoop and walked over to the side of the house where Josh's window perched just above the ground. Their house had been built into a hill, and while half of it was solidly aboveground, the other half was below. It made for good heating and cooling bills, since the ground provided a natural insulation.

It was clear that something had hit the window. When Evan stood in front of his son's bedroom window, he could see an oval spot near the center of the glass. Josh's window had a spray of some white-colored dust around that impact spot, and something that looked like it might be blood dripped down the white painted frame below.

He looked around on the ground near the evergreens and saw the culprit instantly. A seagull. The creature was still alive, but it wouldn't be for long. The wings fluttered, briefly, crazily, with a flap-flap-flap sound that succeeded only in turning the bird's body in a circle. Evan could see the pain in the creature's bright, open eyeball. The thing stared at him from its crooked head and flapped again, moving its bulk in a circle around the broken neck.

"Sorry, buddy," Evan whispered, and went to get a shovel. He needed to put the thing out of its misery and bury it before Sarah came back home. It drove her nuts when birds hit one of the house's windows. "Bad luck," she insisted.

When he came back, the gull was already dead, one open eye stuck staring at the gray sky. Evan shook his head, and thanked the air that he didn't have to smash the thing in the head with the shovel before burying it. Instead, he scooped it onto the blade. That's when he noticed the second one, lying just underneath a long branch of evergreen, near a gnarled twist of root. There *had* been two thumps, hadn't there?

He looked at the bird splayed out on the spade and then at the other bird, and shook his head. "I'll come back for you," he promised, and walked the first bird around the house to bury it in the compost pile. Once back there, he dug a small hole (and was secretly pleased that so far, the fish appeared to have been untouched by the local cats) and dropped in the dead gull.

Then he returned to the front of the house to retrieve the second body.

He was scooping the shovel under the bird when he heard the first sound.

"Eee-ahh-ee! Eee-ahh-ee!"

Evan looked up from the bushes to the sky, and quickly located the source of the sound. Another gull circled overhead, lazily pinpointing the house in its flight.

He raised an eyebrow at the unusual interest gulls were showing in his house today and lifted the dead bird on his shovel.

"Ee-ahh-ee!" came the sound again, only this time it was closer. And then another screech answered it. "Eeeee-aahhh!"

Evan looked up and there were five gulls now flying in the air above his roof. The things did not appear to be en route to another beachside location. The target was right here.

Maybe one of these were a mate, he wondered, stepping out of the bushes with the dead bird.

"Eee-ahhh! Ahhh-eee!"

He looked up again and there were a dozen gulls now swirling around his house; one of them swooped down at his face. It came so close a feather brushed his cheek as it passed.

"Whoa!" Evan gasped, ducking as the bird swooshed by. "What the hell!"

Above his head, the sky suddenly darkened, as scores more gulls joined the flock. The quiet of the morning suddenly turned into a cacophony of screeches and caws, as one by one the cloud of birds grew, and more and more of them peeled off the main flock and dipped in the air to strafe Evan's lawn. He ducked and jumped a dozen times as the birds flew around his yard, bombing his head, screeching as if their babies were being attacked.

"Damn," Evan said. He'd never seen the gulls like this. They normally didn't bother to come in from the beach much, other than for a solo flyby while looking for some easy lunch. He had never seen them circle the subdivision like a flock of vultures that had spotted a kill.

He began to edge away from the house, brandishing the shovel, intending to cart the bird body back to the compost quickly, so that he could get back into the house before too many more birds arrived.

But it was too late.

"Eeee-ahhh!" shouted one gray monster as it dove in the air straight for his face. Evan ducked, but it didn't matter; the bird landed on his head, grasping at his hair with clawlike feet as its beak pecked hard at the soft flesh of his forehead.

"What the fuck!" Evan screamed, and dropped the shovel to swat at the bird. It took off from his head in an explosion of feathers, but then two more gulls dropped from the sky and landed on his shoulders, bending in to peck at his neck almost right away. He shook them off, but the air around him was alive with gulls, shrieking and cawing like mad, and Evan felt the pinch of claws on his head and neck and back, and he didn't stand still anymore. He turned and ran for the house.

Something jabbed him in the back of the neck and he stumbled at the pain, flipping his arms back and flailing at the air, trying to fend them off. Another dart of pain caught him in the neck, and then something reached around and pecked hard at his cheek, just missing his eye.

"No no no!" Evan yelled, turning around in a violent

circle and spraying his hands out like a manic ninja, catching one after another heavy feathered body with the back of his hands. Beaks and claws ripped at his skin; it felt like he'd pulled his arms through a rosebush. The birds bounced off of him and pecked at his hands, and then one was in his face, cold claws grabbing at his lips and teeth for purchase.

Evan literally punched that one midair and felt its claw rip open the inside of his gum as it tried to hold to him before falling away.

"No!" he screamed again and regained his balance from his violent pirouette. He ran again for the door to his house, and quickly ripped it open and flung himself inside. Behind him, thud after thud after thud hit the door.

"Eee-ahhh!!!!" the air outside screamed.

Evan looked up to see a half dozen gulls plaster themselves against the glass, beady black eyes all staring in at him for just a second, as their bodies pounded against the transparent surface, molded to it briefly, and then fell off to pile on the ground outside. He could see wings beating feebly against the ground from the felled animals, and could hear the scrabbling of nails against concrete.

The birds cried and wailed outside, and still more of them came, streaming out of the sky like avian kamikazes. They pounded against the door, one after the next. Each head smacked against the glass with a finality that made Evan's skin crawl, and soon he could see trails of yellowish liquid on the window of the door, and the occasional dots of impact blood.

"What the freakin' hell," he breathed, lying back on his arms on the floor, feet to the door. He could feel the warmth of blood dripping down his neck and back from where the birds had pecked him, but he didn't pay attention. Outside, the air continued to flutter with gray feathers and shrieks of frustration as the birds pounded one and three and five at a time against his door.

He lay there on the floor and waited, wondering if the glass would shatter and the birds would finally plow through the opening and reach him. He could have shut the wooden door, but something made him watch; he wanted to know when the birds gave up. They had to stop eventually, right?

The crashes and thuds against the door did finally start to slow, and soon, he realized it had been a couple minutes since the last bird committed suicide against his front door. Groaning at the pinchlike wounds all over his head and arms, Evan stood and cautiously stepped toward the door. He flinched when the floor creaked as he stepped close. His heart beat faster, and he kept expecting a *smack* to crack against the glass right in front of him. But as he surveyed the piles of bloody feathers that littered his stoop like the remains of a serial killer pillow fight, he began to think that maybe, this attack anyway, was over. Nothing moved on his front lawn. Where his neighbors had been through all of that, he didn't know . . . but nobody was outside down the street as far as he could see.

Evan pushed open the door; it resisted at first from the weight of dead gull bodies piled against it.

Once outside, he peered beyond the frame of the house into the sky, looking hard in all directions for some indication that there was more of a flock coming.

The horizon was gray and roiling with quietly ominous clouds . . . but there appeared to be no more flocks of murderous birds ready to break free of the sky.

He began to count the bird bodies lying all around his

front door, but lost track at thirty. "That's just not right," he mumbled to himself, and then went to get a garbage can. He had originally come out here because he didn't want Sarah to see one dead bird on her lawn. He couldn't let her get a glimpse of this. It was almost biblical.

Evan piled all the birds into the can, and then dug a deep hole next to the compost pile. He didn't want to risk hitting the fish with the spade and this load was going to take some space to bury. The sweat was pouring down his back and chest by the time he was satisfied that he'd cleared enough dirt. He poured the birds from the can into the hole and tamped down the dirt on top of them. Then he returned the can to the garage and went inside to clean up.

He showered for the second time that morning, as much to clean all of the scratches he'd incurred as to get rid of the dirt—and the feeling of dirt. He felt violated, he realized, as he scrubbed shampoo into his hair with extra vigor.

He toweled off in front of the mirror and leaned in to look hard at his face. None of the scratches looked too bad, but he got out some antibiotic cream and rubbed it on all of them. No sense in risking an infection. As he applied the cream, he looked into his own eyes. They were brown and sad, and a little distant. Far away.

"Ass," he told his reflection, watching the bristles of his unshaved beard, now well peppered with gray, move across his cheek as he spoke. "You brought this on yourself."

Then he laughed at his reflection and threw the towel in the hamper. "So what?" he asked the bathroom mirror. "Are you suggesting that she can control the birds? What kind of woman do you believe she is?"

When he didn't answer himself, the house seemed

suddenly disturbingly quiet. He could hear the hum of the refrigerator from down the hall, and the tick of a clock in the front room. The air hung expectant.

"What kind of woman is she?" he asked the empty house more quietly.

Shaking his head, he pulled on a fresh pair of pants and shirt and went back into Josh's room. Then he attacked his mission with renewed intensity, piling all of the trinkets and photos and pictures into boxes and marking them TROPHIES, MOVIES, PICTURES and more in black marker on the side before sealing the tops with packing tape.

In an hour, he had cleared the majority of the room, down to the furniture. Then he got a larger plastic bin he'd been saving in the garage, and began emptying the drawers. He pulled out Josh's top drawer of T-shirts and pressed his face to them, trying to catch just one last whiff of the warm, huggable scent that had once meant the happiness of his son in his life.

But now, the clothes just smelled musty. He stifled a sneeze and dropped the pile into the bin, following it with jeans and socks. When it was full, he pressed down the lid until it clicked.

"I'll miss you, buddy," he whispered, and then rolled it to rest beneath the attic stairs in the hall. Then he got another plastic bin, and brought it into the center of the room before opening the closet doors.

He didn't stop packing until the room was empty of everything but a dresser, desk and stripped bed.

When he couldn't find anything else to box up, he sat on the bed and took in a long, hitching breath. He stared at the faint mark from the bird on the window, and the horror of the morning rushed back at him; he'd been pushing so hard at packing the room that he'd all but forgotten about the birds. He realized that he hadn't slowed down in close to three hours. His shirt was soaked, but when he reached up to wipe his eyes, he realized that it wasn't just from sweat. His face was sopping wet too.

He'd been crying the whole time.

Jensen had then chased the wayward peak out and chased
towards the three tables. His beer was tepid; he
wanted a cold one but there was this . . . thrill that a
friendly inn might enchant. He was stopping off for a
third round or two, he understood.

CHAPTER THIRTY

O'Flaherty's buzzed with laughter, music and the clink
of glasses lifting and resetting on the bar and dozen
wooden tables. Saturday night spelled celebration in any
town, and when you were the town's main watering hole,
well . . . a full house was nearly always a given.

Evan's back and legs complained from all the bending
and crouching and lifting he'd done throughout the day;
never mind the impromptu war of the gulls and subsequent military burial of bird carcasses. Between packing
and digging, he'd put in a week's worth of physical labor
compared to his normal activity quotient.

Sarah had come home after lunch, laden with pack-
ages from the Wal-Mart and Ace Hardware stores. "If
I couldn't help with the packing," she'd explained, "I figured I could be focused on the redecorating. You didn't
have anything in mind, did you?"

When Evan had shrugged, she'd smiled. "Good. Because I found this wallpaper runner and these drapes at
Wal-Mart that I thought would be perfect if we wanted
to go with more of a plum theme . . ."

She'd proceeded to empty her numerous plastic bags
of everything from decorative wall plates to paint
samples on the bare mattress. By the time she was done,
Evan felt more exhausted just from thinking about the

coming painting and redecorating than he had from the actual process of boxing.

At the end of the afternoon, Sarah had plans to meet her friend Melanie for dinner, but offered to cook Evan something first. He declined, opting to call Bill first to see if he wanted to do something. And not surprisingly, Bill had said to meet at the bar. By six o'clock, Evan and Sarah were kissing each other good-bye in the garage and heading in separate directions. "I should be home by ten," Sarah promised, and Evan said the same. If they'd had any inkling of how the night would truly go, they would have kissed a lot longer.

"Hey, Fish Lover!" Bill called from a booth at the back of O'Flaherty's. Evan saw him through the crowded bar instantly; his friend wore a faded, ripped green flannel shirt that would have embarrassed a lumberjack. The thick wave of brown beard that he'd adopted this past winter only exaggerated the effect.

"You applying for a job with a Pearl Jam tribute band?" Evan poked.

"What, this?" Bill grinned, running one hand down his green- and brown-checked sleeve and rolling his eyes in mock enjoyment. "I just want to be in style, you know?"

"Well, news to the clueless," Evan offered. "That shirt probably wasn't in style when it was new, and it sure as hell isn't now."

Bill held up a hand, as if to motion "stop."

"You're just jealous of my hot duds. I know it. I don't blame you." Bill nodded as if he knew the secrets of the underworld. "But it's okay. I'll just slip this off so that you're not seeing the green devil all night."

Underneath Bill's flannel was a T-shirt that unbeliev-
ably was in worse shape than the overshirt. This one had
once been white, with a cartoon bunny adorning its chest.
The rabbit held out a hand as if to shake, while the other
mitt had buried a foot-long cleaver in its own chest. Beneath it, a slogan read LET'S JUST CUT TO THE CHASE.

The shirt looked as if it had been used as a dust rag;
blotchy stains marred it in a dozen places and a couple
holes showed the hair of Bill's shoulders poking through.

"Jeez, man, do we need to take up a collection?" Evan
asked.

"Laundry weekend," Bill explained. "Now you know
why I was wearing the flannel."

Evan nodded. "Yeah, you can put it back on."

"Too late," Bill said. "It's getting warm in here."

"That's just the embarrassment talking," Evan suggested.

At that point, a waitress turned up. "What can I get
you guys?" she asked, bouncing from one foot to the
other while smiling in a way that could only be described
as plastic. Evan supposed the motion was meant to make
her look perky, but instead, the resulting gentle vibration
of her breasts against a too-tight black T-shirt just made
it look like she had to go to the bathroom.

"Red Hook," Evan ordered, while Bill took a Hacker-
Pschorr.

"Leave it to you to drink a haughty beer while looking
like a damn bum," Evan laughed.

"I'm a man of contradictions," Bill answered. "Speaking of which, have you discovered any more fish on your
porch?"

Evan shook his head. "No, but I got a nice crop of rabid
seagulls today."

Bill raised one eyebrow, and Evan quickly related the

day's events. By the time he was done, the waitress had returned with their beers, and Evan lifted his and took a long drink. Telling the story had reawakened the horror of the morning, and his skin felt itchy with the touch of a dozen bird feet and claws.

Bill took a long swig of his fuzzy golden wheat beer before commenting on Evan's gull story. But when he did, he was unsubtle and to the point.

"Dude, you're fucked."

"You have a way with words."

Bill shook his head and reached down into a knapsack he'd tossed on the booth bench beside him. He produced a book with three pink page markers sticking out of its pages. The cover showed a picture of an ancient Greek statue with wings and long, wicked-looking teeth. Above the art it read MYTHS & MURDERERS: A HISTORY OF DEADLY TALES.

"After you told me about the fish the other day, I went and checked this out of the library. I know you have refused to believe anything I've told you about the Siren, so I thought maybe if you saw some of this, you might finally consider the possibility that you don't actually know everything about everything in the world."

"And this is going to convince me . . . how?" Evan asked.

Bill flipped to the first marked section of the book and began to read. "'The Sirens were first noted in early Greek culture as three sisters who took the form of birds. These creatures sang with the sweetest song, but any man who found himself lured by their melodies soon found himself dead at their vicious hands . . . or more exactly, beaks. The Sirens pecked their victims to death, all the while still singing a song described as so intoxicating, nothing but the absolute pain of death could make the victims take notice of their peril. And by the time death throes had set in, it generally was too late for the victim to do anything to save him or herself.'"

Evan nodded when Bill finished, and took a swig of his beer. Then he asked, "And that would convince me that Ligeia is in fact a mythological Siren . . . how? As I think I've explained to you, she's a pretty sexy woman, and I've seen every inch of her . . . she isn't sporting any feathers. She doesn't have bird claws. She's not hiding any vestigial wings; believe me, I would have noticed, no matter how sweet her song."

Bill held up a hand. "Indulge me," he said. "The plot thickens.

"'Over the years, the description of the Sirens changed. While originally depicted as three sisters whose bodies were largely avian, over time the images of the Sirens changed to reflect their affinity with fish. In some accounts, the Sirens took on all of the attributes of the attractive human female. They were described as maidens of exceptional lush beauty, with long, flowing hair, breasts that dripped with fertility and hips that drove men to the verge of insanity. Below the waist, they changed, sometimes displaying the thick black scales of bird feet and other times merging their legs into a single, sinuous fin of flesh capped with blue-green scales—much like the mermaid.'"

"Again," Evan interrupted. "She is certainly attractive, but she doesn't have scales or bird feet."

Bill ignored him and read on. "'Still later accounts eschew the animal aspects of the Siren altogether, simply describing them as three beautiful women who lived on the rocks at the darkest corners of a bay, calling out to weakhearted fishermen in the night and luring them and their crews to their deaths. Their attraction stemmed from their pure, unblemished beauty, and the song that they sang almost unceasingly through everything that they did. The call of the Siren is said to be one that can overcome any denial. Mortal men are doomed to answer the Siren's call, and her call can only mean one thing for a mortal man: death. In the classic text of Homer, Jason steered his ship through the perilous pass occupied by the Sirens by having his ears packed with cotton so that he could not heed the song, and still he had himself tied to the mast until the danger was passed.'"

"Okay." Evan shrugged. "So the myth of the Siren went from birdbrained sisters to rock-dwelling fish women to just really good, sexy singing vixens. I still don't see . . ."

Bill flipped to his next bookmark and read some more, without comment.

"'While the depictions of the Siren have changed through the years, one constant has not. The Siren exists for one purpose; to bring about the destruction of man through his ultimate weakness—sexual desire. Her lure has always been song—the pure, sweet, seductive melody that pretends innocence yet, at its core, is nothing more than a heart trap. And her body, whether sometimes cloaked in animal scales and feathers, or simple, perfect woman flesh, is always described as desirable. Her song demands the attention of the man, while her body demands his lust. In the end, she ensnares him past the point of reason, and he is lost. And then her true purpose is displayed. For the Siren sings not to bring a man's soul to ruin—she doesn't care about such invisible twists of morality. Rather, she sings to bring his body to her for sustenance. The Siren is carnivorous, and her wiles only a means to dinner. Like the black widow spider, the Siren attracts men for the sole purpose of feeding. One famous picture shows the three Sirens lying in repose amid the carcasses of a number of dead bodies, as if sated by the flesh of the nearby dead.'"

"She hasn't once tried to bite me," Evan suggested, smirking.

Bill flipped to his third mark and continued.

"'The chosen habitat of the Siren is the rarely trafficked rocky cliffs near the sea. Here, she is free to commune with the birds and fish by day, while at night she can lure in the unwary male passing by on the water without risk of discovery. The cool air of the sea also aids in preserving the flesh of the victim for her to feed upon longer. Because of the solitary nature of the Siren, she often extends her lure of a man over many days or weeks before ultimately bringing him in for the kill. In this way, she learns the ways of the world through their conversation, and alleviates some of the loneliness of her natural condition, living on the edge of the world. But once her hunger has grown too great, her instinct takes over and one night, the man finds himself the surprised recipient of her sharp and very deadly teeth. She will sing him to sleep one final time, and then drain his blood in the night without compunction. No matter how her tears and words display affection and sorrow, in the end the Siren is a creature without emotion, and she kills without regret.'"

"They paint a pretty foul picture of the old girl," Evan observed, emptying his glass in a final swig. "Though again, I don't see the connection. The ancients believed in a lot of weird creatures. All you've told me is they believed in a woman who lived by the sea and ate men after luring them to her arms with a good tune. Sometimes she looked like a bird, sometimes a fish, and sometimes neither. And, apparently, there are really only three of them, since they were depicted as three sisters much of the time. So are you really going to tell me that one of the three ancient wonders of the world traveled across the ocean and up the California coast to haunt this backwater town? Why?"

Bill smiled. "Come on, Evan—open your mind a little bit. Do you really suppose that after all this time, those three sisters remained the same? Even gods and goddesses have children and grow old and sometimes even die. There are later myths that talk about the children of the Sirens, and their children's children. The Sirens spread from the ancient circle of the Tyrrhenian Sea to sing on the coast of Capri and Capo Peloro. There are stories of a Siren who lured ships to crash on the rocks of Dalkey Island near the Irish city of Dublin in the 1600s. If you pull a detailed map of the European and Asian coastlines from the 1700s, you'll find a number of circled warning spots where captains were cautioned to keep their ships far from shore, lest they be lured in to their deaths from the song of the stones."

"I haven't noticed those on any modern maps," Evan suggested dryly.

"As if," Bill said. "Ask your average dipshit if they believe in UFOs and aliens and they'll probably say yes, and tell you how their mom or their sister saw one last year. But if you ask them about a Siren, they'd probably think you meant the sound on a fire truck. I wouldn't take that to mean anything but that the American populace is a crowd of foolish sheep that follow the fad of the moment, and Sirens haven't exactly been a fad in the past couple hundred years."

Evan shrugged. "Fad or not, you still haven't given me any reason to believe that Delilah has a resident Siren, never mind whether or not I've been sleeping with her."

Bill nodded. "Okay, here's the thing. You know as well

as anyone that Delilah started out as a port town. Kind of a renegade port town, if the truth be known, because we've always catered to those ships bringing in something that might just be a little left of the law. In Prohibition, this was one of the biggest rumrunner ports of the California coast. But even before that, the captains that came through here were often bringing in cargo that no other big-city port would touch. The first reports of the Siren cropped up more than two hundred years ago. You can look them up yourself, if you want to go down to the library and dig through the old local history books. There are a number of stories of ships that went down on the rocks just off Gull's Point. And for nearly every shipwreck story that was documented, there is a story of a crewman who survived and told the tale of hearing a beautiful song that came from the point, and of a woman who beckoned them onward through the night fog to their deaths." Bill paused. "Well, the deaths of everyone on board but the poor slob who survived to tell the tale, anyway."

"I'm sure half the harbors in the world have some ghost story to tell of a lost ship that went down in the harbor," Evan countered.

"Sure they do," Bill said. "But most don't have the same story recur again and again and again over dozens of years. And Delilah—she has a lot of hulls lying at rest out there in the bay. But after a long stretch of those stories, they suddenly quieted about a hundred and fifty years ago. The last ship that went down in the 1800s was the *Lady Luck*, a rumrunner up from the coast of Mexico on its way to Oregon. They went down, all hands, during a bad storm. But while there were no survivors of that ship, there were those on the shore who swore that they heard a song on the waves of the storm that night, and saw strange lights from the ship before she went down. And there are several reports from people all the way into the town that the cracks of thunder that night were punctuated by screams. Nobody knows what happened to the *Lady Luck* other than that she never docked that night in Delilah. And after that, there were no reports of a Siren again off the rocks of Gull Point. Not until the 1980s."

"So what changed?"

It was Bill's turn to shrug. "Nobody knows. But then one night, someone reported hearing strange singing while they were out on the beach after dark, and the next day, someone from the town was discovered dead on the beach with their throat torn out. Nobody connected the two until the same story turned up a few weeks later—someone called the town hall complaining that an opera singer was practicing somewhere down near the water and keeping them awake, and the next day, another body was found lodged in the rocks of the point, its neck and chest and thighs chewed as if it had been found by hungry dogs."

"Maybe they were."

"Maybe. And that was the theory the police put out in the media. But some of the old-timers remembered the stories that their grandparents had handed down about Delilah in the old days. And the stories sounded pretty familiar. They kept their ears out, and started putting two and two together as a string of deaths occurred down by the point. And they noticed when, after the beach started getting some more police attention, the bodies stopped turning up too, but the disappearances continued. And someone always seemed to remember hearing music the night before a disappearance was reported."

Evan felt a shiver crawl across his spine. "So what

brought her back after more than a hundred years of silence?" he asked.

Bill shook his head. "Nobody knows. The beach was quiet for a long, long time, and then all of a sudden people started disappearing there again. And there was always talk of music."

"Well," Evan suggested, "I've heard plenty of music sung by a sexy woman, but I haven't disappeared."

"No," Bill agreed. "But others have. You saw one of them a couple weeks ago."

"She probably just practices out on the beach," Evan said. "She might be in a band or . . ."

Bill held up a hand again. "Spare me," he said. "She has no home and she's not practicing. Face it, Evan, you've been screwing the Siren of Delilah and, for whatever reason, she's let you live up to now. But . . . now she's angry. You told her you didn't want to see her anymore. How do most women respond to that?"

"Not well," Evan admitted. "Not that I have a lot of experience with that."

"Not well," Bill restated. "Well, I do have a lot of experience with it, and I can tell you . . . bitches don't like the word *good-bye*."

"Thank you for that brilliant bit of ghetto philosophy," Evan said. "Though there's another wrinkle to it all that I haven't told you yet."

Bill raised an eyebrow. "Oh good," he said. "There's more?"

Evan nodded. "When I broke up with her on Thursday night, she told me she was pregnant."

Bill snorted into his beer, sending a white froth of foam up the side of the glass. "Tell me you're joking," he gasped, after pounding the glass to the table. "You wore protection, right? I mean . . . you're not stupid?"

"How do you wear protection in the ocean?" Evan asked miserably.

"Oh, buddy," Bill said. "There's nothing like a woman scorned. Nothing but a woman who's *knocked up* and scorned." He shook his head and lifted his glass, in preparation to drain it.

"You're fucked, man. Totally, fully, fucked." And with that, he emptied his beer. Evan followed his lead and slammed the empty to the table.

"Okay," he said. "You know it all about women and mythological sea creatures. What do I do now?"

Bill's lips twitched as if considering one answer, discarding it, hatching another and discarding that one too. Finally he said, simply, "Stay away from the water?"

"The gulls didn't attack me near the water," Evan reminded.

Bill nodded. "I know. But I didn't think you'd want to hear the other answer."

"Which is?"

"Run like hell. Otherwise—and I'm totally serious about this—I think she's gonna try her best to kill you."

CHAPTER THIRTY-ONE

June 10, 1887, 11 P.M.

The *Lady Luck* tossed on the sea like a cork, bobbing up and down in the waves without warning or rhythm. The waves were wild and high. On deck, holding fast to the wheel, Captain Buckley barked orders to what remained of his crew. He hadn't heard from Travers since the first mate had knocked on his cabin, but he had no time to consider the absence. Buckley yelled to Cauldry and Jensen to take down sails, batten hatches and stow nets before they washed overboard, while he tried to follow the troughs of the storm with his rudder and keep them rolling with the march of the storm, rather than against it.

Overhead, the thunder crashed with the report of a cannon, just a second behind the jagged flashes of electric blue that cut across the roiling black clouds. The rain pelted the deck of the ship without mercy, and Buckley shivered at the cold trail of tears from the sky that streamed down his back. "Ah, Ligeia," he murmured. "I could use your song now."

Cauldry staggered his way across the deck, and grabbed at the mast to hold himself steady. "We've stowed everything we can, Captain."

Buckley nodded. "Get below, then, and see if you can find what's become of Travers."

"Aye-aye, Captain," the younger man said, and then zigzagged his way back across the deck to throw himself down the ladder belowdecks. It would be the last time the captain saw him alive.

Cauldry slicked the water off his hair with his hands and shook it off on the deck. He shivered and willed his teeth to stop chattering. This was one of those rare nights when he hated being at sea. The ship was strong, but still in danger. There was no telling whether the waves would rise so high and hard that they rolled the *Lady Luck* over, drowning her and her crew. The captain's struggle to guide her with the tiller was something of a token battle; in the end, the ship would either thread its own way through the waves, or perish. Human hands helped very little in the battle when the hands of Hades reached out of the sky to buffet them like a child's toy.

Cauldry stepped through the empty galley to the corridor that led to their bunks. He passed the captain's chamber and stepped into the crew's quarters. "Travers," he yelled. "Where are ya, man?"

The ship creaked and moaned in answer, but Travers didn't reply. Cauldry shook his head and frowned. It wasn't at all like the first mate to disappear in the heart of a storm. That was all-hands-on-deck time, and he'd been the one to roust the captain. So where had he gone since? There had been entirely too many disappearances from the *Lady Luck* over the past two weeks. A chill spiked through his belly at the thought. What if Travers had suffered the same fate as Rogers and Nelson?

He stepped into the dark passageway that led to the hold, and the ship lurched and rolled. Cauldry grabbed at the wall and tried not to fall. When the deck leveled off, he pushed himself onward, and stepped into the cargo hold.

"Travers?" he called again. This time, his call was answered by a creak. "Travers, are you in here? Are you okay?"

Again, the creak. It sounded like a rusty seesaw, slowly slipping from one side up to the next. Cauldry couldn't figure out where the noise was coming from, but it was unusual; normally, the hold was so quiet your voice disappeared into its dark confines as if muffled like a blanket. So the steady creak felt wrong. He threaded his way through the stacks of wooden crates, blindly following the sound, trying to get to the center of the steady sound.

Reeeeee-Rawwwwwww. Reeeee-Rawwwww.

It seemed to be coming from just ahead of him, and Cauldry rounded the corner of one tall stack of wooden boxes and listened. "It should be here," he said to himself. *The sound should be coming from right about here.*

He stood still, and listened again for the sound. Something dripped on his forehead, and he wiped it off absently. The boat apparently was leaking through the deck; not surprising given the force of the storm. The drip came again, along with the creaking sound.

The sound felt like it were right on top of him. He looked up, and something warm splattered him right in the eye. He wiped it away frantically, and then looked up once again.

"Oh my God in heaven," Cauldry gasped. Above his head, ten bare toes hung limp, droplets of blood hanging like the residue of red rain from each of their tips. Cauldry followed the toes up to the ankles and calves and thighs and the red gash where the man once had shown he was a man; he was a man no longer. From that ravaged private place, a dozen streams of blood trailed down hairy legs to reach the toes, which dripped on Cauldry's face. At that second it clicked that the water in his eyes hadn't been water at all, and Cauldry stepped back and swore.

Then he looked up again and saw the face of his first mate, eyes open in seeming startlement, staring blindly at the ceiling of the hold, where the rope wound around a heavy wooden beam before cinching tight to the dead man's wrists.

The man was naked, but his body still seemed almost clothed given the thick covering of blood that coated its bare skin. The blood seemed to be coming from the man's neck and middle, largely, though there were gored pits on its chest where nipples had once resided as well.

"What happened to ya, man?" Cauldry whispered. Travers had always been a solid man, as far as Cauldry was concerned, and a fair first mate. He trusted him far more than he ever had the captain. His heart turned sour at the idea that somebody could have been cruel enough to torture the man this way.

Something scuffed against the floor nearby, and it suddenly occurred to Cauldry that whoever had done this to Travers was likely still nearby; after all, the captain and Jensen had both been up top for the past hour with him.

He began to back away from the center of the hold, quietly retracing his steps while looking back and forth in the gloom, struggling to make out any shadow that might be the reflection of danger. He kept backing up, while watching the gentle swaying of the first mate's body as it followed the lolling motion of the ship. He backed right up into something soft, and as he flipped around to see what it was, he realized it was not only soft, but warm. He realized this as fingers ran up his arms and cinched around his back just as he came about to face it.

It was a woman. A nude, beautiful woman with breasts

of ivory, and lips that looked rich and full, and red as the fall of Travers's blood. Her arms encircled him before he'd even taken in her features, and as he opened his mouth to protest she whispered, "Shhhhh," and began to sing.

"What did you do to Travers?" Cauldry asked, as her song washed over him like a drug. "Who are you?"

Her hands ran up his ribs and massaged his chest through the cold, wet shirt. Then they slipped over the angry stubble of his cheeks, and she leaned in to plant a soft, sensual kiss on his lips.

"Don't be afraid," she whispered in a pause from the seductive melody. "If you can satisfy me, I'll set you free."

Her hands moved from his face to his trousers, and Cauldry frowned in confusion; she had killed their first mate, but she wanted to bed him? What was this about?

But then the sweet promise of the song filled his head and all he could think about was the warmth of her touch and the scent of her. After spending so long at sea, the touch of a woman trumped all other concerns, and her song seemed to crowd out any fear from his brain. Suddenly the hold reeked of the pheromones of sex, and he felt himself growing aroused at her attentions. His pants dropped to the deck; she lifted the shirt from his body. He shivered with cold and she wrapped herself around him, breathing hot in his ear, "I've needed a real man like you for too long."

He grinned at the compliment as her fingers encircled his erection and tugged to underline her point. He lost all rationality, leaning in to take her tongue between his lips as his hands kneaded at the soft warmth of her ass. As his fingers slipped down, he felt the warm, smooth skin of her upper thighs turn from a sweaty heat to the cool hardness of something else . . . something slippery and smooth but impenetrable; it didn't give way under his kneading like her ass, it felt almost as if he were grasping . . . a fish.

But then she was pulling herself up and onto him, wrapping her arms around his shoulders and forcing him to support her full weight as she moved herself up and over him, drawing his eager manhood inside, and then forcing it out again, over and over, as her lips traveled up his shoulder and neck and ear with hot, moist, panting breaths and a song that refused, it seemed, to quiet.

Cauldry backed her against a stack of crates to help support her weight, and drove his point home again and again. Around them, a cloud of music hid the truth. Ligeia grinned with teeth too sharp for an innocent, and too cruel for a lover.

As Cauldry spent himself with a growing moan inside her, she echoed his passion with cries of her own, and then finished her crescendo by burying her teeth in his neck and chomping down as hard as she could. His flesh parted beneath her teeth like bread, and Ligeia chewed fast and deep, drinking like a glutton from the fountain she opened.

In Cauldry's head, the crimson pain bloomed like a deadly alarm, but he couldn't seem to move as she opened him up for the easy attack of death.

In a flash he remembered the bloody feet of Travers, and for a brief moment, the cloud of her music faltered in its suffocating hold over him. Cauldry saw Ligeia as she truly was—a thin, birdlike woman with an unnaturally long face. Her eyes were brown but shot through with iridescent yellow like a fish. Her nose looked hawkish, and her black hair kinked in ratty knots across bone-thin shoulders that supported tiny knobs of brown flesh; her nipples jutted from a chest almost boyish, while the smooth flesh of her crotch gleamed marble blue with the closeness of veins to its surface. Her thighs changed from the flesh of a woman to the blue-gray scales of a fish, and her feet looked black and gnarled and strange; the claws of a giant bird, not the delicate toes of a goddess.

When she smiled, Cauldry saw the pointed weapons of her teeth. They hungered for flesh, there was no question, he thought, as she leaned into him with desire and promises of protection. "Stay with me," she said. "We'll make babies together."

"But I'm bleeding," he coughed, and something warm leaked into his mouth as he spoke. He choked, and felt weakness coming on.

"I'll take care of you if you promise to stay," she whispered. Her eyes seemed to glow in the darkness, and Cauldry saw the pointy tip of her nose and chin and the sickly bleached tone of her skin and suddenly felt ill. He pushed her away from him. She reached out for his arm and he kicked her, three times, until she stumbled to the ground. With one hand, he held his neck in vain, trying to keep the pump of his blood inside. He threaded his way through the boxes to the corridor beyond.

"I am not going to die in the ship's hold," he promised himself.

Behind him, a scream and a song erupted almost simultaneously. This time the melody seemed tribal, guttural and fast, and Ligeia staggered out of the hold, gripping her belly where Cauldry had kicked her.

"I will love you and kiss you and keep you whole," her voice sang amid the thunder from above. "And I will bed you and wed you and swallow you whole," she continued, her voice growing again in exotic waves. "You will feed me and follow me now 'til the end of your days, and the end of your days is now."

Cauldry felt her claws on his shoulders as he passed the captain's cabin, and he turned into her and kneed her in the belly once more. But Ligeia did not let go. And suddenly the words in his head changed from understandable syllables to an ancient language that he couldn't fathom. But its beauty stopped him. It was as if his limbs were suddenly cased in amber, as she sang and slipped her arms around him, once again pressing her naked flesh to his, and brought her face up to stare into his centimeters away. He could feel the faint fishy breath of her mouth against his lips, and her hideous eyes seemed to draw his into her, inside her, into a dark, heavy place where nothing moved, especially him. He couldn't look away from those cold-blooded eyes, even when he felt her fingernails ripping like daggers at his back. He closed his eyes to block the sight of her and gather his bearings but as he did so the pain bloomed like a gunshot in his neck, and his eyes sprang back open to see the twists of Ligeia's hair against his face as her teeth dug into his neck and struggled to bite deeper, deeper into his very core.

The music was gone now, and all Cauldry felt was the pain and the disappointment that the woman he had briefly coupled with—coupled in a way that had been more satisfying than any girl he'd ever bedded before— had only wanted one thing from him. And despite his enjoyment of it, what she wanted hadn't been the sex. It had been his life.

And she had won it, he realized, as he slipped to his knees, and his head fell to rest against the cold, alien fish scales of her legs.

CHAPTER THIRTY-TWO

The air buzzed. Okay, maybe it wasn't the air, exactly, but rather the space in Evan's head. The space now occupied with four Red Hooks and a night full of laughing, reverberating, unintelligible bar noise. He blinked heavily and walked with a clumsy tread down the sidewalk from Delilah's main drag into his bayside subdivision. He hoped the ten-minute walk would clear his head a bit by the time he got home; as much as Sarah drank and came home to him slurred and shaky, he hated to turn the same trick for her.

When he reached his driveway, the events of the morning suddenly came rushing back; he'd managed to blot it out for the past few hours of chatter. Now the chain of events replayed in his head and his chest tightened. Evan found himself looking into the shadows for the carcasses of seagulls.

But the grass and the drive were empty. He stepped up the walk and took a deep breath before pulling out his keys and unlocking the front door. He wondered if Sarah were home yet; he hoped so, because if she weren't . . . well . . . he might be cleaning up after her at two A.M. after she upchucked the contents of last call in their bed. And he wasn't sure he could handle that tonight.

The living room was still as he kicked off his shoes, grabbing at the door frame for balance. The house felt empty, and Evan groaned inwardly. He knew he'd been out too late himself, and if Sarah weren't home . . .

He stepped into the kitchen and noted the time on the microwave. 12:43. Wherever she was, she ought to be calling it a night soon, he supposed. He walked down the hall toward their bedroom, pausing briefly to look into the empty hole he'd made of Josh's room . . . God . . . just this morning. He could almost see the ghosts of the posters and plaques and CDs and crap that had remained untouched for over a year until today.

Time for a change, he thought. Way past time for a change.

Evan stripped off his shirt and threw it in the direction of the hamper as he walked through the bedroom on his way to the bath. Barely blinking back sleep, he pulled up the toilet seat and let go a seemingly endless stream before flushing and then clumsily squeezing toothpaste onto the brush that didn't want to stand still in his hand.

Finally, after some of the beer had been expunged from his mouth, he dropped his jeans and underwear, and exited the bathroom, tossing the pants in the direction of his shirt. He slipped beneath the covers of the bed, and fully expected the room to spin into motion as soon as he lay back and stopped moving himself.

The pillow felt amazing beneath his head, but as he slipped his feet in and around beneath the sheets, he felt something cold and wet against his knee. "What the hell," he murmured, and reached down with his hand to explore the wet spot. It was cold and *very* wet . . . and he could feel small bits of . . . something . . . in the midst of the damp.

Evan reached out of the bed and turned on the lamp on the end table. Then he threw back the covers and looked at the mattress.

The sheets were definitely wet—a dark stain covered

the half of the bed where Sarah normally slept, and small bits of something silver glittered in the dull yellow light. He leaned closer and picked one up with his fingertips, holding it closer to the light.

A fish scale.

"Huh?" he said to himself.

Something moved in the bathroom, and Evan looked up, pulling the sheets up instinctively to cover himself. "Who's there?"

From the shadows of the bathroom he saw a hint of movement, and then she stepped out into the warm glow of the room, skin glimmering with beads of water.

Ligeia.

"You!" Evan gasped. "What are you doing here?"

She smiled, thinly, and brushed a wet strand of black hair from her face with her hand. "I've been waiting for you to come home," she whispered. "You didn't come to the beach, so I came to you. You're late, you know."

"I was out with a friend . . ." he began to explain, and then stopped himself. "You can't be here," he said. "My wife will be home soon, you have to go."

"I *am* your wife now," Ligeia said, stepping to the bed. Evan's eyes were drawn to the lush promise of her breasts, swaying just inches from his chest, and he gulped involuntarily, trying to swallow his desire and remember his anger. His head buzzed with alcohol and desire and he couldn't stop looking at her, here in his own place, here where for the first time, he could truly take her in his own bed, comfortably intimate, as if she *were* his wife.

She leaned to kiss him, and he almost gave in. But just as her lips brushed his, Evan put his hands on her shoulders and pushed her away. "I can't," he began.

"I am the mother of your child," Ligeia whispered. "You can't deny me this. I've been lonely for too long."

With that, she began to sing, a low, sensual purr of a melody that sent a shiver up Evan's spine. From the first note he felt his resolve slip, as his desire visibly grew. Ligeia dipped her head, encouraging him to look into her eyes, as her fingers slipped up his arms, soft and tentative, begging for him not to deny her.

In the back of his mind, a voice was screaming that he had to get rid of her; Sarah would be home any minute. The last thing he wanted was for her to find him in their bedroom, naked, with an equally nude goddess of a woman. That would end everything between them, no second chances. "Make her leave," the voice pleaded, reminding him that he also needed to strip the bed and clean the sheets before Sarah returned.

But Ligeia's song rippled and moved like honey over his heart, slowly smothering the voice of caution, and drawing out instead the beast inside. The memories of the ecstasy of their sex on the beach overcame him, and he couldn't say no, regardless of the consequence. His mind fogged as his cock ached—physically, throbbingly ached—to be inside her. "Just this last time," another voice whispered in the depths of her song. "Just once here, in your own bed."

Evan's breathing turned involuntarily to panting, as his legs trembled with the force of the need he felt. Now Ligeia's song trilled higher—angelic and ethereal, into the clouds, and she pressed his arms with her elbows down, off her shoulders to hold her waist. "Oh God," he gasped, as his hands slipped along the cool, wet curves of her body. He couldn't stop, but instead drew her tight to him, pressing his need against her groin and cupping her ass in his hands, kneading her, needing her . . .

In seconds she was straddling him on the bed, and Evan blinked and cried at the emotions and sensation.

With every movement of her hips he felt an electricity punch through his balls and up into his belly. She didn't only touch him with her body, she seemed to seep through his pores to touch his very soul. The room dissolved into a haze and all he could see, all he cared about, was Ligeia. He would give up his house, his job, his wife, everything, for one more moment with her. Evan lost himself in the grinding, sinuous rhythm of their sex, running his palms from the smooth point of their union up across her belly and breasts and then back down her ribs. The velvet of her skin amazed him. He couldn't touch her enough.

She never took her eyes from his. She never stopped with her gentle, heavenly song, the soft, whispery music flying above and embracing them invisibly like an angel, and then dipping into the dark, sensual depths of wicked hell to ripple at the back of his spine like a train rumble, almost beyond the range of hearing. She never stopped singing, and Evan never stopped thrusting, struggling with all of his being to draw himself out of his own body to live completely in hers. The golden flecks in her eyes hypnotized him and he felt himself crying inside at her beauty. He needed her.

Evan could feel her rhythm increasing, and her song grew more and more violent, a hissing, animal hunger dripping from every note. He knew she was close, and his own moment threatened to crest.

"Oh God, I want you, Ligeia," he moaned. "I want all of you."

"I . . . am . . . yours . . . forever," she cried, and pounded her body to his. Evan screamed, oblivious to everything, and closed his eyes. As the waves of orgasm slowed, he gazed into her dark eyes and smiled, seeing her in a different light as the moment began to pass.

Now he saw that her face wasn't quite so full and perfect, as he'd imagined just moments before. She still was beautiful in her postcoital exhaustion. Black rings of hair caught and stuck to her cheeks, and perspiration beaded on her forehead, and the long tip of her nose.

He ran his hands down her waist and noticed that she didn't feel quite so silken smooth now. There were scars and bumps on her flesh, just as there were with any woman. She was no perfect Venus, regardless of the allure of her song and her desire. *Still* . . . he took a deep breath, trying to calm the pounding of his heart. Still, he realized, he wanted her with all of his heart. He loved Sarah, but this, this . . . amazing woman was something unlike any he'd ever been with. He wanted to continue to explore her mysteries. He wanted to know more about her desires. He wanted to know why she'd chosen him.

Ligeia smiled and brushed her lips over his, playfully nipping at his lips with her teeth. His hands slipped across her butt again and shook her a little, shifting his diminishing but still turgid flesh inside her. She giggled girlishly with her tongue still in his mouth, and his hands continued to her thighs, and then stopped.

Just below the cusp of her ass, her skin turned cold, brittle. For a moment, he imagined she was wearing thigh-high boots. But then his memory returned. She'd been fully nude when she'd pressed him to the sheets.

His fingers explored and slipped up and down over the divide of her flesh. Ligeia's legs melded from hot skin, with an impossibly soft down of hair to an unyielding, cold span of . . . scales?

"What is that?" he asked, pushing her off him enough to stare down between their bodies to look at her legs.

He gasped. Her thighs glittered silver-blue in the low light of the bedroom, and as she slowly moved one knee up his leg, he saw that her whole thigh and calf were encased in scales. Her foot ended, not in toes, but in the wispy, translucent webbing of fins. As his eyes registered the reality of her alienness, she moved her legs against him, slipping her scales up his leg and then pulling them down to catch him with a sandpapery hint of abrasion.

"This is who I am," Ligeia whispered in his ear. "This is what your child will be. This is what you can be, if you'll only come with me tonight."

The chill that suddenly caught the perspiration on Evan's skin had little to do with the room temperature. He'd laughed at Bill's fantastic stories, even when they rang true. He'd refused to consider whether he believed in them, though in the back of his head, he supposed he had begun to believe regardless of his cynicism. But now . . .

He rolled away from her, rejecting the strange sensual touch of her fish legs.

"You didn't look like this before," he complained.

"I didn't let you see," she whispered, and then let her voice trail into a humming note of song. She breathed notes of slow desire into the air between them and Evan felt his abhorrence instantly slip. At the same time, her face seemed to shine with a fleshier, erotic fullness, and her breasts suddenly looked fuller, and her legs . . . were pale moonlight flesh, creamy womanhood begging for a man to kiss them, inch by inch to where . . .

Evan blinked. "What are you doing to me?" he cried.

He shook his head and Ligeia stopped singing. Her voice grew hard. "I can be whatever you want me to be," she said. "Whatever you need. But you have to agree. You have to say you'll be mine. I can make you happy forever, I promise you that."

"I have a wife," he protested. "I need to make her happy." He shook his head again, and her legs again looked alien; silver-scaled nylons below a pale body that seemed to have shrunk from the fertile woman who had just mounted him with the foggy lens of dream porno. "She'll be home soon," he said, the realization blooming like ice in his bowels. "You can't be here."

"She won't be coming home again," Ligeia said. Her eyes held his, unblinking. The flecks of gold in the depths of brown suddenly struck Evan as fishlike. And cold. "I am your wife now. I will give you back the child that you've lost. Maybe even a son."

"No, you can't replace Josh," Evan exclaimed, pushing himself from the dampness of the bed. He realized suddenly that the room reeked of fish. He could feel his cock shriveling as the smell crept inside him along with the knowledge of what he'd just lain with. A woman who wasn't human. Something of the sea. Something that could change shape. Something untrue.

"You aren't my wife," he insisted.

"The woman who used to live here will not be coming home again," Ligeia said, and stood up on the opposite side of the bed from him. She stepped to the edge of the halo of their dim bedside lamp, scales shimmering weirdly as she walked around the foot of the bed to approach him again. She seemed smaller than he remembered, more wiry. More pointy and . . . somehow . . . coldly, immorally cruel.

The import of her words finally sunk in, and Evan asked, "What do you mean?" His heart suddenly spasmed as he thought of the wet spot in his bed, the wet spot that had been there before he'd gotten into bed. "What did you do to Sarah?"

Ligeia put her arms out, and smiled with a flash of white in the dark room. Her teeth looked sharp, shark-like in the shadows. "Come here, darling," she whispered.

"I'll sing for you and everything will be all right, forever and ever."

With that, her words slipped into the wrenching crescendo of a love song. The first notes sent a shimmer of lethargy up Evan's back, but this time he was mentally prepared.

"Oh no!" he yelled, and sprinted to the bedroom door, continuing to yell. "No no no no no!" he called out, struggling to blot out the sound of the Siren's call from his ears. He fumbled with the sliding glass door latch in the kitchen as her song followed closely behind him, and Evan's legs seemed to waver and fold like jelly. He pulled himself up against the door and pushed it open, falling out into the yard. He didn't care that he was naked, he bolted toward the compost pile, intending to race through the Bentons' yard to the street beyond.

He stumbled forward a few steps but didn't quite make it to the ground where dozens of seagulls lay freshly interred. Instead, something hard slammed into the back of his head, and he went down. He had a faint glimpse of a white rock and two eyes glinting yellow in the moonlight and teeth as sharp as a shark's before the night overtook him, and Evan slipped away with an angry song coiling around his neck like an invisible noose. For a split second he saw Sarah's face superimposed over the feral edges of Ligeia's and his true heart cried and struggled to ask the Siren, "What did you do?" But his lips never quite managed to open before the night came down.

CHAPTER THIRTY-THREE

She swam in a dark blue ocean. She didn't worry about breath; somehow it didn't seem necessary. But there was urgency in her tread. Vicky kicked hard with her feet and pushed with her hands. She needed to find its home. It was important that she got there before it knew she was near. The dark timbers of the old shipwreck came slowly into view amid the murky turquoise of the depths of the sea. This was the place, she knew in her heart. Looking behind her, she only saw the faint disturbance in the water left by her feet. Vicky kicked harder and swam toward the old wreck. Evan needed her.

The deck of the old wreck was black with age and dark green with the anchors of algae and seaweed that trailed and shivered in the waves like a mirage. Vicky swam past the old captain's wheel, looking for a way inside. Below her, she saw a dark rectangle carved in the rotten boards of the deck, and her eyes lit. Maybe there. She kicked and turned in the sea, darting toward it. But just as she reached the opening into the depths of the ship an explosion pushed her back. A hundred silver shapes leaped from the blackness of the ship's belly to dart past her in the water. Vicky flailed in the waves, struggling to hold her position and avoid being hit by one of the foot-long torpedoes that streamed out of the hidden heart of the old wreck.

Then the school of frenzied silver bullets was past, and Vicky began to move again toward the hole. She nosed in and grabbed the edges of the rotten wood, pulling herself down.

That's when something grabbed her by the hair.

Something yanked.

And yanked hard.

An explosion of bubbles sprayed from Vicky's mouth, and she turned to see the glowing eyes of another woman, one who had fins for ears and fangs for teeth. A woman who pulled her close with a sudden grip on her shoulders.

And it didn't feel like the stranger wanted a welcoming embrace. The creature's mouth opened like a trapdoor, wider than any human should be able to open its jaws. Feral teeth gleamed in the dull light and threatened to fasten like a snake's snap on Vicky's shoulder.

Instead, the psychiatrist kicked with her feet and caught the creature in the chin. "Ha!" she laughed, twisting in the water. She kicked and swam hard toward the surface. Take that.

She didn't get far. Needles of pain lanced into her ribs and Vicky felt her flight cease, as the Siren wrapped its cold body around her like a leaden blanket and dragged her down to the cold muck of the sea bottom. She felt the seaweed twist between her legs, and the heat of teeth breaking the skin of her neck. Just before her, inches out of reach, the old planks of the ship loomed like a wall. All this, she thought, and I'm not going to get inside?

Then the Siren turned her to lie on her back in the mud of the ocean, and smiled. When she opened her mouth, Vicky's heart stopped. Long needle teeth exposed and struck, ripping into the soft flesh of her throat . . .

Vicky Blanchard woke up screaming.

Her body was wreathed in sweat beneath the sheets and she threw them off, kicking the covers down.

"Whoa," she gasped as she realized that she was not underwater, but simply lying in her dark bedroom, in her dark bed, after a dark, weird dream.

She lay there, on her back, smoothing the nightshirt down along her waist with her palms, staring at the ceiling for several minutes, willing her heart to stop pounding, and the heat of her flesh to cool.

Finally, when the sweat turned cold, she pulled the covers back up and stared into the corners of her room. Everything felt strange; the comfort of her home alien and dangerous.

"It was a bad dream," she said aloud, trying to calm herself. "Just a bad dream."

But as she lay there, Vicky knew that it was more than a bad dream. It was a bad worry. More than a worry, really. There was a reason that Vicky had gone into psychiatry; she was more than just a good listener, she could *feel* things. Everyone had always said she was a little psychic—she'd think of someone and twenty seconds later her phone would ring. She always seemed to "have a feeling" just before something happened.

Evan had skipped their appointment this week and, strangely, hadn't returned her voice mail. In the year that she'd known him, he'd never missed an appointment without calling. She had worried for the past couple days that something was wrong, and now it was haunting her sleep. All of Evan's stories about a mysterious woman by the sea, and his friend's taunts that she was really the fabled Siren of Delilah had lodged in her subconscious. Now it was keeping her up.

Vicky shook her head. It was dangerous to get involved with a patient at that level. She'd felt sorry for Evan since the day she'd met him and, for a while, she'd thought they had made progress. But over the past month, as the story of his fantastic infidelity had unraveled in the privileged confines of her office, she'd become uneasy. Maybe they hadn't made any progress at all, she thought. Maybe just the opposite. Now his fear of the ocean had grown into an obsession with a woman supposedly of the ocean. It was a thin excuse for cheating on the woman who Vicky knew needed him more than anything now. Evan's wife had become increasingly unstable over the past year as Vicky felt Evan himself was improving. But maybe nothing she'd concluded was, in fact, true.

Vicky shook away the images of the dream. She knew it was bad to get emotionally attached to a patient. She was supposed to remain detached. Aloof. Objective.

Still. She had gone into this line of work because she cared about people. And after a year of weekly sessions, she cared about Evan.

Vicky took a deep breath and forced away the images of the dark ocean. She would call Evan again on Monday. Everything was okay, she told herself. She was overreacting, and he was probably just busy. Hell, if she chilled out, he'd probably just show up for their regular Wednesday appointment like usual.

But she needed to know something before then.

"I'll call him on Monday," she said to the empty room, and pressed her head into the crease in her pillow, demanding comfort in the place where she should be most comfortable.

"For now," she whispered, "sleep."

CHAPTER THIRTY-FOUR

Evan woke in the dark, held in a tight embrace. A woman's arm wrapped around his back and kept his face pressed against the soft flesh of her chest. He knew immediately it was Ligeia. Evan tried to push away from her, but her grip tightened. He turned his head from the cushion of her breast, and saw something that made his throat close.

Ligeia held him close because . . . they were swimming. She was his lifeline, pulling him through the depths of the ocean, kicking steadily with her feet, and guiding them with strokes of her one free arm.

Evan started to take a breath and then stopped. *My God! How deep are we? I'll drown!* The panic rose like a wave and he pushed away from her with both hands, at the same time kneeing her in the gut.

She let him go, instinctively grabbing at her belly, and Evan kicked away from her. But in seconds he went from escaping to flailing. He had never learned to swim; he had always been too petrified of the water to try. Ligeia's body disappeared into the murk and suddenly Evan was completely aware of the weight of the water. It pressed his chest and he struggled not to take a breath. But he kicked with his feet and he could feel the water's resistance. And somehow, instead of rising to the surface, he didn't seem to be going anywhere. He pushed with his hands and kicked and couldn't seem to coordinate. Instead, the panic owned him, and he clawed with his hands, a spasmodic dogpaddle that succeeded only in stripping the last air from his lungs. He needed to breathe and couldn't stop. No, his brain screamed, but his mouth opened. No, he begged himself, but his lungs took a deep pull of breath. And sucked in seawater.

It went down like salty fire and Evan screamed, only sucking in more water. "Oh my God," he cried out underwater, but no sound emerged.

He kicked and motioned with his arms and took another heave of breath that gagged him fully. His stomach threatened to puke, and he struggled to gain some kind of control. His greatest, deepest fear had come true.

He was going to drown. Just like Josh.

"Oh God," he cried.

Two hands gripped him around the waist, and Ligeia swam up from beneath him until she stared at him, eye to eye. She leaned in and pressed her lips to his. Evan began to push her away; but then he felt the pressure in his lungs disappear. Ligeia wrapped herself around him and Evan coughed, choking out seawater. He couldn't hold his breath though, and opened his mouth to suck it right back in.

Only . . . he sucked in air. What the fuck? Cautiously he breathed in again, and he felt his lungs fill with warm, wonderful oxygen. *Impossible.*

"Stay with me," Ligeia said. "I'll take care of you." He could hear her inside his head, under the water. *Impossible!*

"How can I hear you?" he asked, feeling the water fill his mouth as he tried to speak. He couldn't hear his own voice, but she answered him.

"I am *in* you," she answered. "I always have been. I've never spoken a word to you out loud."

Evan didn't think, but tried to speak again through the ocean. Ligeia put a finger to his lips halfway through his sentence as he tried to say, "But we've talked, I heard you . . ."

She shook her head at him, and pressed her forehead to his. "I've talked to you inside your mind. You never had any reason to question it."

Ligeia ran her hand up and down his chest, and Evan could feel the pain and burn of the saltwater in his lungs dissolve with her touch. "With me, you can breathe beneath the waves," she said. "And if you speak in your head, I will hear you, if you're close. We are mated."

She put an arm around his waist and kicked out with her feet, while pushing the ocean aside with one hand. "Let's go home," she said. Evan heard the happy lilt in her voice, and struggled to grasp how she could be talking in his head; her voice seemed so real. So . . . musical and beautiful. He turned her words around and around in his head, trying to fathom how they could sound like . . . sound, but were, in fact, words never spoken.

He let her guide him through the water; what choice did he have—he had already proven that he would drown without her help. Quickly.

As they moved through the waves, the occasional fish darted out of their way in fright. Evan could feel the gentle roll and swell of the current push them gently one direction, while Ligeia dragged him through the invisible wall of water in the opposite.

Something loomed ahead—a dark, shadowy hulk of rock or something; Ligeia seemed to be angling them toward it, and Evan strained to see.

It was an old shipwreck, he realized. The front beams of an old hull curved up and cut into the water like crossing scythes from out of the mud of the ocean floor. The wood that once had held out the water from the space beneath the ship's skeletal beams had rotted away, and Evan could see through the ship to the black water beyond. The ship lay on its side, and Ligeia swam toward a blacker spot in the dark boards that remained of its hull. A school of long, ghostly silver fish swam in a slow zigzag as Ligeia approached the breach in the ship's hull. Then they broke apart like a shower of silver bullets, each speeding in its own deadly course away from them. They opened the way to her.

Ligeia swam into the dark cave of the ship, and Evan held fast to her; a spectator in a surreal episode of some *National Geographic* undersea explorers show. Only, when they filmed those, they used spotlights. Evan strained to see through the underwater night, and caught glimpses of fish slipping just into and out of sight. He could just make out the rotted hull of the ship beneath them. The boards were covered in mud; the timber only periodically peeking through the buildup of a hundred years of surf debris.

Ligeia kicked and dragged Evan through the water just above the sunken floor of the ship. Lying on the mud beneath them, Evan saw the white of bones amid a tangle of sea fronds. His blood chilled. Was it the remains of one of the wreck's crew, left here who knew how many decades ago to be eaten by the fish? To lie here, forever, never to be properly buried and laid to rest by his family? *Like Josh*, Evan's inner voice whispered.

They passed over the ribs of the body, and then Evan saw another set, just barely risen above the silt. The skull lay faceup in the mud, the empty black holes of eye sockets stared at Evan like an accusation. Or a warning.

Another member of the crew, Evan supposed. And then the skeleton was past, and Evan saw the bones of a hand just beyond. And another rib cage. And another. Ligeia swam over an underwater cairn; the jumble and stacks of bones was amazing. Evan swore under his breath as he tried to count the skeletons and lost track at nineteen. There were too many, and the bodies had apparently been stacked on top of one another, three and four deep in some cases. They had decomposed and folded in, one upon and within the other, so it was impossible to tell where one body ended and another began. Only one thing was clear—there were a lot of bodies abandoned down here!

Then he saw one body that still had a rope of black hair attached to a clump of withered flesh on its skull. And just beyond that, fingers of bone pointed up toward the ceiling. While the fingertips were white, Evan could see the patchy remains of flesh still stuck to the emaciated half-eaten corpse's arm bones.

A thick twist of seaweed shivered in the water ahead of them, but as Ligeia swam through it, Evan saw a whole new crop of bodies stacked in various states of decomposition. Those at the bottom of the pile were nothing more than bones. But the bodies stacked at the top of the watery graveyard still had skin on those bones. As they swam over one, Evan could have sworn he saw a viscous cloud of blood disperse like smoke from the corpse's chest.

"Ligeia, who are all these people?" he asked finally.

The Siren didn't answer.

She swam instead farther into the depths of the ship, and finally entered a room with a half dozen bunks that pointed out from the side of the sunken ship like room dividers; because the *side* of the ship was now its floor. She swam around one of the old bunks and in the faint light that leached in from the holes in the hull, Evan could just make out a mess of tangled green sheets and blankets piled in the crook of the bunk in what once had been the ship's starboard hull. She laid him down on the rumpled, watery cushion, and gently pressed herself on top of him. Her eyes bored into his as she held him there, at the bottom of the ocean, at last in her own bed.

"Now you are home," she said. Evan swore that her voice seemed to come from all around him, not from inside.

Evan shook his head to protest, but then there was a sound so beautiful, so warm, that his words stopped before he could finish thinking them. Her music rang again in his head, and she sang of undying, unending love. Of beauty and sadness. Of days that stretched into months and years and centuries of loneliness. And then her song turned to the baser strut of lust, and Evan felt himself instantly respond. Ligeia straddled him and wrapped algae-slick sheets around them as she sucked his tongue into her mouth with the brine.

In his mind, her song changed from lust to selfishness, and seemed to whisper "mine, mine, mine."

And true to her music, it seemed as if she would never let go. When at last she finished with him, Evan had spent himself three times, and his waist ached with the effort, though she had done nearly all of the work. Her sweet soprano whispered a lullaby to him then, and it only took seconds before Evan closed his eyes and accepted the darkness that permeated the old crew quarters into his mind. He slept. And in the soundless, slow current of the bay, ironically, he snored.

Shadows cloaked the room where Evan woke. Shadows and strange gravity. He felt his arms move, almost of their own accord. His body felt weak and heavy at the same time. Fluid and anchored. He knew he'd drank a lot with Bill, but he didn't think he'd toasted himself this bad. But then the fleeting memory of making love to Ligeia in his own bed returned in a flash, and the memory of running from her through his backyard flashed across his mind as well and of bodies at the bottom of an old shipwreck and Ligeia just above him in the tangled sheets of her watery bed . . .

Crap. Evan turned his head and his eyes widened. He was definitely not in his bedroom. What he saw was impossible.

The air loomed dark and thick. Around him, shadows covered everything in a dark light, but the more Evan stared, the more he could make out. And what he made out was . . . that he was, indeed, in a bed of sorts—a rumple of silken fabric cascaded beneath him, and covered his legs and waist. Just out of his reach stretched a wall of dark wooden planks, ascending to a ceiling of equally dark and stained corroded wood.

Everything seemed dark, cloaked in the deepest shadows of night. Evan struggled to make out more details of the room where he awoke, but all he could seem to see were the wooden planks of the wall and the sheets that wound around his legs. And . . . the legs of Ligeia, he realized.

Next to him, hidden in the murk of the room, he followed the curve of a pale thigh up past an indented waist and broadened breast to her thin, aristocratic face.

Her eyes were closed, but it was she. And it was she as he had seen her in his own bed not so long ago. Without the glamour and perfection she normally showed him. Her face and nose looked thin and her belly was covered with tiny but obvious white slashes; scars perhaps from fights that he never wanted to know about.

Evan followed the lines on her belly up the small

swell of her chest. He smiled, briefly, at the rounded lush flesh he'd kissed numerous times over the past month or two, but here, now, it didn't seem quite as enticing as before. And the flesh of her neck looked . . . not "old" per se . . . but . . . weathered. He remembered her skin being perfect—smooth and creamy white. Yet, as he lay here in this strange bed with her and stared, he realized that she was not *all that*.

He reached out a hand to touch her cheek, and saw the hair of his arm pull back, as if in a wind tunnel. And yet, he felt nothing. His arm moved heavily through the . . .

It finally hit him again as he looked beyond Ligeia, and saw the old wooden bunk hung from the side of the wall and the strangely blurred vantage between here and there. He wasn't here with Ligeia in her *house*, with some jealous husband potentially lurking outside. He was here with her in her real home. A home that just so happened to be underwater.

How was he able to be here? Evan wondered, his eyes widening at the realization. His heart threatened to pound in machine-gun panic. He opened his mouth to gasp for air, but felt the cold of water slip inside, and forced it closed again. Still, somehow he breathed as he lay beside her, in this place where no man should be able to breathe.

He was *under*water. The very idea of that sent something shooting into Evan's nerves that felt a lot like ice, only colder. He was petrified.

Water. *All around him.* For a second he convinced himself that he was hallucinating; she had slipped him some kind of drug, and everything just seemed slow and waterlogged. That would explain the whole dream sequence of her talking in his head too, he thought. Evan reached out and tried to swish his hand through the "air," but his rationalization was fractured. It was not air and he was not drugged. No way. He slipped out carefully, slowly from beneath the twisted, algae-stained sheets that Ligeia dozed beneath and looked around the room. Evan followed the faint light that filtered in from the moon above the waves outside out of the room. Moving felt strange; kind of like walking through foam. Everything resisted him, yet, he *could* move through it. As he slipped through the doorway at the far end of the room, Ligeia still slept, and he shifted his feet carefully along the mud-slick floor, hoping not to do anything to wake her. Evan guessed that she wouldn't allow him to leave. After the near-drowning incident last night, he wasn't sure he *could* leave. Still . . . he had to try. So far he could still breathe.

Evan pushed his way through the water and walked slowly down the dark deck of the old ship. He realized that this was very likely the same ship that Bill had seen while diving off the point last month.

He tiptoed slowly away from Ligeia in a surreal slow motion. He didn't understand how he was able to breathe, and the panic of being under the water was making him so upset he wanted to collapse to the ground and cry. But Evan forced himself to hold it together, and to move.

Move was the name of the game. Sometimes life—and the fear of its loss—trumped all other fears. He *had* to get out of here and get home. He had to help Sarah, who had no doubt returned home by now, and was wondering where he was.

He stepped along the deck and looked out through holes in the hull of the ship to an ocean sky; dark shadows rippled and surrounded him, but still he walked, guiding his way by following the line of the decayed planks. They led him to something that looked like an old kitchen, with plates and bowls stacked willy-nilly on a counter, seaweed wavering out of them in the slow movement of the water, as if cultivated in the old bowls like potted plants. A handful of chairs lay on the floor near toppled square tables. Evan walked past these, and that's when he saw the line of bodies.

He had passed over them quickly last night, and the darkness of midnight dozens of feet below the waves had not helped illuminate them well. But now, somewhere above them, dawn was breaking, and the faint light streamed in stronger.

Now he could see the flesh that hung off the bodies and fluttered in the softly oscillating current like so much tissue paper. Evan stepped closer and could see the face of one body—a man. A fuzz of blue-black stubble shadowed his jaw all the way to the ragged hole gored into his neck and shoulder. Evan stared at the violated flesh, wondering what had eaten its way into this man. Had he been attacked by a shark and stacked here by Ligeia for burial? Or had she placed him here and he had been eaten by fish?

Evan refused to think of the obvious.

Refused until it was forced in his face. He walked past the dead man and the moldering bones stacked beneath him to see the nude, gored body of a woman. Her belly had been opened and emptied; Evan could see the yellow bone of her spine through the skin that fluttered just past the edge of her rib cage. Her neck was also mostly gone, and her eyes had been eaten out. She stared with sightless, bloodless pits toward the sun she would never see again.

Evan shivered and stepped past her to see another man's corpse, also half eaten. He gulped at the fleshy hole where the man's sex had once protruded; a tunnel of rippled, faintly pinkish meat ascended beneath the man's hairy skin and met the emptiness that had been dug out of his belly. The body was missing its lips among other things, and Evan had to look away. The association was too jarring.

He looked away to the next in the line of bodies. There he saw the long, curved, still-sexy thighs and still-intact belly and still-desirable breasts and slightly tired cheeks and eyes of a woman he knew more intimately perhaps than he knew himself.

He looked at Sarah.

"Nooooo!" he cried, and tasted the salt of the ocean, but heard none of his scream. Evan pulled her up from the body she lay on, and cradled her in his arms. She was absolutely, unquestionably dead.

His Sarah was dead.

Just as surely as he had doomed his son, his weakness had killed his wife. Evan cried tears that slipped away in the ocean unseen. Her lips were cold, but still he kissed them and hugged her limp body to his chest. His breath came in huge, shivering gasps as he spent his grief soundlessly beneath the surface of his greatest enemy. The ocean had taken everything he had ever loved.

He looked behind him into the dark hole of the ship, where somewhere within, Ligeia still slept. Evan knew he had to leave fast, now, before she woke. Perhaps his cries had already roused her. He carried Sarah past the rotted boards that remained of the ship's outer hull, and set foot on the soft, sucking mud of the true sea bottom. He stepped twice and then tried to mimic Ligeia's form when she had carried him here. He hooked one arm around the body of his wife and kicked his feet off the bottom, swatting at the water with his free hand. He rose a bit from the bottom, but was off balance. He began to lose his grip on Sarah, and then something worse happened.

The weight of the water returned.

Evan shifted to balance Sarah but as he took a breath, he also took in water. He choked, and looked back toward the wreck a few feet away.

Shit! He could feel the "spell" of Ligeia waning fast. Perhaps it was because he had gone too far from her. A convenient—and effective—leash. Or perhaps she had woken and cut the cord herself to stop him from escaping.

Either way, he had to move. In his mind he apologized to Sarah and brushed his lips to hers as he laid her down on the sea bottom. *I'll come back for you*, he promised silently. *But I need to get help.*

The water trickled down his throat and Evan forced himself to stop breathing. He kicked his feet and pushed off with his arms, now too angry and determined to let the fear stop him. Instead of flailing in a panic, Evan swam, truly swam, for the first time in his life. He pushed toward the surface like a cork, and almost made it before he couldn't hold his breath anymore. He took in a big, horrible gulp of water and almost lost his tread with the shock, but then his head broke the surface, and Evan spit out the sea and heaved a wet, sputtering breath of air as he blinked away the water and took in his surroundings. The rocky black finger of the point was just to his right, and the sun hung just beyond on the horizon, a deep orange ball of dawn that would soon be burning hot with the warmth of morning in the late summer.

Evan imagined Ligeia's hands grabbing his feet to pull him down beneath the waves, and before his fear of the water could argue that he couldn't swim, he *was* swimming, desperately stroking toward the black rock and the line of warbling white seagulls that lined its top.

The water was calm and it only took Evan a couple minutes of floundering in raw determination before his hand reached out to touch the edge of a boulder covered in algae hair. The green strands trailed through the water like the hair of a corpse beneath the waves.

Evan pulled himself up and out of the water, scrambling over the sharp points of a jumble of rocks to reach the flat ledge. His teeth chattered in the morning breeze as he stood naked and wet, finally, at the edge of the "lookout" spot on the point.

Evan stared out at where he'd been, where Sarah lay dead, beneath the ocean. He began to cry again, but then his heart jumped when a whitecap frothed just a few yards away. For a second, he thought it was Ligeia's hand breaking the surface.

No time for tears, he pledged, and threaded his way down the path toward the beach. He needed to get away from here before she did come for him. He needed to get home, even if it was only for one last time.

Minutes later, Evan streaked along the beach. He prayed none of his neighbors were up having coffee and looking out their windows toward the waves.

But then again, at this point, he really didn't care. He needed help; he had another fish to fry. A really big, deadly fish.

A Siren.

CHAPTER THIRTY-FIVE

June 11, 1887, 12:23 A.M.

The storm pushed the *Lady Luck* across its surface like a bit of hollow driftwood. She rocked dangerously to starboard and then to lee, and Captain Buckley held the wheel, struggling to roll with the troughs and then turn his rudder in to catch the current to come up the other side without letting their keel break water and capsize the ship. Jensen and he took turns at the wheel; after a half hour or more of pulling and rolling the wheel, a man needed a break. Their knuckles gleamed white on the dark, wet wooden wheel as they rode out the storm.

"I'm going below for a bit, Captain," Jensen announced, and Buckley showed his agreement with a nod. His eyes never left the gray of the tossing waves and the white of their teeth. The ocean was a giant mouth to them now, doing everything it could to swallow the ship whole.

Once Jensen had slipped down the ladder, Buckley's thoughts turned to Ligeia. He realized that he'd been on the deck all night, even when Jensen held the wheel. It was a captain's job to guide them through the storm and he'd been reticent to relinquish his post, even if he didn't hold the rudder. But now he wondered how Ligeia fared through this storm. He'd left her chained to his bunk, alone in the dark. That had been hours ago. A pang of conscience struck him, as he pictured her afraid and trapped in that dark place. Perhaps she was crying. Women got emotional that way when afraid. Not that he'd ever really seen her scared. Or emotional.

An image came to mind of her lifting her blood-spattered face from the crook of Rogers's neck, sharp teeth stained in his crewman's life. It was hard to imagine that face bawling with fear. Buckley smiled, but then thought of another moment with Ligeia, this one when he had first bought her during their last docking in Delilah and brought her on board the ship. He had shown her the cabin, and told her to sit on the bunk as he opened his case to retrieve the bindings that he had purchased from her previous owner. The man had been very insistent that Buckley never remove the bindings—or the gag. "She only needs to sing you one love song and you'll be through," the jittery little Greek had said, over and over again. The man kept cotton in his ears, and so the whole time they were brokering the deal for the fine body of Ligeia, Buckley had needed to almost shout. No matter how much Buckley asked him to remove the cotton, the man refused.

"If you value your life, you will keep her mouth sealed and your ears plugged," the little man said.

Naturally, the first thing Buckley had done was to un-gag the beautiful girl's mouth when he got her back to the hotel. As soon as he had, the girl had begun to sing, but Buckley ignored the sound. He'd always been tone-deaf, and music meant nothing to him. Instead, he let her moan out her little ditty as he stripped off his shirt and pants, and then shoved her down in the bed, finally stilling her song with the force of his tongue.

He saw no danger in her music. Not until he saw her kill a man drawn to her song later that same night.

When he brought her on board the ship and showed her the bindings, she shook her head quickly, her eyes widening in panic. She had not said a word to him since he'd bought her, but now her mouth began to move quickly. Still, she didn't speak, but sang to him.

"I'm sure it's a very nice tune," Buckley said, pinning her arms above her head with the shackles. "But save your breath."

He saw the fear grow in her eyes as he straddled her, and grinned. His teeth held no humor. From what the Greek had said, and from what he'd witnessed with his own eyes, most men swooned at her song, and his complete dismissal of it seemed to bother her more than being tied. She sang louder and pushed her voice into all sorts of shenanigans. Buckley let her go on for a bit, before pulling out the gag and holding it above her mouth. "Enough already," he said.

She was quiet for the next few minutes, as he ran calloused hands over her curves with the rough attention of a man far more used to hauling in nets and managing a band of roughneck men than showing softness to a woman. Her face remained still as stone through most of the act, but as he announced his culmination, a flicker of some pained emotion shadowed Ligeia's face. After he rolled away from her, Buckley saw the trail of a tear down the soft skin of her cheek.

He wiped it off with a thick finger. "Don't worry, girl, it won't be so bad. I won't break ya. And I'll make sure you're well fed. Once we get to know each other, I bet you'll enjoy it."

Buckley shook his head as he pulled the wheel hard to starboard. Even after seeing her attack and kill the man who'd burst into their hotel room the first night he'd owned her, Buckley'd never expected that the term *well-fed* to the girl would mean the blood of his crew. But by the time she had gotten a hold of one of them, Buckley was too enamored of her hips to give her up. He should have thrown her overboard when her mouth had first swallowed the blood of one of his men, but, instead, he'd become her cleanup man, wrapping the bodies of his former crew in sheets and throwing them overboard when she'd eaten her fill.

Over those first couple weeks at sea, Ligeia seemed to grow used to him, and after a few desperate attempts to sing to him, she had given up that gambit. He took care of her needs, and she took care of his. They may rarely have talked but they had an understanding. What words needed to be spoken? Now, she even spoke to him once in a while when he removed the gag to allow her to feed.

Now, in the midst of the storm, he thought back to that lone tear he'd brushed from her face during their first days together, and felt guilty for stranding her below without any communication about what was going on topside. He pledged to go down and talk to her, reassure her, as soon as Jensen returned. He could leave the deck for a few minutes.

He probably ought to check on the hold as well. He prayed that the violent troughs and turns hadn't pulled loose any of the crates of their cargo, or this was going to go from being a very profitable trip to an expensive one. He'd sailed down the Mexican coast farther than usual this time to pick up what was reportedly the finest run of tequila ever produced, along with his usual run of rum. He'd paid handsomely for it, and intended to charge handsomely on the other side, when he reached Delilah. The port chief had buyers lined up for the most expensive spirits, though their identities were never divulged. Delilah served as the clearinghouse for the underground duty-free liquor-import business, and Buckley had no doubt that he could double his money on this hold.

Assuming he could get it to shore.

CHAPTER THIRTY-SIX

Bill's house was still dark inside when Evan pulled up in front with a screech akin to a getaway car on point for a bank robbery. He left the engine running and the driver's door open as he raced up the walk of the small green-sided ranch. He pounded a fist on the flimsy aluminum of the screen door, but then, impatient, threw open the outer door and rapped on the wooden one inside.

It still took a few minutes for a light to finally click on within and the inner door to crack open. When Bill's unshaven face peered sleepily out, his friend asked, "What the hell's going on, man? It's five in the morning!" Bill rubbed a fist in one eye and yawned.

"Five twenty," Evan answered. "Listen, I need to borrow your scuba equipment. Can you show me how to use it really quick?"

Bill choked on a laugh. "You, the guy petrified of water who can't swim, no—who can't even step in the ocean . . . you are going to scuba dive? Have you lost your mind?"

Evan shook his head. Bill saw the look in his friend's eyes and his grin disappeared. "What's happened?"

Evan choked on three of the hardest words he'd ever said in his life. "She's killed Sarah."

Bill's jaw dropped. "Shit. You're sure? I mean, you're sure Sarah is dead?"

"I saw her body at the bottom of the bay," Evan said.

"Her neck was torn out. And she wasn't the only one down there."

His friend's face blanched. "Turn off your car and come inside," Bill directed. "I'll make coffee. I want to hear the whole story before we do anything."

"Not we," Evan said. "She's too dangerous, and this is all my fault. My problem. I have to take care of it."

"Yeah, whatever. Friends don't let friends scuba dive after deadly Sirens alone. *If* I loan you my equipment, I'm going with you."

Evan started to argue but then thought better of it. One problem at a time. He retrieved his car keys and then let himself into the house.

Bill ground the beans and poured the water into the coffeemaker before returning to sit across from Evan, who nervously moved the pepper shaker around and around the salt in a slow orbit. After the fifth scraping, clinking turn, Bill put his hand on the shakers to still them.

"Start at the beginning."

Evan stared up at the ceiling and took a breath. When he met Bill's gaze again, he talked fast, his voice a monotone. "She was waiting for me in the house last night. I thought Sarah was still out and I was alone, but then she came out of the bathroom. She was still wet. I think she killed Sarah and then just laid there in the bath, waiting for me to come home."

"The bed would have been a more traditional choice," Bill observed.

"She apparently had been waiting there before," Evan said. "The sheets were wet and there were scales all over them. I had just gotten into bed and found that out when she came for me."

"Scales?" Bill asked. "What, like fish scales? Did she make some sushi there or something?"

"The scales were hers," Evan said. "Tonight she let me see her true form."

Bill's eyes widened. "Then . . . she really is the Siren?"

"Haven't you been trying to tell me that all along?" Evan's laugh was bitter. "I'm the one who wouldn't believe you."

Bill took a slurp of his coffee. He kept nodding to himself, processing it all. Finally, he said, "Let's go downstairs. I've got an extra suit you can use, but I need to show you how."

A couple hours and many dials, tubes and explanations later, Bill and Evan climbed back up the stairs to the kitchen. Evan sank into a chair, and ran his hand through hair rank with sweat and saltwater. He needed a shower. And sleep.

"Here, drink this," Bill said, turning from the fridge with an Anchor Steam in his hand.

Evan laughed. "It's like seven o'clock in the morning!"

"Yeah, well, we've got the whole day to kill."

"What are you talking about? You've showed me everything you can with the equipment. We can pack it up and go."

"Evan—Sarah is dead."

Evan blinked at the sting of that sentence. It felt as if Bill had slapped him.

His friend nodded.

"Then what you want to do is retrieve a body. How do you expect to explain to the police that you went scuba diving after a lifetime of being petrified of the water, AND that you just happened to learn to scuba dive on the same day that you dredged up your wife's recently murdered body from the ocean?"

"But we can't just leave her . . ."

"We're not going to leave her. But we can't go walking out of the ocean with her body in broad daylight either. This has to be played right. We'll get Sarah. We'll get your revenge. But not during the day."

Bill took a long swig of his own beer, and then belched. "Tonight."

CHAPTER THIRTY-SEVEN

June 11, 1887, 12:51 A.M.

Captain Buckley couldn't wait anymore. He didn't know what the hell his crew was up to down there, but apparently none of them were ever going to return to relieve him. He spit a wad of anger on the deck and shook his head in disgust. Damn louts. The rain was coming down sideways in the dark, and no slicker was going to keep out its cold fingers. His spine trembled with the icy cold and his hands looked frozen in their white-fisted hold on the wheel. The discomfort was made worse because it was something of a pointless hold. With the sails down and the storm in full swing, there wasn't much steering a wheelman was going to be able to do anyway; he simply tried to keep the ship moving with the waves instead of against the troughs. But for a few minutes, it wouldn't really matter if anyone was at the wheel.

Buckley rescued a twine of rope from the wheelhouse, wound one end of it around a spoke of the wheel and lashed the steering wheel to a beam. He grasped the wheel and tried to push it up and down; the thing barely budged. Nodding at the job, he stepped across the slick deck to the shaft leading down to the crew's quarters and holds. Time to get some explanations.

* * *

Belowdecks was quiet; or as quiet as could be with a storm raging above. Everything creaked and moaned. Buckley pulled the leather cape over his head and dropped its sodden weight to the floor. He slicked back his hair, pressing the excess water out with his hands to drip to the deck. His hair drooped then in heavy black ringlets around his neck, and he shook them involuntarily with a shiver. It was, without a doubt, a miserable night.

Buckley stepped into the galley, and noted the remains of dinner still present on the tables. Not only were the damn fools cowards, they'd turned into slobs! He considered the proper punishment to exact for leaving the galley in disarray as he walked back toward the crew quarters. He reached his cabin first though, and paused. He'd be more effective in doling out a tongue-lashing if he weren't shivering in the process. Plus, part of the reason he'd wanted to come down was to reassure Ligeia.

Buckley let himself into his cabin, and after shutting the door to the gangway, he stood at the entry to his tiny quarters for a moment, letting his eyes adjust. "Ligeia," he called out softly.

She didn't answer. Normally she at least groaned an acknowledgment from behind her gag if he called.

Buckley stripped off his soaked shirt and breeches and pulled fresh ones from the drawers built into the cabin wall. He stepped into his pants as he moved toward the dark shadow that was all he could see of the bed.

"Ligeia," he said again, his voice barely above a whisper. "Are you okay? Are you sleeping through it all?"

He saw her lying there in the bed, a darker stain in the dark air of the cabin, and reached out to touch the smooth skin of her shoulder.

Or what should have been her shoulder. His hand met

something that didn't feel at all how Ligeia did beneath him when he decided to indulge. He ran it up the incline of flesh to meet the softer crook of her neck. Only . . . the neck didn't feel soft at all. It felt rough against his fingers, stubbly.

What the . . .

Buckley reached up and grabbed the hair of the man who lay naked in his bed. He pulled on it hard, to force whichever crewman had invaded his most private space to meet him eye to eye, but the body didn't bend or try to meet him. Still, he turned the face and pulled the man close. In short order he realized two things.

One, the man was cold, and very dead.

Two, the identity of the corpse.

"Reg," he whispered.

Call the captain slow, but it was only then that it finally registered that Reg was alone in his bed. The bonds that once held the captain's secret concubine hung loose and free.

Ligeia is loose! The thought hit like a lightning bolt.

"Damn you to a cold, everlasting hell," Buckley cursed at Reg, releasing the man's hair to let the dead head thump back to the bed. "What have you done?"

Buckley pulled the almost forgotten fresh shirt over his head and then back-stepped his way out of the cabin and into the hall again, this time intent not to yell at his men, but to find out if any of them remained. He prayed that they hadn't all met Ligeia.

But he didn't have much hope in his prayer.

Chapter Thirty-eight

The ring of the phone woke Evan from where he dozed beneath a warm afghan on the couch. He blinked in a moment of ambiguity when he wasn't quite sure where he was. And then it all hit him. He'd spent the day with Bill, learning the workings of scuba equipment in the basement, drinking in front of the television and then crashing on the couch to rest until nightfall.

"Hello," a gravelly voice said from the easy chair in the corner. Bill had grabbed the phone.

"No, I haven't seen him . . . Sure, of course I will. Yeah, I'm sure everything's fine; he and Sarah probably just went out somewhere today."

The phone clicked back into its holster on the end table, and Bill announced, "Your shrink is looking for you. Seems you didn't show up for your appointment or return her calls."

"Shit," Evan said, pulling himself into a sitting position on the couch. "I totally forgot. Should I call her?"

Bill tossed a blanket aside and shook his head. "She'll keep. After tonight I don't think you'll need to worry about shrink appointments anyway." He stepped out of his chair and sauntered into the kitchen, rumpling his hair.

"Yeah, maybe not," Evan agreed. "When do we leave?"

Something popped with a hint of fizz in the kitchen and a moment later Bill returned, holding out a beer to

Evan. He took a swig and then set it down next to the four empties on the glass coffee table in the middle of the room.

"As soon as you finish your fortitude," Bill answered.

Bill parked the Range Rover on Fifth Avenue, just past The Sand Trap. The street basically dead-ended into a dune of sand, perfect for two guys who intended to drag scuba equipment from the road to the beach. Bill got out and popped the back door, loading down Evan's arms with flippers, suit, air tank . . . and then grabbing an armful of the same for himself. Bill closed the back door with a shoulder to the metal, and then hurriedly moved toward the ocean.

"Let's not get seen, huh?" he hissed.

The beach was empty when Evan and Bill crested the last dune and began to stumble down the sand toward the water where, just a few weeks before, a woman named Kylie had disappeared after being dumped by her boyfriend.

When they dropped all of the equipment to the sand, Bill turned to Evan and took his friend by the shoulders.

"I can handle this part," he offered. "You don't have to go down there again."

"Yes, I do," Evan insisted. "For Sarah. I owe her that much."

Bill nodded and began to put on the suit and equipment. When he was done zipping and clipping, he helped Evan, who was fumbling with his own. An afternoon of training doesn't breed expert familiarity. Bill turned a knob on the tank, touched a button on the suit hood and something crackled in Evan's ear.

"Can you hear me?"

Evan nodded.

"Then say something. You can't hear nodding under-water."

"What?" Evan answered.

"Two-way radio," Bill explained in his ear. "It's dark down there . . . we need to stay in contact the whole time."

A hand clapped Evan on the shoulder, and then something hard slammed against his rubber-gloved hand. He held it in front of his face and saw the steel tube of a speargun. Bill began to walk toward the dark line where the ocean met the sand. "Are you ready, hunter?"

Evan felt his heart trip as he looked at the cruel, hooked steel barb on the end of his speargun.

"Yes," he said simply and followed his friend toward the water.

He was two steps in when the vertigo hit. "Oh shit," Evan breathed, as he stared at the quiet surface of the water, threatening to suck him down. He teetered on one foot as something inside him struggled to find balance.

Bill's voice echoed through his face mask and into his ear. "I can do this, Evan. You don't have to go."

Rage built in Evan's heart as he thought about that offer. "No!" he wanted to scream. Instead, he gritted his teeth and said, "This is my fight and I should be handling it by MYself."

But he couldn't handle it by himself. The very acknowledgment of that made him feel like sinking to the sand.

"Then handle it," Bill's voice said quietly in his ear. "But if you can't, you're only going to stop me from doing what needs to be done. It's not my fight . . . but I'll fight it for you, if you need me to."

Evan's stomach trembled in shame. He stared out at the quiet black water and forced himself to stand taller. He shook his head and whispered into the microphone,

"This is my fight. This is Sarah's fight. I'll take care of it. Just help me to get there."

Bill didn't answer, but Evan saw his friend's rubber-capped head nod before his feet began to move forward, and his waist sank deeper into the dark of the waterline.

Evan felt his gorge rise in his throat at the idea of stepping another foot into the murk of the ocean. But then his memory focused on the image of Sarah, dead beneath the waves. And suddenly that nausea passed, and he gripped his fingers tight against the steel holster of the deadly speargun.

The ocean had taken his son, the most important person in his life. Ligeia had taken that which was most dear to him after his son.

What did Evan have to be afraid of anymore? He deserved to die, having failed to protect and save his own family.

His stomach flipped as he forced his feet to walk farther into the water. The familiar paralysis began to threaten in his calves, but instead of giving in to it, he closed his eyes and thought of Ligeia, and of how easy it had been for him to walk into the waves when she was near. Now . . . he was walking into the waves to kill her. But invoking her image still made it easier for him to enter that forbidden place. Her spell had broken the ocean's stranglehold on him. Now he drew on the memory of her to give him the strength to do it again. He called on her to give him the strength to kill her. It was twisted, but it worked.

Somehow, Evan forced his feet to walk behind Bill, and step by step, they both disappeared into the surf.

Evan's chest threatened to implode as his face mask dipped below the waterline. But for once in his life, the only time without outside "aid," he was able to go underwater without sucking in brine and nearly drowning.

This time, the thought barely flickered across his mind. This time, his mind was solidly on one thing. Finding the lady of the underwater graveyard. Finding the murderer of his wife.

Finding Ligeia.

Despite the security of the mask and the hiss of the air tank, Evan took a deep breath and let his head slip beneath the waves.

CHAPTER THIRTY-NINE

June 11, 1887, 12:59 A.M.

The crew's quarters were empty. A blanket hung down from Cauldry's cot, and Buckley's militant side made a note to talk to the crewman about cleanliness. A man's bed bespoke his mind. Disorderly linens defined a poor companion for a life-and-death mission; they spoke of a man not paying attention to the details. As far as the captain was concerned, every day on the ocean was a life-and-death endeavor. If you weren't paying attention, the hooks of the deep would catch you unawares.

Captain Buckley moved slowly through the center of the ship, knowing that Ligeia could be waiting in every shadow. A part of him loved her, but none of him trusted her. He knew what she could do to a man. He'd watched her jaws in action, and afterward, had had to dispose of the bodies of men who were much stronger than he himself. If *they* could not resist her unbound hunger, could he hope to?

He might not succumb to her song as the others did, but still, the woman possessed a power, a violence, that he feared.

Buckley stepped on planks that creaked with his weight, as well as the tossing of the ship. His heart screamed at him to move faster, to get back to the wheel above. But his spine insisted on creeping through the guts of his ship like a thief; he wanted to surprise her, not be surprised *by* her.

The dark shadows of the crates of liquor flickered like black ghosts against the wooden walls of the hold, and Buckley stepped inside the crowded room, holding a lantern high. The light would give him away here, he knew. But he would not enter the otherwise black hold without it.

He stood at the entry, watching the orange glow slip back and forth across the wooden slats of the crates. Buckley watched for any movement at the side of the rows of cargo, and his shoulders started, twice, when the shadows themselves seemed to shift. But he quickly saw that those shifts were only tricks played by the light.

Ligeia was not here. Or, if she were, she was still and silent somewhere in the back of the hold. He knew he would have to walk through the room, peering at every crevice to assure himself that she weren't secreted within. But despite his initial belief that she had gone from this place, if she had ever been in the hold at all, his feet were reluctant to step any farther forward.

Something cool dripped down his cheek, and Buckley absently wiped it away. He held the lamp out and tried to tease its light around the corner of the stack of crates nearest him, diminishing the shadow inch by inch.

She did not appear in the disrobed dark.

Something dripped again against his forehead, and this time, he wiped it away and looked up. The storm might be bad, but it shouldn't have opened a breach in the upper deck.

That's when he saw the bloody toes.

Buckley gasped as he took in the hairy legs of his first

mate, hanging just a foot above his head. The thick black
hair of the man's calves was covered in streams of rich
red blood, which ran in rivulets around the curve of his
ankles and down the foot to his toes. As Buckley looked
up, he saw that the blood stemmed from ragged gashes
in the man's belly and neck; his naked torso had been
much violated before being strung up by the wrists from
a beam on the ceiling.

But the first mate wasn't the only one. Next to him,
strung up from the rafter were the naked bodies of Jensen and Cauldry. Their heads all lolled at their chests,
tongues protruding from angry mouths, congealed blood
coating the thick hair of their chests in a sheen of death.
How had he walked into the room without seeing their
corpses hanging there?

"Damnitall," Buckley hissed. He lifted his hand and saw
that it was smeared in the blood of his crew. He wiped it
violently against his pants and stepped away from the
men, a chill running up his spine.

"Damnitall," he said again. Anger bloomed in his
heart. Buckley was not a man with a big heart. Some said
he wasn't a man with a heart at all. But he valued strong
men who were loyal and worked hard. These were good
men. And they had perished because of his weakness.
Because of his need for the dangerous woman who had
shared his cabin these past weeks.

"Damnitall," he whispered, and this time the exclamation brought tears from the corner of his eyes. The rocks
wept. "I will kill you, Ligeia," he whispered. And with
that, he began to quicken his pace, moving around the
crates of liquor with the intent to surprise a deadly killer
who lurked somewhere behind them. His fear at what

surprising her would mean had fled. He didn't fear for
his life any longer.

No matter how good she had made his nights feel over
the past few days and weeks, now he only wanted one
thing.

He wanted Ligeia dead.

CHAPTER FORTY

The ocean was black. It surrounded him like a heavy leaden cape, threatening to close in. To smother him. Crush the breath from his feeble lungs until there wasn't a hint of gasp left in his chest. It crept close and then darted away, a stealth assassin who, despite his quiet threat, was clearly visible everywhere. And creeping closer.

Evan blinked back his fear of the black with a thick throat. In his ears, Bill tried to offer reassurance.

"You're doing great, man. We're under. You're breathing good. All we have to do is swim a little ways down, out to the edge of the point. You can do this."

Evan didn't think he could do this. The panic had returned in a big, bad way. His breath began to come in short, sharp gasps as he thought of where he was. In the water. Beneath the water. Covered by the water. Crushed by the . . .

"Evan, calm down, man. Slow the breathing. You're going to hyperventilate. Move your arms. Follow me."

Evan closed his eyes for a moment, blotting out the claustrophobia of the dark water. When he reopened them, he trained the faint light of his headlamp on Bill's feet, and redoubled the kicking of his flippers. He knew his friend was right. He had to focus on the task at hand and not let the fear own him.

But . . .

The water.

Was.

Everywhere.

Pressing against him.

Trying to find its way into his mouth.

Trying to smother him.

To kill him.

"Evan—fucking follow me," Bill's voice yelled suddenly in his ear. "Think of Sarah!"

The thick suffocation that surrounded his body parted, a little, at the light he played upon it, and Evan focused on the kick of Bill's flippers just a few feet ahead of him. "Follow," he whispered in his mask. "Follow."

"Yes," Bill's voice echoed in his ears. "Just follow. Your suit will protect you from the water. From the Siren . . . that's another story. I need you for that, Evan. I don't know what I'm dealing with here, and you do. You know her. You have to help me."

Evan heard the slight admission of fear in his friend's voice and realized, despite all of his pronunciations of "Siren" before, that his friend had never really believed in the existence of Ligeia. What he'd thought Evan had been doing, he didn't know. Why he had kept insisting that this liaison was one with an immortal, he didn't know. Maybe Bill had simply been trying to give him an "out" for the expression of lust that Bill knew Evan had needed.

Or maybe he just liked to bullshit, assuming he'd never have to face the consequence.

Either way, they were here now, fifty feet below the ocean's waves, swimming toward the woman who Evan knew was more than a woman. She looked enough like a human woman to pass a cursory glance. But he knew that she was more than that.

This woman could breathe beneath the waves and kill men with a song.

This woman was deadly.

And they were swimming toward the very center of her power. An old shipwreck rotted with one hundred years of neglect on the bottom of the bay.

"There it is," Bill said quietly. "This is the ship I saw the last time I was down here. Is this where she took you?"

Evan trained the yellow glow of his headlamp on the green-coated hull of an old shipwreck slowly emerging from the shadows before them. The boat was buried half in the muck of the bay, but Evan recognized it instantly as the place he had escaped from this morning.

"That's it," he acknowledged. "That's where Ligeia lives. That's where Sarah is."

The admission gave him a new energy, and suddenly the feeling of claustrophobia receded as in its place, the anger grew.

She was there. Just ahead. It seemed like a long time since he'd been here last, and at the same time, just a little while before. Evan fingered the tube of the speargun at his side and a slow grin lit his face.

"You're going to die, bitch," he whispered, forgetting that Bill heard his every word.

"Thatta boy," Bill answered, and kicked harder in the dark to descend toward the gaping black hole that their headlights defined in the ship's hull. "Let's go get her."

Evan followed Bill's legs down toward the ocean floor, but when they neared the rotted hull of the old ship, Evan slowed, and then broke away from Bill's lead.

"Wait a minute," he said, and kicked his feet and pushed out his palms, pushing himself close to the bottom. He looked out at the hole in the ship and tried to imagine the trajectory of his escape this morning.

"What are you doing?" Bill's voice asked.

"She's down here," Evan said, and his friend didn't have to ask what he meant. Instead, Bill turned and trained his headlamp on the ocean floor, above where Evan swam, helping to illuminate a wider surface area.

The cold white of her dead flesh was not too hard to find, even in the wide span of the ocean. Evan had known Sarah's body rested near the hole in the hull, and once he began looking, in seconds his spotlight had found her resting place, trailed up the cool flesh of her arm, and then the pale pink hole that showed an unnatural entry to her neck. His light found the open, frightened pale blue orbs of her dead eyes, staring up still toward the sky she would never see again.

In his ear, he heard Bill's intake of breath upon seeing the body.

"I told you she was here," Evan said quietly.

"Let's take care of the reason for that," Bill answered, "and then we'll take her home."

Evan nodded, but still he pushed himself lower in the water, down to the ground. He swam inches from Sarah's corpse, and pressed his face-masked eyes to hers. "I'm sorry," he said. It wasn't enough, but it was all he could say.

Then he looked up at Bill, still hanging just a few feet away. Evan pointed toward the dark opening in the broken ship's hull, and nodded his head in the dull light of his friend's flash. "Let's go," he agreed.

Vicky Blanchard couldn't sleep. Maybe it was because she was afraid of having another nightmare thanks to Evan. She tossed and turned in her bed, alternately kicking the sheets aside, and then pulling them back to hide in the fetal position beneath their warmth. Something about Evan's situation was really bothering her. She felt twitchy; and when Vicky felt that jumpy feeling in her legs and her gut, it usually meant one of two things: either she'd drank one too many cups of caffeine, or her sixth sense was warning her that something bad was about to happen.

And Vicky hadn't had any coffee today.

Giving out one long, exasperated sigh, Vicky got back out of bed and pulled on a pair of sweatpants. She wished her head would either work in full "psychic" mode, or give it up entirely. She hated these feelings that she couldn't do anything about until it was too late, and the reason for her unease became apparent. When they grabbed her like this, there would be no rest until the reason was revealed.

Donning a light jacket, she left the house and decided to take a walk. Perhaps the exertion would tire out her mind so that she could finally get some rest.

She headed away from town, and in a few minutes had passed the din of The Sand Trap bar on Fifth Avenue. For a minute, she toyed with the idea of stepping inside, but she really wasn't in the mood to be social right now, and didn't want to run into one of her patients trying to drown their problems. There was nothing worse than playing bedside confessor to a drunk.

Vicky passed by the bar and stepped up the path of the dunes until she suddenly could see the black sliver of the bay ahead. She shivered in the cool breeze blowing in off the water, and quickly shuffled back down the sand, kicking off her shoes once she reached the flatter, harder packed beach.

Just ahead, she thought she saw a movement down by the water, and she slowed her step. She didn't want to surprise anyone who didn't want to be seen. But as she approached Gull's Point, she realized that nobody was there.

Maybe it had been the shadows of a cloud overhead, or the scuttle of a night bird.

Vicky stopped just short of the long, rocky finger of the point, and stared down its silent length and into the gentle surf beyond.

She considered Evan's stories of meeting a woman here, night after night. A woman who seemed to be *of* the water. A woman who could have passed as the legendary Siren of Delilah. She shivered at the thought and shook her head.

No.

Vicky did not believe in folklore. The facts behind such stories had more to do with the needs of the people telling them than they did of any objective reality. She wondered if Evan's delusion were a way for him to rationalize an infidelity, or if, and this is what she truly feared, that his fear of the water had generated some kind of suicidal fantasy that was ultimately going to end with a police report and a file photo of Evan's corpse, facedown in the water?

She picked up a shell and tossed it into the bay. The breeze was picking up again, and after a few minutes she turned away from the water and began to walk back toward town.

If she had arrived at the point just a few minutes sooner, she might have seen Evan and Bill descending into the dark waves, beneath where her discarded seashell sank. Vicky's sixth sense was definitely working . . . but it simply hadn't woken her to action soon enough.

Behind her, and beneath the waves, Bill and Evan silently entered a sunken ship.

CHAPTER FORTY-ONE

June 12, 1887, 1:57 A.M.

Captain Buckley felt the burn in his chest and couldn't have sworn whether it was from his anger or his fear. His hands felt cold and brittle as he rubbed the circulation into them and stepped quietly around the boxes of the storeroom. His feet slid in something slippery on the floor. He knew without looking that it was a pool of the blood of his crew.

Damnitall. His crew. He had looked the other way at her first kill, and then her second. He had aided her as she began to eat her way through his men. But he'd never thought she'd take *all* of them. He'd never thought that she'd take Travers or Reg. The thought of that made him angry, but also chilled. Any woman who could take down Reg . . . was no woman.

Buckley moved back out of the hold and through the empty crew's bunks. Jensen and Cauldry would never hide a fish beneath the other's pillow here again, he thought.

He stopped at his own cabin and verified that the room remained populated only by the dead. She hadn't slipped back in here after he'd walked past to wait. Buckley pulled the cabin door shut behind him and continued his quiet, deliberate walk forward.

The ship strained against the wind and waves, and

every few steps the captain stopped and held the wall for support until the old boat steadied. He passed the galley, and stared into the shadows at the corner of the room. She was not there. Nobody was there. Buckley continued on down the narrow passageway that was the spine of his ship. He knew this wood by heart; his feet had walked these planks every day at every hour, for too many years to count. But now, in this moment, his ship felt alien to him. Instead of a mother, a symbiotic protector, it felt like a killer. Something waited for him in its hidden depths. Something cruel.

He opened the door to a storage compartment and saw nothing but coils of rope there. There were precious few places belowdecks where someone could hide, and he had nearly reached the end of the options. Buckley ducked his head below a beam and stepped into the smaller hold at the front of the ship. He didn't expect that Ligeia would be here; it was just a room that arched up from the ship's keel to the triangular point of the longest stretch of the upper deck. It wasn't much good for storage, so all manner of odds and ends collected here, from broken crates to fishing nets, strewn along the narrowing, claustrophobic walls like traps. Buckley stepped carefully through the mess, his lamp flickering like a ghost against the stained and blackened wood.

Something moved the wrong way in the shadows on the wall.

Buckley froze.

A bucket set just at the edge of the dark fell over and rolled down the planks to rest at the toe of his boots. The captain drew in a sharp breath, but held his ground. "Ligeia," he said quietly, in the most steely of voices. "I know what you've done. Come out, please."

A shadow slipped past one of the fishnets hanging

from the wall at the narrowest section of the hull. Buckley saw something flash, cat's-eye luminescent, in the dark. He edged toward where the motion had been. "Ligeia," he said. "Stop."

A shuffle just ahead. Wood scraping wood. And a hollow clatter as something fell from the wall to echo on the floor. Buckley took a chance and leaped forward at the noise. His stomach caught in his throat as he took the leap, praying that his fingers would connect with flesh, and not a net full of hooks.

Instead, he connected with nothing. His hands grasped empty air, and Buckley stumbled forward off balance, before one hand touched the rough-hewn planks of the hull. And then something sharp and cool slipped along the back of his neck.

Buckley drew in a sharp breath and flipped around. The glow of his lamp reflected off the rusted metal of an old hook dangling from a rolled length of fishnet propped against the wall and crooked at its top as it reached and tried to exceed the ceiling.

He grumbled in disgust and pushed past the hook back out to the passageway. She wasn't in the storage room. She wasn't in the hold. Could she have decided to make a run for it, now that her meals were done here? Could she swim to shore from this far in the ocean? Did the distance matter to one such as her?

Buckley began to walk toward the galley. He'd have to go back above deck and see if she'd hidden out in the wheelhouse or some such. But he doubted it. She was gone, the wicked bitch. And she'd taken his crew with her.

He stepped forward just as the ship shook, propelled first up one watery swell and hanging almost sideways before getting sucked back down into the trough of its negative force. He had to get back up top and take the wheel again, Buckley realized, or very soon, it wouldn't matter if Ligeia had eaten his men. Because if there were no ship . . .

Movement again, just ahead. The flash of skin in the dark. The swirl of black hair in black shadow.

"Ligeia," he breathed. She was here. She hadn't gone above. Buckley hurried after her. It was ironic that all he could see of her in the dark was the sheen of her black hair, the darkest part of her, as it caught the faint ray of his lamp and then moved, twining in the air as she ran, always just out of range.

She darted through the crew's quarters and he saw the white skin of her fingers pass like a ghost's over the crate nearest the entryway to the hold before all hint of her disappeared to the left of the entrance.

"Ligeia," he said for the fourth time as he stepped over the threshold. "I demand that you come out of there at once." He stepped cautiously into the hold once more, wishing that he still held his lantern.

A hand reached around his neck from behind, holding his chin in a vise grip. "Ah, my vile, brutal captain," a voice whispered in his head. "You cannot demand anything of me, I'm afraid. But I have a lot to demand from you."

Buckley started to turn but something sharp dug into his neck and Ligeia's voice gritted, "Don't move, my sweet. Or we'll be mopping your life off the floor and hanging you on a hook. I've gotten quite good at that, as you can see. But one can always improve one's technique."

"Release me," Buckley demanded.

Ligeia ran a daggerlike fingernail along the soft underside of his chin and whispered again, "You don't hold the chains anymore, my captain. *I do.* This time, the chains are on you."

There were some things that Captain James Buckley

III could swallow. He could take the guff of a crewman one step over the line. He would dig into his wallet and pay the tariffs imposed by the port authority though he knew they were simply skimming half of his toll off the top for their own pockets. They knew what he carried in the hold and he knew they knew. He didn't fight them, simply paid them off, a gentleman's blackmail.

But what James Buckley (don't ever call him Jim) could not swallow, was the threat of a woman besting him. That's why, when self-preservation would suggest that he remain still and hear her terms, Buckley did exactly the opposite. As the tenor of her threat sunk in, the image of his men hung naked and bleeding filled his head, and Buckley lashed backward with the point of his elbow, catching Ligeia somewhere in both the flesh and the ribs—perhaps a breast?—at the same time as he threw the rest of his body forward, down to the floor to roll between the crates until he could come back to his feet in a crouch.

"We can talk," he said, breathing hard, "but you will *not* hold me."

A rope slipped under his chin from behind and pulled tight, eliciting a gasp from the captain. He gripped at its rough threat and tried to pull it looser, but it only cinched tight.

"Tell me that again," Ligeia's voice whispered as sweet as honey in his ear. Honey with blood in it.

His answer was a gasp.

"Yes, I thought as much," she said. Her voice couldn't hide a cloying flavor of turnabout. "A typical man. All talk, no action."

Ligeia pulled the rope and Buckley staggered backward, forced to follow as she led him like a calf to the slaughterhouse. He knew that wherever she dragged him, his end would be the same. The tables had turned. She was no longer tied to his bed, helpless to do anything but his will. For a moment he speculated about his treatment of her. Had he been so bad? Had he made her so unhappy that she'd . . .

He stopped that thought when, again, he remembered the bloody feet of his men hanging overhead.

Then he thought of all the times he had come back to his cabin and forced himself upon her with no pretense of foreplay or civility. He recalled the wetness that frequently trailed across her cheeks when he was done, and the smoldering sparks that passed across her eyes as she lay there restrained and staring at him, unmoving. Biding her time.

That time was now.

At that moment, Captain James Buckley III knew, unequivocally, that he was going to die. At the same time, he resolved that if he had to go, he was going to take her with him.

CHAPTER FORTY-TWO

Sometimes, no matter how much you want to avoid it, you have to be the one who goes first. For Evan, this was one of those times. He had been here before; he had been here this *morning*. Bill could back him up, but in the end, this was his fight, and he had to step up.

Swallowing the bile in his throat, Evan kicked hard with the strange, clumsy rubber flippers on his feet, and moved ahead of his friend as they crossed the black boundary of the rotted ship's hull. "I know where we're going," he explained simply, and pushed his arms through the water as he'd watched his son do countless times. Josh had taught him how to swim, and he'd never even set foot in the water during his son's life. The bile rose again, but he forced it back.

Evan swam just inside the hole in the old wreck's hull. He was looking for something, and it wasn't hard to find. In seconds, he saw the faint ivory of bones poking through the muck of the ocean sediment on the floor of the boat. They curved along the drift of muck, containing or conforming to it, was hard to tell. But Evan knew what they were. Rib bones. And just beyond, more evidence of yellowing death poked through a frond of wispy seaweed caught in the light strapped to his forehead.

Evan pointed out the half-buried skeletons to Bill, who grunted in his headphones.

They swam on and quickly the submerged bones became stacks of visible, layered skeletons. And then the corpses grew more recent—half-rotted, gray-chewed, flesh-somewhat-on-the-bones bodies, again, stacked gruesomely one on the other. Evan lingered for a moment at the corpse of one with nothing but a skull atop the ragged cotton of a faded black T-shirt. The dead man's hand lay upon the remains of the shirt and there still were flecks of flesh bleached gray and dead clinging to the bone like old gristle. His mind refused to accept that this had once been a living, breathing person; this was not a Halloween prop, this was death. The real *final* deal. His chest grew tight, and he forced his eyes to look away.

Evan swam on, and the orange of his lamplight glinted off something near the head of another stack of bones. He started to kick past, but then something made him linger. He looked again at the metal that flashed as he turned his headlamp toward it.

"C'mon, man, we don't have all night," Bill's voice urged.

"Wait," Evan insisted. His hand reached out toward the medal and he prayed, prayed, prayed it wasn't what he thought it was when the light played across it for the first time.

"Please, no," he whispered, as his hand picked up the silver chain with the ragged charm attached. "No," he said again, as he turned it over in his hand, staring both at the words broken in half by the artificial division of the jagged W rift down its center. It was a medal meant to be joined with another. As Evan stared at the empty eye socket orbs of the skeleton's skull, he unzipped his wet suit just a hair, and pulled out the silver chain that hung around his own neck. Then he matched the edge of *his* ragged charm to the W cut of the one worn by the dead bones. They fit seamlessly together. The reunited medal read LIKE FATHER, LIKE SON.

Tears welled up in his eyes and a sound rose in Evan's throat—a low, pained howl of shock and disbelief and anger and a dozen other unclassified emotions that all boiled down to one horrible burning pain. "Oh my God, Bill," he whispered. "She killed Josh too. He didn't drown. She took him."

The voice came very quietly in his mask, as a hand gripped his shoulder, trying to offer support. "Are you sure that's him?"

"How many people wear the other half of this medal and died in the surf of Delilah Bay?" Evan asked bitterly. And then he pointed to the green-crusted remnants of the bathing suit around the skeleton's midsection. A faintly red-striped scrap of blue cloth still clung to the empty bones of the body. "And that sure looks like his suit. I used to joke that all he needed was a Superman *S* on his chest."

"But he was surfing in broad daylight," Bill argued.

"Then she was under the waves, waiting for someone to fall," Evan said. The tears welled up again and, for a moment, he couldn't see anything at all but the shadows of anger. "She's taken everything that ever mattered to me. And there I was fucking her like a goddamn idiot."

"She probably doesn't even know Josh was your son," Bill suggested.

"I don't think that really fucking matters," Evan screamed.

With that, he pushed off with both hands catching the water and swam toward the place where he knew Ligeia slept. He had slept there with her. The thought of that made his blood run cold.

"Is your gun ready?" he asked softly in the radio.

Bill answered simply, "Whenever you are."

Together they swam into the dark of the rotted ship.

Evan led them past the rotted beams of what once had probably been a cargo bay and then up past an old beam to where the Siren's nest lodged, along the rotted broken planks of ancient wood that protruded crazily from the hull of the broken boat.

Maneuvering in the bowels of the ship was difficult; his feet slapped at the low ceiling and then he used his hands to guide him along the crumbling spongy wood of a passageway wall. He imagined himself as an astronaut, floating through the abandoned hull of an alien spacecraft, exploring. When he thought of an alien, tentacles whipping through the gravity-free air and catching him in the face as it leaped out from the unknown corridors ahead, his spine trembled. Perhaps his predilection for science fiction wasn't helping at this point. No—the unknown here was the where, not the who. He knew *what* he faced here, but where she was . . .

Evan drew a startled breath as his light suddenly illuminated a billow of graying fabric floating just ahead of them in the water.

Was that her?

"What is it?" Bill asked in his ear.

"Not sure," he whispered, and forced himself to move closer. The edge of the material seemed almost to shimmer in the slight current of the water, and Evan swallowed hard as he reached out to grab the thing, to unveil whatever hid behind it.

The stuff almost slipped through his hand as he grasped at it, but then he gave a sharp tug and like a matador, he succeeded in deflating the sheet of ancient rotted cloth and then it was hanging from his arm, at his side, and nothing was revealed beyond it.

"Just some old tablecloth," Bill suggested.

"On a fishing boat?"

"Okay, an old prom dress, shed like a . . . prom dress," he suggested lamely.

"I repeat . . . on a fishing boat?" Evan hissed. He batted the thing aside and swam ahead, faster now, angry for being spooked by an old sheet.

"Ligeia was here recently, and stirred this up or left it behind," he insisted. "There's no other reason for it."

They turned a corner and Evan pushed ahead, spotting the nest where he'd lain with Ligeia, both as her prisoner, and lover, not even twenty-four hours before. But as he reached the pile of old sheets and blankets, his heart sank. The bed was clearly empty.

"Shit," Evan breathed.

"Forget to take your vitamins again?" Bill suggested helpfully.

Evan ignored him. "This is where she sleeps," he said. "I'd hoped we might find her here again tonight. Corner and take care of her while she slept."

"Would've made it easier," Bill agreed, kicking past Evan to peer into the dark room beyond. "What's down here?" he asked in the earphones, and Evan shrugged before remembering that body language didn't work well in the dark, underwater. Nausea threatened to overwhelm him at that thought. "Didn't go there," he answered. Bill didn't give him time to obsess about the water.

"Whoa," his friend whispered in the headphones. "You've got to check this out, man. This ship did not have a happy crew when she went down."

"What are you talking about?" Evan asked, while pulling himself away from staring at the mess of sheets in the corner. He kicked off to follow Bill just ahead. When he reached him, Evan followed the point of Bill's arm, and his headlamp joined with Bill's. The narrow yellow cones painted a gruesome picture, as they trailed down the chains from the ceiling to the well-padlocked loops that curled around the necks of skeletons.

"Well, maybe that's why she went down," Evan whispered. "The crew were all hanging around down here."

Bill laughed. "Gallows humor at its finest," he said. "Nice! No, I think *that* is why she went down." He pointed to the giant rip through the ship's far wall.

A shattered, jumbled pile of wooden crates rested near the rift. The wood at the edge of the breach was blackened and jagged. Evan shone his light from the hole to the crates nearby, where the light picked up the glitter of broken glass. He swam closer, and reached into one of the crates, and pulled out a single, unbroken bottle. Unconsciously, he whistled.

"How much do you suppose an unopened bottle of 1887 rum is?" he asked.

"Depends who bottled it," Bill answered, with a caution. "Doesn't matter though. After more than one hundred years in the ocean, that shit would burn its way right through your throat, splash out on your lap and eat its way back in to arrive at your stomach from the outside," Bill pronounced, grabbing the bottle away.

"Damn," Evan said, and then kicked past Bill to exit the room. "Have to come back for one," he said. "Meanwhile, we need to keep moving. She's somewhere close. I can feel it."

As Evan exited the *Lady Luck*'s hold, something slipped around his neck and with a jolt, pulled tight. His eyes bugged at the sudden pressure, and he coughed as he tried to call out for help. With his cough, the noose only pulled tighter.

"Shhhhh, my sweet," a familiar voice whispered in his

brain. "I knew you'd come back. They always come back. I've been waiting for you." Her voice took on a darker tone then. "But you really should have asked me before you invited a friend into my home. Let me just deal with him, and then we can talk, okay?"

The rope pulled again on his neck and Evan kicked out against her, flailing his arms and then grabbing at his neck, trying to pull loose Ligeia's knot as she dragged him along by it. And then her hands were pushing him into a tight, dark place. She wrapped the rope around his hands and then tied the end off on a clothes hook anchored to the wall. And then she slipped away, closing a door behind her, locking him in. In his headphones, he heard Bill call out, "Hey, Evan. Where did you go?" before his head was filled with a hollow gasp, and then a grunt of startled pain.

"Uh-oh," Bill said. "Evan, wherever you are . . . I could use a hand? This fish does not look at all happy to see me." He yelped and swore, and then after a short, not very macho scream, Evan heard him say, "And the damn bitch bites."

CHAPTER FORTY-THREE

June 12, 1887, 2:07 A.M.

There were worse things than falling in love, Captain Buckley found himself thinking. He'd avoided the weakness like it were a plague after watching the varied circles of hell that the darkest, most deceptive four-letter word had put his shipmates through over the course of a lifetime at sea.

But now, as Ligeia dragged him to tortures unknown with no love whatsoever burning in her heart, he knew that maybe love, that emotion he'd so long spurned, might have helped him this time around. If he had used her better, and brought to life that fickle flame in her breast, maybe she would have played him easier now . . .

No matter, he thought. His chance at winning Ligeia's heart was long, long gone. The proof was around his neck. The rope tightened again and Buckley felt his tongue thicken. He gagged as his throat constricted and clawed first at the coarse rope around his neck and then, when that did no good, at her hands. He had to stop her from throttling him! She slapped him back, hard, and he fell to his knees, wheezing now and holding the rope to stop it from tightening any further. His eyeballs felt swollen, ready to pop. The pressure in his head was horrible; he could feel every beat of his pulse. Sweat beaded on his forehead and he gasped one word, "Please."

Ligeia laughed, and with one hand, bent to pat his head. "It's a very different feeling when you're on the other side of the bonds, isn't it?" she said.

The ship rolled at that moment, and Ligeia grabbed for a crate to steady herself. Buckley fell to the deck as her hold on the rope relaxed, and as he righted himself, he also reached into his side pocket, slipping his hand over his most prized possession. The weight of his scaling knife felt good in his hand. It was the one thing he could always count on. He raised it fast, but instead of taking the opportunity to stab at Ligeia, he opted to bring it down on the rope that held him to her. Freedom was more important than revenge in that moment and there was no guarantee that stabbing at her would end in his release. If she managed to deflect him, his chance would be gone. If he were free, he would likely have more than one chance to best her.

The blade caught in the heavy fiber of the rope halfway through, and Buckley pulled it out and then brought it down again. The motion tipped her off as she recovered from her stumble. Ligeia grabbed at his knife arm, but he pushed her back with a knee, and sawed again with the knife.

A handful of dagger-sharp fingernails raked down his neck and shoulder, and then her other hand closed on his neck, finally getting a solid hold on him.

The last threads of the ropes parted, and Buckley coughed a victorious "Yes!" as her stranglehold on him was severed. He threw his whole body away from the dig of her claws and rolled across the floor with the knife, cracking his head on the wood case. The ship took that moment to roll hard again and this time the room filled with screeching sound of crates shifting and sliding across the hold's floor.

Ligeia let out her own screech and lunged for him. Buckley was ready. He'd weathered a thousand storms at sea, and the yawing of the deck didn't inhibit his stability at all. He was back on his feet in a crouch by the time she came; he waited cold and ready. She was a banshee. Angry as fire and beyond control, she dove at him with nails ready as her weapons and teeth bared to shred.

His knife slipped easily into her gut, as her hands clutched at his neck. The warmth of her poured over his hand as he pulled out the knife so that he could stab again. She shrieked and raked his cheeks with her nails as she pulled away to clutch at her belly. He could feel the warmth leaking down to pool at his chin.

First blood for both, though he wagered that the stab he'd given her was far closer to mortal than what she'd given him.

The noose still choked him, and Buckley took advantage of her wound, and her nursing of it, and backed up a few feet. He never took his eyes off Ligeia, who lay on the ground, cursing in a foreign tongue filled with sibilant syllables and fricative staccato rasps as she rubbed at her abdomen. As she struggled to raise herself back off the ground, Buckley held the knife in his teeth and worked on the knot of the rope with his fingers. She'd only worked one twist and then pulled when she'd captured him, and in seconds, he had it out, and dropped the loop to the floor, heaving in a giant gasp of unimpeded air.

Then he moved in for the kill. Now he was ready.

But he was too late.

Just as he stepped forward, Ligeia collapsed facedown

on the deck and lay still. Buckley approached her slowly, knife in the air, poised to strike. As he stood over her prone form, he couldn't do it. How could he stab someone in the back who wasn't even moving?

His hesitation did him in. It was all a feint.

Ligeia scissored her legs and caught him in the back of the knees. He began to fall and she took the opportunity to flip and kick him, hard as could be, in the gut. Buckley lost the knife, which skittered away on the floor into the dark.

And then she was on him, all fury again. She grabbed him by the head, slipping a fingernail into his left eye and pushing, as she levered her body over his to pin him to the ground. Buckley felt her finger slip beneath and around his eyeball, her nail digging into the soft nerves and flesh just ahead of his brain. The immediate sensation was strange, uncertain, squishy . . . and then the pain began as the eye lifted from its socket.

Buckley screamed and thrashed away from her with manic power as the fire lit in his eye and burned its way back into the very core of his head. Tears and dark blood coursed down his face and all the pretense of civilized behavior was vanquished by the pain; he punched at her with all his fifty-six years of ship-working might, connecting with her chin. He heard bones crack, and then slugged her again. He struck again, but with the blood of his ruined eye slicking his face and blurring his remaining vision, he dealt only a glancing blow.

The force of his attack didn't seem to affect her at all. Ligeia only came down harder on him, this time with teeth bared. She went for his jugular like a wild dog, and he screamed as she chewed into the soft flesh below his ear. Something in his neck gave, and Buckley cried out, now in true terror as he felt the blood before the pain. He began to fall, unable to hold himself up, but true to his promise, he took her with him.

He gripped her by the hair and rolled, slamming her head again and again against the deck, as drops of crimson fell across her face like molten wax. She mewled and moaned, her eyes rolling back to show their whites as he slammed her against the ground. From somewhere she found the strength to gouge at his face again with her nails, drawing a new thread of blood across his cheek. The ship seemed to lift and plummet with the force of their fight, but neither even noticed anymore.

Buckley pulled out of the reach of her fingernails and she used the moment to kick him away from her. Scuttling like a crab she moved toward the exit of the hold, but Buckley didn't let her go. He staggered up and leaped over her, grabbing the black iron handle of the hold's door and pulling it shut with a heavy thud. Then he pressed his back against it as she crawled toward him, eyes alight with hate.

"You're not leaving here," he said simply.

"Neither are you," she hissed. She leaped, but Buckley was already in motion and her body barely touched his as he launched to the right. She grunted and struck the door, holding on to the wall for support. Her belly and thighs glistened with blood from the knife wound, and Buckley saw that his own shirt was stained forever with the blood of her life.

Or maybe it was his own. His neck and eye pulsed with pain and he could feel the hot stickiness of his own blood running down his ribs. "Damnitall," he gasped.

Buckley pushed himself off the deck, using the ship's own yaw to help him as gravity momentarily shifted. He staggered backward until he collided with a stack of crates, and screamed out as the shock of impact stirred the exposed nerves of his eyeball. He could barely hold his head up straight but Ligeia was not giving up the fight, and neither could he. He would not be bested by a woman. Would NOT.

To his left, he saw one of the stacks of liquor crates that had shifted and spilled to the deck, shattering bottles of precious cargo. Inwardly he cursed at the loss, but then the reflection of the broken bottles from the light of his abandoned lamp caught his eye. He had an idea.

A smile lit his gored face. Ligeia held her gut with one hand, but the determination to kill was obvious in her eyes as she staggered toward him. Just before she reached him, Buckley lunged for the deck and came up with the neck of a broken bottle in his hand. Not slowing at all, he stabbed at her with all his waning might.

The jagged shards caught her in the right breast, encircling and ruining what just yesterday had been his favorite oral toy. The glass tore into her soft, milky flesh and blood sprayed Buckley as he twisted his hand. Ligeia's scream was deafening, but it didn't slow Buckley, who wrenched out the makeshift knife. One glittering brown shard remained lodged in her chest. He stabbed at her again, but this time her arm blocked him, and the glass ripped open a gash across her biceps before slipping out into the open air beyond.

The force of his stab unbalanced him, and Buckley fell into Ligeia's arms for the last time. She did not embrace him as she once had. Instead her teeth sunk deep into his shoulder and then gored their way up his neck. She ripped at his flesh with hunger, anger and desperation. Buckley could feel her strength waning; but he was on the brink of exhaustion himself. He shoved her away, and they both fell from each other to the deck, unbalanced.

Around them the ship lifted and dipped with a force that would have turned Buckley white twenty-four hours before. But now, he barely noticed. All that mattered was the final duel between him and Ligeia. He no longer played to win. He only played to make sure that he wasn't the only one to lose. And as he stared at Ligeia gasping and panting on the floor, blood coating her naked belly, his eyes lit on the one thing that might absolutely seal her fate. But the gambit would seal his own as well. As Buckley held a hand to his neck to stem the flow of his own blood, he found he no longer cared. His one overriding thought was simple.

Ligeia must die.

CHAPTER FORTY-FOUR

Bill kicked at the woman with his right leg, trying to hold her off and gain enough separation to pull the speargun from its "holster." She'd come at him out of nowhere, a nude flash of unbridled femininity with a mouth of teeth that were definitely not being shown simply to smile. She came at him with full intent to kill and eat, not necessarily in that order.

Now she circled him like a shark, waiting for him to make the wrong move.

"Un-fuckin'-believable," he whispered. "He's really been bonin' a Siren. Or a really pissy mermaid with a great voice."

One thing he knew she wasn't, was human. She hung just out of his reach in the dark, slow current of the ocean, black hair rippling gently in the water behind her, eyes slitted to vengeful threats. Her breasts were bare, depending from her taut frame like an invitation, nipples already pointed and pink, waiting. And below the smooth white skin of her belly, he saw the smooth white skin of . . .

He stopped his admiration of her sex when his eyes saw the rest of her. Her thighs changed from the alluring milky skin of a woman to silver-blue scales that glinted like metal at the touch of his headlamp's glow. He whistled in his face mask.

She lunged at him then, and Bill gasped and fumbled

for the speargun. He didn't risk firing the gun with no chance to aim, but simply jabbed it at her. Ligeia dodged him easily and disappeared into the dark passageway from which she'd come.

"Evan, come out, come out, wherever you are . . ." Bill said into the microphone. "Your fishy friend just asked me to dinner. Problem is, I'm the main course."

Static filled the headset for a moment and then Evan's voice crackled in, for just a moment. "Workin' on it," Bill heard. "Hang on!"

Two arms slid up and around his side from behind, and a hand grabbed hold of his wrist holding the speargun. Bill struggled to turn, but she was strong. He couldn't free his arm, couldn't even move it. His only salvation turned out to be his oxygen tank. It barred her from chomping down on his neck, unless she released her hold on his arms. To solidify that difficulty, Bill pushed his legs backward and then brought his feet together. Effectively, he now held her TO him, preventing her from doing any fancy acrobatics to get around his air.

And then she spoke to him.

"You shouldn't have come," she said. Her voice was liquid sweet. Beauty with a razor-blade smile.

Bill opened his mouth to answer, and then realized that she couldn't have spoken to him . . . they were under-water.

"How . . ." he began, and then faltered.

"My voice is within you," she answered his unvoiced question. "I only need to touch you once to know you enough to talk. Of course, if we were above, I wouldn't have to know you at all. I could simply use the air and sing. That always makes them try to know me."

"Why did you kill Sarah?" he asked.

From his headphones, Evan's voice crackled. "What

are you talking about, Bill? I didn't kill Sarah, Ligeia did . . ."

"I know," Bill answered. "I was talking to her. Anytime you want to join us . . ."

Ligeia whispered coolly in his head. "She was in my way. Just as you are. I don't like things to come between me and my husband."

"Husband?" Bill choked. "Evan's been married to Sarah for years."

"Exactly," she answered. "That's why we had a little talk last night when she came home. She wasn't very receptive to sharing Evan. Neither, I have to admit, was I. With her . . . or you."

"With me?" Bill struggled to turn to see the face of the woman speaking silently to him, but his effort was cut short by one critical problem.

His mouth suddenly filled with water, not air.

And as he coughed out the cold brine, Ligeia let him go. He pushed away from her as soon as her grip relaxed, and that's when he saw the true evil in her eyes. They almost glowed red in the amber beam of the low-beam flashlight.

But her eyes weren't the focus of Bill's panicked feeling. No. The focus was in her hands. A thin black piece of corrugated plastic tubing.

The tubing that fed him his air. In his head, he could hear Ligeia laughing, cold and reptilian cruel.

Bill started to scream, but the intake of water put a quick end to that.

CHAPTER FORTY-FIVE

June 12, 1887, 2:17 A.M.

The lamp remained where he had left it. Its light shed shadows over the dangling corpses of his crew . . . hell, of his friends . . . above.

Buckley decided that he would reach that lamp if it was the last thing he did. Okay, second to last. There was one thing he had to do after he reached it.

He crawled past Ligeia, feeling the strength wane with every movement. He could barely see with his remaining eye, the pain was so bad. It crashed over him in waves of cold, hot and nausea. But it drove him too. He was sinking, that was clear. But he would not go alone. Behind him, he heard Ligeia struggling to move too . . . but he kept his eye on the goal and forced one hand in front of the other across the deck.

When he put one hand on the lantern, Buckley turned to see where Ligeia had crawled to. At first, he didn't see her, but then his eye was drawn to his first mate's corpse and the shadows surrounding it. Ligeia was there, hands gripping the dead man's calves. When Buckley saw her head between the man's legs, he scowled in disgust. What kind of foul creature could take pleasure in a dead man, a man she herself had killed . . .

But then she turned to look at him, lips and chin

awash in blood. When she smiled, her teeth were shockingly white in the gloom, and then she turned back to Travers's thigh. Buckley could see her mouth bite down on the man's flesh, and her head twisted and pulled with obvious relish at Travers's leg until a slab of still-red meat came back for her effort.

Ligeia smiled again and swallowed.

"I needed my strength back," she explained.

Buckley shook his head. "You're a desecration!" He spit a wad of blood-seamed saliva to the deck at her feet. "You've killed them, can't you leave them to eternity in peace?"

"I killed them for food," Ligeia said. "And after this day, I am going to need a lot of it. But every bite helps."

She pointed at the ragged wounds in her ruined breast and with the palm of her hand wiped away the trails of fresh blood there. The wound had begun to close already; no fresh blood was flowing.

At the same time, Buckley noticed that her belly had ceased to flow. "You've stopped bleeding?"

Ligeia laughed and stepped away from the body, and toward the captain once more. "I'm immortal, you foolish man. Do you think I would go through eternity bleeding from now on? You hurt me, yes, but now it's time to heal. You, on the other hand . . ."

She didn't finish her sentence because at that moment, the ship took another stomach-lifting plunge into an ocean trough before shooting back out, nose in the air, and then smashing down hard on the cap of a new wave.

In the hold, boxes moaned and shifted. Something smashed against the back wall and Buckley lost his footing and fell, sliding down the suddenly inclined deck along with bits of wood, glass and a pile of other debris.

He moaned as his back smashed into the corner of a wooden crate, but held on to the lantern for dear life. Ligeia held on to Travers, mouth grinning wide with a horrible surety. She looked like a rookie soccer player who'd just scored the winning goal.

"You haven't won yet, bitch," Buckley growled, and rolled himself off the crate to retreat into the shadows of the hold. He knew she'd follow. But before she did . . .

Buckley toppled a crate to the ground; as he'd bet, the fall shattered the lid, as well as a couple of bottles inside. Grabbing an unbroken one from inside the opened box, he held it by the bottom, and cracked off the top of its neck against the ship's hull. Then he stepped past the crate to wait. He didn't have to for long. He'd barely leaned back against the wall when she came for him.

Naked and beautiful as she'd been on their first night together, Ligeia stepped around the liquor crates and stopped. With one arm gently resting on the top of a wooden box, she leered at him, pursing her thick lips with exaggerated intent. Her belly glistened with perspiration, while her breasts heaved slightly, flushed as if from sexual exertion. Her sex also begged his attention; smooth as a schoolgirl, but achingly, swollenly mature, she lifted her leg to stretch, resting her foot on the ship's wall so Buckley could see every inch of her with the last strength of his tortured eye.

"Will you miss me?" she asked in a dangerously false tone.

Buckley nodded, almost hypnotized by the full glamour of her flesh. She hadn't looked so good to him in weeks. So vibrant. So lusciously fertile. So . . .

"I'll spare you that," she threatened, and kicked her naked toes off the wall to walk through the glass toward him, oblivious to any pain from the splinters. Ligeia had only one purpose now, and nothing would stand in her way.

Buckley waited until she was just a yard away before he sprang. He thrust hard with the broken bottle top at her groin, connecting for just a second before she dodged out of the way. But she wasn't fast enough; he'd cut her. The blood came fast, spilling out in seconds to coat and run down the delta of her thighs. Buckley was ashamed at the reaction the blood on her nakedness invoked in him, but it didn't matter now. He knew that he'd be paying for all his sins soon enough.

Ligeia didn't stop with just a feint away. She turned and attacked, hands clawed and teeth bared. Suddenly the glamour of desire was gone and her face seemed longer, meaner; her breasts tighter, pale. And Buckley caught the reflection of scales from her legs where the blood had not dripped.

She smashed into him full body, rolling him against the hull and to the floor. But Buckley countered with another stab from the bottle. It glanced off her arm, and she ignored it, teeth aiming straight for his neck. She pinned him there, half sitting, half fallen, with her incisors buried in his flesh. Buckley struggled to scream, but more so, he struggled to raise his arm. He could feel the rip of something in his throat, and a scalding cold constricted in his neck. Then his confused nerves dropped their hot-and-cold analogies and just spasmed, sending an unbroken jolt of pain through his spine. Buckley slipped one arm back, and then raised it up along the wood of the hull. As Ligeia chewed on his living flesh, he brought down the arm again, smashing the half-full bottle as hard as he could against the back of her head. The force of the blow sent her teeth deeper into him, and he gagged as she broke through to his windpipe. A splash of rum trickled across his throat, burning like molten fire.

The blow stunned her, for a second, and Buckley pushed her body off him, all the while wheezing and crying bloody tears.

He pushed himself backward, crablike across the floor, and then undid the latch on the lantern he still had managed to hold on to. Ligeia raised her head, still obviously groggy from the blow, and blinked her eyes several times.

Buckley set the lantern down on the deck, and then slowly tipped it over, letting the oil spill out to mingle with the rum. There was a slight huff, and the alcohol and oil caught fire from the wick, and spread with a blue tongue across the deck.

"Good-bye, Ligeia," he said, picking up another loose bottle. Her eyes widened and she began to rise, but not before Captain James Buckley III rose to a crouch and swung, connecting the bottom of the full glass of spirits with her head. The bottle didn't break the first time, or even the third. But on the fourth, as Ligeia lay unconscious in a pool of immortal blood, the glass did shatter, and the alcohol dripped down her beautiful skin with a golden kiss.

That's when the fire really caught.

The room was spinning for Buckley, and his breath came in wet gasps, but he forced himself to stand one more time, to push against one of the last towers of crates standing in the hold. He was weak, and his arms wouldn't stay stiff. Finally, he simply used his whole body and threw himself at the stack. With a little help from the toss of the ship, they went over, smashing down on Ligeia's body, and giving the flames more fuel to burn. Buckley lay on top of the pile, spent, as the wood of the crates began to crackle.

"Get up from this, bitch," he mumbled, as the flames singed at the back of his hair. He tried to push himself off the wood, but his body wouldn't respond. His heart trembled at the thought of being burned alive, but then, he was going to be no matter where he lay, wasn't he? "At least I'll die on top," he chortled to himself.

The flames had now spread throughout the hold, following the splashes of alcohol and then gripping onto the wood beneath. In seconds, the room became an inferno, flames licking at the feet of the corpses hung in the entry, and roasting the body of Captain Buckley as he lay still half alive, near the hull.

From beneath him, a low, keening wail erupted, and then a high, searing song.

The Siren had awakened again, and called for help. There were none left on the ship to answer. But from outside the hull, a pounding began. It began almost silently, and then grew as if an army rattled on the hull of the burning *Lady Luck*.

Inside the hull, the crates burned with a white-hot fire, and bottles exploded like fireworks, feeding the fury. With every pop of glass, the orange of the fire magnified, rose, and then died back, until another explosion of fresh fuel came to take its place. When the precious cargo was fully consumed, the fire continued to burn hot, now consuming the very wood of the ship's skin itself until its ferocity met with the anxious pounding from without.

And then the hull itself imploded, and the cool, lifesaving waters of the sea poured into the hold of the ruined *Lady Luck*, along with a host of sharks, small whales and other large fish, called by the song.

But the song of the Siren was long since extinguished, her body a blackened husk on the hold's floor. The ship sank fast, the hold's walls collapsing further with the inrush of waves, and as it settled to the bottom of the bay just outside of Delilah's port, the body of Ligeia spilled out to rest in the mud of the sea's cool bottom, one blackened hand upraised, as if in a last plea for help.

It would be one hundred years before that help came, in the form of the blood of a young woman named Cassie.

CHAPTER FORTY-SIX

Sirens were not Boy Scouts, Evan thought, as he worried the rope off the hook in the dark closet of a cabin. Thank God.

Ligeia had essentially hung him on a hook to come back for later, but he'd quickly realized that he could loosen the knot enough to bounce it off the hook. The next step was to find a way to get the rope off his wrists, and there, she'd done a pretty good job of imprisoning.

Evan heard a gurgling scream through his tiny headphones. Bill was in trouble and needed his help, but he was literally tied up.

He looked around the cramped space to see if there was any sharp edge he might wear the rope against, but couldn't find anything. Wood and bones did not a knife make.

Bill's voice began to sputter, as if he were swallowing water. Evan swore. He couldn't stay here and let his friend face Ligeia alone. Though what help he could be without hands, he didn't know. Determined to find a way to do something, he gripped the door handle with both hands and twisted. It opened to a slight swoosh of displaced water, and Evan shambled out toward where he'd last seen his friend.

The twisting shadows of two people circled each other in the dark water just ahead. He moved closer, still trying to figure a way to free his hands. In his earphones, he heard Bill choking.

"Hang on, man," he answered. "I'm right nearby. I can see you, I just have to figure out how I can help."

Evan held his wrists over a jagged piece of wood sticking out from the broken hull. He tried sawing the rope back and forth on it, but quickly realized that it would take hours to free himself that way. No real edge, no friction. He shrugged and decided to at least try to buy Bill some recovery time.

"Coming in," he announced, and dove off the floor toward the two. He kicked hard with his feet, pushing with his bound hands for steerage through the otherwise quiet water. He saw the black air tube hanging off the back of Bill's oxygen tank, a chain of bubbles rising from it toward the surface. Evan kicked his way closer to his friend, and with both hands reached out to the tube, shoving it toward the hole it should have been connected to. In his zeal, he collided with Bill and sent the both of them sinking toward the bottom.

Bubbles still rose from the tube and Evan saw Ligeia darting through the water straight at them. He fumbled again with the tube, positioning it over where it should connect, and then pushed hard, again. This time Bill rolled away, but Evan saw that the trail of bubbles seemed to have stopped. In seconds, he heard Bill's coughing again, and a raw whisper of "Thanks, Evan. That did it."

And then Ligeia was there in front of him.

Evan twisted himself around 180 degrees and readied his feet to kick. As she turned with a smile to look at him, he unleashed his best right foot hook, straight to her jaw.

But Ligeia didn't go down.

She didn't even flinch.

"You'll have to do better than that," she laughed in his head.

She reached out and pulled him close to her, kissing him quickly on the mouth before pushing him away, and then delivering a hard kick to his forehead. Evan saw stars, and fell away from the two of them, as Bill yelled in his ear, "Evan, are you okay?"

"Yeah," Evan answered blurrily, as he sank to the floor.

Above him, Bill took the opportunity Evan had given him and stabbed hard at Ligeia with the speargun. When she turned back to face him, he swung his hand through the water to punch her, but the natural fighting motion of a man aboveground does not translate to a workable fighting motion below waves. Ligeia captured his fist in midswing and laughed in his head, twisting his arm away from her and toward himself. With a knee, she delivered a blow to his groin, and Bill gasped and contracted to a fetal ball as she connected, nearly dropping the speargun in the process. She grabbed onto him and pulled him closer, opening her mouth to follow the blood of her last bite, and enlarge the source. She was hungry, and Bill offered fresh meat and fear. Plenty of fear, and Sirens loved the taste of that. Fear and lust were Ligeia's favorite seasonings.

"You're all the same," she told him, as her eyes widened, and her teeth grinned like a shark's maw. "So cocky you think you own the world, and you don't even know the first thing about the world." She reached down to cup his groin and whispered, "You all think we want to suck one thing, but you're *dead* wrong. I can tell you this: I will enjoy sucking your soul."

Then she leaned into his neck and encircled him with her arms; arms that were tight as cords of steel. This was a black widow of a woman, not one to let her prey walk away. She pressed her mouth to his rubber-sheathed neck and bit through the ragged wound she'd gouged there before. Bill brought his arms around to pound as hard as he could at her back but it did no good. He tried to bring the tip of the speargun around to catch her, but instead, she bit down hard on his neck and he dropped it, the black metal slipping quickly into the dark green of the waves to disappear on the bottom of the ship's floor.

Evan didn't miss it. He watched the speargun plummet, and pushed his way toward it as soon as he saw where it was likely to land. He couldn't fight Ligeia hand to hand in his current state, but if he could get a finger in the right place on the gun, he could find a way to operate it.

As Bill screamed out in pain in his headphones, Evan scooped up the black metal of the gun as it touched the slick, dark wood of the ship's floor, and hugged it to him as he positioned his fingers in a way that could operate the mechanism. Satisfied that he had the trigger ready, Evan kicked off the bottom and returned to the fray, this time ready to really help.

"Evan, this is no Ophelia," Bill groaned in his headset. "This bitch is mean." His friend coughed and gasped before adding, "I don't know what you see in her."

A tear slipped from Evan's eye at that, as he considered what Ligeia had done to his family, and now his friend. "I don't know either," he answered. "I'm sorry."

"Don't be sorry," came his answer. "Just stab the bitch!"

Evan kicked his way closer to the embracing couple, and saw the fog of Bill's blood beginning to cloud the water around them.

Instead of swimming all the way up to her, Evan checked his ascent and positioned himself directly behind her, until the soft globes of her buttocks were level with his eyes. Then he fumbled the speargun up until the point of its hook stared down the spot just between her shoulder blades. In his mask, Bill screamed again. Closing his eyes, refusing to watch the decimation of the woman he'd loved, Evan squeezed his finger against the trigger of the gun, and reeled backward at the kickback as the spear ejected. It slipped through the water and connected with a small plume of red against the cream between her shoulders.

As he tumbled in the dark water, the orange of his spotlight shone against the white skin of Ligeia's back and Evan couldn't help but see the silver steel of his spear protruding from the center of her back. Her arms lifted and reached behind, grasping for the thing that had bit her. As she did, Bill pushed away from her to freedom. Ligeia turned corkscrew in the water to see her attacker, and her eyes widened.

"You're mine," her voice said in his head. "You will always be mine."

Evan shook his head as Ligeia drifted down, blood coloring the water in her wake. "No," he said. "I will always be mine."

He kicked away from her toward Bill, who left his own shadow behind in the water. "Are you okay?" he asked, as he pushed a shoulder into his friend's wet suit.

"I'll be better when we get away from her."

"I'll second that," Evan agreed. He looked behind to see Ligeia settle to the muddy deck of the ruined ship, her body shuddering and kicking as she struggled to remove the spear from her back. "Let's get out of here?"

Bill nodded, and then choked as he did so.

"Bad move," he gasped.

"Can you still swim?" Evan said.

"Yeah," Bill answered, but then added, "Shit."

"What's the matter?"

"I don't think we're out of this yet."

Evan followed Bill's gaze down to the deck of the ship and swore himself. Ligeia was gone.

"What the fuck, man. I hit her with a spear that would take down a shark."

"She's more than a shark," Bill answered.

"She wasn't when I knew her," Evan said.

"Women are deceiving," came the somnolent answer. Bill's head started to slump, and Evan pushed at him with his twined fists.

"Come on, man," Evan begged. "Don't lose it now."

Bill coughed. "It hurts."

"Let's go home," Evan said. "But you've gotta stick with me. I can't do this one on my own."

Bill groaned.

"I mean it," Evan insisted. "I can't swim, remember?"

Bill coughed again. "You're going to have to now," he said. "I don't feel very good."

The sound in his headphones wasn't good. Kind of like a gasp and an asthmatic wheeze combined with a cry.

"Come on," Evan urged, and kicked his feet. An overwhelming sense of desperation overcame him then. How could he save his friend when he himself couldn't swim, and didn't even have the use of his hands? But he knew, at the same time, that he had to try. He couldn't let Bill die here, for him. This was Evan's war, Evan's mistake. His folly.

Evan kicked hard, using energy in lieu of skill to push the two of them through the hole in the ship and out into the bay. They had just made it through when he felt something touch his back. Evan turned away and looked into the sea-soft eyes of Ligeia. She locked into his gaze and in the back of his mind he heard her say, "We will always be together. You were meant to be mine."

He shook his head as she wrapped her arms around his.

"No," he insisted, and reached around her to feel the steel tip still protruding from her back. "No," he said. "You killed everything that I love. I could never be yours."

With that, he grabbed the haft of the spear and pulled it toward himself. He could feel it move within her, and Ligeia's eyes widened as it made its way through her ribs and belly to exit her flesh. When Evan felt the tip of his own spear poking him in the stomach, he released her.

"Die," he said quietly, and pushed his feet off her chest as he held on to Bill and pressed them both toward the open water of the bay.

He looked back only once, to see Ligeia collapsed on the black wood of the old boat's timbers as they swam out.

"Sarah," Bill said after they left the shadow of the boat, and Evan nodded, kicking as hard and fast as he could to aim them at the bay's bottom, toward the place where he knew his wife's body lay.

Sarah's face looked peaceful in the false twilight beneath the waves, and Evan hesitated to even touch her. But then Bill whispered in the microphone to "pick her up" and he found that he couldn't resist. He had to hold her one more time, even if they didn't bring her to shore.

Evan slipped his arms into the mud beneath Sarah and pulled her close. She hung away from him, slack and unresponsive in death. But Evan pulled her tighter, trying to find some last magic of Sarah trapped in this dead flesh. This was the woman he had loved all these years. She had been his friend and lover and sparring partner. They had hated each other and loved each other in ways that nobody would ever understand. They had created Josh, and they had almost died in the loss of Josh.

And now . . . as he looked at the still-quiet features of

her here, beneath the strange foggy current of Delilah Bay, Evan finally totally realized that he had lost her too. That mouth would never share coffee with him in the kitchen at five in the morning. She would never put on lipstick in the bathroom and leer at him to ask if she looked "like a slut." She would never kiss his lips and then his nipples and then his cock again, and her eyes would never look up at him from a position of submissiveness and say, "I love you."

The million times that he had played her poorly slipped through his head and in a heartbeat he wept for them all and begged forgiveness. And then he slipped his roped arms over her head in a sling and held her to him, and struggled to lift her from the ocean floor before saying quietly in his microphone, "Bill, I'm going to need your help."

Somehow, Bill slipped his arms around the two of them, and with weak but experienced feet, he guided the three of them toward the shallow expanse of Delilah Bay, and eventually, when they were close, Evan was able to take over, and in the end it was the power of his feet that dragged the three to shore. Sometimes, it is the least likely who find that the only way is the way they would never consciously take.

Evan found his way, as he held on to the body of Sarah, and the gasping form of Bill. And as he pushed them toward shore, he thought once more of Josh, and of skipping stones on a quiet bay.

"Let me touch you now, forever." He whispered their old favorite song. "Just this one last time." He cried just a little as his head finally broke the water.

Epilogue

Sarah had a lot of clothes. Evan had never appreciated exactly how many until she was gone. Unlike the way that she and he had dealt with Josh's death, he decided on his first night home alone that he was not going to turn their house into a memorial to her. He knew better now, after the past year. A week after her funeral, Evan began to open Sarah's dresser drawers and sort her things into boxes for the Vietnam Veterans or Salvation Army to come take and haul away. Better that someone benefit from her loss than that her clothes hang as food for moths in a closet. She would never wear them again, so why should he care about her clothes? This time, he was going to meet death with determination. A determination to let the past go.

Bill had been there at his side for her funeral. Thank God for that. Evan didn't think he could have given a eulogy on his own, but Bill had been there, pushing him on, and saying his own words when Evan's had failed him. Dr. Blanchard had been there too, with a look of confusion about her as much as sadness. When she told Evan "I'm sorry," she sounded as if she herself had killed Sarah.

It was a small funeral, because Sarah had had no sisters, really no family at all. So the packing was his to do, and his alone. He pulled a purple blouse from a drawer with random words strewn in false script across it and held it to his lips to kiss, and to smell the remnants of her scent. He'd miss that, he knew. But he couldn't hold her here. That perfume would only turn to alcohol over the next few months, and he didn't want to remember her that way. His memories of Sarah should always be of fresh smells and cheerful jokes and secret glances that led to kisses requited in so many places he squelched the train of thought. If he began to remember their time together, he'd never finish packing her drawers.

Sarah was gone.

Bill was recovering at home from his neck wounds. Hell, Darren had even given him a couple weeks off from the dock until he'd gotten strong enough so that he wasn't inadvertently moaning every time he took a step and his stitches shifted. The police had bought into his story of being the victim of a shark attack as he discovered the body of Evan's recently ravaged wife and swam it to shore.

Evan knew better. He folded a turquoise shirt and a tear slipped down his face as he thought of the time Sarah had filled out that shirt and pressed herself against him through its thin fabric at a movie, and asked if he wanted to cop a feel.

At the time, in a public theater, he'd laughed her off, embarrassed.

Now he wished he hadn't.

But wishes don't rescind reality. And the reality was, Sarah was gone.

Evan slipped the last of her clothing into a cardboard box, and drew a piece of packing tape over the gap to close it. Sealing the last of her life in a box.

"I miss you," he whispered at the cardboard. As the tears started, he dropped the tape gun, and left their bedroom for a while. When he returned, it was with a determination that only death can engender. One by one, he carried eight boxes of Sarah's things to the garage, and stacked them there in a pile, ready to be taken away. After he was done, he went back in the house, turned off most of the lights, and then slipped out the back door. He didn't bother to lock it when it closed. Somehow, he didn't think it would matter.

Across town, Vicky Blanchard awoke with a start. Images of fish and swarming birds and a nude, shadowy woman swam in the fading light of the dream memory—a kaleidoscope of the bizarre. In the center of it all had been Evan, naked and dripping with the ocean, walking down an endless beach.

Shaking away the nonsensical vision, Vicky rolled over and closed her eyes again. She'd been especially worried about him and how he was dealing with the loss of Sarah, though he'd seemed to be holding up well at their last session. "He's going to be fine," she told herself again and again, as she slipped back into an uneasy sleep.

Evan walked barefoot down the beach. The black of the horizon was a ghost in his vision that bled on forever. He looked away, and stared instead at the point where the ocean met the sand. The point where infinity touched now.

"Everything I loved is gone," Evan whispered to himself. "But here I am. Still. Why *me*?"

He walked in silence for a few minutes, and the cold dampness of the sand on his feet was as bracing as it was soothing. Here, at the lip of dusk and dawn, he could let his real emotions out. There was nobody here to see him break.

And it was in that moment, as he approached the point,

that he finally realized what his true emotions of the past month had been. And where he was headed. Really.

He loved Sarah, he had. But . . . he had loved Ligeia too. A Siren. A deadly killer.

Evan stopped at the spot where he had first met the darkly mysterious nude woman from the bay, and looked out over the cold black water.

Where was she now? Had he really killed her? Was she dead, in the casket of an old ship, thanks to his own vengeance? Could someone like her even *be* murdered by someone like him?

He had never been a man of violence, but stabbing her through had felt right at the time, and when he thought of Josh and Sarah, his eyes filled with angry tears at what she'd stolen from him.

Yet, despite all that, his body responded at the very thought of her . . . he'd done nothing but dream of her these past few nights.

When he remembered the nights beneath the moon, his hips moving with hers, he couldn't refute the love he'd felt for the strange woman who'd approached him every night clad only in her own skin. For the woman who had sung to him in tones that only a deaf-mute could ignore. Who had made him feel like a real man when she'd dragged him down to the beach and ultimately beneath the salty blanket of the waves. A *man* after a decade of hibernation.

He thought of her lips on his, and of Josh at twelve, skipping stones across the bay, and of him and Sarah in San Francisco, rediscovering what had made them *them* after so long. He thought of these three disparate things and desperately wanted them all back.

"Just this one last time," he whispered.

The ocean replied with a rush and a slow roar.

A tear slid down his cheek as he looked out at the edge of Gull's Point and remembered the time that he had first met Ligeia there, embarrassed at her nakedness, or so it seemed, when she dove back beneath the waves.

"Come back to me," he wished.

From somewhere beyond the point, at the place where the black sky met the darkest shadow of rock, a sound began to keen. A sound that spoke of wanting and need and desperation and hunger and desire. Maybe it was the answer to his song. Or the answer to his wish.

It sank and swam and rose and died. And resurrected again with a ray of unquenchable hope. Forever was now.

Evan began to walk toward the sound, oblivious to the water at his calves.

On the edge of the point, something vaguely human twisted toward the bay, and dove with a flash of silver scales and naked cream into the whitecaps nearby.

Abruptly, the sound of ethereal music stopped, but Evan did not.

"I'm coming," he said to the dark. "One last time."

And despite the fear that had driven him and defined him through all of his life, moments later, his head dipped beneath the waves and his eyes opened wide beneath the sea as he swam without fear to meet his destiny.

His lust.

His bittersweet, deadly love.

His Siren.

RICHARD LAYMON

"If you've missed Laymon, you've missed a treat!"
—Stephen King

The Funland Amusement Park provides more fear than fun these days. A vicious pack known as the Trolls are preying on anyone foolish enough to be alone at night. Folks in the area blame them for the recent mysterious disappearances, and a gang of local teenagers has decided to fight back. But nothing is ever what it seems in an amusement park. Behind the garish paint and bright lights waits a horror far worse than anything found in the freak show. Step right up! The terror is about to begin!

Funland

"One of horror's rarest talents."
—*Publishers Weekly*

ISBN 13: 978-0-8439-6140-9

Valley of the Scarecrow

The legend of Joshua Miller has chilled residents of Miller's Grove for seven decades. The town's children all know about the man who sold his soul to the devil and his macabre death at the hands of outraged townspeople—bound to a cross in a desecrated church, sealed away and left to rot.

But he didn't rot. His skin withered and his body mummified until he resembled a twisted human scarecrow. And he didn't truly die. And now, after seventy years, blood will revive Joshua Miller. He will finally be free to exact his unholy revenge. With a burning hatred born in hell . . .

THE SCARECROW WILL WALK AT MIDNIGHT!

GORD ROLLO

"A talent of horrific proportions."
—The Horror Review

ISBN 13: 978-0-8439-6334-2

INTERACT WITH DORCHESTER ONLINE!

Want to learn more about your favorite books and authors?
Want to talk with other readers that like to read the same books as you?
Want to see up-to-the-minute Dorchester news?

VISIT DORCHESTER AT:
DorchesterPub.com
Twitter.com/DorchesterPub
Facebook.com (Search Pages)

DISCUSS DORCHESTER'S NOVELS AT:
Dorchester Forums at DorchesterPub.com
GoodReads.com
LibraryThing.com
Myspace.com/books
Shelfari.com
WeRead.com

□ **YES!**

Sign me up for the Leisure Horror Book Club and send my FREE BOOKS! If I choose to stay in the club, I will pay only $8.50* each month, a savings of $7.48!

NAME: _____

ADDRESS: _____

TELEPHONE: _____

EMAIL: _____

□ I want to pay by credit card.

□    □ MasterCard   □ DISCOVER

ACCOUNT #: _____

EXPIRATION DATE: _____

SIGNATURE: _____

Mail this page along with $2.00 shipping and handling to:
Leisure Horror Book Club
PO Box 6640
Wayne, PA 19087
Or fax (must include credit card information) to:
610-995-9274
You can also sign up online at **www.dorchesterpub.com**.
*Plus $2.00 for shipping. Offer open to residents of the U.S. and Canada only.
Canadian residents please call 1-800-481-9191 for pricing information.
If under 18, a parent or guardian must sign. Terms, prices and conditions subject to change. Subscription subject to acceptance. Dorchester Publishing reserves the right to reject any order or cancel any subscription.